Cold Echo

William Mark

Published by:
Southern Yellow Pine (SYP) Publishing
4351 Natural Bridge Rd.
Tallahassee, FL 32305

www.syppublishing.com

ISBN-13: 978-1-59616-137-5
ISBN-13: 978-1-59616-142-9 ePUB

Cover Design: Gina Smith

First Edition
April 2026

Printed in the United States of America

Dedication

To the persistence of my readers who kept me writing.
Thank you.

Other Works by William Mark

From Behind the Blue Line

Crossing the Blue Line

Lost in the Darkness

Where the Light Cannot

Prologue

"Don't move!" he screamed.

I froze. The black void of the shotgun barrel inches from my face was enough motivation to keep me kneeling on the wet ground, motionless. I could feel the moisture seeping through the knees of my pants. "Don't move!" This time, I could sense the sheer panic and heavy anxiety in his voice. "Dammit, I said don't move," he barked.

Frozen, but still gasping for air, I struggled to catch my breath. I was doing my best not to get shot. Still on my knees, I slowly lifted my arms in surrender. Glancing down at the empty holster on my hip, I realized my gun was lying elsewhere.

In twenty years as a cop, this was my first time with a gun pointed directly at my face. While investigating countless shootings, murders, and deaths, and hunting down the worst killers society had to offer, I had never been in a situation like this. I didn't care for it, and I sure as hell knew I hadn't missed out. My thoughts swirled as I attempted to analyze where I'd gone wrong. What did I miss? How did I end up like this?

A smirk bent the corner of my mouth as one thought broke through all of the confusion, even at a time like this. It wasn't of life's regrets, uncontrollable panic, or thoughts of the afterlife. Nothing flashed before me, and only this thought brought me calm in such a dire situation. It was of her.

Had she not died of cancer, none of this would've ever happened. With death looming in the form of a shotgun blast to the head, the eerily clear, vivid image of her face brought me peace. I could see every perfect imperfection as if she were in front of me. Was this the end? Was I on my way to see her? I lowered my arms in submission, and suddenly everything became clear. Everything aligned. I heard the echo.

Chapter 1

Six Months Earlier… Spring, 2018.

As Victoria's condition worsened, the doctor suggested that a little spontaneity could lift her spirits. I planned something certain to brighten her day; so, I let her sleep in a little longer than usual. I used the morning to pack everything and get it ready so that when she awoke, we could begin our day.

The clock read ten o'clock in the morning. I made my way up the stairs with a hot cup of coffee in one hand and a half grapefruit with sugar lightly sprinkled on top in the other. I slowly pushed open the bedroom door to see the late morning sun had burst through the windows, brightening the room. Even though she was dying, the sun brought life into our bedroom. Lying on her side, she faced me as I stood at the door. I paused.

I watched her stir as she felt my presence. Victoria always seemed to know when I was there. Her eyes blinked open, and she inhaled that first deep cleansing breath of the day. The silk wrap around her head had loosened during the night. She adjusted it so that it covered her baldness.

"Good morning, beautiful."

"Aww, Hank, you're just being sweet. I'm sure I'm quite the sight," Victoria replied.

"I'll always see you as nothing but the most beautiful woman in the world."

She smiled. Her face beamed despite her pallid tone and sunken eyes. The battle had taken a physical toll on her body, but her spirit still burned bright. Her once vivacious body flourished at a healthy hundred and thirty pounds, and now, she was reduced to a sickly ninety-five.

As she sat up, I held out the coffee until she carefully took it with both hands. I set the grapefruit on the nightstand and slid into the bed next to her.

"I've got a surprise for you today." I was attempting to build suspense. "An adventure, if you will."

After a sip of coffee, she replied, "An adventure, huh?"

"Yeah."

"That's what we used to say to Katie when we took her to the museum or a hike or something."

"Oh yeah, we did tell her that."

"Hank Trescott! Are you taking me to the museum?"

I laughed at Victoria's exaggerated seriousness. Her clever humor always made me laugh. My attempt to build suspense gave way to a witty retort.

"No, but if you're a good girl, we could stop for ice cream afterward."

Her smile returned, dazzling the room more than the sunshine. Then she let out a strained giggle, which led to a series of coughs. I silently regretted making the joke. She settled and took another sip of the hot coffee.

Times like these were numbered and running low. My heart ached as I watched her trying to enjoy the moment. I struggled to suppress the tears beginning to well up in my eyes, but she had scolded me enough times for doing that. She would say she wanted my love, not my pity. Sensing my emotions, she leaned her head against my chest. I swung my arm around her and held her close until she gained the strength for our outing.

⌘

"How do I look?" she asked.

Drawn in by the floppy, oversized straw hat, complete with a floral print ribbon and bow on the side, I chuckled at her choice of headwear. The enlarged sunglasses under the brim reminded me of a nineteen-fifties starlet out for a stroll down Rodeo Drive.

"Does it look silly?"

"Yeah, it kinda does, but I don't mind."

"Well, fine. I'll just take it off and let my hair down. Let the breeze blow through it."

Victoria's humor was strong. This was going to be a good day. There had been too many bad ones, especially of late. We were due for a good day.

The bright sun warmed our spot on the ground. Kids playing off in the distance provided welcome sounds of energy and life. Ever since the city opened Cascades Park in the downtown area, Victoria loved to visit. It had become one of her favorite spots. Specifically, she cherished this spot atop the hill, overlooking the amphitheater. The panoramic view of the city's modest skyline, the majestic oaks, and the pristine landscaping of the park brought her a satisfying relaxation.

"You hungry, Torey?" I asked, propping the picnic basket in front of me.

She gave me an indifferent look. Her appetite had nearly disappeared and regularly caused me to worry.

"We can wait for a bit. It won't go bad," I said.

A breeze swept over the park, bringing a brisk chill to the air. Victoria shivered, even in her thick cardigan and the blanket I had draped over her legs. All the weight loss kept her in a constant cold state.

"You need another blanket, honey?" I reached into the day bag for the other blanket.

The breeze moved on, and the sun's warmth radiated down through the stillness.

"No, Hank. I'm fine. You've got me bundled up just fine."

"Here." I took a thermos from the basket and poured a cup of hot chocolate. "Hot cocoa, your favorite."

I held out the cup until she took it with both hands.

"Oh, wait." I rummaged through the basket and pulled out a mint chocolate candy to add to the drink. "Here, just the way you like it."

Her face was appreciative and endearing, but she wasn't interested in the hot chocolate.

"Hank, I love you."

I smiled. "I love you too, babe."

"And thank you for taking such good care of me."

"Well, I kinda vowed to do so, remember? The preacher, my parents, your parents, a bunch of friends at the church?"

"Yes, of course." She looked off into the distance. "It's one of my most cherished memories."

Blood rushed to my face and an involuntary grin creased my face.

"Well, most cherished over all my other wedding days, that is." She smiled. "Top three for sure."

Torey elbowed me in the ribs and giggled at her own joke. It had been a long-time, running joke that I was the favorite of all her husbands, even though we were high school sweethearts who married after college. I always played my part in the joke. It was one of the many things I would miss.

After a series of grapes, cheese slices, and crackers, Victoria lay across my lap as we looked over the rolling hills of the park. Fixated on the waterspout on the far lake shooting a hundred feet into the air, it brought a sense of tranquility to our little picnic. I hoped the moment would last forever.

"I'm worried about you, Hank."

"Me?" Torey sat up to face me. Her face was tender. "You don't have to worry about me? My concern is taking care of you."

"And you're amazing. Hank, I'm not going to be around much longer."

I hated the words as soon as they came out of her mouth.

I looked away, back to the fountain.

"You need to hear this." She reached over and squeezed my hands. "I'm dying, and I will be gone soon. I worry that you won't move on; I do. I love you, Hank. You have been the best partner, best friend, best father to our child, and best husband I could have ever asked for, and I pray you find peace after I'm gone."

"Torey, let's not—" I choked up.

"Talk about it? Yes, my love. We need to. Not for you, but for my sake, please?"

Holding my stare at the waterspout across the park, I desperately wanted to enjoy the moment, not talk about my wife's inevitable death. Anything but that.

"I don't want…." I wiped the tear before it fell. "Can't we talk about something else?"

"Promise me you'll do something you love after I'm gone."

"I love you."

"Hank!" She snapped. "I need to know you'll be okay after I'm gone. I won't find peace unless you promise me, please?"

"Well, I worry about Katie." I spat out the first excuse that came to me. "She needs her mother."

"I don't have to worry about Katie," she said.

"Why not? You're her mother. You don't think she needs you?"

Torey reached up and gently rubbed the side of my face. "I don't worry about her because she has you, my love."

This time, I let the tear roll.

"Okay, but do something like what? Get a job? Collect stamps?" I asked.

"I don't know. Anything. Whatever it is that you want to do. Just so long as it makes you happy, promise?" Victoria held out her right pinky. It was something she shared with our daughter when she was a kid. It solidified the event when there was a need for a solemn oath.

"Hank, promise me. Please?"

I hooked her pinky with mine and gave it a gentle tug. "I promise, Torey."

"Thank you." She lay back down in my lap. "Now, feed me some more grapes, like I'm Cleopatra and you're my servant boy!"

⌘

"Okay, I got it opened. Now what?" I asked, staring at the screen.

"Okay, you need to search for the song. You can do it by album, artist, or title," the screen said back.

"This is silly, Katie."

"Dad, c'mon. No, it's not."

"I'm talking to you face-to-face on a screen about getting music on my phone. It's a little silly. There was a time I'd just go to the music store and buy a CD." I gave my daughter a derisive smile.

"It's called technology, Dad," she said. "Embrace it."

"Seriously, whatever happened to CDs?"

Katie rolled her eyes. "When you're done with this, Google the nearest music store, and let me know how many you find. Just type the name of the song in the search bar."

I hunted and pecked the miniature keyboard until I finished spelling the name of the song I wanted to download. I hit search, and the song popped up on the screen.

"Hey!"

"Told you it was easy."

"Not out of the woods yet."

"Yes, you are. Just hit download." Katie moved offscreen, and I heard shuffling in the background. "I gotta get going, Dad. Those tax forms aren't going to get done by themselves. Give kisses to Mom."

"Okay, punkin. Go be the best accountant you can be. Love you."

The iPad screen went black, and I turned back to my phone. It was a gift from Katie last Christmas. It has taken me almost a year to figure out most of its functions. The little circle next to the song title was almost finished circumnavigating. With coffee steaming and the grapefruit sliced, including the necessary sprinkle of sugar on top, everything looked ready, so I headed up the stairs. A hopeful smile broke out on my face, knowing that she'd like the surprise.

She wasn't awake yet. I placed the coffee and fruit on the nightstand and watched her sleep. As I listened to her breathing, I imagined, just for a moment, it was possible for life to stand still. Her face, peaceful and content, appeared to be lost somewhere in the far reaches of the dream world. A place where cancer and pain didn't exist. She stirred quietly within the sheets. I set my phone down on the nightstand and poked at the screen until the song was queued.

The soft piano keys began to play. I waited for the verse to begin, and as Elvis Presley's deep velvety voice started, I sang along. The words were just as true now as when we first heard it together. I could not help falling in love with Victoria. She was my whole life. Victoria stirred and her eyes blinked open. The daylight radiating in through the windows gave her an angelic glow. Like every day, I could see her beauty through the scars of cancer.

I knelt down to her eye level and whispered, "Good morning, beautiful." Elvis continued singing.

She smiled at the greeting, and it warmed my heart.

I kept singing. *I can't help falling in love with you.*

"I love this song," she said, groggy from sleep.

"I know." I smiled back.

"Take my hand, Torey, take my whole life, too."

We let the song play as Victoria sat up and took the first sips of her coffee and a bite of the grapefruit. I sat next to her, letting her awaken. It was my favorite part of the day. It meant I had another day with her.

"Wait!" Torey was suddenly aware of the song. "Where's the music coming from?"

"Um, my phone."

Torey got suspicious. "Your phone?"

"Yeah. I downloaded it."

Victoria took another sip of the hot coffee and gave me a *yeah, right* look.

“What? I did, I promise. All by myself.”

Another sip. “And Katie sends her love, I presume?”

Busted, I let out a guilty laugh. “Can’t get anything past you.”

⌘

Our nights were spent quietly at home. By the end of each day, Victoria was exhausted, and it made for early nights. I never argued. Her appetite, once voracious and diverse, had been stripped away during this battle. She loved to cook and would spend hours upon hours in the kitchen, preparing meals for Katie and me. In comparison, as a chef, I came in very short, but as the cancer progressed, her meals required less and less effort.

“It smells good,” she said.

She was just being sweet because it was canned soup heated on the stove. I added some extra spice, but it was still the canned version and far from the hands of a gourmet chef.

“Thanks, it’s my secret recipe.” I raised an eyebrow for emphasis.

I put our bowls on the table and sat down next to her. Our kitchen table was small and intimate. Victoria’s preference was to have a smaller table as opposed to a larger one, wanting our family of three to be close not only in proximity but also in life. It had worked, proving she was a genius with no equal.

Victoria took her first sip. She looked at me with a knowing smile that instantly made me feel guilty.

“It does smell good. But there’s something else.”

“Uh,” I stammered a bit. “I uh…added some spices that you normally like.”

“No, that’s not it,” she quickly responded. Her wit never slowed with the sickness.

I gave her my best dumbfounded look.

She covered my hand with hers. With mock sincerity, she said, "Junior Whataburger?" She paused as she contemplated something else. "With onions. Definitely, with onions."

I couldn't hide the bashful grin as she spooned more soup, letting me wallow in my own guilt.

"I guess we know the cancer didn't affect your sense of smell at all."

Victoria smiled and winked at me.

"You don't have to eat what I eat all the time, Hank. Just promise me when I'm gone, you'll be careful, and try your best to watch what you eat?"

I nodded. I didn't want to continue this line of conversation, and suddenly, I remembered something to get me off the hook.

"Oh, I forgot the bread."

I stood up and fished my phone out of my pocket. I had downloaded another song. This one she was going to love. I grabbed the bread out of the toaster, put it on a plate, and sat back down at the table. Propping my phone against the napkin holder between us, I angled its face toward her and hit play.

A rush of sweet stringed instruments spilled out of the tiny speaker, and Victoria's expression lit up. For a moment, her pale face became flushed with life.

The smooth and silky voice of Etta James entered.

I lip-synched acting out my best crooner style with "At Last" by Etta James as she sang about her love coming along. I smiled and took her hand.

"Oh, now you're just showing off, Hank Trescott."

She was right. I stood with an inviting smile and gave her fragile arm a gentle tug. She checked her head wrap, folded her robe tighter, and finally gave in to the moment. I helped ease her out of the chair and took her in my arms.

I started singing again about love and blue skies.

I pulled Victoria in close, holding her in my arms so she didn't have to exert herself. We swayed slowly to the music and lost ourselves in the song.

"Oh, Hank!" she cried, with tears welling in the corner of her eyes.

"Shhhh. Just dance with me, Torey."

She nodded, doing her best to hold off her tears, and melted in my arms. It was the song we danced to at our wedding. At the time, Victoria had an affinity for the classics, and James's song had regained popularity with its resurgence in several movies and television shows. But to Victoria, the song was about finally finding love and being happy, something our wedding day had solidified for her.

I was absorbed in the music as I allowed it to guide me around the kitchen's simple tile flooring, granite counters, and white appliances. But in that instance, I was transported to a grand ballroom with crystal chandeliers, velvet drapes, lit candelabras, and a full orchestra on stage, playing our song, just for us.

While I did my best to sing in tune with Etta, my gaze remained fixated on Victoria's eyes.

"I could stay here a while," she said. She smiled, but there was disappointment in her eyes. It came with hiding a tremendous pain from within.

"What's wrong?"

"Nothing, Hank. Nothing." She squeezed as tightly as she could and let loose to sit back down.

"Are you tired? Was that a little too much?"

"No, dear. That was wonderful. It felt like we were in some enchanted ballroom, just the two of us, and you know I love that song!"

I didn't say anything, allowing the moment to fade, and let her finish dinner.

After a few moments, she became noticeably tired. The dancing, albeit slow and soft, had drained the little energy she had left for the day. She struggled to lift herself out of the chair, so I got up to help.

"Maybe I just need to lie down on the couch for a bit."

"No, it's time for bed," I said. She was more tired than she realized.

I reached under her legs and lower back. She tried to stop me, pleading for me not to hurt myself. Her frail and fragile body was light, like a child, and I lifted her out of her chair with ease. She draped her arms around my neck and nuzzled her head on my shoulder.

It had been decades since I last picked her up in this manner, but I felt strong and protective. Like a new groom on our wedding day, I made my way up the stairs. Although she didn't weigh much, my own abilities waned as I neared the top. The aches in my muscles reminded me of my age, but I pressed on, willing to carry her anywhere.

As I laid her gently on the bed, I noticed she was looking up at me.

"There. It's been a while since I did that, huh?"

"You were always my knight in shining armor, Hank Trescott."

"And you, my fair princess."

"I'm tired, my love. I'm going to sleep now."

"Okay, Torey."

I fixed the bed and got her settled for the night. As I leaned in to kiss her, she reached up and held my face with both hands.

"I love you." She moved her arms out and pulled me down on the bed for a hug.

"I love you, Victoria."

⌘

After a restless night, I was up early, before dawn. Before heading downstairs, I stood in the doorway, letting the hall light fall gently across the room and watching her sleep. Her chest slowly rose and fell, giving me relief. After several minutes, I tiptoed downstairs and started my morning.

The morning news cycled over on the television and repeated the top stories. More murder and mayhem were on tap for Tallahassee. Some politics and special interests were interspersed, but the violence always headlined the news. That and sports. I took the news in stride those days.

Once on the front lines of the violence as a homicide detective, my priority quickly changed from investigating murders to being Victoria's caretaker. After she was diagnosed, nothing else was as important.

The coffee pot steamed out, letting me know Victoria's cup was ready. A blast of citrus emanated as I sliced open the grapefruit. A pinch of sugar, and I was set. Halfway up the stairs, I realized I left my phone in the kitchen, primed with another favorite song. With the food tray in my hands, I contemplated whether or not to get it. I decided to leave it and headed up. The song would be for later.

I toed the door gently, and it swung open. She was still asleep. I set the tray down on the nightstand and reached out for her.

"Good morning, beautiful."

She didn't move. I repeated my words and gently roused her. She rolled over, but something was wrong.

"Hey, Torey?" Panic washed over me. "Hey, honey?"

Her eyes opened, giving me relief. She looked at me; however, she strained to find words. Her eyes urgently searched the room but found solace as they focused on me. Still, no words came, as if she'd lost the ability to speak.

"Hey, what's wrong?"

She didn't answer. For some reason, she couldn't.

I threw back the sheets and climbed into bed with her, scooping her up in my arms.

"Torey, what's wrong? Should I call for help?" I reached into my pocket for my phone and remembered I'd left it downstairs. I would have to leave to get help.

"I need to go get my phone, honey."

Her stare back didn't waver, and I stopped moving. I fought against everything inside of me to get help, but my heart was tethered to hers.

"Tell me what to do. Torey?" I stroked her face and held her tight. "What should I do? I don't know what to do."

Her look said everything. In an instant, and with a sense of calm erasing the panic, I accepted the reality. We'd shared a lifetime together, and I didn't need words to know she was saying goodbye. I coveted the moment, letting everything else wait.

I squeezed her tight, willing myself to stay strong. Tears rolled down my cheeks, but I mustered enough strength just to keep our eyes locked. The vibrant emeralds that sparkled with life and love stared up at me for the last time. I watched as they slowly faded, and she passed. Her body, her vessel, gave way in my arms, as her soul, free of any earthly pains, ascended into heaven where she belonged.

For a moment, I wanted to go with her, but as if she was already reading my thoughts from beyond, a joy radiated from within which could only be her reminding me of how much love we'd shared. There were no alarms, no sirens, and no help came. I let loose a cascade of tears as I held Victoria in my arms. She died in peace, as she'd wanted.

Chapter 2

I never counted the days after Torey got sick. Every day with her had been a blessing. Since her passing, I noticed with much disdain that days moved at glacial speed. Maybe it was the fact my days had been full of her, and now that she was gone, all I had was time. Nothing but empty time. Her funeral was five days later, and the days leading up to it were agonizingly slow. It had been a nice ceremony. Her sister came from Orlando and sang a favorite childhood song. Several friends and former co-workers said sweet things about her and shared their favorite memories. In life, Victoria avoided funerals, but she would have liked her own.

I had her cremated; a surefire way the cancer wouldn't follow her into heaven. I was presented with the urn like it was an extension of her, which bothered me. She was my wife, a flesh and blood person I loved, and to think a ceramic jar full of ashes was somehow an equal replacement felt wrong.

After Victoria's death, I explained to everyone that she simply passed in her sleep. I didn't want anyone to know the truth, as it was a moment just for us. A moment that I would forever hold next to everything dear in my life. If I explained the truth, everyone would look at me strangely, like I had endured some horrific tragedy, when, to me, it was a beautiful moment. Our last moment together. I didn't want or need anyone's pity. When the eulogist shared the alternate version with the congregation, there were joyous smiles and tears shared at the thought of her going in such peace. It was my gift to our friends and family.

The process was surreal, and I often had to remind myself that she was actually gone. Every time I realized we were *celebrating the life* of Victoria Trescott, I felt a pang in the underside of my heart. I imagined that was where her death had created a hole. When I thought of her, it ached in that very spot.

A parade of people, family, friends, neighbors, nurses, and doctors all came by the house to pay respects. Katie never left my side, tugging on my arm much like she did as a shy little girl in unfamiliar settings. Her husband busied himself by receiving the overabundance of food and casseroles brought by everyone. It was comical because Victoria Trescott hated casseroles, citing their existence as the lazy way to make food. I could hear her snicker in my ear at the irony.

"How you doing, Daddy?" Katie asked.

Surprised at the sound of, "Daddy," something she stopped saying the day she started high school, I gave her a look.

"Daddy?" I questioned.

"Yeah, I'm just checking on you." She said with a comforting smile. "Do you need anything?"

In a hushed voice, I said, "Someone needs to eat all those casseroles. I think your mother would disapprove if I ate any of them."

Katie tried to stifle a giggle, but a smile managed to crease her face. She had her mother's smile. "Yeah, Mom hated those."

"Shhh, don't tell anyone. We don't want to hurt their feelings."

"No, we don't want that."

I nodded to her husband. "Does Kevin like casseroles?"

"Oh, my goodness," Katie said while rolling her eyes. "That's all his family ever makes."

"Well, he's in luck then."

The rush of people, the din of their conversations, and the feel of a packed house had all ceased by nightfall. Katie and Kevin retired early into her old bedroom while I sat in the living room alone. The television provided background noise as I was numb to the world. I didn't know what to do. Five days earlier, my life had direction and purpose, but that withered away the moment Victoria died. *How would I adjust?* I fought the urge to go check on Victoria and make sure she was comfortable. That had been my life for the better part of a decade. *She* had been my purpose. The pang on the underside of my heart reminded me she was gone.

Realizing I should at least attempt to sleep, I checked the house and turned off all the lights before heading to bed. Upstairs, I paused before going into the bedroom. It was easy to pretend she was sleeping quietly just beyond the door. The pang hit again. At the door, I leaned my head against it, summoning the strength to turn the knob.

I pushed through to an empty room. The bed sheets were pulled tight; the room was clean and tidy. I remembered our last moments and shed another tear as I replayed the scene in our bed. Even though it was her last moment, I vowed to hold on to the memory and let it forever live in my mind. However, at the time, it was too visceral and too fresh of a wound. Overwhelmed, I came to the realization that I was unwilling to face it. Not yet, I told myself. The pain was too much and still very new. I headed back downstairs for the couch.

⌘

A week later, I was in the house alone. Katie and Kevin had gone back home to live their own lives. I had promised Katie I would get out of the house, so I ran a few errands and picked up a bagel for breakfast. I passed by my preferred Whataburger and heard Torey's voice scolding me for even thinking about eating fast food. Instinctively, I looked over at the bag containing my whole wheat bagel as my rebuttal.

Is that how it was going to be? My late wife still nagging me from the afterlife? I was sad for a moment, but then I chuckled. She would have found my dilemma funny. But I would have given anything to have her nagging me in person.

After eating, I moved around the house anxiously. The time on the microwave read 9:30. I had set out at eight o'clock hoping to waste the morning with distractions, but it proved to be a failed attempt. Putzing around, I couldn't find motivation, so I resigned myself to the living room, my recliner, and the incessant noise that is daytime television.

As I settled on one of Torey's favorite house remodeling shows, something caught my attention to my right. Under the staircase were built-in bookshelves that descended with the steps. Torey had them decorated with books on some shelves, knick-knacks and pictures on others. I hadn't noticed, but Katie had placed her mother's urn tastefully in the middle of the shelves. I stared at it, hoping to see her face materialize, so I could see her smile one more time. After a while, nothing happened, and I felt foolish. A shroud of depression settled over me, and I questioned if I could handle the role of a widower. Standing at the base of a mountain of self-doubt, I wondered if I could even move forward. These were the things Victoria was good at; now I felt lost.

Something propped under the urn further caught my attention. I jumped out of the recliner to get a closer look.

It was a card with my name written on it, accompanied by a sticky note. The sticky note read: *She wanted me to give you this, after. Love, Katie.*

Confused, I opened the flap and slid out a note folded inside. As I unfolded it, the scent of Victoria's favored perfume wafted up, flashing an image of her. It was from a date night we shared at the Silver Slipper Lounge many years ago. It was the night she told me I was going to be a father. It was the first time she'd worn the scent, and she'd kept it as a staple ever since.

I read the note, handwritten by Victoria, and dated a week before her death.

My dearest Hank,

I can feel my time is coming to an end. I had a few thoughts that I wanted to write down. I figured if I told you in person, you would argue with me, but if you're reading this, I've passed, and you have no choice but to listen. I always get in the last word, don't I?

I pulled the note away and nodded in agreement. "Yeah, you did."

Don't let this cancer affect you as it did me. Once I'm gone, I want you to go out and live your life as if I were right next to you. In a way, I will be. You've put your entire life on hold to take such good care of me; you deserve to do something you love. Travel, learn a new language, take up a hobby that gives you joy. One of the reasons I fell in love with you is that passion you carry inside. That is what makes you such a great husband and father and one hell of a detective. Except with Katie and I, I never saw you burn as bright as you did when working as a detective. The case, the chase, the truth was what drove you. Find something that returns that fire, Hank. I fear that I've taken many of your best remaining years, but I'm confident that you have many more left.

I have no regrets, Hank. None. I love you with all my heart. Never doubt that you were a good husband, friend, or partner. Always yours, I love you.

Victoria

P.S. You better do as I ask, you know I'll be watching from heaven.

I giggled at the postscript and failed to notice a tear had leaked out and rolled down my cheek, leaving a wet stain on the note. I flipped over the note, looking for more wisdom, but it was just the one letter. I scanned the rest of the bookshelf and did a hand search through random books I knew were her favorites, looking for any more letters. After a thorough search, I didn't find any. I reread the note several more times, each rendition letting her voice fill my inner thoughts.

Chapter 3

Fulfilling the promise to Victoria was harder than I realized. After making a list of interests that would bring me joy and direction, I spent the next few weeks trying them out. I slowly managed to cross them off, one by one, as they ended in miserable failure.

Walking into what they call a *Globo Gym*, I shook off the initial intimidation when I saw other people my age on the treadmills. My only other gym experience had been back at the police station. After shifts, and as a much younger man, I would work out with my squadmates. At the time, I was usually surrounded by muscle-bound ex-jocks that left me feeling inferior, so I relegated myself to the cardio machines and light weights for toning. Never did I consider myself a physical specimen by any means, but I would argue I was *in shape.*

Greeted at the door by a fit and toned twenty-something-year-old blonde, I was welcomed right in. After explaining the membership requirements, she invited me on a tour of the gym. As I followed her around, she bounced as if she walked on springs with seemingly unlimited energy. *Bubbly* was too mild a description for my tour guide. Effervescent was more apt. We stopped at each machine, and she demonstrated how to use them. She explained that I needed to find something called "maximum burn." Even after listening to her, I wasn't sure what that meant, but I clearly wasn't as excited about it as she was.

Little Miss Bubbly was my complimentary fitness consultant that came with my new membership. The friendly purple and gold logo, the spacious floor, the overall cleanliness, and the presence of other retirees had been my deciding factors for joining. I liked the idea of improving my health, and when I stood in front of the mirror, I was confronted with the older version of who I was. Hair was a little grayer, eyes were more tired, back was tighter. Not that I was disappointed, just noticeably older. Looking at myself, I could see the hidden sadness that brought me here. Moving on, I gave myself a once over and decided I could stand to lose a few inches around my midsection.

I could hear Torey say, “You’re perfect the way you are.” I countered silently that this was not for anyone else. It was for me. As she requested.

I spent an hour or so with the trainer finding this “maximum burn” she was so adamant about. I moved to each machine and lifted what I felt was a comfortable weight for an ungodly number of repetitions. She seemed impressed and even said so a few times. But I was convinced, behind all of her encouragement, what she meant to say was, “Not bad for an old guy.”

Leaving the gym, I had sweat marks down the center of my shirt and around my collar. I wasn’t out of breath, and surprisingly, I felt more energized than I did walking into the place. I even bought a smoothie from the juice bar, following a recommendation from Little Miss Spunky. It contained kale, which I’m pretty sure I remember Torey comparing to seaweed. It tasted okay.

When I got home, I felt productive and tackled a few house projects I had been ignoring. I prepared a dinner with grilled chicken and sautéed veggies, a meal that would’ve surprised Torey. This was the beginning of a change. I fully embraced the idea of me being a gym person.

However, the next morning, I hated life. I couldn’t move. It hurt to breathe. I cursed every repetition that little pixie sprite made me lift. My entire body felt like one giant muscle ache. It was agony just to get out of bed. It even hurt moving my toothbrush back and forth as I brushed my teeth. At the top of the stairs, I weighed out the pros and cons of just hurling myself down the steps because moving my legs seemed a worse option. I was willing to take the chance of a broken neck, given the way I felt.

After managing to get down the stairs, I ate a minimalist breakfast and chased a palm full of pain relievers with orange juice. I waddled into the living room and waited on the couch for death to come carry me away.

I looked over at Victoria's urn with a pathetic whimper.

"Sorry honey, I don't think I'll be going back to the gym."

⌘

I was not to be discouraged. After the gym fiasco, I had to wait a few days before my muscles were able to work again to take up my next venture. Instead of the gym, I felt that I could flex my creative side to find joy and direction.

At the local hobby store, I found myself wandering up and down the aisles. I felt compelled to build something. To have a finished product of my own creation sounded satisfying. Ambling along the do-it-yourself section, and mulling it over for way too long, I settled on a two-story birdhouse. It was fancy, and a certain upgrade to the little aviary death trap Katie made in third grade Sunday school that we'd hung on the back porch. On the way home, I made a quick stop at the hardware store and stocked up on some essential tools required for my new endeavor. Visions of moving past the stock, prefabricated homes, and creating a design all on my own, complete with a signature piece, certainly gave me some direction. I was excited.

Seven hours later, staring back at me in my garage, earlier dubbed my workspace, was a lopsided, rudimentary version of the image on the box. I had started over twice, not quite figuring out the right angles and where certain tabs met certain slots. A few times, I accidentally dropped a few of the pieces, breaking them. I hunted around for makeshift replacements but had to settle on slathering it with glue. Not the woodworking glue I knew existed, but some ancient Elmer's glue I found in the junk drawer. My patience had eroded completely away. At one point, I stared at my hammer, wondering selfishly if it was the problem and not me.

"Holy crap!" I murmured to myself. I stepped back, and it looked like a one-armed preschooler had done the construction. The only resemblance it had to an actual house was the slight pitch of the roof, which was uneven and barely discernable. It was terrible. I was devastated.

The weeks went on as I tried various other hobbies and interests, but I managed to fail miserably at all of them. Some were fleeting and desperate ideas that turned out to be extremely boring and left me emptier than when I started. It felt as if life were playing a viciously cruel joke on me in my mourning state.

I stopped at the grocery store and slowly pushed the cart, as I was in no hurry to get back to any of my projects. I saw an ad for a cooking class the store was offering at night. They would teach you how to cook a certain meal, pair it with wine, and then the class would eat the meal together. It reminded me too much of Victoria and how she used to float around our kitchen preparing gourmet meals. Plus, given my luck of late, I would probably start a kitchen fire that would burn the store down.

"Hank?" A voice called from behind me. I turned to look at who it was. An instant flash of recognition came.

"Mike! Hey, buddy. How are you?"

Mike Durgenhoff was an apprentice of sorts when I worked homicide for the police department. A tall fellow, his dark hair had receded back a few inches and turned gray. His belly had expanded a couple of inches, but overall, he had aged well. When we met, he was new and eager as hell to learn. A little bit too eager, and I had to teach him the methodologies for solving crime.

"Not bad, Hank. Not bad." His extroverted smile suddenly became sympathetic. "Listen, I'm sorry to hear about Victoria. I know that was a long battle for the both of you."

"Yeah, it was tough." I didn't need a reminder and wanted to change the subject. "So, what are you up to? How are things at the department?"

"Oh, yeah. I mean, some things never change, but a whole lot has changed, too. But they finally made me sergeant and stuck me back on the road."

"Oh, you're not in homicide anymore?"

"No. I figure they let me sweat it out on the road for a few years then put me back in. Especially when Polk retires."

"Melvin? Oh my goodness, he's still there?"

Durgenhoff let out a hearty laugh that echoed through the entire produce section. "Yeah. Believe it or not, that SOB is still there."

"Wow. That's great." Melvin Polk's dark, chubby face popped into my mind. He was another stellar investigator who had come in while I was there.

"Hey, listen, I got to get this food home, but are you free for lunch?"

I pretended to sort through a full calendar in my head, knowing full well I didn't have any plans for the foreseeable future.

"Yeah, today?"

"Sure. I'm buying." Mike said.

"Okay, name it."

Mike blurted out a casual barbeque joint we used to abuse on a weekly basis when we worked together. Back then the waitresses all knew us by name. The tables were all picnic-style, and the plates were dented-up metal tins that looked as if they were Army surplus circa World War One. But the food was good, and they liked cops.

"I'll see you there."

⌘

Even though it had been ten years, when I stepped through the front door to *Jim and Milt's*, it was like I was toting a badge and gun again. The dining area hadn't changed a bit. The picnic-style tables were still holding strong and the Florida State University memorabilia on the wall, recent ten years ago, was now faded.

I glanced around the room and spied Mike sitting at our usual corner table. It was the perfect spot to watch both the front and back doors, not only for any trouble that might wander in, but for the college girls who would come in from time to time. I waved and walked through the line of tables to sit down.

"This brings back memories," I said.

"Shit, Hank! I think it was you who first brought *me* here," Mike said, searching his memory. "Being a South Florida boy, you said I had to try some real southern barbeque and brought me here."

"I did?" I couldn't place the memory.

"Oh, yeah. Sure was."

"You remember that early morning hit we did on the bank robbers who shot the teller? It was that duplex down off Gamble Street?"

I vaguely made the recollection. "Kind of."

"We let TAC hit the house, and the guy ended up having all those bills with sequential serial numbers from the bank robbery? Hell, you found the gun in the air-conditioning vent, remember?"

"Oh, yes!" The memory stirred excitement. After the suspects were secured by the TAC team, we brought them back into the living room and interviewed them separately, but neither ended up talking. However, when I brought up the gun, one of the suspects inadvertently looked up and past me. It was his tell. Even though he denied knowledge of the weapon, his eyes told the truth. I was just paying attention. So, I looked behind me and up to see the air-conditioning vent. The screw was loose and there was spackling on the ground below it, as if someone had messed with it recently. It was something noticeable only when close. So, I got one of the TAC guys to rip it off and send a pole camera up there to look around. That's where they had hidden the gun that shot the teller.

"Well, since it was early morning," Mike said, "it was wrapped up just after sunrise. So, we came here and had breakfast before heading back to the station. Best steak and eggs I ever had."

"That's right. We did come here a lot."

The waitress came and took our orders. She knew Mike by name but obviously didn't recognize me. Mike had fun with the girl and explained that I was America's version of Sherlock Holmes. An "American Icon," he said. I blushed, and I don't think she cared, but she played along anyway.

"So, Hank." Mike's tone was more serious. "What are you doing these days? I mean, you working anywhere or doing anything?"

"Well, I was taking care of Victoria full-time and living off my pension. With that and what we had saved, we did fine, even with the medical costs. Victoria's company helped take care of things."

"Oh, right. Right," he said, "but, I mean, now. What have you been doing, you know, since? You staying busy with anything?"

I felt myself deflating. "I tell you what, Mike, I've been doing a bunch of things. You know, trying to find something that fits?"

"Sure, sure."

"Cause, and you'll like this, Torey writes me a letter, from before, but I don't get it until after."

"After she's gone?"

"Yeah."

"What?" Mike was fully invested. "How eerie was that?"

"Well, it wasn't, really. I mean, I didn't expect it, that's for sure, but I can't say I was surprised."

"So, what did it say?"

"Well, it says she wants me to find happiness. To find direction in my life."

"So, you're going around trying a bunch of stuff to see if you find this direction?"

"Pretty much."

"And?"

I let out a self-deprecating laugh. "I've found that I pretty much suck at everything."

Mike joined in with his hearty laugh.

"I'm serious. I joined a gym and after one workout, I can't move because my body hurts so bad. I bought one of those pre-fab birdhouses, and it's an utter disaster. I swear the bird police would've shut it down because it was too dangerous. I tried painting; I tried taking a class at FSU, collecting coins…." I shook my head in embarrassment. "I suck at everything."

"Oh, Hank! Don't tell me that, brother. I need hope. If the great Hank Trescott is struggling, I got no chance at survival! My time is coming around shortly. I mean, Shelly just started college, so as soon as she's done, I'm pulling the ripcord."

Shelly was Mike's youngest of three daughters. Katie had earned enough for a down payment on her first car babysitting for Mike and his wife.

"Well, I wish you luck, but I *am* struggling."

"Hank Trescott, struggle?" Mike said with reverence. "You taught me more about homicide work than anyone ever has. You definitely did not suck at working murders. You ever think about coming back? I mean, what are you, like fifty-four or something?"

"Fifty-five." I took a sip of the sweet tea the waitress brought. "But I don't think my body could handle being a cop again."

The failed experiment at the Globo Gym sent shudders throughout my body. Even the basic physical requirements of police work sounded insurmountable.

"What about teaching?" Mike asks.

"I don't know, Mike. I tried that for a couple of years. It was fine and all, but I was more of a hands-on instructor than a classroom guy. Plus, anything I got is going to be outdated. I've been out of the game for too long."

"Okay, fair enough." Mike thought for a minute. "What about consulting?"

"Consulting? Like on cases and stuff?"

"Sure. I mean, with your experience, someone's gotta have a need for that, right?"

"We never used one," I answered.

"Yeah. You're right." Mike thought for a minute. "We never needed one, cause we always had you!"

I smiled at the compliment.

Mike continued, "But you're right, we usually didn't need one or we were too stupid to think of it at the time. Tight asses on the third floor wouldn't spend the money even if we did want one."

The third floor was where the top brass, the chief and his command staff, had their offices. The term "third floor" was usually synonymous with incompetence and the birthplace of bad ideas.

"No, I wouldn't think so."

The waitress interrupted and placed our food down on the table. Mike got the barbeque beef lunch platter while I faced a steaming bowl of their Brunswick stew. It was my old go-to meal. As I inhaled my first few spoonfuls, I was grateful the recipe had remained the same.

A few minutes passed and the waitress returned to ask if the food was in order. With full mouths, we nodded, and she smiled back at me. I thought nothing of it, but Mike began to stir.

"That smile was a little extra, don't you think?" Mike asked.

"No, Mike," I said, "I don't. I'm old enough to be her father."

"Maybe she's into that," he joked.

I took another bite of the stew, ignoring his statement.

"But seriously, Hank," Mike said. "You think of maybe seeing people? You know, when you're ready, of course."

"Ready for what?" I asked.

"You know, dating, or at least just seeing other women?"

Honestly, I hadn't even considered the thought of dating. I felt as if I was past that stage in my life. Losing Victoria was hard enough, I didn't think I would ever be ready to be emotionally involved with another woman.

"Oh, I don't think so, Mike," I answered.

"Why not?"

I had no answer for him. "I don't know why," I said. "It doesn't seem right, I guess."

Mike stopped the line of questions while he ate a few french fries.

"Let me ask you this, Hank," he said, "and answer honestly. If the roles were reversed and you were the one in heaven, wouldn't you want Victoria to move on?"

"Well, yeah," I said without much thought. Victoria's happiness was always important. "Of course, I would want her to move on and be happy."

Mike opened up his arms, palms up, and shrugged his shoulders. "That's my point, my friend."

"I don't know, Mike. It seems different."

"It's not, Hank. Allow yourself to move on and be happy. You know deep down that's what Victoria would've wanted."

As we finished lunch, we shared a few more memories of cases we'd worked on and suspects we had arrested. It was therapeutic being back in that world, albeit for the span of a meal, but it reminded me of some good I'd done in the world.

"Thanks for lunch, Mike."

"Anytime," he said. "You were a mentor to me, Hank. It's not until you get to the end of a career that you start thinking of all the people who truly molded you into the person, or cop, you are. You, brother, were one of those people who helped me along the way. I was just lucky I ran into you at the grocery store."

⌘

I did it again. Strangely, I found comfort in the error. As I prepared breakfast for Torey and brought it upstairs on a tray, I realized my mistake halfway up. I climbed the rest of the stairs and stood outside of our room. I knew she wasn't asleep on the bed, but I cracked the door anyway and watched the empty bed as if she were there. I missed watching her. I missed her. I wanted to hear her voice again, but there was only silence. The kind of silence that is consuming and, although quiet, manages to drown out the world.

I don't know how long I stood there, but eventually, I returned downstairs with the tray. I had an idea to help fulfill her request for me to find direction. I thought a lot about what Mike Durgenhoff had said about moving on and being happy. I wasn't sure I was ready for any level of companionship. But it was what Mike had said about consulting on cases that gave me an idea. It was a long shot, but it was worth a try.

I showered and dressed. I stood in front of the mirror, hoping that my choice of clothes didn't portray my inner desperation.

Walking into the police station, I immediately noticed how many things had changed. There was thick ballistic glass protecting the duty officer, whereas before it was a sliding pane much like the reception desk at a doctor's office. The security leading away from the lobby had been upgraded with proximity readers and remote locks. Even the décor had changed from the dated wood paneling to sleek walls with gold framed pictures of the current members of the city council. But somehow it felt like the same police station I had known for twenty-three years. It was like walking into a childhood home where some other family lived. I asked the duty officer to speak with the Commander of the Investigations Bureau. When he asked me for my name, there was no sign of recognition when I answered. I checked his name and "serving since" pin. He'd been a cop for three years and didn't look a day over twenty-five.

"You can have a seat, sir. His secretary said it may be a minute," the kid said.

I turned to find an open seat in the lobby. The notion of explaining who I was to garner a speedier response seemed like a wasted effort, so I took a seat and waited.

Ten minutes later, a face from the past appeared in the lobby, Bobby Jessup. Bobby had started a few years after I did, and we managed to parallel our careers going in different paths. He had jumped from the COPPS squad to Vice, and over to interdiction, while I anchored myself in homicide. He was a good cop with good instincts on how to find drugs, but he was still a slick sleeve when I retired. To make commander from the ground level in ten years took some doing.

"Hank?" Jessup said with surprise. "It is you. I thought they were kidding with me when they said you were here to see me."

"Bobby, how are you?"

Jessup grabbed my hand in both of his and shook wildly, holding a grin across his face. It was a nice reception.

"I'm good, Hank. I'm good." He let go of my hand and leaned back showing off his Class A uniform, "They made me Captain! Can you believe that?"

"Ha, no. Not really."

"Me neither." We shared a laugh, drawing the attention of the young duty officer. "So, what brings you in today, Hank? You're not here to report something, are you? Did something happen?"

"No, no. Nothing like that."

"Oh, okay. That's good. So, what can I help you with?"

"Well, I'd—" I hesitated with embarrassment. Jessup read my face and thankfully invited me up to his office. "C'mon up, I'll show you around. I promise it looks nothing like it did when you were here."

On the walk up, I noticed the Hall of Heroes was still something the department kept going. As I scanned the plaques, I saw they had been decorated with more recent and younger faces. Faces that I didn't recognize, all doing heroic acts in the line of duty.

Jessup led me into the Investigations Bureau, and I sat down in a chair across from a gigantic cherrywood desk. The top shined like glass and held nothing while a smaller computer desk in the corner was crammed with paperwork and notes. The cherrywood desk was his show desk, I figured, the latter his actual working desk.

After informing Jessup of Victoria's death, he apologized for not knowing, but I used it as a segue to my request.

"I have a lot of time on my hands, and as a promise I made to her, I'd like to consult on some cases or even help work some of the big cases when manpower is an issue. I think my career speaks for itself, and I'm well qualified to help."

Jessup smiled, but it was the fake smile of a politician. He was thinking of an answer that wouldn't hurt my feelings. I could tell already his answer was going to be no.

I hit him with a preemptive, "What?"

"Sorry, Hank." Jessup readjusted in his leather chair. "It's just that— How long have you been retired?"

"It's been ten years, but if you're worried about the advances and techniques being used, I've always been a quick learner. I think my experience would account for that."

"No, it's not that. I'd love to have you, but it's been ten years. Did you let your standards lapse?"

Shit.

I hadn't thought about that. All law enforcement officers in the state are required to keep up their standards, basic credentials that say they are competent to uphold the law. Once you separate from an agency, it's incumbent on the officer to keep their standards valid as a retiree. I hadn't bothered to keep up with my standards because I was busy caring for Victoria. To get reinstated, at this point, meant I would have to attend the basic recruitment academy at the age of fifty-five.

"Yeah. I did," I answered. "But, what about volunteering? You don't need standards to do that."

"Hank," Jessup steepled his hands together and gave me a consoling look. "You know the mundane crap we ask the volunteers to handle. Callbacks and harassing phone calls? Gas skips and vandalism cases. Do you really want to do that?"

It stung, but he was right. If I didn't dive into a homicide, my attention would dissipate, and I would get bored.

"Yeah, you're right. I wouldn't be able to stand that for very long."

"And I can't let a volunteer, no matter who he is or what his experience is, in to work on a homicide. If anything goes wrong, that'll be the first thing that blows up."

"I understand." It was fine, I told myself. It was one more thing to fail at.

Jessup escorted me back down to the lobby, and we said our goodbyes. I sat in my car for a moment, shutting out the world.

"Shit." I leaned back in my seat and looked up. "I keep failing Torey. I'm trying, honey, I hope you see that I'm trying. I just keep failing."

There was no answer. Only silence. It seemed to find me frequently. I cranked up the car, pulled out, and headed home. A moment later, my cell phone rang. For an instant, I hoped it was Bobby Jessup with the news that after consulting with the chief and command staff, they found a loophole and I could get back to homicide work.

It was Katie.

"Hey, Katie. What are you up to?"

"Hey, Dad. I was just calling to check on you."

Subconsciously, I must've let out a disparaging sigh, because she instantly picked up on it.

"What's wrong, Dad?"

I told her. Sparing her most of the details, I let her know about the debacle that was the gym experience, the artistic neanderthal I turned out to be, and the rest of the failures, including the latest at the police station.

"Oh, Dad, I'm sorry. It's their loss, for sure."

"Thanks, Katie. So, tell me something good?"

"Wait, Dad, what about those spontaneous road trips you and Mom used to take? You guys would always tell me how much fun you had exploring the little towns and stuff. You know, off the beaten path."

I smiled at the memory. "Yeah, we did have a lot of fun doing that. But that was something she and I did together. I don't know if that's something I can handle alone."

"Okay, well. It was just an idea."

We spoke for another five minutes until she had to get to a meeting. When I made it home, I walked into the empty house and was greeted by more silence.

⌘

Normally reserved for special occasions, I poured a glass of bourbon to calm my anxiety. I pulled out my phone and finger-tapped my way to the songs Katie helped me download. I no longer felt like a novice navigating my smartphone. Maybe I wasn't lost on modern technology. Elvis Presley began to resonate from the tiny speakers of my phone as I sauntered around the house. I remembered playing his records on an actual turntable at one point in my life after Torey and I were married. I'd come home after a shift, and we'd let the music fill the house while we danced, talked, and enjoyed life.

Ignoring the television, I let myself get lost in the framed pictures of our most treasured memories. I moved along the bookshelves, reliving each picture and smiling at the memory it captured. I moved to the books that filled the shelves, mostly from Torey's collection. She loved books. She called them portals to a new world. I ran my fingers across the spines, spot-reading a title here and there.

After the books, I stopped at Torey's urn. The inscription on the base read: *Beloved wife and mother.* She was so much more than those four words, but they rang true, nonetheless.

I finished the bourbon and decided to read one of Torey's books. I ran my finger down the shelf like a glissando slide on a piano and grabbed one at random. It was a crime thriller Torey had raved about, so I was excited to get started.

I poured another drink and sat down in the recliner ready to dive through this portal. As I peeled open the book, a bookmark fluttered down into my lap. I grabbed it to set it aside, but the logo caught my attention. It was beige with black lettering and read *The Old Bookstore.* Instantly, I was pulled back into a memory of when Torey and I visited a quaint little bookstore in a small town in north Florida between Tallahassee and Jacksonville. We had come across it during one of our aimless wandering adventures Katie had just spoken about. The store had been one of the treasures we found along the way.

I set down the book and stared at the bookmark. I shot a look back at the urn as if it were Victoria's face waiting for me to finally take notice of something she had done.

"So," I said into the silence, "you want me to take a road trip." I nodded, finished the bourbon, and added, "Fine, I'll go."

Chapter 4

On road trips, our mantra had always been: Stay off the interstate. Taking the back roads and the less traveled highways increased our chances of stumbling across some piece of Americana that was worth experiencing. To keep tradition going, I left out of Tallahassee east on Highway 90. I buzzed through a few small towns and came upon my first designated stop, Madison, Florida.

It had been at least fifteen years since Victoria and I had last visited, obviously making a stop at the Old Bookstore where she had received the bookmark. My recollection of the visit had grown vague, but I imagined that like most cities and towns, much had changed, while much had stayed the same.

Following the signs that led to the downtown area, I entered a nine-square block area of small-town America. The buildings were well-maintained holdovers from a different era but modernized to fit today's culture. The area was centered around a magnificent courthouse that was an operational relic. I marveled at it as I drove by. A modest two-story building with a dome centered on top and a clock face on all four sides sat proudly in the square. Out front were white marble steps leading to the front door centered between four columns that ran the height of the building. It was a mix of Southern and Roman architecture. In comparison, it paled in size to the courthouse back home, but what it lacked in size, it made up for with southern charm.

I parked in an empty spot along the side of the courthouse. Checking my watch, I noticed it was nearing lunchtime. I couldn't remember what we did for meals on our last visit, so I was in search of food. Scanning the block, my eye caught a neon sign sprawled across a building's facade. It read: *Lucile's*. The two-story brick building had the look of industrial intentions, but I assumed that as the years went on, it took on various other roles to stay relevant. Now, with a window front and a fashionable metal awning stretching over the sidewalk, it housed a general store with a pharmacy, and apparently, a small deli. A small handwritten marquee out front offered a lunch deal consisting of a sandwich, chips, and a drink for six bucks. With few other options in sight, I crossed the street and entered.

If I focused on the aisles and merchandise on the shelves, I felt like I was in present times, but once I looked up and took in the surrounding walls of the building and the décor, I was thrown back to the fifties. The rim of the deli's counter was rounded chrome and matching stools with vinyl seats were spaced out along its length. An actual jukebox sat in the corner playing small 45s. I couldn't remember if this place was around on our last visit, but either way, I knew Torey would have loved it.

I ordered a chicken salad sandwich and asked the girl who took my order if the Old Bookstore was still open.

"Oh yeah, it's steel goin' strawng." She answered with a sweet southern drawl. "It's just down this street, he-yeer." She pointed to the back entrance of the store, away from the courthouse. "Okay?"

"Okay, I got it," I answered. "Thanks."

I worked on the sandwich as I walked down the sidewalk to the end of the block. The chicken salad was surprisingly good, and I finished it rather quickly.

From across the street, I saw the black and orange laminated "open" sign that was facing out through the glass door. I crossed the street and pulled the door. A chime dinged above as I stepped inside. I glanced around but saw no one at the disorganized roll-top desk in the corner. As I stood there, my nostrils were greeted with that distinct musty smell of unread pages that line the shelves of a bookstore. I moved further into the store and around the front counter. An open threshold connected the front area to the main floor of the bookstore, and I could see it went much further.

A stirring came from the back, and I could hear someone moving forward. Footsteps grew closer and were accompanied by a mysterious metal click. Before I could see him, a voice called out, “Hello, welcome. C’mon in and look around.”

The voice belonged to a younger man, not the old man I recalled on our last visit. As soon as he broke the corner of a bookshelf, he smiled a friendly grin.

“Hi, there. Welcome to the Old Bookstore.”

“Hello,” I answered, “and thank you.”

The man was in his mid-thirties, with graying hair on the side, and would’ve stood much taller if not for a cane he used to significantly favor his right leg. He was otherwise very fit and healthy looking, which immediately told me his handicap was the result of an injury, not congenital, and given the well-worn handle of the cane, I would say it had happened many years ago.

“Looking for anything in particular, sir?” he asked.

“Uh, no,” I answered. “Not really. Just thought I’d come in and browse.”

“Okay, well, I’ll let you to it then.”

The man stepped out to the front area, and I could hear the squeak of a chair under pressure. I moved up and down the aisles, spot-reading the spines, waiting for something to jump out at me. It was usually Victoria who fueled these searches while I just followed patiently. The more I thought back, it was she who found and suggested books for me to read, not me making a thoughtful selection for myself. As I realized this, I began to understand why I felt so awkward.

After about ten minutes of browsing, I had a few books that seemed like good investments. The young man shouted back, “Still okay back there, sir?”

I detected some level of authority in his voice but let it pass.

“Yes, sir. Thank you,” I shouted back.

After a moment, I stepped to the open threshold and asked, "Hey? There used to be an older gentleman who worked here, right? The owner? Is he not around anymore?"

He gave me a consoling smile, burdened with sadness. "Yeah, my grandpa. He's who you're asking about, no sir, he passed away a few years ago. He left me the bookstore, and I've been trying to keep it going ever since."

"Oh, I'm sorry to hear that." I thought back and remembered the owner was a charming, nice man. "I remember he was very kind."

"Thank you. That's very nice of you to say," he answered. "Since I've been doing this a while, I get a lot of long-time returning customers who ask about him. It lets me know just how many people's lives he touched, and for the better."

"Right," I nodded. "Well, he sure was nice to my wife and me last time we passed through."

"Oh yeah, where from?"

"Tallahassee. We would take spontaneous road trips and travel the back roads looking for places like this."

"That's nice. I'm glad it warranted a return trip. Is your wife with you?"

It was my turn for the consoling smile. "No. She um—" It was actually hard saying it out loud to a complete stranger.

He leaned forward in his chair. "Oh, I'm sorry, sir. Forgive me for asking."

"No, it's okay." I waved off his unnecessary apology. "She loved places like this. So, I figured I'd come back for a bit."

"Well, like I said, I'm glad you came back."

"Thank you."

The young man grinned and leaned back in his swivel chair. He looked at me expectantly.

"What?"

"You said, Tallahassee, right?"

"Yeah."

"By chance, did you used to teach at the police academy?"

The fit physique, authoritative voice, and the mysterious injury all blended together in my thoughts, and now he was asking about the academy? Did he used to be a cop, I wondered.

"Yes, I did. Briefly. Were you in one of my classes?"

"Yes, holy shit. I remember you." He squinted his eyes and waved his hand around like he was conjuring a thought from decades past. "Trousdale? No. Treskill…no…."

"Trescott, Hank Trescott."

"Yes!" His eyes beamed, and I couldn't help but smile at the recognition. "Yes, that's it. You were a great instructor. I loved listening to all of your stories. I remember being so tuned in when you taught." The guy didn't register even a spark of memory, but somehow, I'd managed to make an impression on him, enough that he remembered me over a decade later.

"And, I'm afraid I must've taught over two hundred cadets in my time teaching, so I'm sorry I can't recall your name."

"That's okay, it's Cade McCoy." He strained to lift himself out of the chair without his cane to shake my hand. I stepped closer and met him halfway.

"Nice to meet you again, Cade."

"Yes, nice to see you again."

"You still going to browse some more, or are you ready to check out?" He nodded to the handful of books I was holding.

"Oh, um—"

The door chime gonged and a woman police officer walked in purposefully. She nodded politely to me and stood at the counter. Flecks of auburn intermingled with her light brown hair, loosely tied up in a bun. I pegged her for late-thirties and noticed she carried a tired sadness in her eyes. A quick glance at her left hand told me she was not married.

"Hey, Jewels," Cade greeted the officer.

I looked over at her name pin. It read Haywood. The bright blue patch on her shoulder said Madison Police Dept, and the phrase, "Four Freedoms," was centered below some sort of a gold symbol.

"Cade, I need a good one for tonight. I'm pulling a double over in dispatch."

"Yeah, go knock yourself out," he said matter-of-factly. "I got some more Michael Connelly books in this week, you know, if you haven't already read them all."

Officer Haywood nodded again as she walked past me and disappeared through the threshold, her tight, slicked back bun belying her loose uniform. It was folded over in the back and tucked tight in her belt. Clearly, it was larger than she needed, indicative of a hand-me-down shirt from a small-town department.

Cade turned his attention back to me and reached out for the books I was holding. As he rang up the order, he explained that he had worked as a police officer for the Jacksonville Sheriff's Office before getting hurt in the line of duty. It explained the mysterious injury, but he didn't elaborate on exactly how he was injured. There was something awful behind its creation, and I knew not to ask if he wasn't willing to divulge.

"So, I take it you're retired now? Or close to it?" he asked.

"Yeah, I've been retired for just over ten years now."

"Oh, really." He placed my books in a recycled plastic grocery bag. "Doing anything else or just enjoying retirement?"

"No, I was doing something to occupy my time, but that…." The *something* was Victoria's well-being, and I had to stop myself before I got emotional. "…that chapter is over. So, I'm looking for a new chapter, so to speak."

Cade gave me a smile as he handed over my purchase. "No better place to start a new chapter than in a bookstore." The young man gave me a wink, and I let out a relieved laugh.

I said goodbye and pushed open the door, setting off the chime again.

"Hey, Hank?" I heard Cade's voice call out.

I turned and stepped back into the bookstore. Officer Haywood was standing by the front desk, her back to me.

"Yes, did I forget something?"

"No, um—" Cade looked intently at Haywood.

There was something going on between the two that I wasn't in on. Haywood kept her back to me, but Cade was insisting that she do something.

"What's going on?" I asked.

"Ask him," Cade prodded the officer.

"You do it," she whispered, although I was close enough to hear.

"Hank, um…would you be willing to help out with a case Officer Haywood is looking into?"

I was caught by surprise and had no answer.

"No, it's okay. I'm sure you got better things to do," Haywood answered.

Cade gave her a scolding look of disappointment.

"It's fine, sir," Haywood twisted around to face me. "Thanks anyway."

Unsure of what exactly was going on, I didn't feel the need to inquire further. "Okay," I said, flatly. "Have a nice day."

Leaving the store, I heard Cade's voice get loud toward the officer. I kept walking down the block toward the courthouse, and their voices faded. There was nothing else of interest on this block. I turned toward the drugstore diner to see what else the downtown offered. Passing a few boutiques along the way, I realized that, had I been with Victoria, we would have stopped in and spent at least an hour in each. Relegating myself to window shopping only, I made quick work of the block and made my way back to the car.

Confused about what transpired in the bookstore, I replayed the scene in my mind. Why was the former-cop-turned-bookstore-owner telling a current police officer to ask me about a case she was working? My mind swirled at the possibilities. What kind of case was it? Why were they asking a seemingly perfect stranger passing through town to help? I admitted that I was intrigued.

Passing on the odd exchange, I noticed it was getting late, and I wanted to get home before dark. Before I could open my door, a soft voice called out from behind. It was Officer Haywood.

"Excuse me, sir?" she asked.

"Yes, Officer?"

Officer Haywood looked hesitant to ask for whatever it was she wanted.

"Is everything okay? I know I'm not here on official courthouse business, but I thought it was okay to park here."

"No, it's not that," she said. "It's just that—" She hesitated again. She hung her eyes low, studying the ground.

"What is it, Officer Haywood?"

"I need your help."

"My help?" I asked. "Is it the case you're working?"

"Yeah, I need your help to solve a murder," she said. "A murder that's twenty-five years old."

Chapter 5

"I'm sorry?" I asked, "You want me to help you solve a twenty-five-year-old murder?"

"Yes," she said. "Cade told me that you used to work homicide in Tallahassee. He said you were pretty good at it, too, and I thought maybe you could take a look at the case. I mean, I've been through the files back-to-front dozens of times, and I don't have a clue as to how to continue."

There was a certain arrogance that came with homicide detectives, and Haywood didn't have it. It seemed odd that a uniformed officer would be seeking help on a homicide case. Plus, I heard her tell the bookstore clerk, Cade, that she was working a double shift in dispatch, something that would be beneath most death investigators.

"Forgive me for asking, but…is that what you do for the police department, work homicides and cold cases?"

Haywood picked up on my skepticism and looked down at her uniform. The sorrow I saw in her eyes earlier had returned. "Well, I'm on patrol, sure, but as you can imagine, we don't have enough manpower to dedicate officers solely to cold cases."

I nodded. Made sense with most small-town agencies barely able to muster double digits for sworn officers. They had to stick to the problems at hand, rather than the past, no matter how terrible the crime. It was a resource allocation problem, not laziness.

The pleading and desperation in Officer Haywood's eyes gave me the answer I was looking for. The sadness I noticed earlier wasn't heartbreak of the normal man-woman variety, but heartbreak from the loss of someone very close.

"You don't work cold cases at all, do you?" I asked.

Haywood didn't answer, shocked by the question. After a moment of recovery, she replied, "No, but the case *is* technically assigned to me."

"It's personal, isn't it?"

Haywood let out a sigh as she appeared relieved. Tears welled up in her eyes as she replied, "Yes."

In an instant, the absence of police work from the last decade vanished. Standing with a victim once again, I felt a compulsion to help without question. I opened my car door, tossed the grocery bag of books onto the front seat, and swung the door shut. "Buy me a cup of coffee, and let's see what you got."

⌘

Madison, the county seat, lacked many options for coffee. Still in the downtown area by the courthouse, Haywood suggested Lucile's, now that the lunch crowd had moved on. The same young girl with the sweet country accent from my lunch visit called Officer Haywood "Jewels" and served us two cups of coffee, on the house.

Haywood picked the table in the far back corner of the dining area for the most privacy.

I held up the coffee. "Police perks?"

Haywood smiled.

"So, how does this work?" she asked.

"Um, I don't know," I answered. "I guess just tell me about the case."

"Well, it happened back in 1993, and she was shot twice in the chest."

"Wait, no." I stopped her.

"What's wrong?"

"Nothing, it's… I'm sorry. That's not what I meant. I meant to ask, why is this case so important to you?"

"You don't want to hear about how it happened, evidence, and statements, and whatever?"

"No, not yet," I answered. Haywood was confused and looked hurt. "Listen, if I help you, I need to digest the case my way, not some regurgitation from someone else, sorry."

She didn't like my use of the word "if" but found acceptance with the rest of my statement.

"It's okay."

"So, why is the case so important to you?"

"Well, to be honest, this case is why I became a police officer."

Officer Haywood wasn't speaking as an officer; she was speaking as a family member who had tragically lost someone close. Also, doing the math, a twenty-five-year-old case meant this happened when she was around ten to fifteen years old, not someone on the verge of a career choice.

"You knew the victim, didn't you?"

Haywood nodded her head. "Yes. Her name was Crystal, and we were very close."

Chapter 6

Officer Julie Haywood had spent her adolescent and adult years living with the loss of the person she was once closest to, Crystal Daws. Crystal was more of an older sister to Julie than anything else, being just three years older. Julie told me about their adventures as young teenagers growing up in rural Madison County. They turned private ponds into their luxury pools. A wood thicket just beyond Julie's home became protective castle walls to the fair maidens, and homemade lemonade was their royal tea served on hand-me-down coffee mugs that were, in their eyes, the finest china.

As they grew older, Julie clung to the regal fantasy while Crystal became more interested in boys. Julie abandoned the pretend regality to stay close to her friend, tagging along when she could, trying to understand the attraction to the opposite sex. The year Crystal turned sixteen, she got a job at the Woodard Theatre, the only movie theatre in town. Crystal would sneak Julie into the movies, and sometimes she would help her clean the theatres afterwards.

That's when Julie's story of her friend ended. Crystal was murdered after closing the movie theatre one night. She had been the victim of a robbery gone bad as she was leaving to take the day's earnings to the night deposit. Instead of depositing the money, she was found dead, and the money bag was missing.

"There was only like two hundred dollars in it." Julie relived the moment and fought away tears. "Her life was worth so much more than two hundred damn dollars. Hell, I would've given them more to just not hurt her, but…."

"I've never quite understood the senselessness of it all. Even after all those years in homicide, I could find the who and how, but rarely did I ever find the why."

"Yeah, well, I was supposed to help her that night, but I was a brat and didn't want to see the movie that was playing, so I stayed home. Had I been there…."

I'd seen this plenty of times before in homicide survivors. Self-imposed guilt was a tremendous burden to carry and even harder to alleviate.

"It's not your fault, Julie. Really. If you would've been there, you could've gotten hurt too, or worse."

"Well, not sure the alternative was much better."

I didn't know Julie Haywood beyond what she had just shared, but her comment was off-putting, and I didn't know how to respond. I just let her wallow in whatever self-loathing pit she was in.

"I'm sorry," she apologized. "It's still hard for me to deal with. Plus, here I am a police officer because of what happened, and I can't even figure out who did it."

"I get it," I answered.

"So, will you help me?"

I hesitated. This was just what I was looking for, but I was quickly reminded of what it took to work a case. That's the part they don't tell you about. Following the leads, making the arrest, and living on adrenaline was exciting, but for every ounce of effort put into a case, it was that much harder to recover afterwards. Being out of the game for so long, I worried about the toll it would take.

"I got a place where you can stay, and the chief said he'll pay per diem while you work the case."

"You talked to your chief about me, already?"

Julie looked away, sheepishly. "Well, sort of."

"Sort of?"

"Okay, I've had a deal in place for a while, it's just that…" she paused. "We can't actually pay you."

"Oh, I see." I hadn't thought about compensation. Never did before, but it was my actual job. It was how I provided for Victoria and Katie for twenty-three years.

"But, as you can see, I don't exactly have a line of people waiting to work for free on this case."

"No, I don't suppose you do."

Julie leaned back in her seat and let out a frustrated sigh. She was easy to read. She was desperate for answers, desperate for closure–something all homicide survivors have in common. Unfortunately, some had to live this way, not knowing the who or why. I imagined her frustration was amplified as a police officer.

The sun had just ducked under the tree line, signaling the start of dusk. It would be well after dark by the time I got home.

"I need to get home, Julie."

"Okay." Her disappointment was obvious. "Sorry to waste your time."

"No, I enjoyed meeting you. I think your case is intriguing; it's just that—"

"You won't help," she interrupted.

"No, it's just that, I need to think about it. There's a lot for me to consider."

"Alright. Well, the case isn't going anywhere. She'll still be murdered tomorrow."

⌘

By the time I made it home, it was well after dark. I mulled over the offer to essentially work a twenty-five-year-old murder for free, in a town I hardly knew anything about. I didn't lie when I said I was intrigued. She didn't describe some ill-advised drug deal gone wrong, or high-risk victim getting in over her head. Crystal Daws was a genuine victim, and that sincerely grabbed my interest. Not that it ever mattered what kind of person a homicide victim was; it's just that she and Julie Haywood deserved justice. On the other hand, could I even deliver? There was a reason I had never wanted to work cold cases. They were cold for a reason. Who was I to think I could do any better of a job than whoever first worked the case?

Another thing they don't tell you is how to deal with that *look* from the victim's family when you can't make a case. It was a combination of world-crushing devastation, disappointment, and anger all in one. It's a look that cuts straight into your soul, letting you know that you weren't good enough.

I couldn't help but remain on the fence about this decision. It would provide me with some direction in my life, but the last case I worked was over a decade ago. I wasn't so sure I was up to the challenge. Ironically, it was decisions like these where I usually depended heavily on Victoria's opinion.

I picked up some orange chicken for dinner from our favorite takeout Chinese restaurant. Out of habit, I ordered enough for both Torey and myself, so I was surprised when I had so much leftover. After storing the rest in the fridge, I cleaned and put away the dishes. Placing the last cup in the cabinet, there wasn't enough room. Torey always kept it straight and organized, and I did a miserable job of trying to maintain it. With a quick shove, the cup fit; however, it spit out another cup to make room. It was a thermos that fell from the shelf, hitting me on the arm. It clanged around on the tile floor, making a terrible racket.

As it rested, I instinctively knelt down to pick it up. On the thermos, facing up, was a police badge with my badge number etched under it. I paused and smiled. Then, I laughed to myself. I leaned back for a view into the living room, catching a glimpse of Torey's urn. I half expected to see her looking back with a slight grin on her beautiful face.

"Really?" I asked.

The thermos was a personalized Christmas gift she'd gotten me a handful of years before retirement. I remembered that on several of the unfortunate, middle-of-the-night calls, she would get out of bed to make me coffee. Half asleep, wrapped tight in her robe, she would soldier the wake-up call just to see me off. Standing by the door as I left, she would hand me the thermos and give me a kiss goodbye.

Be safe. I love you, she would always say.

"Fine," I said. The message was obvious. "I'll go back in the morning."

Chapter 7

There were only two chairs to pick from. I chose the furthest from the door. The chubby-faced man working behind the reception desk kept looking my way. I hadn't decided if it was out of curiosity about me or the smell emanating from the bag of bagels in my lap.

I checked my phone; nothing. I had called Katie, letting her know my plans, but had to leave a message. I figured she would call back and be excited for me.

"She's usually in by now," Chubby Face said. "I can check the CAD to see if she's logged on."

"Thanks," I replied. I smoothed down the lapel of my suit jacket. I had chosen the light gray one with a plain white shirt, no tie, for my first day. First impressions were important when on someone else's turf, so my intention was to look sharp.

A moment later, "Yep, she's on. Want me to radio her?"

"Um, no. That's okay. I can wait until she makes it in." I checked my watch; it was nearing nine o'clock, and I was sure the bagels were beginning to lose their freshness.

"Okay," Chubby Face turned back to his computer screen.

The lobby of the Madison Police Department was not exactly a lobby, but a reception area for what was originally intended to be a doctor's office or law firm. It was clean, tidy, and held the air of professionalism, but there was also a quaint, small feel. I liked it. Unlike what I had been accustomed to back in Tallahassee, it was quiet.

Chubby Face answered a ringing phone and introduced himself to the caller as "Tyler." He snapped to attention and began writing notes, looking panicky. I hoped it had nothing to do with Officer Haywood, but I didn't get that sense. It was something else. He repeated, "Yes, sir," a few dozen times, hung up the phone, and jumped out of his seat.

"Um, sir…, are you good here?" He clearly needed to do something for the caller and couldn't stay.

"Yeah, I'm fine," I said. "Do what you need to do."

"Okay, great." He smiled and disappeared somewhere beyond my vision. I checked my watch again. It was ten past nine.

A car door shut somewhere out in front of the station house. I turned to see Officer Haywood walking up to the front door. Her gait was slow, and she hung her head in the bright morning sun. Clearly, the double shift in dispatch had slowed her down this morning.

As she stepped through the front door, I stood to greet her, offering the bagels as an apology for my hesitation. Her eyes popped open, and she froze in the doorway.

"Hey, what are you doing here?" She asked, confused.

I thought the answer was quite obvious. "Well…, I thought, I could—"

"The case? Oh, right. Shit! Does this mean you'll help?" A spark ignited inside Officer Haywood.

"Yeah, I gave it some thought, and yes, Officer Haywood, I would like to help you."

She grinned, then smiled and completely reversed her mood. "Call me Julie, please."

Julie reached out and shook my hand, then glanced down at the bag.

"Here, for you." I lowered my voice. "I noticed there weren't many options for a good bagel around here, so I brought you these."

"Aw, thanks." She took them, and we stood awkwardly in the tiny lobby.

"They're from a little bakery in Tallahassee; my daughter is friends with the owner," I explained. "They're pretty good."

"Awesome," she said, peeking inside the bag.

Julie looked around. "Where's Tyler?"

"Dunno. He got a phone call and then took off back there somewhere." I pointed to the doorway where I last saw him.

"Oh, okay." She waved off whatever breach of protocol he'd made. "Come on, back. I'll show you around."

I followed Julie through the doorway, which was unlocked using a key card reader. She swiped her card against the reader, followed by a beep and click. She pulled the door leading into the back room. Offices lined the perimeter of the open space. Several desks were situated against each other in the center. A long bench ran about fifteen feet in the corner, with large, iron eyelets screwed into the seat every three feet. A podium stood next to the bench stocked with paperwork, fingerprint cards, and black ink. On the wall was a large, gray-colored square with two footprints outlined on the floor below.

I felt like the new kid at school, being shown around the campus by another student. However, after a minute, I realized Julie and I were alone in the station house. I knew the department was small, maybe twenty or so sworn officers, but it was completely empty. There should've been at least a few other people.

"Here," she pointed to a room in the far corner. "We can use the conference room." Julie led the way. The room had a large oval table surrounded by cushioned chairs sitting in the middle. In the corner was a refrigerator and a microwave next to a small sink.

"Conference room?" I asked, looking at the appliances.

"Yep, slash break room," she said with sarcasm. "Welcome to the Madison Police Department."

She flipped on the lights and pulled out a chair for me. "Have a seat, and I'll go get my files." Julie reached into the bag and fished out a bagel, considered it, and then took a bite before exiting the room. Following suit, I slathered some melted butter on an everything bagel and had it nearly finished before she came back.

Julie brought in a small box, the size a toaster oven would come in, as opposed to what I had expected, a thick three-ring binder.

"What?" she asked. She must have read the confusion on my face.

"It's a box?"

"Yeah, so?"

"What's in it?"

"Files and stuff."

"Stuff?" I did not like her use of the word. "What does that mean?" I stood up to inspect the inside.

"You know, pictures, logs, evidence."

"Wait, what?" I snapped. "Did you say evidence?"

"Uh…, yeah." Julie looked hurt.

"What kind of evidence?"

"Most of what was collected at the scene, but not everything."

"Why would there be evidence in the case file, er, box? Why isn't it locked away in an evidence locker?"

"Okay, well, um…," Julie backtracked and squinted her face as she searched for an answer. "So, I checked it all out for safekeeping. I didn't want anything to happen to it, you know?"

"What the—" I stopped myself from yelling at her. What was done was done. I reminded myself that this case was personal to her, and she asked for my help. I just hoped the mistake wasn't irreparable.

"I'm sorry. Should I not have done that?"

"No, not really," I said, but with as little admonishment as I could. "Did your chief okay that?"

Julie looked away.

"He doesn't know, does he?"

"No."

"Okay, let's move past this. We'll discuss evidence handling and safekeeping measures later."

"Okay."

"Well, it's clear we start with organizing everything into a working murder book," I said.

"Sounds like a plan."

Over the next ten minutes, I had Julie separate all the actual files from the evidence in the box. I sent her to Lucile's to fetch a proper binder. Aside from the huge evidence snafu, I found a little comfort in seeing the evidence was at least still properly sealed in evidence bags. The reports were handwritten and mostly on the top copy of carbon-copied report paper. They were the originals and appeared to be in fair condition, considering how old they were. I noticed most of the files, report-wise, were in good condition overall, with little to no wear on them. That stirred something inside of me.

Carefully, I handed her the stack of reports and said, "Go immediately make three copies of each of these reports."

"Copies?" she asked. "And why three?"

"Julie, these are carbon copy paper reports."

She didn't understand my point.

"You're lucky they're still in good condition. But I can assume there isn't an electronic backup file anywhere, right?"

"No," she said.

"Thought so. Go make copies."

When Julie returned, I tasked her with putting the original files in a large black binder, categorizing them into the patrol response, investigative follow-up, evidence collection with property receipts, witness information and statements, any media releases, and any valid suspect information.

"That'll be easy," she said, regarding the last category. "There are no valid suspects."

I looked up at her. There was a perpetual sadness that followed Julie Haywood, and it seemed to resonate from this case. Hopefully, my involvement could change that.

"Hey," I said, optimistically. She looked up, and I winked at her. "Not yet."

As the binder was nearly complete and the evidence properly cataloged, a commotion drew our attention outside of the conference/break room. Tyler hustled past, fiddling with a ring full of keys, while loud voices shouted. Julie stepped out of the room to see. I hung back, watching from the doorway. Two handcuffed suspects were being led past the lobby and forcefully tethered to the eyelets of the bench. Each was trying to buck their escorting officer, offering choice swear words and empty threats. The officers maintained their cool as much as they could, but they were losing the upper hand.

Julie shouted out, "What's going on?"

The other cops ignored Julie while they struggled to get the suspects under control.

"Nothing, we got it, Haywood," one of the men said.

A back door swung open sending the bright morning sun through the middle of the room like a giant light beam. In strode a tall, well-built man in his late forties wearing a tactical uniform and dark sunglasses. His serious scowl scanned the room and fixed on the ruckus in the corner. He marched right over to the two suspects and, anticipating an unjustified beating, I started to look away. I had heard rumors of how smaller agencies operated, especially in the deep south. However, as the man neared the prisoners, he removed his sunglasses, and they instantly complied, sat still, and let the officers attach their cuffs to the eyelets. He didn't say a word to them; his mere presence shut them up. Then he leaned in and said something to the two wild suspects in a low, hushed tone, just out of earshot. Whatever it was, he had their attention and respect.

Julie helped with the prisoners while I stayed in the room and watched. The missing personnel I wondered about filed in soon after the arrival of the suspects. Several were in matching tactical gear, others in plain clothes. One, dressed in a formal uniform, who I assumed was the chief, came in with a beaming smile. I learned by eavesdropping that they apprehended the two men in the act of committing a crime, of which type I hadn't learned yet, but with all the commotion, I was willing to bet was some type of violent felony. Watching everything, I noticed the tall, well-built man was at the center of it all.

He handled the suspects, as well as his colleagues, with the mastery of an orchestra maestro, delegating responsibilities, giving out orders, and taking control, all to help follow up with their ongoing case. He was sharp. I was impressed with this man, who I heard someone call "Ryder."

"Excuse me? Can I help you?" A voice asked from behind.

I spun to see a small compact man, dressed in a police uniform, with a large bulge in his right cheek and a dark brown liquid sitting on the rim of his bottom lip. Waiting for an answer, his eyes glared at me as if I were a threat. His stance was bladed, keeping his right hip farther away from me than his left.

"Uh, um…," I stammered. "I'm here with Officer Haywood." I nodded toward the conference/break room, assuming he knew I was working on the cold case with her.

"You ain't got no visitor badge," he said.

I looked down, but realized Julie had swiped us in with her card and never provided me with one.

"Yeah, um, I never—"

"Boone!" Julie yelled from across the room. "Leave him alone. He's with me."

The compact man she called Boone relaxed a bit but didn't bother moving back. He still held his glare. The scene drew everyone's brief attention, and now everyone noticed my presence. I couldn't help blushing.

"Where's his badge, Haywood?" Boone asked.

"I didn't have time, and Tyler was too busy with this mess to make him one, okay?"

"He needs a visitor badge if he's to be back here." He scolded Julie. "'Specially, if he's working on that lost cause of yours."

Julie took the rub with little response. "I'll get it taken care of asap, alright?"

"Fine," he answered her and stepped away. "But make sure you keep it with you at all times, ah'ight?"

"Yeah, sure. Not a problem," I answered.

As the diminutive officer walked off, I heard him say, "Damn right, not a problem."

"Don't pay him no mind, he's got little man syndrome," Julie said.

"Yeah, we had guys like that, too. I guess every department does."

I shook off the awkward introduction to Officer Boone and sat down at the conference table.

"Who's the other guy? Tall, older, has his stuff together?"

"Oh, you mean Super Cop? That's Ryder Langston; he's somewhat of a local hero." Julie spoke about him with reverence. "He's a legend around here. He's who stirred up the mess out there. He got information that those two clowns were going to rob the First Community Bank this morning. So, he and most of our guys set up on it and caught them before going in."

"Wow, really?"

"Yeah, apparently they're good for several other bank robberies, too."

"That's a helluva good cop," I said.

"Yeah, like I said, he's super cop. Not a lot goes on around here without Officer Langston knowing about it."

"How come you weren't in on the operation?" I asked Julie.

"Someone had to stay behind," she said with some aversion. "Hence the double shift in dispatch."

"Oh, okay," I said. "Wait, you said Officer Langston? He's not like, a captain or something?"

"No, he's a slick sleeve. He's turned down many promotions over the years, and I've lost count. He just doesn't want management; says he loves being a street soldier. Been doing it like twenty-five years."

I nodded in astonishment. I was truly impressed.

"So, getting back to the case. Now that we're organized, where do we get started?" Julie asked.

The uniformed man with the proud smile I had pegged as the Chief stepped through the door of the conference/break room and coughed, announcing his presence. Julie turned around to see who it was.

"Chief!" she said. I was right. "Hey, I figured we could use this room for a little bit and then…Oh—" She stopped and looked back at me. "Sorry, Chief, this is Hank Trescott. He's a retired homicide detective from Tallahassee."

I stood up and reached over the table to shake his hand. He smiled a politician's smile and offered a firm handshake.

"Chief Randall Pitts. Pleased to meet you."

"Chief, thank you. It's nice to meet you, too."

Chief Pitts scanned the table to see why we needed the conference/break room and gave Julie an expectant look to explain my presence. She was slow to read it.

"I'm here to give Officer Haywood some help on the Crystal Daws murder."

His face turned serious for a moment, but the politician's smile slowly reappeared. I didn't know what to make of that, but then again, I knew nothing about this town or the people in it.

"Officer Haywood did not let me know you were coming." His voice was sharp and professional.

"That's because I didn't really accept her offer until this morning," I answered.

"Yeah, he just showed up here at the station, then everyone, including you, were busy with the—"

"Julie, it's okay," the chief said. "So, I take it the arrangement we agreed upon was acceptable?"

He was referring to the no pay, but free room and board for working the case.

Julie turned from the chief to me with a puzzled look. Her round face crinkled at the eyes and nose attempting to lessen the oversight. "I never officially asked. Does that work for you?"

"Yeah, that'll be fine."

"Great!" the chief boasted. "I'll let you two get crackin'."

⌘

While the robbery investigation moved along in the main room, Julie and I managed to complete the binder by lunchtime. She had run out of the station several times to answer minor calls for service but quickly returned to the station to provide what assistance she could. Tyler made me a visitor badge, and I clipped it on my shirt collar so that when Officer Boone walked by, he'd see it.

On Julie's last return, she brought in a white bag and a drink carrier with two drinks.

"Lunch," she announced. "From Lucile's." It was a turkey sandwich on wheat, chips, and a homemade chocolate chip cookie covered in Saran Wrap, with sweet tea to drink.

As I started my lunch, I began to scan over the reports, eager to learn about the details of the case. Trepidation set in as well because I knew that once I dove into a case, I would fully immerse myself and not come up for air until it was complete. It was the only way I knew. The main source of trepidation came from wondering if I would ever come back up for air.

"What do you look for?" Julie asked.

"Look for?"

"You know, it's a cold case. It's been worked already. I mean, if there was DNA or something super obvious, I would've dealt with it already. I'd like to think so anyway. So, now that you're here, what do you look for?"

I thought about her question. "For me, it's deeper than simply looking for the missed clue. It's about reliving the case and having it speak to me," I said. "Every case has a voice, of sorts."

"So, we have to find the right voice?" Her eagerness to understand my method was naïve but welcomed. "I'm not sure I follow."

"No, we have to find the echo."

Julie's face crinkled in confusion. I chuckled. It wasn't the first time I'd seen that reaction when explaining my method. Victoria did the same thing after asking a similar question.

"Ever stand at a canyon or at the start of a long hallway and shout something only to have it echo back at you?"

"Yeah, sure."

"Where does that echo go, you think?"

Julie gave it an earnest thought. "I don't know. It disappears or whatever."

"See, I don't think it does. It just goes on and on until it's too far away for us to hear, but it has to go somewhere, right?"

Julie didn't answer.

"So, with this case," I continued, "we need to listen for the echo. It's out there somewhere, this *cold* echo. We just have to find it."

Chapter 8

Before I left my department, we had transitioned to electronic, typed police reports. One of the advantages is that I no longer experienced the frustration of having to decipher hieroglyphics and chicken scratches that some officers called handwriting. I was constantly having to catch up with the officers and get them to translate reports, which unnecessarily slowed down the process. I considered myself fortunate that the majority of the reports from the Crystal Daws murder were well-written and legible.

Julie provided me with several legal pads for note-taking. She sat across the table from me, typing reports from her calls on a Toughbook laptop. She had offered to check one out for me to use, but I admitted that I was more comfortable handwriting my notes.

"Keeping it, *old school*, okay," Julie said.

I had heard the term before, but given the context, I didn't care for it.

Starting in chronological order, I began with all the responding officers' reports. Out of habit, my eyes scrolled down to the bottom of the report to see its author. Not that I would recognize any of the names. However, I was surprised that the first report I grabbed had Ryder Langston's name on it.

"So, Super Cop was first on scene?" I asked Julie.

"Yup. Sure was," she answered. "He calls it 'the one that got away'."

"Oh yeah?"

"Yeah."

With the first impression I had of Officer Langston, I knew one of my first moves was to interview him and get his perspective on the case. *That should bode well,* I thought, *once I get him to jump the emotional hurdle. Especially, if it's his "one that got away" case.*

After reading through the first batch of reports covering the initial response and the start of the investigation, I began digesting the case. Visualizing the crime, as retold by the officers' observations and witness accounts, I had a decent handle on how everything went down. I jotted notes down on the legal pad and charted the area with little marks on a printed map.

On March 14, 1993, Crystal Daws was working the late shift at the Woodard Theatre on SW Pinckney Street. The two movies playing that night were *A Few Good Men* and *Groundhog Day*. She was tasked with making the night drop after closing. Her coworker that night, Maynard Preston, left before Crystal at 10:02 p.m., according to his timecard. She was found shortly after reports of gunshots were heard at 10:16 p.m. Daws never punched her timecard, as she was making the night drop and still technically on the theatre's time. I wrote Maynard Preston's name down along with "alibi?" next to it. In a separate column to the right, I wrote the two times down to establish a timeline.

Officer Langston was working patrol that night, parked two blocks away, situated on the north side of Four Freedoms Park, when he heard gunshots. He was on scene in less than a minute. He wrote that when he got there, Daws was on the ground in front of the theatre, with labored breathing. He called for medical help, but she died moments later before any help arrived. Langston wrote in his report that he didn't see anyone in the area as he responded.

I couldn't help but realize that the last thing Crystal Daws saw in this world was a strange cop hovering over her, unable to help. Then I imagined how this report read to someone like Julie Haywood and what emotions it stirred. I glanced across the table at her as she typed behind her laptop. She felt my stare, looked up, and gave me a sporting smile.

I checked the map and saw that Four Freedoms Park was located in the center of town. Being a central location for call response, it offered an ideal place to park a patrol car in the middle of the night.

As other officers arrived, they set up a perimeter, and a K-9 team from the county sheriff's office was called to start a track. It was noted that the dog did find a track that ran east for a few blocks but then trailed off. The consensus was that the suspect or suspects had stashed a car at that location for their getaway. Unfortunately, dogs cannot track cars.

Langston wrote that the bank bag with the night deposit was missing, along with Daws's purse. I jotted down under the timeline, "Daws's purse taken with night deposit." The manager was called to the scene to verify the deposit wasn't left in the theatre, as was a bank employee to verify it never made it to the night drop. The theatre manager totaled the deposit at $212.50. Not much of a take by way of a robbery, so it made sense the suspect targeted Daws's purse to maximize his efforts.

In regard to the body, Langston described Daws as lying on her back with two apparent gunshots to her chest and stomach area. She was found in the street in front of the theatre, a few feet away from the curb. He later noted that Daws's vehicle was parked across the street, halfway down the block. I consulted the map, although it was current, and I agreed with Langston that her location was consistent with being interrupted on the way to her car.

I thought about the significance of Daws's vehicle being present on scene, and made another note in the right column, Keys? If Daws's purse was taken, were her keys in it or elsewhere?

After finishing Langston's report, I picked up the next one. The officer's name obviously wouldn't register, so I skipped straight to the narrative. This officer located the witness who called in the report of the gunshots. She'd let her dog outside and heard the shots from her porch. She told the officer she didn't see anyone fleeing the scene. She explained to the officer that she kept the cordless phone on her when out at night, in case she needed to call for help. She had remained outside the entire time. I noted the witness's address on the report, Hancock Street, and found it on my map. It was one block east and slightly south of the theatre. Recalling the direction of the K-9 track, I was curious as to how this witness only heard the gunshots but saw no one running. I jotted down her name with a note, "didn't see suspect flee?"

"Hey?" I called to Julie. She lifted her head from the laptop. "Is this officer still around?" I showed her the supplemental report, and she shook her head after reading the name.

"No, he retired a while ago. Pretty sure he moved somewhere far away."

"Okay, we may need to track him down."

Julie's eyes gave me an incredulous look. Apparently, this was some monumental task for her.

"Really?" she asked.

"Yeah, there's going to be a lot of that in this case. Especially with it being twenty-five years cold."

"Twenty-five years *cold*?"

"Sorry," I said. "Pathetic attempt at humor. I'll stop."

She gave me a pitying smile and went back to her laptop.

I read the last officer's report, which detailed his canvass of the area and his follow-up with Maynard Preston. The officer, Cedrick Fallon, had made several block loops, checking each business surrounding the theatre to see if it was open, if there were any customers or employees working, and if there was any functional video surveillance. Before I left my department, video cameras weren't as prevalent as they are now, but in a small town like Madison, it was hard to imagine that they ever needed security cameras. Nonetheless, the officers checked, and, as Fallon wrote, "negative results on any open businesses and no cameras operating that covered the outside of the businesses." He noted the few residential homes in the area but still had negative results.

I kept reading, wanting to know how Maynard Preston was dealt with. Officer Fallon noted that Preston's grandmother vouched he made it home at approximately 10:15 p.m., because he interrupted her news program. Also, he noted that Preston was very cooperative and described him as emotional when he was told of Daws's death.

I scratched a line through "alibi" by Maynard Preston's name. Still, I wanted to talk with him if he was reachable. As it was, Preston was the last person other than the killer to see her alive.

"You good?" Julie asked. I didn't notice she had collected all her things from the table and was standing by the door.

"Yeah," I answered. "You're leaving?"

"Oh, no. I just need to get these reports turned in. It's technically end of tour time, but if you want to keep going, we can."

I checked my watch. It was nearly four o'clock. Finished with the officer's reports, I was eagerly awaiting the chance to pour into the crime scene photos. The anticipation of opening the folder of eight-by-ten glossy photographs brought excitement because they were not on a disk or flash drive. Soon after I joined homicide, we went digital, so I never got to experience the grit of thirty-five-millimeter film.

"Well, I'd at least want to go over the photos, if that's okay?"

"No, that's fine," she said. "I need to get my son from school, and then I'll come back to help."

"Oh, okay," I said, surprised, but unsure why. The fact Julie Haywood had a child felt unexpected. But then I realized that I knew very little about her, the person, outside of what I had learned the last few days. Determined in her job, despite being timid around her co-workers. She carried herself well, but it felt forced, like she was fueled by a resolve that she was unsure she deserved.

"I'll tell Tyler to keep an eye on you," she added. "Everyone pretty much leaves the station in the next thirty minutes, anyway. It won't take me long."

I told her I would be fine, and she left after giving Tyler a heads-up at the front desk. For the most part, everyone had stayed busy on that robbery bust from the morning, leaving us alone in the conference/break room. I was sure I would continue to stay under the radar.

The folder with the crime scene photographs was nearly an inch thick. They weren't as worn as the rest of the case reports were, and I imagined that was because seeing her close friend dead on the street wasn't a welcome sight for Officer Haywood. Obviously, I didn't blame her. However, I have always believed that the crime scene contains the most information in any case. It is the origin of the echo.

I peeled open the folder, and the first photo was of the theatre, taken from across the street. They call it an overall range picture. In the foreground was the yellow crime scene tape, mid-ground was Crystal Daws's body lying on the street, with the theatre façade further back. The tall vertical neon sign stretched high into the air, and although turned off and dull in the picture, I imagined it looked magnificent during its time.

In the far corner of the picture was the back of an officer and the profile of a man who I assumed was the lead detective. He wore plain clothes with slicked-back hair and a cigarette hanging out the side of his mouth. I could see the butt of a revolver sticking out from his waist. They were too busy to notice the photographer and failed to get out of the way. What I identified as the front bumper and hood of a 1993 Chevy Caprice patrol car was to the far right of the picture. My eyes bounced around the picture, taking in the captured moment. Looking at the photograph was like looking through a time portal. The eerie part was that it was a time I existed in when I was living my own life elsewhere.

Flipping through the next few photographs, they captured the overall scene and both east and west down Pinckney Street. To the west was a sea of police cars, marked and unmarked, stacked deep along the entire block. Given what I knew about the case this far, I imagined that, for the small department, it was all-hands-on-deck. I moved quickly through these and slowed when it came to the close-ups of Crystal Daws.

Lying supine, her shoulder-length hair was scattered above her head, tossed wildly on the ground. Her eyes were grayed, lifeless, and still. There was no trauma to her face or neck, but blood trickled from the corner of her mouth and ran down the side of her cheek. One of her arms was out to her side, the other was folded across her stomach, palm down. Her blouse was saturated with blood from her chest down. The palm of her outlying arm was covered in blood. I imagined that she was holding her stomach with both hands at some point, a futile attempt at stopping the blood or just grabbing for the wound. Her legs were positioned awkwardly, but as I imagined the victim falling backwards from the impact of two quick gunshots to the abdomen, it made sense. She would've, most likely, been backpedaling, lost her balance over the sheer violence of everything, and fell. Langston was on the scene pretty fast and reported that she died moments later. Even without reading the autopsy report, I imagined the bullets did quite a bit of damage internally, causing her to bleed out quickly, thus losing the ability to get away from her killer.

I took my time with each picture of the immediate crime scene. I let my eyes wander around each one, taking in the various angles, putting the different pieces together in my head, and getting a grasp of the scene. I knew I would never walk the crime scene in person, something I normally required when I worked a case, but that wasn't possible. I had to live through the photographs.

"What do you think?" A strong, deep voice asked.

I looked up from the crime scene photos to see Ryder Langston in the doorway. His short-cropped hair was mostly gray, but he looked younger than his age. His eyes were serious, and he carried an air of competence that went well with his athletic build.

"Oh, um…," I let the question register. "What do I think? About this case?"

"Yeah, I heard you were looking into a cold case for Officer Haywood."

"Oh, well. It's too early to tell. I'm just getting my bearings right now."

"Okay, fair enough." Langston entered the conference/break room and stood on the other side of the table. "I hear you're former homicide from Tallahassee."

"Sure was. About fourteen years." I stood up and reached across the table. "Hank Trescott, nice to meet you." Langston extended his hand, and we shook. As expected, his grip was firm and strong.

"Ryder Langston, welcome to Madison," he replied. "Fourteen years, that's a long time. We don't really see that level of violence over here. Obviously, I try my best to keep it that way."

"Looks like you're doing a pretty good job of it." I nodded outside toward the main room.

"This morning?" He was being modest. "That was a little bit of luck and good timing. I'll take the win, though. Thank you."

"Sometimes, that's all you need," I answered.

Reviewing the scene from earlier in my head, I wanted to ask Langston a question.

"Can I ask, what did you say to those suspects to calm them down?"

Langston thought hard, sifting through the events of the day. "Oh, at the bench?"

"Yeah."

"Those boys grew up around here, cousins, and I've been chasing them around for years," Langston said. "So, I told them that if they continued assin' up, I was going to call their granddaddy to come to the station."

"Oh?"

"Yeah, their granddaddy served in Korea and Vietnam, one of those born tough guys, you know?" Langston explained. "So, they ain't scared of cops, but they damn sure scared of their granddaddy."

"Wow," I said, "that'll do it." The working knowledge of the community Langston held was quite impressive.

"I'm just glad it worked," he said.

Langston hung in the doorway, and something told me that he had a message for me but was unsure how to deliver it.

"Is there something I can help you with?" I asked.

"Well, I just wanted to give you fair warning."

My guard immediately went up. Stepping into someone's backyard, not knowing all the rules and none of the players, I could have easily made missteps, unknowingly.

"About what?" I asked, cautiously.

"Look, Officer Haywood means well, but this case has been an obsession of hers since it happened. Don't let her drag you down into her mess, okay?"

"Oh, okay." I knew the case was personal to her for obvious reasons, but to blindly fall into someone else's obsession was not a possibility I foresaw. Again, not knowing all the players, including Julie Haywood, was something I had to deal with.

"Thank you, Officer Langston."

"Call me Ryder."

"Okay." Unsure of his motivation for warning me, I decided to try something. "She said for you, Crystal Daws's murder was the one case that got away, is that right?"

His eyes turned serious and then somber. "You could say that, yes."

"Can I ask you something about the case?"

His eyes widened. "Sure, but as you know, it's been a while."

"Like I said earlier, I've just read the first few reports, yours included, and studied most of the crime scene photos, but there is one thing that is already bothering me. You know, from the initial look."

"Okay, shoot?"

"The K-9 track, it says they tracked a few blocks east."

Langston looked up, searching his memory. "Yeah, sounds right."

"The witness that called 911 about the gunshots, she lived one block to the east. You know, the lady out walking her dog? She told the officer that she was standing on her porch when she heard the shots and then said she didn't see anyone run by."

Langston nodded, seeing the contradiction.

"What do you think? I mean, the lady stayed outside from gunshots to police arrival but never saw a suspect run or pass by or anything."

"You know, I thought about that same thing back then."

"What'd you come up with?"

"Well, it was a robbery gone bad, right?" Langston paused. "You did see where the bank bags and purse were taken, right?"

"Oh, yeah."

"Okay, well, I figure there were two suspects. The doer and the driver. So, the driver lets out the doer two blocks to the east, and he walks up before the lady takes the dog out, robs and shoots the girl, and then runs to the west where the driver goes and picks him up, then they haul ass. The driver moves so he's not seen waiting around drawing attention."

"But the K-9 track went east?" I said out loud. Langston didn't respond. But then, as I absorbed his scenario, it clicked.

"The track got him coming in, not out."

"Right!" Langston said.

"Of course, the track is the track. The dog can't tell if it's coming or going. You guys just assumed he ran off to the east. Plus, you figured he was walking slow, creeping up to the theatre to wait until closing. That would lay a thicker scent than if running at full speed."

"Exactly." Langston agreed.

"Okay, well. That's plausible." I remained impressed by Super Pop, Ryder Langston.

"Well, I gotta get home," he said, backing out of the room. "But remember what I said. Be careful."

"I will."

A moment later, Officer Haywood entered the conference room.

"You will what?" She asked, clearly catching the end of the conversation with Langston.

Realizing I needed to remain on guard with everyone until I knew who I could trust and not trust, I decided not to divulge what Langston had warned about.

"Oh, nothing. Just let him know if I need any help with the case."

Julie's face scrunched up and her brow furrowed. "Really?"

"Yeah, really." Needing to change the subject, I asked, "So, dinner? You said something about a per diem?"

"Oh, right." She thought a moment and then responded, "How's pizza sound?"

Chapter 9

Apparently, there are not many culinary options in the town of Madison. Looking around the restaurant Julie selected, it was easy to tell that it had once been a convenience store. The mason brick walls, large front windows, and the slight overhang from the roofline were all obvious clues. But the food smelled great, and the locale gave it character.

"Did this used to be a convenience store at one time?" I asked. We sat at a small table for two in the back corner. Although I moved to it first, I let her face the front door with my back turned. I figured it was her town, so I gave up the seat.

Julie smiled at the question. "Actually, yes." She took a nibble from a garlic roll and continued. "It was the Swifty Mart when I was a kid. Matter of fact, there's a lake a few blocks from here, Lake Francis, where I grew up. Crystal and I used to ride our bikes over here sometimes after school or on the weekend."

Julie smiled at the memory, and then her cheeks flushed slightly. "There was this cute high school boy named Beau who worked there. We used to go up there and flirt with him. Well, we called it flirting, but I'm sure he called it something else. And we knew he would never give us the time of day. But we still went."

Julie stared off into the past, a content grin resting on her face.

"I can imagine how close you two were," I said.

Julie went silent for a moment. I looked toward the kitchen. A large man with dark hair and a bushy mustache covering both corners of his mouth tossed circles of raw dough in the air, spinning them faster with each catch and toss.

"Hey," I asked, "didn't you say you had a son to go get?"

"Yeah, he's at baseball practice right now.

"Oh, right. I forget about all the extra-curricular activities kids have."

"Oh, don't get me started. If it's not baseball, it's football or basketball or judo or Lord knows what else."

I fought the urge to bring up Victoria. She used to complain about all of Katie's after-school commitments and how draining it was to keep up. I wasn't ready to talk about my late wife to Julie, so I let the conversation go silent.

The din of the small restaurant filled the silence at our back-corner table. I had brought in the binder and crime scene photos, hoping to ask Julie a few questions about the players involved and whether they were still within reach. After placing them on the table, I reached down in my bag for my notepad. When I sat back up, I noticed Julie's terror-stricken face. She was staring at the folder of photos.

"You okay? I asked.

She blinked and averted her eyes away from the photos. "Yeah," she said, "I'm good. You get through all the reports?"

"Just the responding officers," I answered. "I spent most of the afternoon studying the crime scene pictures."

"Oh," she said. Her tone told me she was afraid to ask. "Find anything useful?"

"Well, except for the written confession they missed? No."

"What?" Julie Haywood shot up straight in her seat.

"I'm kidding. I'm kidding," I admitted.

"Oh, sorry. I'm a little out of it. When it's just me going over the case, it's easier to deal with, but reliving it with someone new is proving harder than I thought."

“It’s okay. I’m still working on my humor,” I said. “But, to answer your question, no. Nothing that I would say is useful, but then I’m just soaking it all in right now. Something may stand out later.”

“Okay, let’s hope so.”

Soon, our pizza was brought to the table and placed on a metal holder. As we ate, I inquired about several of the witnesses and cops mentioned in the reports. Julie told me one of the officers had moved away, and I’d already met Langston. That left Cedrick Fallon.

“Yeah, he retired and started working as a part-time bailiff for the sheriff. I see him up at the courthouse every so often.”

“Okay, good. So, he’s still around.” I made a note.

“What about the co-worker, Maynard Preston?”

“Yep. He’s an assistant football coach at the high school, teaches history.”

“Excellent. That’s a start.”

After a second slice, I wanted to ask Julie about one other person. I opened the photo folder and thumbed through until I found it, then slid it out with the back toward her. I used the top picture to cover up Daws in the picture I wanted to show Julie.

“I can’t, Hank.”

“No, wait. I just want to ask about the detective in the corner of this picture. I just want to show you the edge. I’m covering up the other parts.”

Julie’s anxiety subsided only enough to look. “Detective Byrd.”

“Okay, Detective Byrd. Was he the lead? Is he still around?”

Julie gave me a crooked smile. “Yes, Holcomb Byrd was the lead, but no. He’s been dead for twenty or so years.”

I let the answer process and then scribbled a line through “Lead Detective?” on my notepad.

After finishing up, Julie paid the bill, and we walked the two blocks back to the police station. Afterward, she had me follow her to an apartment she had set up. I offered to commute the hour back and forth to Tallahassee if she would cover gas expenses, but she insisted on the apartment. I felt foolish taking up an apartment to consult on a case, knowing most likely I wouldn't be there long, but I didn't want to seem ungrateful.

"Alright, I turned on the air, set out fresh sheets for the bed, and made sure the TV remote had charged batteries."

The apartment was on the bottom floor of an eight-unit brick building that ran along Duval Street. The red brick had an industrial look with wrought iron and black accent shutters. I stood in the living room of the small two-bedroom apartment and figured it would work. The last time I spent the night away from the house without Victoria was before she was diagnosed with cancer. It was the time Durgenhoff and I were working on a case that led us down to Miami. We hooked up with the local marshals to take a murder suspect into custody early the next morning.

"It's fine," I said. "I'm planning on reading through the rest of the case file tonight. We can make a game plan in the morning."

Julie held a wide smile. At that moment, the sadness that she carried with her seemed to have disappeared.

"Sounds good. Good night, Hank."

⌘

I had packed light, not expecting to stay very long. I changed out of my suit, made the bed, and put away the few clothes that I'd brought. As a final touch, I set a framed picture of Victoria next to the TV in the living room. It was a photograph that I had taken of her on our trip to Hawaii, just after Katie went off to college. Her long, beautiful hair was flowing in a sharp breeze; the sun was radiating down on her flush skin, and her smile was wide and full of life. It was my favorite picture of her. It was also about a year before we found out. It was a perfect time but seemed like a lifetime ago.

Once I had put my touches on the place, I settled on the living room couch with the case file's contents spread out across the coffee table. I picked up the binder and pulled out all the investigative reports. Holding them together, they were a little over an inch thick.

I set the stack of reports down on the table in front of me and stared at them, unable to focus. I had been a cop for twenty-three years, and I wasn't naïve enough to believe that I could just waltz into a case that had been unsolved for over two decades and magically figure it out. I knew that once I read all those reports, there was a real possibility that what the detectives did was exactly what I would've done. They might have made the decisions I would've made. Which meant I had nothing to offer, and Julie Haywood would forever know that sadness.

I cupped my face in my hands. Suddenly, I felt exhausted and inept. In my suitcase, tucked in the front zippered pouch, I brought Victoria's letter she'd written to me. I reread it. Her warm voice resounded in my head.

One of the reasons I fell in love with you is that passion you carry inside. That is what makes you such a great husband and father and one hell of a detective. Except with Katie and I, I never saw you burn as bright as you did when working as a detective. The case, the chase, the truth was what drove you. Find something that returns that fire, Hank.

The fire.

I sat up and started reading. I was going to give the case my best, because fresh or cold, Crystal Daws deserved my best.

⌘

Holcomb Byrd was very formulaic. He stuck to the script as far as homicide investigations go. I was fine with that approach, except that it wasn't all-encompassing. Following this style could lead to success, but it wasn't guaranteed. There were always exceptions to the rule. The dogma wasn't appropriate for every situation, and I believed that each case held a unique identity and had its own voice.

Byrd had conducted a canvass of the area to include a four-block radius. He'd interviewed Daws's parents and close friends, including

Julie Haywood, inquiring about any issues she may have had at the movie theatre or anyone suspicious following her around in the days prior to her death. It was eerie reading Julie's interview, knowing how this event shaped her future. Byrd also interviewed each of the movie theatre's employees, inquiring about suspicious characters hanging around the theatre in the days prior. He even pulled the theatre's phone records from the day of the murder.

During a secondary canvass, Detective Byrd located video surveillance from a nearby bank. He noted that the captured video was from an hour before to an hour after the murder, but that no suspect leads were developed.

All moves were standard procedure, and each netted negative results. Byrd had put stops on all her checks and her credit card the day after the murder. He noted in a later report that no checks ever surfaced, and her credit card was canceled with no unauthorized uses. Obviously, the little amount of cash she'd had in her purse along with the theatre's deposit was untraceable, so there was just a brief mention of it in Byrd's report.

I keyed into a section of the report when it mentioned uncovering a robbery trend in the area that was possibly related to Daws's murder. Byrd received information from neighboring Jefferson County that they had pursued and arrested three suspects for committing a late-night robbery of a clerk leaving a consignment store. They had waited until after the store closed, snuck up on her, and robbed her at gunpoint, before fleeing in a silver sedan. A Jefferson County deputy spotted the car leaving the area and gave chase. They crashed out as they crossed over the Leon County border and were taken into custody. In the car, deputies found a gun, the stolen cash, ski masks, gloves, and some personal use narcotics.

The entry date for the robbery information was March 19, 1993. The next entry date was March 22, 1993, and Byrd stated that the lead didn't pan out and that the Jefferson County robbery suspects had been ruled out in the murder of Crystal Daws. I kept reading and then reread this part over but never found information as to why these suspects were dismissed. I jotted down a note to follow up with Haywood in the morning.

Byrd's report tapered off in the following months, citing follow-ups of tips and loose information that amounted to nothing. The last entry he made was August 20, 1993, in which he followed up with an informant at the jail who claimed to know who killed Crystal Daws. The snitch was brought from the jail to the police station in an attempt to protect his identity, but Byrd succinctly put that the snitch's information was worthless and a waste of time. He didn't include what the information was, but given the circumstances, I had to give the detective the benefit of the doubt.

Letting Byrd's investigation digest, I concluded that he did a thorough job with what he had to work with. But as I feared, he'd made moves that were logical and common sense, and they didn't pan out. Being able to manifest anything out of it was going to be difficult.

Amongst the case box was a bound printout of computer paper, continuous form paper with perforated holes along the sides. It had data printed in several columns and corresponding handwriting off to the side. Atop the page was AT&T's logo. I scanned the front pages and read a column of phone numbers, next to another set of phone numbers, a time, a date, a second time, and then some other indiscernible numbers and text. Handwritten off to the side were names and addresses, each followed by a checkmark.

I sifted through the printout and noticed that each and every phone number had a handwritten name by it. Any repeats had "x2" or "x3" by the name. Going back to the front page, I saw the latest times were from earlier on the night of the murder. I referenced one of the earlier reports and confirmed the AT&T printout was from the movie theatre's phone line. I was astonished that Detective Byrd had gone down the entire list and identified each caller. Since no real suspects were identified, I could only assume that the check mark meant their non-involvement. Double-checking the length of the printout, there were only check marks, no deviating marks that would indicate something else.

I moved on to the forensics side of the investigation. DNA was coming online in the early nineties and was being used in criminal investigations. Back then, they needed a voluminous sample of blood to obtain results. Over the years, the science progressed exponentially, providing law enforcement with a powerful tool for proving cases, especially cold ones. If not in the investigation itself, maybe I could manifest something from the physical evidence.

The autopsy report wasn't much of a surprise. Daws died from sharp forced trauma to the abdomen and exsanguination, which meant two bullets ripped through her torso and caused her to bleed to death. It was a gruesome way to be killed, but mercifully, it was quick. Reading through the medical examiner's report, it was noted that the shots were from an intermediate range. That meant, up close and within approximately eighteen inches, not point blank, which was inside of six inches. The trajectory showed them on a slightly downward, front-to-back path.

I set the autopsy report down and sifted through the crime scene photographs toward the end of the stack. The forensic tech had taken Daws's bloody clothes and draped them over a table for additional pictures. I pulled these from the stack and studied them closer. Powder burns surrounded the entry points from the bullets, speckling her blouse in a spread the size of a bread plate. This was consistent with the suspect standing just out of arm's reach when she was shot.

Closing my eyes, I imagined the moment just before the killer pulled the trigger. The robber was standing only a few feet away, demanding the bank deposit, and aiming the gun at her mid-section. At some point, either through Daws's defiance or the excitement of the suspect, the gun fired twice, knocking her down.

The jeans and shoes Daws was wearing were on the table next to the blouse. The pants were blood-soaked around the waistline. They had been cut down the side, something done by either the medical examiner or EMS as they attempted medical intervention. Other than the blood and intervening cuts, there was nothing obvious. I checked the blouse, and it had been cut down the side as well.

Pulling the property receipts from the crime scene, I made a note of every piece of evidence. I disregarded the clothes and swabs of blood. Those were expected. I noted both projectiles were recovered from the autopsy and measured to be .38 caliber.

“Revolver,” I noted. I pulled out the best overall picture of the crime scene, yet one that was close enough for a look at the ground around the body. Scrutinizing it closely, I noticed the lack of any shell casings on the ground.

Moving back to Byrd’s report, I scanned down to the part of the Jefferson County robbery suspects. There was no mention of the type or size of the gun found by the deputies following the arrest. I made another note, “Jefferson County gun.” This may have been why Byrd dismissed them as suspects, simply because they didn’t have the right type of gun.

My eyes grew heavy, and my mind slowed. I checked my watch, which read ten minutes after midnight. I cursed the late hour and cursed my body for not shutting down sooner. There were only a few more reports to read, but they were the peripheral reports of tasks delegated by Detective Byrd and unlikely to contain the smoking gun or signed confession. I decided to catch up on those in the morning and headed off to bed. I quickly gathered up the files and put them back in the binder. Noticing their clean condition again, I grew concerned and knew I would have to address something with Julie in the morning.

Having spent most of the day engrossed in the murder of Crystal Daws, I had ignored my phone. I checked the screen, and it was lit up with missed calls and unanswered texts from Katie.

“Whoops,” I said out loud.

I listened to her voicemail.

“Hey, Dad, that’s great to hear you took on a job. A cold case sounds so interesting. I’d love to hear about it. I had to look up where Madison was, not gonna lie. Anyways, I’m excited for you and know you’ll be good at it. Just, you know, be careful, okay?" There was a pause in the message. "I know Mom would be happy for you. I'll check in with you later, love you."

I sent a quick text back to Katie and set the phone on the nightstand.

Before heading to the bedroom, I grabbed the picture of Victoria off the TV stand and set it on the nightstand. Before falling asleep, I stared at her beautiful smile. Even in the dark, in a picture, she lit up the room.

Chapter 10

Managing a few hours of solid sleep, I awoke in a strange place. It took me a minute to get my bearings and remember. The compulsion to fix Victoria breakfast hit me, but I shoved it aside and started my day as a consultant on a cold case. The new change was odd, but I was excited to get started. I wanted to get hands-on with the Daws murder investigation, so I asked Officer Haywood if she would meet me at the crime scene. To my surprise, she was only a few minutes from the apartment.

"Hey, Hank. I brought you some coffee."

I thanked her and invited her in. Out of what I assumed was curiosity, she took a visual inventory of the place. She probably thought I didn't notice, but I did. Julie was out of uniform, which completely changed her look. Her hair was still swirled up in a loose bun, but her clothes, a tucked-in blue polo and blue jeans, fit her differently. Her badge and paddle holster hung from her belt, completing the *cop look*, but she looked more feminine than when on patrol.

"No Starbucks?" I asked.

"Nope! Ain't got no fancy Starbucks here. I got my Keurig and a case of French roast K-cups."

I smiled and took a sip. "It's fine, thank you."

"I was thinking we could take a look at the crime scene," I said. "I know a lot has changed, obviously, but I would still like to go to the scene. I want to see it for myself."

"Yeah, okay."

I grabbed my keys and the binder with photos and headed for the door.

"We can just walk if you want?" Julie asked, noticing I was headed for my car. "It's not that far."

"Oh…," I didn't realize when studying the map that I was staying only a few blocks away. "Okay, sure."

I locked up the apartment, and we set out for the crime scene.

"You off today?"

"Yes, sir." I looked down at the badge and gun on her hip. "Pretty much, but we're allowed to wear our gun and badge whenever."

"Of course," I replied. "And you don't mind hanging out with me?"

"No, of course not," she replied. "I mean, you're here to help me find answers, and I'll do whatever it takes."

"Well, let's go get started."

We continued down an old sidewalk headed deeper into downtown. We passed by the post office and a few residences. I paused and confirmed with Julie that this was where the K-9 track led. She advised that this particular block hadn't changed much in the past two and a half decades. I scanned the area, looking, overlaying what I knew had happened that night. The suspect crept up from this direction while his getaway driver circled the block. At least in theory.

Letting the scene absorb, I could feel Julie waiting for some sort of magic trick that would reveal some long-hidden clue. Her stare bore into me to the point of embarrassment. When I turned to look at her, she looked down.

"Okay," I said, then pointed. "The movie theatre is this way?"

"Um, yeah."

Ever since Ryder Langston gave me the heads-up about Julie and her obsession with the case, I was on guard. My initial assessment was that I didn't think she would be reckless. However, I noticed something last night that bothered me, and I wanted to clear the air.

"Can I ask you a tough question, Julie?"

She was caught off guard but accepted. "Sure."

"I'm the first one, besides yourself, to look into the case after it went cold, aren't I?"

She didn't answer.

"I am, right?"

"Yes," she said. "But, how? Did someone tell you or something? Was it Boone?"

"No."

"So, how did you know?"

"I didn't know how to take the Chief's reaction at first. There was no way for him to know I was coming, but when I told him why I was here, he had absolutely no clue that was a possibility."

"You got that from a look?" She was astonished.

"No, the case file, too."

"What do you mean?"

"I worked twenty-three years as a cop. I've been around reports and case files and evidence for my whole career, and those pages are way too pristine for having been used by more than just one person." I stared directly at Julie. "And that one person," I said as I stared directly into her eyes, "probably cracks open the case once, maybe twice a year? Probably to refresh her memory and hope something sticks out."

Julie Haywood hung her head and slowed her step.

"My guess is on the anniversary of her death and her birthday."

She nodded while looking down.

"Listen, Julie." I stopped and put my hand on her shoulder. "I'm not mad. It's just something I noticed."

"You probably think I'm pathetic," she said.

"What? No, of course not. Desperate and under-resourced sure, but not pathetic."

"Yeah, that I am," she agreed.

"Just don't lie to me, Julie," I said. "In cases like these, especially with such a personal connection for you, we have to have trust."

"Okay, Hank. I'm sorry."

"Let's move on. How much further until we're there?"

"We *are* there."

The red brick building to my left caught me by surprise. Unlike fresh cases, I had built up the crime scene to be some sort of spectacle in my mind, but it was normal. Not the macabre sight that most of my murder scenes had been. I craned my neck up to take in the rest of the building, halfway expecting there to be a marquee with movie titles and a vertical neon sign spelling out the theatre's name. Instead, four white columns held up the front eave, with "Courthouse Annex" stenciled across the facade. The building had a boring government feel. A few curious heads watched us from inside and behind a counter.

Stepping back to take a wider look, I could see the modifications done over the years to cover up the markings of the old movie theatre. They were subtle but became obvious the more I studied. I pulled out one of the pictures taken from across the street in 1993 and held it up in comparison. The movie theatre was still there, but it had undergone a facelift.

Scanning the ground, just beyond the curb, I found the spot and moved over to it. Julie instantly recognized it and stayed on the sidewalk. I knelt down as if Crystal Daws was still there, trying to read what I could from the cold scene. Twenty-five years had passed since she last lay here. My mind became fluttered with visions of multiple road resurfacings, thousands of rainstorms, cars coming and going, foot traffic to and from the courthouse annex, and life moving for over two decades. It was everything that would and could carry away evidence, making the echo nearly impossible to hear.

Breaking away from my thoughts, I looked across the street, where the main courthouse sat in the middle of a square. From this side of the historical building, a giant silver column stretched high in the air, looming over the courthouse like a detached chimney.

"What is that, exactly?" I asked.

Mentally, Julie had left the scene. "What?"

"That." I pointed. "Is that like a silo or something?"

Julie found what I was talking about and looked back at me. "I actually don't know what it is. But I know it's not a silo."

"Right," I replied. "Well, I don't know why, but I had imagined the other side of this street to be business fronts too, not the backside of the courthouse."

"Does that change anything?" she asked.

I quickly applied the facts of the case as I knew them to the physical scene twenty-five years later. Surveying the scene and beyond, I imagined Langston's arrival, the K-9 track leading away, and Detective Byrd delegating responsibilities. Across the street from the movie theatre felt more open than I had imagined. I could see all the way to the main highway that ran east and west through town. Past that, I could see a white gazebo centered in what appeared to be a park.

"What's that? One block over?"

"Four Freedoms Park. Kind of our hallmark for the city."

"Ah, okay." Something felt off about her answer, but I passed over it for now. There was much more to learn about the case first.

The morning sun began to warm up the day. I shaded my eyes and looked over the scene one more time. It wasn't the same as a fresh crime scene, but I was satisfied with my visit.

"Okay, we can go," I announced.

"Where to?"

"Do you think Maynard Preston is at school?" I asked.

"Probably not," she answered.

"Why not?"

"It's Saturday, Hank."

I felt foolish, not even knowing what day it was. I felt even more foolish for having Julie Haywood work on her day off, even more so due to the weekend. She must've read this on my face.

"It's okay. I don't mind." She smiled, relieving my guilt. "Not much to do on Saturdays as a single mom in Madison. Working a twenty-five-year-old murder seemed like a good way to spend the day."

Maynard Preston lived out of town on nice, open acreage off Route 6. He was one of the few people involved in the case who was still around. I wanted to talk to him in person and had to explain this to Julie Haywood.

"You think he's a suspect?"

"Not really, but you can't be too sure."

"I don't know, Hank." Her skepticism was obvious.

"In cold case work, you either find missing or new evidence, or you have to change the theory."

"The theory?"

"Yeah, the reason why," I said. "And this was a robbery, and most robberies of businesses are inside jobs in one way or the other."

"Really?"

"Yes," I answered. "I don't know how many boyfriends of robbery victims I've caught or ex-employees I've arrested for robbing their old employers."

"Interesting." Julie looked concerned as she turned down a dirt driveway.

"I'm not saying he's involved; I just want to get a feel for him."

As we pulled up in Julie's Jeep, I saw a man and a young teenager in an expansive yard, throwing a football back and forth. The man paused to see who was pulling up but went back to tossing the football when Julie waved through the windshield. He had an athletic build under the added weight that came with age, although he looked younger than he was. He smiled and waved back.

"Hello, Jewels. How are you today?"

"I'm good, Maynard. I'm good." The two embraced in a friendly hug. As he moved away, he looked at me. "Maynard, this is my friend Hank Trescott."

Maynard Preston had a firm grip, friendly and welcoming. "Nice to meet you, Hank," he said. "Are you a police officer, too?"

"Well, kind of. Retired."

"Good for you. Hope to be there one day, too," he said.

"So, we wanted to ask you some questions," Julie said.

This confused Maynard, but he moved on. "Don't tell me one of my guys did something stupid last night."

"Oh, no. No, nothing like that," Julie answered. "We're actually here on a different matter."

"What's that?"

"Hank is helping me look into Crystal's murder."

Preston's face, which I could tell in our short interaction normally held a joyful smile, turned sullen.

"Oh," he said. Preston looked down, and his body began swaying back and forth. He was clearly uncomfortable talking about Crystal Daws.

"You were there that night. You were the last person who saw her."

"Hey, MJ!" he called out to the teenager. "Go inside for a bit and let me talk to them, okay?"

The kid nodded and took off for inside.

"I don't really want him to hear any of this stuff."

"That's fine. We can go somewhere else, if you like." I offered.

"No, this is fine," he answered. "What do you want to know? I mean, that was like twenty years ago."

"What *do* you remember of that night?"

Preston began walking away from the house. Julie and I followed, walking with Preston in the middle.

"Well, I remember working at the theatre with Crystal. I cleaned up theatre two after the movie was done, while Crystal was counting the money from the concessions. It was just the two of us there. When I finished up, she was done, too."

Preston got quiet and remembered something painful from that night.

"What is it?"

"You know I think about her all the time, Jewels?"

"Really?"

"Yeah, I mean, every time I take the boys to the movies, or hell, when Felicia makes popcorn in the microwave, I think about her. She was my friend. I miss her."

Julie Haywood nodded and smiled. "I miss her, too."

"Anything else about that night you can remember?" I interjected.

"Um," Preston thought. "Not really. Just that I double-checked the doors like I was supposed to, and we left after I clocked out."

"Wait, 'we'? You left together?"

"Yeah, well, I offered to walk with her to the bank, but she went back inside for some reason."

"Did you normally walk with her?"

"No, but she didn't normally make the night deposits," he said.

"Oh? Who did?"

"Well, usually our manager did, but he took the night off for some reason. Sundays were usually slow, so he let Crystal take care of it."

"Oh, okay." I let the information sink in. That wasn't in the report. It wasn't game-changing information, but it could play later depending on how the case worked out.

"So, you didn't see anyone hanging out or standing nearby when you left?" I asked.

"Nope."

"The report said you went home to your grandmother's house, right?"

"Yeah, I lived with her until I left for college."

"Is that east or west from where the theatre is?"

"West. Why?"

"Just trying to put pieces together."

We had circled the front yard and were approaching the house. I replayed Preston's answers and couldn't think of any follow-up. Julie thanked him for answering questions and said she looked forward to the next football season. Before we got back in her Jeep, I thought of one more question.

"Mr. Preston?" He turned around. "You said you guys walked out together, but she went back inside."

"Uh, yeah she did."

"Do you remember why?"

Preston thought hard. He searched his memory and squinted his eyes as if looking back into the past.

"Did she forget something?" I offered. "Like her purse or jacket or something?"

"No, no. Nothing like that," he said. "Oh, the phone rang. She went back to answer the phone. It was probably Mr. Elden checking in."

"Mr. Elden?" I looked at Julie and back at Preston. That name wasn't in any of the reports I read.

"He was the manager," Preston answered.

"Oh, okay," I said. "Alright, thank you again, Mr. Preston."

"Sure thing." He waved and walked inside.

His answer about the phone ringing bounced around in my head for a minute. I waited to see if something would spark an idea or notion to help with the case, but it fell flat.

"Damn."

"What?" Julie asked.

"It was just a phone call."

"Yeah, so?"

"Byrd pulled the phone records and exhaustively went down the list. I saw it in the file. It's a road that's already been traveled and led to nowhere."

We drove in silence on the way back to town. As we pulled up to the apartment, Julie asked, "You still think it was an inside job? I mean, with Maynard?"

"No, my gut tells me that guy's pretty genuine."

"Good. I agree."

Chapter 11

After a few phone calls, Julie Haywood managed to track down Cedrick Fallon. He had pulled babysitting duty at the jail and would be there until after dinner time. But first, I asked Julie to take me to Mr. Elden, the manager of the Woodard Theatre.

"So, we're just retracing steps at this point?" Julie asked.

"Pretty much."

"Okay." Her flat answer was telling. It was as if she said, *I could've done that.*

"Tell me what you know of Mr. Elden?"

"Um, well… He's probably in his late sixties by now, managed the theatre back in the eighties and nineties, until it closed, pretty much after everything happened. Then, he worked at a grocery store as a manager until he retired a few years back. Widower for about five years, has grown kids that moved away. Not sure where."

The term "widower" struck me. I had never considered that word would be used to describe me if anyone were to ask. I didn't like it.

"Okay, that it? Did you know anything about him, like what kind of person he was?"

"Oh…," Julie thought again. "He was usually mean to me, always yelling at me and watching me, but Crystal seemed to like him. Always told me not to worry about him."

"Hmm. Okay. Maynard said that Elden took the night off, and I never saw it in the reports. Do you know why?"

"No."

"Alright then." I gave Julie a wry smile. "Let's retrace those steps."

Mr. Elden lived in a neighborhood behind the community college on the west side of town. Modest, older homes with families gave it character and surrounded the area. Each house had a small step-up porch and an awning that supported bench swings and rocking chairs. The yards were well-manicured, and I felt like I stepped into a picture of Americana from decades past.

Julie led the way up to the porch and knocked. Up close, I noticed the exterior paint was chipping and the floorboards were over-worn.

After a second knock, I heard footsteps shuffling toward the other side. A voice mumbled and Julie answered back, "It's Officer Julie Haywood, Mr. Elden." I noticed that she straightened the badge on her belt and adjusted her stance to show off her credentials.

The old door peeled open, and in it stood a white-haired man with sunken eyes, a wrinkled face, and bifocals perched at the end of a long, thin nose. The sight gave me pause.

"Yes?" he said in a soft voice.

"Hi, Mr. Elden, it's me, Julie Haywood, and I've brought a friend with me." His tired eyes moved to me, and I introduced myself. His hands were large, but his grip wasn't as firm as I expected when we shook hands. He invited us in and offered us a seat on the couch. He slowly eased backward into a recliner and turned the television off with a remote.

I leaned toward the former theatre manager and said, "We're here to ask you about Crystal Daws, Mr. Elden."

His face registered confusion at first, but then recognition followed. He leaned back in his chair. "Yes, Crystal."

"Yes, sir. What do you remember of her?"

"Good employee, she was. Easy to train, dependable, and nice to the customers. The only thing I didn't like was that she had this little girl always following her around, helping her around the theatre."

Julie appeared surprised when I glanced over at her.

"I knew she was letting her sneak into the movies when I wasn't around," he added.

Julie's expression of surprise turned to embarrassment. Mr. Elden leaned forward in his chair and winked at Julie. "Didn't think I knew, did ya?"

She let out an embarrassed laugh, and I couldn't help but giggle. The old man was having fun with Julie.

"Oh, my goodness, I thought you hated me."

Mr. Elden waved her off. "Pish-posh, girl. I didn't care. Like I said, Crystal was a good employee. I only gave you the stare-down so the other kids would think twice."

I let the moment take its course, and then I interjected.

"Mr. Elden—"

"Jimmy, please call me, Jimmy," he corrected.

"Yes, sir, Jimmy," I said. "Did you ever have any problems with any other employees around that time?"

He gave it an earnest thought. "No, sir. Can't say that I did. Didn't have too many employees at the theatre. Mostly high school kids to run the booth and counters, then clean up the theatres after each show."

"What about anyone else? Anyone make trouble outside or inside the theatre?"

"I mean, we had some issues pop up every now and then, but nothing I would consider dangerous."

"Like what?" I asked.

"Oh, well…," Jimmy searched his vast memory. "Kids sneakin' in, sure. Maybe a spat over money or something would come 'round every blue moon, but nothing serious." He continued searching. "I mean, we'd have some kids come in drunk and get rowdy ever' so often, but nothing that gave me too much concern."

"Okay." I thought about my next question carefully, as the answer would lead us down one of two paths. If the robbery was an inside job, then Elden would be at the top of the suspect list. He had separated himself from the theatre that night, giving him the appearance of being uninvolved, and with proper questioning, he could reveal the actual culprits. Or he could provide a plausible answer and kill that theory where it stood.

"Why did you take off that night, Mr. Elden?" I asked.

He bowed his head and leaned forward. A move I'd seen in many suspects just prior to a confession. My heart thumped for a few beats, and I saw Julie sit up straight, too.

"You know, that's haunted me for a very long time," he said. "I used to lie awake at night thinking about how that could've been me. But, Mr. Trescott, I took the night off to celebrate my wedding anniversary with my Sarah."

Through welled-up eyes, he peered across the room to a picture of a lovely woman in a tasteful portrait. "She had complained of me working all the time and even threatened to leave me. We didn't have much, so I was always working, which clearly didn't leave much time for our marriage. So, I made sure I took that night off, and we set off to Tallahassee for a much-needed night together." He smiled at the memory. "Ate at the Silver Slipper like we were a couple of movie stars, we did."

Julie looked over at me, and I gave her a shrug. I remembered the Silver Slipper. Victoria and I had spent a few dinners, and glasses of wine there, too. It was a fine dining establishment with sectioned-off booths and an exquisite menu. The posh ambiance catered to those looking for a fancy evening. Like Mr. Elden, many people from the outlying counties came to Tallahassee for more of a dining experience.

Jimmy Elden smiled and looked up at me. "Hell, we conceived Jimmy, Jr. that night. It was a great night until we got home." The smile vanished. "The machine had a message on it from the police department; said something had happened at the theatre, and I was to get down there ASAP."

Jimmy nodded, reliving that night twenty-five years ago.

"I thought maybe it was a break-in, or a fire, or something. Not *that*." He shook his head. Tears followed. I saw Julie wipe her own eyes. "I wasn't prepared for *that*. So..., they needed me to figure out how much money was taken and to get access to the bank deposit to make sure it was missing. They said it was some sort of a robbery."

Silence gripped the room. Jimmy Elden, like Julie Haywood, harbored his own guilt surrounding the murder of Crystal Daws.

"She was just lying there..., in the damn street." He began sobbing, and Julie jumped up to hold him in the recliner. Eventually, she calmed him, and he excused his outburst.

"I didn't mean to bring up painful memories, Mr. El— Jimmy, I'm sorry."

"Oh, no, not necessary." He winked back at the picture of his wife. "I'm just glad someone is looking into it again. It's a shame they haven't caught the man responsible."

"We're trying our best, sir," said Julie.

Searching for any last questions, I paused, replayed what I had asked, thinking about anything I'd missed.

"One last thing, Jimmy. Do you remember calling the theatre that night?"

Mr. Elden's eyes narrowed at the question.

"It would've been around closing time, perhaps?" I had to be careful not to lead him too far.

"Honestly, that's something I did quite frequently when I wasn't there, but I couldn't tell you if I did or didn't that night." He answered. "Sarah and I splurged on a bottle of wine that night, and I don't remember much from the tail end of dinner, Mr. Trescott. I'm sorry."

"It's alright. Thanks for your time, Jimmy. We'll get out of your hair." I stood up and met him at his recliner, so he didn't have to get up. "We'll see ourselves out."

On the way out, I caught sight of a porcelain plate hanging on the wall by the door. Pink-colored flowers and gold trim made it stand out, but the two hands holding in the middle with the date March 14, 1977, stamped at the bottom confirmed Jimmy Elden's anniversary was the night of Crystal Daws's murder.

"Still think it might be an inside job?" Julie asked.

I thought for a minute. Jimmy Elden had been plagued by his guilt about Crystal Daws's murder, even after all these years. It contradicted the theory that he could be involved. The possibility of another employee outside of Elden and Preston still existed, but the likelihood was dwindling fast.

"How many other employees were there?" I asked, before answering.

"Um, six. At the time."

"Not including Crystal or Maynard?"

"No, including them."

"Oh. How long will it take to track the others down?"

Julie perked up.

"I've actually already done that."

"Really?" Her proactive approach surprised me. "When did you do that?"

"Before I met you. It was something I thought I'd do when I took over the case."

"And?"

"I wrote it all down, but nothing stood out."

Julie gave a rundown on the four remaining theatre employees at the time of Daws's murder. One moved across the country and was working for a tech company in California. Two of them wound up marrying each other and moving to Tallahassee to raise a family, and the other followed Jimmy Eldon into the grocery business. She worked as a cashier at the grocery store and was the only one with a criminal history, catching a DUI back in 2003.

"Alright. We may need to revisit them later, but to answer your question, no. It's not looking like an inside job."

After answering Julie's question, I let the idea that the motivation for the robbery was not an inside job settle. However, this discovery added a wave of depression. Normally, the elimination of a theory was a good thing. It narrowed the focus of the investigation. But, in this case, theories were scarce and dismissing them inched us closer to a dead end. The realization started to sink in that this was a robbery of opportunity. Unfortunately, that created endless possibilities with endless suspects who'd been hiding for a quarter of a century.

Next, I told Julie I wanted to inspect the physical evidence collected in the case. I wasn't hopeful after reading the property receipts from the case file, but another look wouldn't hurt.

"Alright. I've got them at the house."

⌘

Ten minutes later, we pulled up to an open field with a white prefabricated home situated near the front of the road. A large oak tree rose from behind the house, and landscaped shrubbery encircled the foundation. A shed sat behind the house, and a small johnboat was parked off to the side. It was modest but well-kept, much like Julie Haywood.

She cut the engine to her Jeep and said, "Home sweet home."

I followed her in and took a seat at a kitchen table. She buzzed around the house for a moment until she came back carrying the original case box she'd presented yesterday. She pulled out a few plastic bags and some paper bag packages adorned with red evidence tape. The labels of the paper bags told me they contained clothing that Crystal had worn the night of her death. I set them aside and focused on the few pieces of evidence encased in clear plastic. One bag held her personal effects: a watch, a ring, and earrings. The other bags contained video cassette tapes. The label on the tapes read "surveillance video." With a closer look, I saw the original evidence tape had been replaced.

"Those are from the bank on Main Street," Julie explained. "They had a camera aimed toward the street. It was pretty much the only surveillance system in town at the time."

I turned and looked up at her expectantly. "And?"

"Hank, I've watched those videos for hours and hours." She had a depressed tone. "There's nothing there. I mean, there is a gray truck that drives by five minutes before, but the angle and lighting don't allow for any actual detail. Best guess, it's an early nineties model Ford F-150. I've actually pulled all registered trucks that match the description from Florida and Georgia."

Julie let out an exhausted sigh.

"Wow," I said.

I was beginning to see how Ryder Langston could have misconstrued her exhaustive follow-up for an obsession. Her tenacity genuinely impressed me. But I could tell she was grasping for something that wasn't there.

"Do you know how many trucks match that description according to the Department of Highway Safety and Motor Vehicles?" Julie asked.

I blanked, "No, how many?"

"Over ten thousand in Florida alone."

"That sounds about right."

"And, I found that the majority of those from Madison County don't exist anymore, so I can't really follow up with them. It was a friggin' wild goose chase."

Her tone turned into a frustrated whine. I understood her pain. At times, detective work was tedious and fruitless, and because the task was often necessary, it doubled the frustration.

"You did a lot of work, Julie. Be proud of that. Have faith that it'll pay off."

"I hope you're right, Hank."

I smiled and handed her back the tapes.

She dug into the box, pulled out a manila envelope, and handed it to me.

"I had a friend at the State Fire Marshal's office try to enhance the video of the truck. Here are the still shots.

Her phone buzzed on her hip.

"Hello?" she answered.

I perused the pictures. They were of a fuzzy, dark gray truck, taken at an odd angle from the bank out toward the street. The truck was nondescript, and above that, there was nothing that indicated it was even involved in Crystal's death. It was simply a picture of a truck.

With regard to the other pieces of evidence, I looked them over and knew this was another dead end. I hid my concern from Julie as she talked on the phone. There just wasn't enough to generate a new lead. Absent a time machine, what was laid out on her kitchen table was all there was, and all there was ever going to be.

The kitchen door opened behind me, and I turned to see who it was. A young brown-haired teenager stepped through the door. A flat-brimmed ball cap hid most of his face and feathered hair stuck out from the sides. He looked at me but didn't say anything as he walked past. Julie locked eyes with him and nodded toward me. Begrudgingly, the kid turned around.

"Hi, I'm Bryce. Her son." He stuck out a skinny arm.

I shook his hand. His grip was surprisingly strong for a young man. "Hank, nice to meet you, Bryce."

"Alright." he replied, then vanished down a hallway. I heard a door shut and muffled music started playing.

Julie ended her conversation and clipped her phone back to her belt. "Fallon is about to leave the jail. We can meet him over there if you want."

"Yeah, sure. Sounds good."

"Sorry, that was Bryce. My son."

"Seems nice," I said.

"Ha. Most of the time," she said. Julie yelled toward the back of the house that she was leaving but would be back before dinner. "C'mon, let's go."

⌘

Officer Cedrick Fallon was now *Deputy* Cedrick Fallon. He was leaning against the side of a shiny silver truck, waiting in the parking lot of the jail. He stood, arms folded, but with a friendly smile on his face. He spied us pulling into the parking lot. He was a stout man with a dark complexion and graying hair on the sides.

"Hey, Fallon," Julie said as we climbed out of the Jeep.

"Hey, little Jewels, good to see you."

"Good to see you, too." The two hugged quickly, and Julie introduced me. We shook hands as Julie explained that Fallon had acted as her unofficial training officer when she'd first started. They reminisced about the importance of the complimentary coffee from the local convenience store when working the long and boring midnight shift.

"So, you guys are looking into that murder, huh?" Fallon seemed relieved.

"What do you remember about it? Anything stick out now?" I asked.

"Wow, what are we talking here, twenty-five years now?"

"Yeah, it has been," Julie answered.

"Well, I remember that night pretty well. We don't get too many homicides, and the ones we do get tend to stick with ya."

I nodded, letting him figure out where he wanted to start. Several images from past homicides I'd worked flashed through my mind, as those were the ones that stuck with me. When you live the cases, they never close. They become a part of you.

"Well, I remember hearing Langston calling out that he'd heard shots fired, and then he found the girl on the ground. I came to the scene and helped him secure it. Uh…then…, oh yeah, I did a canvass of downtown after Byrd made it to the scene. Checked all the businesses but came up empty."

"Did anything stick out that maybe wasn't worth mentioning at the time?" I asked.

Fallon scrunched his face and started shaking it. "No, nothing really stuck out."

As a detective, I put beat cops in two categories, trailblazers and followers. Trailblazers were the cops who relentlessly pursued the truth and toed the line of acceptability to get bad guys off the street. They usually went on to find success up the ladder of rank and opportunity, assuming they never crossed the line. Followers were just that. Capable cops that could get the job done, but with minimal effort. Cedrick Fallon was a follower.

"Do you remember speaking with Maynard Preston that night?"

"Oh yeah, that's right. Coach Preston used to work at the theatre," he remembered. "Yeah, I went out to his grandmama's house to talk to him. I remember he didn't take the news real well."

After having met and spoken with Maynard Preston, there was no need to continue asking him about the witness he'd interviewed.

"What about any of the other employees? Any of them stick out as weird?" I asked.

"No, not really. I mean, Byrd and Langston were the ones mostly working the case. I just helped when they needed it."

"Do you remember the news of a robbery crew getting arrested in Jefferson County soon after the murder? They did a robbery that was similar in M.O. as this one."

Fallon's eyes went wide in search of one memory shuffled and filed amongst twenty-five years of others.

"No, I got nothing for ya," he said. "I mean, it was a robbery. Why they had to kill that poor girl, I ain't quite figured." Fallon then asked, "You think the 'A Team' missed something back then?"

"Probably not, but we need to check, right?"

Cedrick Fallon nodded.

Standing next to a cop who was there when the case was fresh, I wanted to get a feel from him, but all I felt was static. This was a dead end. Fallon had moved on. Being a follower, he'd distanced himself from the fact Crystal Daws's murder went unsolved. No other questions came to mind, which created a sense of despair. It was slight, but I felt it in the pit of my stomach. Fallon and Julie exchanged hugs, and I thanked him for his time.

Dusk was giving way into night, but there was one more box I hoped to check. Something to spark life into this cold case.

"Do we have time for one more stop?" I asked.

"Uh, sure," Julie answered. "Where?"

"Who, actually," I said. "Crystal Daws's parents. Are they still alive?"

The hesitation before answering my question was obvious. Clearly, it was a sore subject given that Crystal Daws was Julie's cousin, making her parents Julie's aunt and uncle. Thankfully, I'd never had to deal with any of my family during a murder investigation, so I understood her pause. Yet, speaking to them was still necessary.

"I wouldn't ask if I didn't think it was important," I offered. Julie Haywood still didn't answer. "Listen, I can go alone if you like."

"No, no," she said, "it's fine. Uncle Steve passed a few years ago, but Aunt Carol still lives in the same house. It's just that..., I really haven't been over there since."

"Really?"

"Yeah, when things got somewhat back to normal, we never went over to their house. When we gathered as a family, it was always somewhere else. It would've been too weird."

"I bet," I said. "You think it's too late for a visit?"

"No, shouldn't be," Julie said.

A few minutes later and several turns into an unfamiliar neighborhood, we pulled up to a quaint home sitting atop a small hill. Concrete stairs led from the road, and boxwood hedges lined the sides. There was a small, screened porch in front of the house, and there were plenty of lights on.

Julie led the way up the narrow steps and knocked on the outside porch door. A shadow from inside the living room moved toward the door.

A woman in her early sixties, with stylish short gray hair and a trim figure opened the door. She had a quietness about her. A small but concerned smile creased her face as she recognized the late caller.

"Hey, Jewels," the woman said as her eyes darted toward me.

"Hi, Aunt Carol," Julie said. "Sorry to bother this late, but um…."

Julie stuttered awkwardly, with an uncomfortable search for words.

"Who's your friend, Jewels?" Carol Daws said.

"Oh, yeah." Flustered, Julie introduced me. "Sorry, this is Hank Trescott."

"Hello, ma'am." I said in my most inviting tone. "Nice to meet you."

Carol's eyes scanned over Julie, looking down her side. With narrowing eyes, she said, "Did you want to come in?"

"Oh, no ma'am," Julie said quickly. I figured her decline had more to do with the past memories than the late intrusion, so I didn't say anything. But asking a family member about the twenty-five-year-old death of their daughter is not an ideal conversation for the front porch.

"We're looking into the case, Aunt Carol," Julie blurted.

"Oh," Carol said. "You are, huh?"

"Yes, ma'am," I added.

Carol turned to address me. "I assume you're helping?"

"That is correct."

Carol folded her arms and leaned against the door frame.

"We're in sort of a retracing of footsteps mode at this point," I explained. "So, I find it necessary to speak with the family, as I would any other case."

"Alright," she said. "You're some sort of detective, then?"

I smiled. Julie scoffed.

"Are you or aren't you, Mr. Trescott?" she asked.

"Well, yes, but I'm retired," I said. "Julie asked for my help and that's what I'd like to do, help."

"He worked lots of murder cases over in Tallahassee for the police department there, Aunt Carol," Julie informed. "He knows what he's doing." Julie's voice rose convincingly as she boasted about me to her aunt.

"I see," she said. "Well, as Jewels will tell you, there's nothing I didn't give or haven't given to the police about my daughter's death. So, I'm afraid I can't give you any more insight than I have already."

"Okay, that's understandable," I said. It was clear that Carol Daws wasn't up for a rehash of her daughter's death, and I was not one to change that.

Julie chimed in. "Well, we really just wanted to touch base, Aunt Carol. Basically, to let you know we were looking into the case."

Carol Daws nodded but kept her emotions quelled.

"I'm very glad to see that she is still remembered, Jewels. Mr. Trescott, thank you. Even after all these years, it is still a source of great pain."

"Mrs. Daws, if there *is* anything that should come up, will you give Julie or me a phone call?" I asked.

"Certainly."

"Good night, Aunt Carol," Julie said.

"Good night, Jewels."

Back in the Jeep, Julie took an exaggerated breath in before turning the ignition.

"Was that weird, or is it just me?" I asked.

"No, that was strange," Julie admitted.

"Thought so."

"I haven't seen her in a couple of years, so I imagine showing up like that… telling her we're looking into Crystal's case…, yeah, it was weird."

⌘

The Jeep ride back to the apartment was silent aside from the rush of wind coming in from the sides. Mired in the unknown of the case, my thoughts were clouded with doubt, and any real answer felt out of reach.

There were no witnesses, no real physical evidence existed, and the killer had a twenty-five-year head start. The only aspect of comfort the case held was a solid theory of what had happened, but that wasn't enough to yield any possible suspects, not even from back then. Looking at the case as it stood, I feared the echo had become lost in the void.

"What's that look for?" Julie asked. I hadn't noticed we were parked outside of the apartment, and she was staring at me.

"Huh?" I asked, confused.

"That look on your face, it's like you ate something that spoiled. You okay?" she asked.

"Yeah. Just lost in thought that's all." I wasn't ready to share with Julie Haywood that her case wasn't getting solved.

Chapter 12

Awakened by the same unfamiliar sensation, like a splash of cold water tossed from a bucket, I quickly scanned the room. I remembered. Madison, murder case, Julie Haywood. I wiped my face and headed for a shower.

After dressing, I checked my phone. There were no messages or missed calls from Julie. I found that odd as she set the hospitality bar pretty high. I ignored the thought and stepped outside of the apartment building. The sun hung low in the eastern sky, showcasing a warm shade of orange that was chasing away the dark, purple dawn. It was going to be a pretty day.

Out on Main Street, two blocks down from the apartment building, was the familiar image of McDonald's golden arches. Breakfast sounded like a good idea. Given the culinary limitations of the town, I rationalized my menu choice with Victoria in my head.

I tried Julie's cell phone, but the other end of the phone rang until her voicemail kicked on. I began leaving a message when a strange noise beeped in my ear. I pulled the phone away to see a text message from Julie floating on the screen. It read: *Sorry, I can't talk right now*. I looked back at my breakfast option and figured I could eat while she finished up whatever she was doing.

The small town's fast-food restaurant was just like any other I had visited. In the corner of the dining area, a group of elderly men, probably in their early seventies, gathered to gossip, embellish, and waste time.

As I walked in, they perked up and followed me with their eyes. I ordered a hot coffee with my food and found a seat by the window, across the room from the men. I could hear parts of their conversation but couldn't put anything together.

As I ate my breakfast sandwich, I kept checking my phone. It had been twenty minutes since Haywood's text response. What could be keeping her? Was it something with the case or something contemporary she had to deal with? Moving on without her, I rolled through my internal checklist of the Crystal Daws murder. Despite the setbacks from regurgitating the case, I needed to be thorough. I needed to comb through everything and would hate it if I missed a small detail that proved crucial down the road. What I'd wanted from the beginning was to talk to the lead detective, but unless he could be resurrected from the dead, that was an impossibility. There was no way around it. But that didn't mean he hadn't stored away his notes and thoughts somewhere.

I remembered the dozens of notepads from my cases stored in my attic back in Tallahassee. Had I joined Detective Byrd in the afterlife, my notes would be available, if they could be found. I realized I'd never told Victoria or Katie or anyone where I'd put them.

"Detective?" A soft, aged voice interrupted my thoughts. One of the elderly gentlemen from the corner was standing before me. It was strange that he pegged me as a detective, but I had been traipsing around town with Julie Haywood for the last two days. That must've been their link. It was impressive how fast information moves in a small town.

"Yes, sir?" I said. "Well, used to be anyway."

"Once a cop, always a cop, right?" he said, looking back at his crew.

"Something like that." I smiled. "What can I help you with?"

"Well, I wish I woulda recognized you sooner, woulda bought your breakfast. Would you mind joining us?" he asked. "For just a bit, please?"

"Um, sure." Still no alerts on my phone, so I got up and joined the group in the corner. They all introduced themselves, and I tried to commit their names to memory: Mark, John, Lorie, Prentiss, and

Herman. They were all long-time retirees who met at the fast-food chain for breakfast to "philosophize" as one of them put it.

The one who introduced himself as Herman asked, "So, you're the big shot from Tallahassee that's helpin' little Miss Haywood with that murder case?"

"Yes, sir. Something like that," I answered. "Although I wouldn't call myself a big shot. I am trying to help."

"How's it goin' so far?" asked another.

"Um, it's slow going right now," I said, noncommittally. "But looking over any case that's been sitting for this long is going to take some time."

"Any new leads?" asked another one in the group.

"Well, now, John. You can't rightly ask the man that point blank, you old goat!" Herman chimed in. The group chuckled at the insult. John waved off his counterpart in dismissal. But I was glad for the interjection. I had never discussed the limitations of what should be kept confidential and what could be shared from the case. I made a mental note to hold that conversation with Haywood.

"He thinks he knows all, since he used to *be* the police chief," Mark stated about Herman.

"Oh, yeah!" I said. "When was this?"

"Oh, shoot, boy. A long time ago. Back in the sixties, probably when you were a little fella. But yeah, I used to be the police chief, fire chief, and city manager all rolled into one."

"Okay, wow. All three at once, huh?" I asked.

"Yeah, small town like this. Didn't take much to do all three. I left it all and went to FDLE soon after it was put together. Bout nineteen-se'emty-two, I went over."

Doing the math, Mr. Herman may not have had any influence over any of the players of the Daws's murder. I thought back and realized I was in grade school at the time he'd left Madison.

"Did you ever work with Holcomb Byrd?" I took a shot in the dark.

"Oh, shoot yeah, the Byrd man? Course I did. Good peoples, he was," Herman answered. "Damn shame he had that heart attack when he did."

"So, he was the lead on this case."

"Yeah, that's right. He was, wasn't he?"

"He always walk the line?" I asked Herman, cop-to-cop. "Stay righteous?"

Mr. Herman squinted and held my stare. His jovial demeanor turned serious, and I feared I may have insulted the memory of his friend, but it was something I needed to know.

"Yes, sir. I would say so. No reason to think otherwise?"

"Okay, good," I said, relieved. "I'd love to talk with him about the case, you know? To get his feel for everything, but that's not happening." I sighed and added, "Or at least get ahold of his notes on the case."

"Well, hell, son. Why didn't you just ask?" Herman laughed toward the bunch.

"What do you mean?" I asked, left in the dark.

"His widow, Mary Anne. She lives just outside of town on 145. She prob'ly hep you out."

⌘

After getting directions to Detective Byrd's widow, I walked back to the apartment to grab my notepad and the case file. In my haste, I'd missed a call from Julie Haywood. There was no message, so I called her back. Voicemail again.

My message was short, "Phone tag, you're it."

Driving around town, the old men provided landmarks instead of an actual address. However, with someone who's lived in this town for generations, I had high confidence they could accurately depict which tree and bridge to look for before making a turn.

Following each step with literal precision, I found myself pulling down a dirt driveway and up to a white, farm-style house with a large porch stretching across the front. “Byrd” was painted on the side of the mailbox. The home was a well-maintained holdover from a different era. It was like looking into the past with my own eyes. A large metal structure with a giant weathervane towered over the side of the house. A gust of wind kicked up, spinning the wheel and pointing the arrow due west. I heard chickens clucking as I walked up, and I swore I heard a cow moo off in the distance. The air smelled clean, which inexplicably brought a smile to my face.

The front door was between a pair of wooden rocking chairs that adorned the porch. I knocked on the antiquated screen door to announce my presence. The main door was open, and the sunlight shadowed the inside, making it difficult to see. But I could hear someone coming.

“May I help you?” a woman’s voice asked. As she neared the other side of the door, I could see she was in her late sixties, healthy, wearing an apron over her clothes. The skeptical look on her face made it obvious to me that she didn’t get many strange visitors.

“Hello, there. My name is Hank Trescott.” I started with, “I got directions from this gentleman at the McDonald’s in town, name of Herman. He said this is where I’d find you.”

The widow studied me for a moment and opened the door. I had passed some kind of test, something I assumed she’d picked up from all those years of being married to a cop.

“You found me,” she said flatly. “Now, what exactly do you want?”

I told her I was helping Julie Haywood look into the murder of Crystal Daws. When I worked a murder, especially involved cases, Victoria would often act as a sounding board for my thoughts. For the cases with sex appeal that were not the run-of-the-mill street shootings, she could have probably recounted the facts better than any other cop on the case. I hoped Detective Byrd had done the same with his wife.

“Well, Holcomb never really went into detail about his cases, except for that one.” She paused. “That one was different. It had a whole different feel to it, he’d say. You see, there aren’t many murders in Madison, and not ones like that of that poor girl, Mr. Trescott.”

"Please, you can call me Hank."

Mary Anne Byrd unceremoniously waved me in and moved to a reclining chair in the corner of a living room.

"That's the one at the movie theatre, right?" She said over her shoulder.

"Yes, ma'am," I answered. "The young girl who worked at the theatre. It was back in nineteen-ninety-three."

"Yes, I remember." She nodded and sat down. She crossed her arms at her chest. "Holcomb talked about that one. Said it bothered him to the end that he couldn't make an arrest."

"Yeah, I can imagine that."

"He spent a lot of time on that case. Had another policeman helping him, did you talk to him?"

"Ryder Langston?" I offered.

"Yes, Langston. Holcomb liked him. Called him his protégé."

"Yes, ma'am. I've spoken to him a little bit about the case."

"Well, okay. I'm not sure I'll be able to help ye' much."

"That's alright, Mrs. Byrd. I've read all the reports about the case. But, you know, when I was a detective, I kept notes in a notepad." I held up the notepad I brought with me. "Just like this one. It helped me keep everything organized for later, you know, reports and court and such."

Mary Ann Byrd nodded in understanding.

"Did your husband do that, too?" I asked.

"Yes, I believe he did."

"Did he, by chance, keep them around or in a box or drawer or something?" It was a longshot, but I was hopeful.

She perked up. Her eyes widened, and I grew excited.

"Um, hold on, Mr. Trescott." Mrs. Byrd stood up and walked to somewhere else in the house. I followed her footsteps on the floorboards and could hear items being shuffled around in another room.

"Can I give you a hand, Mrs. Byrd?" I called out.

"Oh, no thank you. I got it."

I sat patiently in the living room and let my eyes wander. A portrait of Holcomb Byrd hung over a modest fireplace. He was tall and thin, just like he was in the crime scene pictures. His ruddy complexion and mild demeanor told me he was a no-nonsense type of person outside of the job. Someone who carried the same personality over into his role as a detective, which was evident in his report.

"Here, I found this," Mary Anne Byrd announced. She was carrying a small box, much like the one Julie Haywood had the case file in originally. She set it down on the nearby table and waved me over.

"I'm not sure if this is what you're looking for, but it's the only box full of stuff mixed in with all his police things. I assumed the box because it was his biggest case."

Assessing the contents of the box, Mrs. Byrd's assumption was correct. The tabs on the folders were labeled with the name *Crystal Daws*, and the same case number I had now committed to memory. I mused over Madison Police Department's affinity for boxes in place of actual murder books.

"Yes, ma'am. This is exactly what I was looking for."

"Alright, well, I'll leave you to it, if you don't mind. I got a roast to prepare for the church later."

Flipping through the folders and files, I could see Holcomb Byrd had made his own copies of the files. Maybe he had ideas of working it after retirement, but apparently, his health had stripped him of that opportunity. I was curious about his death but knew it was inappropriate to ask his widow, seeing as I had just barged into her life.

The papers in the box were clean and much like the original. The last set of eyes that read over these files were probably Holcomb Byrd's. I set each folder aside and took inventory of what was present. I excused myself for a moment and retrieved the case file from the car. Next, I compared what Haywood had presented me with to what Holcomb Byrd had made copies of. After I was done, it was the same exact report. Nothing different.

"Dammit," I said.

"You alright in there?" Mrs. Byrd asked from the kitchen.

"Yes, ma'am," I answered, hiding my frustration.

Before replacing the folders of Byrd's copy, I discovered a notepad at the bottom of the box.

"Jackpot!" I whispered to myself. It was an ordinary yellow mini legal pad with notes scribbled on the majority of the pages. Being at the bottom of the box, the pad and pages looked to be in adequate shape. The corners of the pages rolled upward and felt frail in my hands. I sat down at the table and carefully deciphered the notes. For an old, country detective, thankfully, Holcomb Byrd had good penmanship.

The first pages were the basics. The address of the theatre and the time of the call were written along with two names I recognized. Langston and Fallon. Next was his description of the crime scene with his own, accurate drawing. He even drew in a suspect at arm's length with a gun. The next pages had witness information, contact numbers, addresses, and even school grades. Below each name were notes from what I assumed was an interview. I opened up Byrd's report and found the corresponding information.

I scanned the next few pages of the notepad as the information was synched to the report, something of which I had a good working knowledge. I stopped at the pages where I saw a deputy's name next to *Jefferson County Sheriff's Office*. I assumed that was who called him about the arrest of the robbery suspects soon after the murder. Below it, Langston's name was written with an arrow pointing to "9mm" which was circled with a line through it.

This coincided with my theory that the gun from the robbery suspects didn't match that of the homicide, so that lead was a dead end.

Moving on, the notes got more and more sparse. On the last page, at the top, was a name I didn't recognize, Jarret McKeirnon. I recalled the case as a whole and was confident that name had never appeared. There was a five-digit number and a time written next to the name. As I compared the notes chronologically to the report, my best guess was that it referred to the informant he'd spoken with about the case.

I dug around the box for any last shreds of information that could've slipped through the cracks but found nothing. This new name was something to follow up with, but again, I didn't have high hopes, as Holcomb Byrd had proved to be thorough.

"Mrs. Byrd?" I called out, "I'm headed out. May I keep this notepad?"

Mary Anne Byrd stood at the threshold of the kitchen, wiping her hands with a small towel. She studied the notepad for a moment, giving the request some thought. Reading the look on her face, I felt like I had asked for a sentimental piece of her husband's legacy. I felt intrusive until she answered.

"Sure. Take it all if you need to."

⌘

After thanking Mary Anne Byrd for her time, I headed back to the police department. If McKeirnon was the snitch referenced in the original report, there should be a corresponding file on him. It could have more information that might help in this investigation.

I thought back on the numerous times I'd talked to snitches at the jail. Everyone snitched. We joked about how the code of silence on the street never translated into the correctional system. Once they sat in jail for a few months, they realized that doing years on top of years in prison wasn't so appealing and began to clamor for ways to get out early. Snitching was the fastest. Especially on a murder.

Ten minutes later I checked in with Tyler at the front desk and made sure I had the correct visitor badge before heading to the back. It was strange without Haywood as my escort, but I had been on foreign soil long enough. I moved with purpose like I actually knew where I was going. But I needed help to find what I was looking for.

I walked around the cubicles outside of the break/conference room, and only one was occupied, a heavy-set man with a balding head and bushy mustache. I hadn't been introduced to him, and he was on the phone. I passed on interrupting his call. I looked around the large room and there was no one else. I turned and glanced up the stairs toward the executive suite. The chief had given me an open invitation for help, so I figured I could impose for a moment. Even though I pegged the invite as superficial, all I needed was to be pointed in the right direction.

The front door clicked open, and Officer Boone walked through.

"Hey, Officer Boone!" I called out.

He looked over at me and sneered once he realized who was calling. He put a Styrofoam cup up to his lips and spit out a dark liquid.

"You got your visitor badge, yet?" he asked.

"Yep." I flipped it up from my lapel. "Listen, can you help me out? Officer Haywood seems out of pocket."

He smirked at my mention of Julie. "What is it?"

"Well, I came across a name and wanted to see if he was a documented source for you guys."

"A what?"

"A snitch." I explained.

"Oh, yeah. No can do, partner. That's intel and is not to be shared with…" he looked me up and down, "civilians."

"But, whenever Haywood gets done, I'll get her to do it, so you might as well save me some time."

Boone spat again in his cup. Now that he was closer, and with my height advantage, I could see it was half full of tobacco spit. The menthol flavor wafted up from the cup, making me nauseous.

"Then I guess you'll have to wait until she gets back," he said with condescension.

"But it's just a confirmation of a name, Officer Boone?"

"I don't care, civilian," he said. "You'll just have to wait."

"Right."

Boone walked away with his head up proudly, and I was left with an unanswered question. I started back to the conference room when I heard a familiar voice.

"He's just intimidated by you, 'tis all."

Ryder Langston had come in through the back and set down a briefcase.

"Yeah, I guess. He's still an irritating little shit."

Langston chuckled. "Yeah, he is."

"What is it that you were asking him?" Langston asked.

"Oh, I paid a visit to Mary Anne Byrd today, you know, Detective Byrd's widow? She let me keep his personal files on the Daws murder, and when I was going through it, I found a name that I wanted to cross-reference in your confidential source files."

"Oh, yeah?" Langston's interest peaked. "What name?"

"Jarret McKeirnon," I answered. "Was he the snitch Byrd mentioned in his report? The way it reads is that he talked to him but gave no viable information."

"Yeah, I remember he said he had a snitch at the jail. The name doesn't ring a bell, but it was twenty-five years ago."

"Do you guys keep files on your sources?"

"Mostly. But if he was just a songbird at the jail, we wouldn't document that. Unless it panned out, of course."

"Oh, I see." I thought for a moment, figuring out the situation. If McKeirnon was like most snitches who came across a nugget of information on a murder and tried to sell it to get out of jail, he would've barely been worth mentioning. Nine times out of ten, they never panned out. It usually turned out to be stale, unsubstantiated, or a false lead. From what I've learned about Holcomb Byrd, if McKeirnon had anything worth saying, he would've used it.

"Well, do you mind if we check, anyway? Just for my sense of completeness?"

Ryder Langston smiled. "Sure. Follow me."

He led me upstairs to Chief Pitts' office, knocked on the open door, and stepped in.

"Hey, boss!" he said to the chief.

"Hey, what's going on?"

"Nothing. Mr. Trescott wanted to look up a name in the confidential source file. He wants to confirm something he found in Holcomb's case file."

Chief Pitt's brow furrowed in contemplation. He steepled his forefingers together and pressed them to his lips while he gave the request further thought. After a moment, he reached down, grabbed a file from his desk, and slid it across the top. "Knock yourself out."

It was an accordion file, about three inches thick, with manila files within. I thumbed the top and looked for McKeirnon's name. I spotted it, pulled it, and opened it up on the chief's desk. I could feel Langston and Pitts staring at each other over my back as I followed a dead-end lead. Maybe it was my own insecurities I sensed, but I felt like they were simply humoring me in this futile endeavor.

The file was bare bones. It had McKeirnon's biographical information, his unimpressive rap sheet with even less impressive crimes, and a few notes about drug information dated twenty-three years prior. He wasn't even a *good* snitch. But there was nothing in the file that could help me with the murder of Crystal Daws.

"Okay, well, that wasn't helpful at all," I said, closing the file and returning it to the chief.

"Sorry, Mr. Trescott," Pitts said.

Langston excused himself, and I thanked him for his help, anyway. He was much more accommodating than Officer Boone.

"How's everything else going?" asked the chief.

"It's going. I'm still in the review stage."

"Ah. I see," he said. "I take it you haven't found anything glaring or overlooked?"

I didn't want to concede just yet, but it almost seemed as if the chief wanted my involvement in the case to be finished.

"Um, well, I don't think I've crossed all the t's just yet," I answered vaguely.

"Okay, like I said, if you need anything, just ask."

I walked back downstairs and sat down in the conference room. I checked my phone and there was nothing from Julie Haywood. I began to dial her number when she trudged through the doorway and plopped down on a chair, exhaling loudly. She looked exhausted. Her face was flushed red, and her hairline was beaded with sweat. I focused on a smear of brown across her forehead and hoped it was just dirt. An odd animal smell emanated from her side of the room.

"Hey, I was just about to call you," I said. "Where the hell have you been?"

"Don't." She was upset about something. "You don't want to know."

I sat up. "Oh, no," I said, now intrigued by her being standoffish. "Now I gotta know. What have you been doing all day?"

She let out a sigh of exhaustion and irritation. "Wrangling fucking cows, that's what."

Chapter 13

The infrequent, yet not unusual occurrence of mischievous cows breaking through a fence and wandering dangerously close to the interstate had occupied Officer Haywood's morning. For some unknown reason, she was tasked with assisting the sheriff's office when this happened despite the area being out of her jurisdiction. I assumed it was a manpower issue solved with combined attention from both agencies. She had been out all morning with the owner and two deputies getting the cows back on the property and getting the fence mended. This explained her disheveled appearance.

"Have fun out there, Elsie?" Officer Boone walked by with a grin from ear to ear. Julie's reaction was of disgust. I could tell she was holding back and swallowed a retort. She sneered at Boone as he walked off with an *eat-shit* look.

"Elsie?" I asked.

Julie shook her head slowly. Her lips were pursed tight and her jaw clenched. A story of great embarrassment hid behind this reaction. She was upset, and I could tell she was at her limit.

"Don't worry about it," I said. If she wanted me to know, she would tell me. I'd learned in my twenty-plus years that holding people's past over their heads was petty and detrimental to their growth. If they were a constant fuck-up, then that's what they would do, and the problem would take care of itself. But rehashing past mistakes did not allow others a chance at redemption.

After a moment of calming thought, Julie sat up, put on a more pleasant face, and asked, “So, what have you been doing this morning? I saw I had like five missed calls from you. Find anything good?”

I ran through my morning of follow-ups, including the trip to Detective Byrd’s house and finding the notepad. I pulled it out and slid it across the table for Julie to look over. I continued with the discovery of Jarret’s McKiernon’s name on the last page and confirmed that the snitch angle was a dead end.

“Jarret McKiernon, huh?” Julie said.

There was recognition in her tone. “You know him?” I asked.

“Kinda,” she said. “We went to high school together. He dated one of my friends but nothing too serious. He was kind of a loser. Drug user, petty crimes here and there.”

“Capable of murder?” I asked.

“No.” she said flatly. “He never had the necessary brain power to do anything like that.”

Never one to casually pass off a name when it came to a murder investigation, however, Julie had insight into this person, and I felt comfortable shoving him off to the side for now.

“Anything else?” Julie asked.

I shook my head. “No, that’s pretty much it.”

“So, nothing?” she said.

“Nope,” I said.

“Well, that fits. It’s been a shit day already. Why the hell would it get any better?”

I felt bad for Julie Haywood. It made me think about my time in her town, investigating the case that meant so much to her, and how I hadn’t made any real headway. Breaking down my time in Madison, I had basically retraced the same steps taken by Holcomb Byrd twenty-five years before.

“I’m sorry, Julie.”

"No, it's okay." She tossed Detective Byrd's notepad on the table. Leaning back in the chair, she looked up to the ceiling. I saw her eyes water, but she wiped the bottom of her eye before the tear leaked.

"Listen, Julie, cases like these are tough, but that doesn't mean we give up."

She shut her eyes, and her eyelid squeezed out a tear. Silence fell upon the room.

Guilt enveloped me. Julie had entrusted me with this case, and I was letting her down. I knew from the beginning that the death of Crystal Daws was more than a cold case for Julie Haywood; it was part of her story.

"I'm going to head back to Tallahassee tonight," I said to break the silence. "There's a few things I need to take care of. I can be back in a few days, and we'll pick up where we left off, okay?"

"Sure," she said, flatly. "Whatever."

I let the insensitivity of her response fade away. "Sometimes you have to step back from a case and come at it renewed to gain ground."

"I thought that's what you had been doing, fresh eyes and all, looking for the noise or whatever."

"Noise?" I asked. "Oh, you mean the echo."

"Yeah, whatever. The echo." She stood up, ready to end the conversation, and I felt stupid for what I thought was a poetic analogy. "Listen, I gotta get back out there."

Julie Haywood walked out of the conference room without any further words, leaving an awkward silence hanging in the air.

"So, I guess I'll see myself out," I said to the empty room. I gathered up a few things, grabbed Holcomb Byrd's notepad, and headed past Tyler out the front door.

"Here," I said, placing the visitor badge on the counter. "I should be back in a few days."

"Alright. See ya, Hank." His friendly tone was contagious.

"Bye, Tyler."

After a quick stop by the apartment, I was on the interstate, headed westbound back to Tallahassee. My thoughts circled around Julie Haywood's bitterness. I had approached her with the mindset that she was just a fellow cop working a case and not what she really was—a murder victim's survivor. For that fact alone, she was allowed some grace.

During my career, I had come across several cops who decided to become law enforcement because they, too, were homicide survivors. One fellow officer from my early years told me he'd become a cop to find the man who'd murdered his father. I thought he was kidding at first because it sounded too Hollywood, but his demeanor quickly told me he was serious. He was a child when a random encounter left his father shot over the contents of his wallet. At the time he'd shared his story, I lacked the experience to help him. So, when it came to Julie and her connection to Crystal Daws, I didn't want to disappoint her, and I wanted to help her find closure.

Being driven by the death of a loved one was understandable. Victoria immediately came to mind. Taking revenge on her killer would bring me happiness because it would help so many others suffering from fatal cancer diagnoses. However, the extent of my knowledge surrounding cellular biology and oncology was limited to what had been explained to me by Torey's doctor. The more I thought about it, I wasn't sure which was worse, losing a loved one to an unknown subject or a named killer that can't be stopped.

Pulling up to my house, I was again reminded that Victoria was gone when I realized she wasn't inside waiting for my return. I recalled her waiting for me after work, walking in, and being greeted with a loving kiss. Moving through the memory, it was hard to focus on her beautiful face. Even after a moment of clarity, her image became hazy. It was like I couldn't see her in my mind. I glanced at her portrait over the mantle as I walked through the house and held the stare of the picture. She was still breathtaking.

I sorted through the pile of mail and tossed the junk into the trash. Dutifully, I filled up a watering can and watered what was left of Torey's plants. I had done a pitiful job at keeping them alive and could hear her voice getting on me to take better care of them. Checking on the rest of the house, I unpacked the little clothing I had taken to Madison and then ordered some food.

The drone of the local news was on in the living room as I ate alone in the kitchen. Nothing of note, a politician making promises, violence reported, local sports teams playing, and the weather was hot and rainy.

After I finished eating, I retired to the living room, turning the television to a baseball game. The Crystal Daws case and Julie Haywood took turns intruding on my thoughts. I questioned if I would be able to actually help them. I brought Detective Byrd's notepad in and studied it, reading through his detailed notes once again. New blood was needed if I was going to move the case in any fashion. My earlier doubts about working a cold case weighed heavily. Looking over Byrd's notes, I was left with the same conclusion. He had run a thorough investigation, and who was I to think I would be able to do anything differently?

I tossed the notepad on the floor and wiped my face in frustration.

"Ugh!" I let out my anger to an empty house. "Who am I kidding?"

DNA processing wasn't an option, absent a time-traveling forensic scientist. All the witnesses were contacted and interviewed. I thought it was a miracle that most were still around a quarter century later. However, they'd offered no new information. The physical evidence was limited to Crystal Daws's clothing, and the projectiles recovered from the autopsy, which could hardly be considered a smoking gun. After letting all these factors settle, I felt stuck. Mired in the silence of a twenty-five-year-old unsolved murder case.

The trill of my cellular phone saved me from my spiraling thoughts. The screen read, "Katie."

"Hello?"

"Hey, Dad. Just calling to check in." She sounded happy, but worried. "How's everything going with the Madison thing? You defrosted that cold case yet?"

I chuckled. "Ha, no. Unfortunately, not."

"Oh," she sounded surprised. "Everything okay?"

"Yeah, it's fine." I wanted to spare her my frustrations and failure.

"Doesn't sound fine."

Another chuckle. "Goodness, you sound just like your mother sometimes."

"I'll take that as a compliment." Her ear-to-ear grin was somehow audible through the phone. "But I'm right. What's wrong?"

Victoria had possessed an uncanny ability to sniff out when I was stalled on a case; it stood to reason that Katie was able to follow suit. I gave in.

"I just feel stuck with this case. I've gone over it several times, reviewed the evidence, and tried to find any missed steps. Hell, even most of the witnesses are still around. That never happens, and of course, it still doesn't lead to anything."

"Oh, wow. So, what happened?"

"Like, how the murder went down?"

"Yeah. Maybe as a civilian, as you cops put it, I could offer a different perspective."

I hesitated for a moment. "What the hell, can't hurt."

"This high school girl, Crystal Daws, was working late at a small movie theatre one night. Her manager took off to celebrate his wedding anniversary, so she was responsible for making the night deposit. There was another employee with her that night, but he left minutes earlier while she was going to make the bank drop."

A realization just popped into my head, but it was hard to decipher at the moment. It had to do with something Maynard Preston said about the night of the murder. I would need to go back and read his statement carefully. It felt like an unchecked box.

"Dad, and?" Katie asked. "You tailed off there."

"Oh, sorry," I continued. "So, as she leaves the theatre, she's confronted by her killer armed with, most likely, a revolver. I imagine he demanded the money, and she probably froze in fear. He probably mistook that for defiance and shot her at close range twice, then took her purse and the bank bag."

"Oh, my God."

"I know. She was just a kid."

"How much money did they get?"

I let out a sigh of disgust. "A little over two hundred. Most of it was from the theatre earnings. There wasn't much in her purse."

"Ugh, that's terrible. Someone's life…for nothing." Katie was getting emotional, and instantly I regretted telling her about the case. Victoria had grown alongside me in my career, and as I moved along from the streets to the investigations, she'd learned how to take the hard stuff. Katie's indoctrination was by jumping into a pit of fire.

"Listen, we don't have to talk about the case," I said.

"No, no. It's okay. It's just terrible to think about how it's so senseless."

"They're all senseless," I said.

"And you worked these cases for fourteen years. Wow," she said. "Now I feel bad for being a brat all those times."

"Ahh, no. Katie, you were a great kid."

"Thanks, Daddy."

"So, you got anything for me, you know, from the civilian perspective?"

There was silence on the line while Katie was thinking. I wasn't expecting anything of value, but it was sweet that she was willing to help.

"You said her purse was taken?"

"Yeah."

"You said a high school girl, how old was she?"

"Seventeen."

"Did she have a credit card?"

"Yes," I said, "actually, she did."

"Run a credit report on her," Katie said matter of fact. An accountant by trade, cop's daughter by birth, Katie couldn't help but resort to what she knew. I had been ready to decline her idea as ineffective and uninformed, but she said it with such conviction.

"But, she's been dead for twenty-five years, honey. Doesn't that sound like a waste of time?"

"Not really, plus, you said yourself, you're stuck. What do you have to lose?"

"But still, a credit check?"

"Sure. I've seen it a bunch of times. Scammers get deceased people's social security numbers and open a line of credit, only to let it sit for a while. They'll buy something small, make the payments, and actually build up credit. Months or even a year later when they wait out anyone who would check, then, bam! They go on a shopping spree and abandon the card with boatloads of stuff paid for by stolen credit."

"You've seen this happen?"

"Yeah, earlier this week, actually. My firm helped the Jacksonville Sheriff's Office on a credit card fraud case where the bad guys were doing just that."

"But doesn't the credit card company get a death certificate and know not to open up any credit?"

"Sure, but do you know how many credit cards there are out there?"

I thought of just the one in my wallet, but knew that, at one time, I had a gas card, two other credit cards, and Lord knows how many Torey had for her *legitimate* shopping sprees.

"Yeah, I guess you're right. Worth a try, right?"

I spent the next ten minutes on the phone convincing Katie that I was taking care of myself. She was so much like her mother, and the thought always brought a smile to my face.

After turning on my computer and clicking open the internet search engine, I glanced at the clock. It was late, but curiosity made me want to see if, by chance and a long shot, someone had used Crystal Daws's credit cards following her death.

I pulled out the case file and plugged in Crystal's biographical information to run a credit check. I hit send and went in search of something sweet to eat. Guilt about what Torey would say dissuaded me from destroying the package of cookies I'd bought at the store, but I bargained with my conscience for just two and a glass of milk. After a time allowing the calculations to churn, the computer screen bleeped, and I was provided with an answer I wasn't expecting.

Chapter 14

I lost count of what number cup it was. For some reason, homicide work and an unhealthy addiction to caffeine-heavy coffee went together. Whatever number it was, it was too many, because my leg wouldn't stop twitching. It was that, or it was because I was sitting on a fresh lead from a twenty-five-year-old murder case.

"Where is he?" I impatiently checked my watch. Another sip. It *was* early, but the midnight shift should've ended already.

After I heard a rush of air from the door opening, I turned. It wasn't him. Another sip. Another glance at my watch.

The Honey Bear Bakery was a popular breakfast spot in the mid-town area. Morning commuters and early-rising students stopped in for their choice of bagels, breakfast sandwiches, homemade donuts, muffins, and top-notch coffee. A friend of Katie's had opened the shop a few years ago, so I stopped in as often as I could. Pictures of cuddly looking bear cubs in various stages of frolicking, sleeping, or staring at the camera adorned the walls. Victoria had called the place *cute*.

"Hey, Hank," a familiar voice said.

I turned. *Finally*, I thought. "Mike, thanks for coming."

Now Sergeant Mike Durgenhoff stood before me in full police uniform. His newly earned gold badge gleamed in the bakery lights, but his eyes were dull and tired. Midnight shift was not treating him well. It was a promotion and a demotion at the same time. Better pay, but shittier hours.

"Sure, Hank." Mike sat down across from me. "What's going on?"

"Well, I need some help," I started.

"Wait," he said, putting his hand out in front of him. "How many cups of coffee have you had?"

Apparently, the jitters were more obvious than I thought.

"Ha!" I smiled. "Too many. But, seriously, I took your advice about the consulting and just tripped over this case from Madison, you know? Little town about an hour east of here."

"Yeah, I know it," Mike answered. "You 'tripped over a case'? What the hell does that mean?"

I explained how I came across Officer Julie Haywood and the death of her childhood friend and cousin, Crystal Daws. I went on about how the twenty-five-year-old case had been worked thoroughly by then, Detective Byrd, and that I went back through the case with negative results. Until last night.

"So, the credit check paid off?" Mike asked, "That actually worked?"

"Yeah, I was surprised, too. After running the check, I found that one of her cards had been active in 1995, two years after the murder."

"Right, but how'd you get a name? Don't those credit score sites just give you a score?" Mike asked.

"Yeah, I owe Katie big time. She had some contacts at the credit card company that she schmoozed for a favor last night. I'll just have to get Julie to send a subpoena later."

"Okay, so?" Mike said, with anticipation plastered on his face. "You got a name?"

I smiled. "I got a name."

"Well, hot damn. Anyone you know? Anyone from the initial look?"

Many times, Mike and I had found, especially in prolonged investigations, that we often came across the suspect in the initial part of the investigation, during the initial look. Most of the time, we knew the person was the suspect but lacked the proof to act. There was an extra level of satisfaction when we connected enough dots to make the arrest.

"No, completely new name," I said. "I'd spent an hour meticulously combing through the case file, writing every single name in the investigation down. I even subcategorized them under witnesses, cops, and others. Unfortunately, there was no one in the suspect column."

"Ah, that's where I come in, right?" Mike had surmised correctly. Without a badge and credentials, my authority was that of an average citizen. I needed Mike to run the name.

"You got it, buddy," I answered. "Wha'd'ya say?"

"Sure," he said. "Does he have ties to Tallahassee?"

"Yeah, the address on the charges in '95 was on the southside, so I figured we could start there."

"Alright," he said, "thanks for the coffee and donut."

"But I didn't buy…Oh, right. I'll be right back."

Mike got up from the table. "I'll grab my laptop."

I headed back to the front counter to place his order. I ordered a cinnamon swirl bagel for myself.

"Hey!" Mike called.

I turned to see what was so urgent. "Chocolate sprinkles."

I smiled as he stepped outside.

A few minutes later, I had Mike's coffee and donut ready, and he had his laptop queued.

"Darrell Banks." For the first time, I said the name aloud. "Should be in the neighborhood of forty-six years of age." Saying a suspect's name aloud was always followed by a surreal feeling. It meant the hunt had begun, and he was out there looking over his shoulder. In this case, though, he had one very long head start.

"You're in luck my friend," Mike answered after a minute of typing. "The cat's on paper for burglary. He did seven years starting in 2005, followed by ten years of probation. DOC (Department of Corrections) has a current address that jives with what we have in records management."

"Burglary, huh?" I asked. Having a property crime for his criminal history wasn't giving me positive thoughts. A murderer tends to have more violent crimes in his past. In this case, preferably robbery.

"Yeah," Mike defended. "That don't mean he ain't capable of murder, Hank. C'mon, you taught me that."

"You're right." I shook off the feeling of disappointment. Often, some of the most heinous murders were done with people who had little to no criminal history. And the argument still holds; people can change in a very short period of time. Darrell Banks could've been a trigger-happy robber back in 1993, and for some unknown reason, took up credit card fraud and burglary in the following years.

"Banks?" Mike said with thought. "You think he's related to Neville Banks?"

"The old doper we busted for attempted murder?" I said, remembering the name.

"Yeah. That's the one," Mike answered. "He went for a gun when the patrol went to pick him up, got shot, and wound up in a wheelchair for life."

I recalled the memory. It was a good case because the gun Neville went for was the same gun he'd used to shoot a rival drug dealer the day before. We tied it back forensically, and he was later convicted. However, due to his incapacitation, his sentence was on the light side of only ten years. Not that steep for a solid attempted murder case, but when drug dealers shoot other drug dealers, there is seldom any public outcry.

"They could be related," I said. "Neville had a lot of connections, but I'm not sure about the family."

"Yeah, just spit-ballin' for ya," Mike said. "It's getting late, er…" Mike glanced outside at the rising day. "Early. Whatever, midnights suck, Hank. I'm exhausted. You need anything else?"

Mike had written down Darrell Banks's address for me, which was plenty. "No, I think I'm good."

I gathered up my things and walked out with him. He was driving one of the new, marked patrol SUVs. It was a far upgrade from the Chevy

Lumina I drove when last on patrol. Mike showed off the bells and whistles of the newest police technology. The patrol vehicles were essentially mobile desks with mounted computers and printers. Absent any Polaroid pictures, I remember having to beg the jail to fax over pictures of inmates when working cases. When I did get assistance, the quality of the dark and grainy images was horrendous and worthless in an investigation. It was a new age, for sure.

"You're not going to go talk to him, are you?" Mike asked.

His question made me pause. I was dead set on talking to Darrell Banks in the matter of Crystal Daws's death, but now Mike made me second-guess my plan. Mike was still the sworn officer, I was not.

"Um, well—" I stammered, not sure what to say.

"Jesus, you are, aren't you?" he asked. "Do you even carry a gun anymore?"

"What if I just sit on him?" I offered. "Keep working the case. You know, plug him in the holes and see where we can build a case."

"Hold on." Mike turned to his mounted laptop, clicked on a few things, typed briefly, and then something began to hum somewhere inside the SUV. Mike ripped something and turned back to me, holding out a piece of paper. I took it and looked it over. It was a printed-out rap sheet for Darrell Banks, complete with all of his charges and his most recent jail photograph. He was a dark-skinned man with wild dreadlocks and an indifferent look stamped on his face. A look of the disenfranchised I had become very familiar with over the years.

"Be careful, Hank," Mike said. His sincerity was welcomed. "I wrote down his listed employer at the top."

I extended my hand, and Mike shook it before leaving. "Thank you, my friend."

"I'm glad you're on the case, Hank." He shut the door but rolled down the window. He smiled. "This Haywood chick, she doesn't know how lucky she is that you two crossed paths."

With Sergeant Mike Durgenhoff off in dreamland, I went in search of Darrell Banks. I had to see the man. Like before, when I worked cases, after identifying a suspect, I needed to see them in person. It was a step in my process of figuring out who they were, what made them tick, and why they committed murder.

The morning sun had lifted well into the sky, casting short shadows on the trees that lined the back of Darrell Banks's listed address. It was a modest home, well enough maintained, with a neat but simple yard. It was one of the better homes in an otherwise less-than-desirable neighborhood on the southside of Tallahassee. A few slow drives past the house garnered no activity, so I parked down the street. Being a weekday, I assumed most of the residents were at work and kids at school, so I took my chance in this spot for a stakeout.

I passed the initial time reading Banks's rap sheet, starting with the latest. Multiple counts of burglary, dealing in stolen property, and theft. All of the case numbers were the same, meaning he had been charged with a cluster of crimes at the same time. The date of the crimes was 2005. He had done seven years in prison according to Mike's search on the DOC website, followed by ten years of probation. Meaning he was still on probation. This was always exploitable. If probationers sneezed wrong, they could get the full sentence of the original charge and go away for a long time. That was the incentive for staying straight.

Going backwards on the list, Banks had a few minor drug possession charges in the early 2000s. I kept going back in time and the charges were all similar, a burglary charge, trespassing, theft.

My skepticism mounted. "He's a thief," I said aloud. I quickly shook my head, telling myself, those were just the crimes he was caught doing. It doesn't mean he's incapable of murder.

I looked at the last page and the earliest charges. My eyes widened as I read charges from 1993 that read *Burglary/Hold for Madison County.*

"Hot damn," I celebrated. That at least puts him in Madison County around the time of the murder. Unfortunately, rap sheets don't include the offenders' release dates, but the information was still promising. It was no smoking gun, but I was getting close.

After a few hours of watching Banks's house from various spots along the street, I decided to move on. There had been no activity at the house, and I still had another viable place to check—his place of employment.

Darrell Banks listed his employer as one of those big box electronic stores. Unsure of what particular job he filled at this place, I found a shaded spot in the back of the parking lot and watched the storefront. The electronics giant anchored the strip mall that also housed several small restaurants, a cell phone store, and some other service providers. Customers of all shapes and sizes came and went. A few employees arrived for work or returned from a break, and I compared them to Banks's description and photo in the corner of the rap sheet. None matched.

I looked down at my phone and debated whether or not to call the store and ask if he was working. I passed on the idea. Getting a strange phone call, however random and innocuous, could put him on guard. I wanted to catch Darrell Banks by complete surprise.

Staring at my phone, for some unknown reason, Julie Haywood popped into my mind. Instantly, I felt as if I was betraying her by working the case without her. I had come across a lead and immediately jumped on it, treating her like an afterthought. She should be here, I realized. She should enjoy this moment alongside me. I unlocked my phone, scrolled down my contacts, and hit Julie's name, placing the call.

Holding the phone to my ear, it rang as the call connected. My gaze was unfixed, but exiting the front of the store was a forty-year-old black man wearing the electronic store's well-known blue polo and khaki pants. His hair was high and tight, not unkempt dreadlocks. His demeanor looked purposeful, not the lazy indifference from the jail photo, but it was Darrell Banks. As I focused on him, I noticed he kept looking around, specifically at the front of the store. He did it on the sly, not overly obvious and paranoid, but extra cautious. He walked with determination toward the deep part of the parking lot at the middle of the strip mall. Suddenly, he stopped and knelt. From my vantage point, I could clearly see what he was doing. He was pretending to tie his shoe, but his head and eyes were angled toward the storefront.

"Hello? Hello? Hank?" I heard Julie's voice through the tiny speaker in my phone. I needed to focus on Banks, so I replied, "Hey, sorry. Gotta call you back."

There was an audible groan from the other end of the line just before I hit the *end* button.

Keeping watch on Banks, I blindly groped the passenger seat for my binoculars. Finding them, I moved them to my face. Banks finished tying his shoes and was walking toward a car. After another quick glance around, he reached into his pocket, removed a small black plastic-looking item, and leaned into the passenger side of the car. I could see another head moving from the driver's seat. Banks handed him the item. They shook hands inside the car, and Banks instantly shoved his hand back into his pocket.

The car drove off, and Banks stood back, pulled out a cigarette, lit it, inhaled, and let out a puff of smoke into the air. He milled about for another ten minutes and headed back into the store. After processing what I witnessed, I was unsure of what happened. However, my mind was made up, I was going inside.

The blast of air-conditioning was welcoming as the automatic doors slid open. I got a head nod from a greeter just inside and continued on. Banks was still outside finishing up his cigarette, so I just hit the first section I came to, computers. I pretended to read the labels of each model, comparing prices while I watched the front through my peripheral vision for Banks to return.

Five minutes later and waving off help from an associate, Banks strolled back inside. I watched him walk down the middle of the store. He walked with confidence, and I wondered if that was from getting away with murder twenty-five years ago. I moved unsuspectingly throughout the store until I saw Banks stop in the cellular phone area. He talked with another associate in the same area while I watched from the printer section. I kept moving, pretending to browse for electronics, trying to get a feel for my suspect.

Banks moved around the cell phones and accessories and addressed several customers who all declined assistance. I moved toward the center of the store and began to browse.

"Can I help you, sir?" A younger Asian girl asked from my right.

"Um, no thank you. I'm just looking," I answered.

I moved through the section, closer to the middle with the cell phone cases. They had all sorts of decorated cases, from superheroes to pop culture music icons, and even some '80s-themed cases. I smiled when I spied a case with *My Little Pony*; it had been Katie's favorite. If cell phones had been prevalent back in the '80s, Katie would've wanted that cover.

"Can I help you, sir?" The voice was coarser than the Asian girl…aged. I turned and Banks was standing a few feet away.

"Um, well…." I had to improvise to keep the conversation going. "Yeah, I was wondering, what's the storage space on this model?" I handed him whatever phone was in my hand.

"Well, none of the newer models really have 'storage space' since everything goes in the cloud. It's really unlimited storage when you consider it."

"Oh, okay." My ignorance of cellular phones was more than apparent to Banks. "I forgot about 'The Cloud'."

"Is that what you needed help with, or was there something else?"

There was an implication in his voice.

"Are the cameras in these things pretty much all the same?" I asked.

"I would say there isn't much of a difference, but it all depends on what you're using it for."

"Well, taking pictures, what else?"

"Right, but like action shots versus homemade movies and social media use, things like that, would require a higher resolution and pixel for clarity. Otherwise, you end up with a blurry mess."

"Ah, okay," I replied. "Makes sense."

"So, you a PI or something?" Banks blurted out.

I looked around, caught by surprise. "Excuse me?"

"C'mon, man." Banks's professional tone gave way to his street persona. "I saw you eyein' me since I walked in from break. You slowly make your way over here, decline help from the Asian hotty but talk to me?"

"But I'm not a PI, I'm just looking for—"

"Whateva', man," Banks cut me off. He stepped closer to keep the conversation from unwanted ears. "You too old to be a probation officer, so maybe you a PI. Cuz, you don't need no phone. That's the newest model iPhone clipped to your belt, so try again?"

I decided to drop the ill-fated ruse. He caught me. I hated that I had been figured out so quickly. "Fine. I'm here because I have some questions for you."

Banks scoffed. He folded his arms, pleased with his ability to sniff out my ulterior motives.

"You a cop?"

"Was."

"Then you know, I ain't gotta answer shit."

He was right. As a subject on probation, he was required to cooperate with law enforcement. However, that does not apply to former homicide detectives looking into a cold case. I had lost all credibility and had no leverage, but I couldn't leave without answers.

"I gotta get back to work," Banks said. He turned to walk away. Short of grabbing him and dragging him outside, I was out of moves.

Suddenly, I was reminded of earlier in the parking lot. I took a blind stab in the dark.

"I'm sure your actual PO would like to know about your side hustle."

Banks froze. His shoulders sagged. My blind stab hit something vital. It was a cell phone that he slipped the man in the car for cash. That's why he was being so careful, he had slipped it out of the store and past the theft sensors. The slight bulge in his pocket was probably the cash he got in return.

"Yeah, shouldn't be hard to convince him a convicted thief was running a scam on his employer."

"Okay, fine." Banks spun around, his eyes wide, pleading for me to be quiet. "You win, but not here."

Feeling redeemed from the earlier failure, Banks ushered me through the back of the store and out to an empty loading dock. I noticed there were no cameras or other employees around. I kept my back to the wall and held a stance to defend myself, if needed. Desperation knows no limits, especially ex-cons facing a return trip to prison.

"What do you want?" Banks asked.

"Madison, Florida. 1993?"

Banks's face crinkled in confusion. "What the hell does that mean?"

"Tell me about your stay there in 1993."

"You serious?"

I pulled out my phone. "Hold on while I'll look up the state probation number."

"Okay, okay." Banks held out his hands, palms down. "Just let me think a minute. That's a long time ago."

Banks thought for a minute, arms folded. Moving his left hand to his mouth, he chewed on a fingernail. "Madison, right?"

"Yes. Small town east of here."

"Okay, okay, yeah. I remember a little bit. I did a few licks there. Got pinched. Did time in county. So, what?"

"That it?" I asked.

"Yeah, that's it," he retorted. "What's this about, man?" There was desperation in his voice.

"You tell me what *you* did, that's how this works. I don't show you my hand."

"C'mon, that was a lifetime ago. You gotta gimme something."

"You came across a credit card of a victim I'm helping, used it quite a bit a few years later."

"A credit card?" Banks said. "This about a credit card?"

I flicked my thumb to open the screen of my phone. I feigned typing, but said, "State…probation…," as if I was typing it in the search bar.

"Yeah, man. I took a lot of cards back then. Shit was a lot easier to use back then."

"Think back; the card I'm asking about belonged to a girl." I didn't want to mention Crystal's name. I was hoping the use of the word *girl* as opposed to *woman* would help jog his memory.

With stress and panic washing over his face, Banks's memory failed him. "C'mon, man. I can't think of every last damn card I stole."

"Okay, fine," I said. I put my phone to my ear and looked at him with deadpan eyes. "It's ringing."

"Shit, okay," he said, searching deep into the recesses of his mind. "Gimme something else."

"I can't spoon-feed you, Banks. That's not how this works."

"Um, okay…." He strained to think. He paced a bit, still chewing at his fingernails. "Man, I can't. Okay, I can't."

"You better, Darrell."

"Call my PO, hassle me all you want over some bullshit credit card shit from twenty-something damn years ago. I can't tell you anything I don't remember."

Banks ripped his cigarette pack from his pocket, fed one into his mouth, lit it, and took a long drag. He blew out, letting the smoke billow out. It calmed him, but I still needed him on edge.

"It was from the girl you shot, asshole." I dropped the hammer on him.

His eyes bulged. The newly lit cigarette almost fell from his mouth. I widened my stance in case he got any bad ideas.

"The girl *I* shot?" he said incredulously. "What in the hell you talkin' about?"

"The card I'm asking about, it belonged to the girl you shot."

His body relaxed. He took another drag and seemed to gather himself. "Man, I ain't shoot no damn girl. I don't even like guns." He blew out more smoke. "I stole them, sure. Sold them, hell yeah. But use them? Nah. Not me."

"Then how come you ran up the credit card that belonged to a girl who was shot to death?" I barked at Banks as I stepped closer, invading his personal space. It worked because he went back on edge instantly.

"Wait, wait, wait," Banks said. "Hold on, man. Just hold on. I ain't shoot no girl."

"Then how'd you get her credit card?"

"Wait!" he shouted. "Madison, 1993. Credit card, yes. You said I ran it up?"

"Yeah, it wasn't until a few years later, but I figured you held on to it until the coast was clear. Updated the information and went on a spending spree."

"Yes, I remember now," he said. "I found that credit card. It was in a purse. Tossed the purse, but kept the card, like you said. Ran with it for a bit until I got locked up."

"So, you remember using the card?"

"Yeah. I do now. I got a lot of mileage out of that card. That was my *gold deluxe* card."

"And you said you found it?"

"Yeah, I found it. Cuz, I ain't shoot no girl."

I didn't want to believe that Darrell Banks simply found Crystal Daws's purse after the homicide. It was one of the notable items that was missing from the scene. The killer removed it. It made too much sense the killer would have it, but Banks was muddying the waters.

"You're a liar, goddammit. Now tell me the truth."

"I am, man. I am. I found the purse."

Everything about Darrell Banks told me he wasn't a cold-blooded killer. His rap sheet, his job at the electronics store, and his steady probation record all pointed to someone who steered clear of violence.

Even when I stepped up to him, he submitted. Most killers wouldn't submit; they'd challenge my authority. My instincts were to believe him, not press him further as a killer.

"Fine," I said. "Where?"

"Shit. I ain't going to remember that." Banks finished up the cigarette and stamped out the butt. "Wait, when this girl get shot?"

I really didn't want to answer his question, so I hesitated before answering. "Late at night."

"No, no. Like the date?"

"March 1993."

Banks straightened up. "There ya go. Believe me or not, but I found that purse. Sure, I used the card like you said, but I didn't shoot anyone, especially not some girl in Madison County. Look for yourself, Mister-I-ain't-no-PI, but I was locked up in county for burglary in January. Didn't get out until late August."

Chapter 15

"He found it?" Julie Haywood was pacing around her living room. "That's what he said? He found it?"

Dusk had cast its reaching shadows over Haywood's house. Sitting in her living room, I had just told her about the credit check leading me to Darrell Banks and the fallout from our conversation.

"He's got to be lying." She began to rationalize his guilt. "We know she had her purse when she left that night or else it would've been left inside the movie theatre. The killer took it. Banks didn't find it. He took it *after* he shot her."

"I didn't want to believe it at first either," I said, "but the fact is, he was locked up in the county jail the day Crystal was murdered. I swung by the jail and verified he was there before I came over."

I presented Julie with a printed-out page of Darrell Banks's Madison County Jail information, complete with his detailed timeline while in custody. Julie sat down in a huff, struggling to accept the fact that Banks couldn't be in jail and murder her friend at the same time.

"Then how in the hell did he get her credit card?" she demanded.

"Well, when he said he 'found it,' he meant he stole it when he burglarized a house or someone's car."

Julie's face lit up. "So, he must've stolen it from the actual killer." She stood up and resumed her pacing. "We just need him to tell us where he stole it from or what car he took it from or…."

Suddenly, the spark of excitement faded back into disappointment. I had already worked out this same problem and waited for Julie Haywood to catch up.

"Wait…," she figured it out. "Shit. He doesn't remember where he got it from or what car, does he?"

"Nope." I shook my head.

"Yeah, we wouldn't be talking about it in my living room if he had remembered."

"We can't expect a guy like Darrell Banks to remember a detail like that. He was just a burglar passing through town. He's likely to remember the score, not the vessel. He got caught a few months before Crystal's death, served a seven-month sentence in jail, got released, and put this town in his rearview mirror. But he obviously grabbed the purse in mid-August on his way out. That would've been the earliest he could have gotten ahold of it."

I pointed to the jail printout of Banks's release date.

"But he told you he couldn't remember where he took it from, how do we even know it was in Madison that he took it?"

"Yeah, that is a good question, but he called Crystal's card his 'gold deluxe' card. I think we just have to operate as if he stole the purse from somewhere in town until we find out different."

"Okay, but how does that help us in this case?"

"I don't know," I said.

"We should go charge his ass with credit card fraud," Julie spat.

The statute of limitations on that specific transgression was well expired. Only the crime of murder has no shelf life. She knew that too, but I understood her anger and the compulsion to punish him for something. Darrell Banks had gotten away with a litany of charges during his life, one that hit particularly close to home for Julie Haywood, so I explained that a phone call was made to the district supervisor of the electronic store, informing them of a scam one of their employees was running. I figured the company would take care of business, and I'd let the chips fall where they may.

"It'll all work out in the end," I said.

The house fell quiet as the last oranges and pinks of the day gave way to the indigo and black of night. The flicker of hope I'd found in the Crystal Daws's murder investigation had extinguished as quickly as it had been lit. Was hope really a good thing, seeing that when it didn't work out, it bored an even deeper hole into your soul? To me, this had always been a nagging question, but for someone like Julie, extinguishing that flicker of hope could be devastating.

"So, where does this put us? Can we even use this?" Julie asked.

This was another part of the lead I had already thought through. However, I wanted to explain it to her as opposed to having her catch up. She had been through enough.

"Well, this is a new fact of the case, yes. Not much we can do with it, but we'll leverage it as best we can."

"Okay, how?"

"Well, we don't have enough information to retrace his steps from twenty-five years ago, and even if we did, it's not like we can go back and track down video surveillance or cell phone data. We're still in the dark with that."

"Doesn't sound like we can leverage anything, Hank." Julie plopped down on her sofa and leaned back, closing her eyes, exhausted from the situation.

"Well, not exactly."

"I'm listening." Her eyes remained shut.

"We confirmed it was Crystal's card through the credit bureau, right?"

"Uh huh."

"And we determined it was stolen sometime in August of 1993 and then later used by Darrell Banks, right?"

"Yep." Her eyes were still closed. "If we believe the word of a felon."

"So, where'd it go between the times of the murder and when Banks lifted it?"

Julie sat up. Something stirred in her mind, as I knew it would. I smiled as she processed the question.

"It stayed here." Her eyes widened with the realization. "It stayed *in* town."

"Yep." I could almost see the wheels turning in her mind.

"That means the killer lives here. Or lived here at the time of the murder, for at least those five months."

"Narrows the focus, right?" I said. "That's something."

"Yeah, I guess." Julie was still put off and with good reason. If it was the proverbial needle we were looking for, it only made the haystack smaller.

"Hey," I said, catching her attention from the sofa, "it's more than we had yesterday."

"Ugh, true."

⌘

Julie Haywood offered spaghetti for dinner. Due to the hustle created by the lead, I hadn't eaten much. After her mention of food, I realized I was very hungry and accepted the invitation. She began buzzing around the kitchen after we settled on a plan for her to dig up as many old auto burglaries from August of 1993 as she could find. The murder case had been preserved by someone from the time it left the meticulous hands of Holcomb Byrd until it fell into the care of Julie Haywood. But run-of-the-mill auto burglaries from twenty-five years ago would've been long forgotten. Haywood questioned their existence but mentioned a storage room in the basement of the courthouse and their possible whereabouts stored on microfiche film.

"Where would we even find a microfiche machine around here?" The skepticism in my tone was obvious.

"That's easy," Julie replied from the next room, yelling over the boiling pot of noodles.

"Oh?"

"Cade's bookstore. He's got one." Julie's matter-of-fact response surprised me. "His grandfather was an old college professor; he kept stuff like that in the store."

"He did?" I tried to recall if I saw one of those machines during my last visit, the day I met Julie Haywood, but I couldn't place it. I remembered the collection of old cameras adorning several shelves in the area by the desk, but the rest was fuzzy.

"Sure," she said, "you didn't see it in that back room, in the corner?"

"Must've missed it."

"I'll call him after dinner. If we're able to find any of those cases, I'm sure he'll let us use it."

Auto burglaries were rarely isolated events. Darrell Banks explained that he was looking for what he called, "get out of town money," so he would hit several cars in a row until he found money or something with enough street value that he could liquidate into cash. Oftentimes, they looked random and unconnected because they were reported at different times of the day. Maybe one of the victims didn't realize they were burglarized and drove home, believing the crime took place at the house and reporting it as such. This skewed the statistics. I hoped we could grab as many auto burglaries as possible from that time frame and piece them together to retrace Banks's steps. With any luck, the killer might have reported a burglary himself. It was the longest of long shots, but it was a new lead, nonetheless.

As the meat sauce aroma emanated throughout the house, I strolled around, ignoring my grumbling stomach, taking in the mementos and pictures Julie had on display. The images put forth in a home tell a personal history of the occupants.

Many of the framed pictures were of Julie's son in different stages of youth. From toothless soccer player to mop-top fisherman to high school baseball player, she had them all. She adored him, and he seemed like a good kid.

Beside the fireplace, set back on a bookshelf, I saw a picture of young Julie Haywood. Not quite a teenager, arm-in-arm with two other girls about the same age. Cute, innocent and carefree. Unaware of how her future would turnout. One I recognized as Crystal Daws. She was slightly bigger than Julie, beautiful and confident. The other girl I did not know. She appeared the same age as Crystal, but thin with stringy blonde hair and bangs teased out over her forehead. Braces gleamed as she smiled widely with the other two in the picture. There was history in this picture. This was a part of Julie as well as Crystal.

I grabbed the frame off the shelf and walked it to the kitchen.

"Who's this?" I held up the picture for Julie to see.

She squinted through the steam rising from the pasta. "Oh, my goodness," she responded. "Me, Crystal, and that other girl was the third musketeer back then. Hope Bennett."

"Okay." The name meant nothing.

"We were the 'Crown Jewels'."

"Huh?"

"Well, you got Crystal. That's obvious. I was 'Jewels' and then Hope, you know? Like the Hope Diamond."

"Ah, how cute."

Julie shook her head with embarrassment. "It sounds stupid now, but we loved it back then."

I examined the picture, taking in the captured moment. It was like many of the photographs I had taken of Katie and her friends after birthday parties, trips to the beach, trips to the mall or movies, or wherever I chauffeured her and her entourage.

"When was this taken?"

Julie gave it some thought. "Um…," She stepped next to me and looked at the picture again. "I'd say late '92. Maybe around Christmas time or something."

"So, Hope was close to Crystal?"

"Yeah, they were the same age. Same grade."

"But you and Crystal were closer?"

"Yep."

"Did Byrd ever talk to her about the case?" I didn't recall seeing her name in the files.

"No, I don't think so. Maybe he did, and she had nothing."

From what I understood of Holcomb Byrd, if he did anything with regard to this investigation, it was in the file. But not talking to a close friend of the victim was kind of a big miss.

"We should talk to her," I said. "Is she still around? I take it you're not still friends?"

"No, she pretty much fell in a bad way the next school year."

"Bad way, huh?" I said. "What's she like nowadays?"

Julie rolled her eyes and put her hand on her hip. "She's a fucking mess."

⌘

"That was really good spaghetti, Julie." I wiped the excess sauce from my lips.

"Thanks, Hank. It's really the only thing I know how to cook well."

"Well, you gotta stick with what works, right?"

Julie smiled and began cleaning up the dishes. At that moment, I was reminded of Victoria and our quiet dinners alone. I missed them, and I missed her. I missed taking care of her when she was sick.

An odd sensation washed over me as I took in my surroundings, wondering how far removed I was from Victoria's death. It seemed like just a blink of an eye that we were dancing to Elvis Presley in our kitchen. Now, I found myself dining with another woman in her home. I felt guilty. Guilty of what, I didn't know. I thought of Torey looking down on me, and I felt ashamed. I tried thinking of her beautiful face to make amends, but it was a struggle to imagine her clearly in my head. My guilt turned to anger.

"You alright, Hank?" Julie's voice was soft and concerned.

I snapped out of the trance and looked up at her from the table. She was drying a dish by the kitchen sink.

"Um, yeah," I stammered. "Yeah, I'm fine. Just got lost in thought is all."

Julie gave me a skeptical look and turned back to the dishes. "Okay."

After a moment, I spoke up. "Hey, Julie, I'm going to head back to the apartment to get some rest. We should start early in the morning at Cade's bookstore."

Julie didn't reply. Her head bowed as if something was wrong. I blanked at what it could be.

"Sorry, Hank," she said.

"Sorry for what?"

"You can't go back to the apartment."

"What? Why not?"

"So, it doesn't belong to the department. It actually belongs to the chief's brother."

"Okay?"

"He got a tenant and moved them in today."

I was confused. I didn't know how to process that.

"Wait?" I said. "Where's my stuff?" It wasn't much, but the few things I brought with me were important to me. Namely, the picture of Victoria.

Julie smiled sheepishly. "In a box. In my garage?"

"Well, damn."

"I'm sorry, Hank. I didn't know if you'd actually come back, so I told him that he could have the apartment back."

"It was one day, Julie. One day!"

"I know. I know. I'm sorry."

"I mean, it wasn't mine to begin with, so I'm not mad or anything. But, damn, Julie. You've got to quit being so damned pessimistic."

She nodded. "You're right."

I checked my watch. It was late.

"Well, I guess I better get going. It'll be pretty late by the time I get home."

"You could stay here if you like. You could take my bed, and I'll sleep on the pull-out in the living room."

My full stomach, the long day, my exhausted body, and heavy eyelids didn't care, but I wasn't going to kick her out of her own bed.

"I'll take the pull-out."

Chapter 16

"You spent the night?" Katie's tone was insinuating. "At this lady cop's house?"

Waiting at the bookstore while Julie hunted down those stored files at the police station, I called Katie to tell her how her credit check idea panned out. I mentioned how Darrell Banks had stolen Crystal Daws's credit card during an auto burglary several months after the murder and that Julie and I were going to sort through any available reports from that time. I let where I spent the night slip, and that was the part of the conversation she chose to dwell on.

"Well, yeah," I replied. "I didn't feel like driving home, and I slept on the couch, Katherine. What's the big deal?"

I used her full name, hoping to end the discussion. Guilt from the transgression began to weigh on me.

"But after she cooked dinner for you, right?"

I was wrong. Unable to see the existence of a romantic relationship, I replayed the night before. There was nothing obvious, I thought. Although, I probably wouldn't be able to tell if a woman was interested in me or not. Since I'd met Julie Haywood, I'd considered her a colleague.

"Well, yeah, but I don't think—"

"It's okay, Dad." She cut me off, her voice on the edge of laughter.

"Plus, I'm sure she's into another guy," I said.

"Oh yeah, who?" Katie asked. "Or are you deflecting and making that up?"

"No, there's this ex-cop who runs the bookstore. I think they may be a thing."

"Did she say they're dating?"

"Well, no," I answered. "Not specifically."

"Did you ask her?"

"No."

"Did you ask *him*?" Katie asked.

I paused, obviously having no basis for what I said about Julie and Cade being an item.

"No."

"If she hasn't mentioned it and she let you spend the night..., after cooking dinner for you..., c'mon, Dad. Aren't you supposed to be this great detective? Open your eyes."

Uncomfortable didn't begin to describe how I felt at that moment, and I desperately wanted the conversation to end.

"Well, I doubt she's interested, Katie."

"Well, I doubt that she isn't, Dad!" she said. "Anyways, I got to go. Let me know how the lead goes."

"I will, Katie."

"Oh, don't forget to have her send that subpoena, Dad. I don't need any backlash from that, okay?"

"You got it, honey."

I pressed end at the same time as I pulled up to the bookstore. Cade McCoy was walking up to the store, a drink tray with three coffees in one hand and a tight grip on the handle of a cane with the other. There was a distinct limp to his walk, something I missed during our earlier meeting. I remembered the cane, just not the gait. He balanced himself carefully, fished out his keys, and unlocked the bookstore door.

Julie arrived, parked, and followed Cade in. She grabbed the coffee tray from him as he sat down behind the desk. I watched their interaction closely through the window, as they were unaware of me just outside the store. Paying closer attention to their body language, positioning, and conversation, it was obvious they were simply friends with no level of romantic involvement. That meant Katie was right.

"Shit," I said out loud.

Exiting the car, I made my way to the door, welcoming the chime from above. Julie had finished her stop at the courthouse hunting down those old burglary reports. By the thin folder in her hand, I assumed she managed to find something from the lead.

"I got you plain black coffee, Hank," Cade said as I walked in. "Not sure how you took it, but I have creamers and sugars and whatnot in the back."

"I'll manage. Thank you very much, though."

"It's nothing. Just my way of helping with the big case." He smiled and shot Julie a wink.

Julie gave a quick smile back, but it was clear that she was anxious.

"You think your Grandpa's old microfiche machine still works?" Julie asked.

"I hope so," Cade answered. "It's just been sitting back there collecting dust for who knows how long."

Julie took the thin folder and disappeared toward the back of the store.

I sipped on the fresh coffee. The plain black was oddly satisfying, almost cleansing. Cade busied himself turning on a computer by the roll-top desk and arranging his workspace for the day. I sat in a chair at the front of the store and took in the collection of oddities displayed around the room. Along with the old cameras on the wall behind me were hung pencil-drawn pictures of working pack mules and their handlers. Various glass containers of different colors lined the top of the wall partition, and a framed collage of geometric wood pieces hung by the door entrance. Odd, indeed.

"How's she doing?" Cade's voice was soft and low.

"What do you mean?" I asked. He stood up, leaning over the counter for support and to be closer to me while trying to remain out of Julie's earshot.

"This case, it means a lot to her, obviously. She can be...," Cade searched carefully for his next words. "Involved, if you know what I mean."

"Obsessed?" I clarified.

"I think that's a little harsh, but not exactly untrue. I mean, a loved one is murdered, wouldn't you be obsessed on some level?"

I instantly thought of Victoria. Cade was right. If cancer could be legally defined as a criminal, there's nothing I wouldn't do to bring it to justice.

"I see your point. But why ask?"

"She's looked over that case for the last decade. She's never gotten anywhere until now. I'm excited for her, but also, I know these things have a way of building up false hope. I just want you to be careful."

In homicide work, hope can be a double-edged sword. Hope creates faith that justice will be found. However, that same hope can be exponentially devastating when justice is lost.

"I told her my expectations from the beginning, and she signed on. I didn't make any promises, but I also know how shortcomings in this work can be disastrous."

Cade held back a response, but it was clear he was concerned about Julie Haywood.

"Okay, I lied," Julie's voice yelled from the back of the store. "I have no idea how to work this thing!"

Standing over Julie's shoulder, I stared at the antiquated machine. The over-sized monitor screen was a fuzzy bright gray, and I could hear a hushed whir coming from somewhere inside. Julie huffed as she manipulated a thin strip of film on a small panel in front.

"Wow, it still works," I said. "I haven't actually laid eyes on one of these since—" I thought back to a task I had as a patrol officer in the early nineteen-nineties where I was analyzing a crime pattern of robberies. It was what impressed the powers that be who brought me into the investigations bureau. I finished my statement. "The early nineties."

"Whether it works is still debatable." Julie fell back in her seat in defeat. "I can't figure this damn thing out."

After a quick scan, I reached over Julie's shoulder, picked up the film, and fed it into a small slit on the side of the panel. An image of a handwritten report illuminated the gray screen. It was clear as day.

"User error?" I asked playfully.

Cade McCoy giggled from behind.

Julie snapped, "Shut up!"

Still unsure how to proceed, Julie let out a sigh as she searched around the machine for something.

"Okay, I give up," she said. "How do you move it around? There isn't a joystick or something to move it around."

I leaned over her shoulder once more. "You see that glass panel the film is under?"

"Yeah."

"Move that. It's on a track system, and it'll move around like a joystick."

Julie carefully moved the glass panel side to side, blurring the image across the screen as if it were being fast-forwarded.

"Whoa!" she said.

"Yeah, slow it down just a bit."

"I barely touched it."

"It's reading microscopic words on a sheet of film. It's like scrolling across Google Maps when you're panned out too far."

Julie nodded. Cade adjusted his stance with an agreeing, *hmm*.

The next hour was spent reading over the reports from August 1993, looking for traces of Darrell Banks and his get-out-of-town burglary spree. Being a new lead in the death of Crystal Daws, Officer Julie Haywood ensured nothing was overlooked. There weren't many reports to sort through, but Julie took her time. When she was finished, she reported that starting on the day Banks was released from jail, there were eleven reported crimes in the following week. When she called out that three auto burglaries were reported the same day Banks got out, I knew the seemingly far-fetched lead had a possibility of going somewhere.

"Three reports," Julie said. The bookstore was empty of customers as we sat circled in the front area by Cade's desk.

"You think one of them belongs to the killer?" Cade asked.

"Hard to think someone would've called in a burglary to their own car where a homicide victim's stolen property was hidden," I offered, trying to process everything.

"Weirder things have happened," Cade replied.

"True." I looked at Julie. "Who are the listed victims?"

She consulted her notes. "The first one was a black female, nineteen years of age, student at the community college who reported it happened at the Winn-Dixie parking lot. Said her backpack and Walkman were stolen."

"Okay," I said. "Walkman, really?" It had been a long time since I'd heard that brand name. I remembered buying Victoria one for her birthday decades ago. The thought of downloading music to my phone as Katie had instructed would've been pure science fiction back then.

"What time?" I asked.

"The listed window was an hour between 1:00 p.m. and 2:00 p.m."

"Is the Winn-Dixie near the jail by chance?" I asked.

"Actually, it's not too far at all," Julie answered. "Maybe half a mile?"

"Alright. What else?"

"The second was a woman, white female, thirty-three years old who reported it from her house," Julie said.

"Does she live near the Winn-Dixie?"

Julie went back to her notes. She looked up. "No. Not really. She lives on the other side of town by Lake Francis."

The answer irritated me for some reason. "Other side of town?"

"That's what's on the report."

"What does the narrative say, like how'd the burglary happen?"

She scanned her notes for a moment. "She got home around three-thirty from running errands and stated that as she got into the house, she realized she'd forgotten her purse. She went back out to the car, and it wasn't there. Assumed it was taken soon after she got home because she'd left the door open."

I let the information Julie read off settle in my mind. Then, an obvious glaring question came to me.

"What errand was she running just before she got home?"

A quick glance at her notes left Julie blank. "I don't know."

"Check the report again."

Julie got up and walked back to the microfiche machine in the back room. She came back three minutes later with an embarrassed grin.

"What?" Cade asked.

I already knew.

"Grocery shopping at the Winn-Dixie."

Another giggle came from the bookstore owner, and I just smiled.

"That's two. What about the third?" I asked."

"It was off Marion Street, reported by a white male, age 38, who was eating lunch at Doris's Diner. Parked his car down the road, and when he came back from lunch found his door open and the glove box rummaged through. Reported loose change and a few cassette tapes missing."

"Doris's Diner?" I asked, unfamiliar. "Is that anywhere near Winn-Dixie or the jail?"

Cade was quick to answer, "Yeah, it's like a block or two from the Winn-Dixie, just on the other side of Highway 90."

"Alright," I felt the lead fading away. None of the reporting victims seemed to fit the bill of robber and murderer. None of them felt right.

"That's it?" I asked.

Julie gave a submissive smile. "Yeah. Looks like it."

"Any other burglaries reported later in the week?" I asked.

"Um…," Julie scanned over her notes. "No, none. You think maybe they delayed making a report?"

"Possibly," I answered. "You think you can check the following weeks for any delayed reports?"

"Yeah, sure."

Cade McCoy chimed in. "Well, what about those three burglaries you mentioned? You don't think any of them are who you're looking for?" He had a point. We were looking at the reports at face value and not going deeper into their backgrounds.

"Right." I turned to Julie. "We're going to have to look into these three burglary victims just to make sure. They could have had some connection to the killer. If it's there, we need to find it."

"Now?"

"Soon, yes. But can you take me over to the Winn-Dixie? I want to get a feel for it."

Julie stood up and began to grab her things.

"Oh, one more thing." I had a question from earlier. "What were the other reports that came in that week? The other eight?"

Julie sat back down and flipped a few pages of her notebook. "Um, a couple of thefts, animal abuse, a couple of batteries, and a criminal mischief. Sounds like not much has changed in twenty-two years."

"Thefts of what?" I asked.

"A car and a horse."

"A horse?" That was something I had honestly never heard in my career.

"Yeah, it happens," Julie answered.

"Wait, could Banks be good for the auto theft?" I asked.

"No, it was a boyfriend and girlfriend thing. She got mad; he took her car, blah, blah, blah."

"Okay. What about the criminal mischief? Was it graffiti or something like that?"

"No, someone threw a rock through the back window of a car."

I let the information from the old cases process, but nothing was glaring or obvious, which left an uneasy feeling in my stomach. The frustration of this lead vanishing before it proved fruitful began to weigh heavy. Listening to the information available, I was doubtful.

⌘

As it neared midday, Julie pulled into a shopping center anchored by the chain grocery store. A sandwich shop, a hardware store, and a consignment clothes shop filled out the rest of the strip mall. The warm sun radiated down as I stepped out of Julie's Jeep. She parked in the middle of the parking lot, and I stood and turned, taking in a three-hundred-sixty-degree view.

The parking lot sat at the beginning of a shallow valley with three sides that opened to the west.

Across the highway, sitting on top of a series of hills were the academic brick buildings of the community college. To the east, another hill led back into town. To the south, an outcropping of old, dilapidated houses rose just above the roof line to the shopping center.

"The jail's back that way, about three blocks past those small houses over there." She was pointing to the south where I was looking.

"Okay," I acknowledged.

Standing in the area where, twenty-five years ago, Darrell Banks stood, casing cars to break into, provided me a sense of connection, but that was it. There was nothing else to gain from this place. According to Julie, the area hadn't really changed in the last two decades. A few businesses and some of the people had moved in and out, but the infrastructure was essentially the same.

"It makes sense though," I said.

"What does?"

"The location." She gave me a questioning glance, so I explained my logic. "He leaves the jail and finds this place. It's probably one of the bigger collections of people and cars in this town at any given time. Maybe the courthouse would have more, but that also has cops coming and going. Not here. So, it's perfect for him to sit and watch. He sees the college girl park and get out. Notices she probably doesn't lock it. Goes right behind her, takes her stuff, and waits for the busy mom to do the same. Then moves on and hits the last one on his way out."

Julie stood beside me but didn't say anything.

"You don't think any of those are the killer do you?" she asked.

I didn't want to say no, but the more I thought about it, it would've been careless for the killer to make a police report of Crystal Daws's purse being taken. Being elusive for over two decades proved the killer was patient, methodical, and extremely careful. It didn't fit, and that was frustrating. He would've just chalked the theft up as a loss and hoped it didn't bite him in the ass.

"We still have to look, right?" I answered.

"So, that's a no, the killer didn't make a police report. Got it."

Standing in the hot parking lot for a moment was peaceful. A pleasant, warm breeze rolled off the hills to the east. It also pushed the sweet aroma of barbeque downwind. The smell of chicken and ribs broke my concentration. I looked toward its source and saw a modest wood building at the edge of the parking lot. Gray smoke billowed into the sky from a screened-in porch at its rear.

"What's that?" I asked, eyes fixed on the restaurant.

"Ronnie's Barbeque," she said. "One of the few locally owned restaurants in the area."

"They got good food?"

"Sure, not bad."

"Good, it's lunchtime."

⌘

The place reminded me of Jim and Milt's back in Tallahassee. Food was served off the same style of tin plates, and the menu was close to the same; they even had Brunswick stew. I could make the argument that they were run by the same owner.

As we finished our lunch, I noticed Julie was growing anxious. She sat across from me, facing the door. I had my back to the door since she was the official gun-toter between the two of us. Her anxiety spiked after I heard the door chime, and her eyes followed someone behind me. Not wanting to give it too much attention by turning around, in my peripheral vision, I saw two deputies from the Sheriff's Office sit at the other side of the dining hall. They sat in the corner, ignoring Julie Haywood, and I grew confused as to why she was apprehensive.

I ignored the behavior change, and we finished our lunch.

Standing in line to pay our check, I heard the two deputies finish and get in line behind us. Julie's body tensed. I turned and looked at the deputies with a smile.

"Hey guys, how are you?" I asked.

"We're fine, thank you, sir," one of them answered.

I turned back around as the cashier addressed Julie. When Julie handed her money, someone made a low, but noticeable, "moo" sound, followed by a quick giggle.

I still didn't understand, and Julie lowered her head. She didn't turn. She snatched her change out of the cashier's hand and bolted for the door. I turned back to the deputies. One had a grin on his face, the other was watching Julie move toward the door. The grinning deputy let out a louder "moooo" as Julie disappeared through the door. I handed my check to the giggling cashier. Outside, Julie was already sitting in the driver's seat of her Jeep, the engine running.

I climbed in. She was mad. Whatever the joke was; it was personal. I kept silent.

Julie pulled out on the main highway, heading back toward town. Her vise-like grip on the steering wheel did little to calm her down. Her breathing was quicker than normal, and I hoped the awkwardness would dissipate during the drive.

"You ever do anything back in Tallahassee that no one ever lets go?" she asked.

I thought for a moment. Mistakes, I've made. But compared to the next-level fuck-ups that sometimes came around in law enforcement, they paled.

"Not really," I answered.

"I shot a cow," she said flatly.

I didn't say anything. But that clearly explained the "moo," and when I thought back, Officer Boone's "Elsie" comment back at the station now made sense. And then, the next thought hit me hard.

"That's why they call you when cows get loose?"

"Yup," she said. Her face was growing red with embarrassment. "It's my penance."

"Really?" That seemed a little too backwoods. "Why? Just to be assholes?"

"No." Julie deflated. She didn't want to explain anything, but for some reason felt compelled to tell me. "It was a deal the Sheriff made to keep me out of trouble."

"Oh?"

"Ugh…," Julie groaned. She whipped into a parking spot in front of the police station. "So, one night, I got dispatched out to the county to help with a report of a prowler. It was my first week."

She stopped and inhaled a deep breath.

"So, my first week and I have a chance to catch a prowler. Some real action." She shook her head, reliving the moment. "So, I get there, and there are two deputies on scene. The place is a farm, and I head toward the barn, which is next to the cow pasture. I hear something moving inside and withdraw my firearm. I go in, hoping to catch the guy inside. Prove to all those male deputies that I got what it takes. But, in reality, I'm scared shitless. But I go in. Gun up."

Julie stopped again and bowed her head in self-pity.

"I swear it was footsteps of a man, but when I ran after and turned the corner, that fucking cow was right in my face. I must've scared it as much as it scared me. She mooed, and I fired."

I didn't know what to say, but given the context, it was quite humorous. But it was a mistake, nonetheless.

"You kill it?"

"No." she answered.

"No?" I was surprised. "Then why the penance?"

"The reason that cow was locked up in the barn was that she was about to give birth. The calf came from a bull whose bloodline was high dollar, and she was the owner's top breeder."

"Oh…."

"But the damage was done, and they had to put her and the calf down."

"Oh," I said. "Damn. So now you have to help round up loose cows."

"Yeah. And now those asshole deputies think it's funny to tease me. Hell, I'm not convinced they don't let those damn things loose when they're bored just to see me out chasing them around like some idiot."

"Is that why you're trying to solve Crystal's case?" I asked. "To prove yourself?"

Julie didn't answer right away. I imagine she'd never been asked that before. She gave the answer some thought and considered the prospect. "Somewhat. I mean, it's personal to me in one sense, but on the other hand, if I could solve it, not only do I get justice for Crystal, but I also get respect from all these clowns. In a way, it would show them that I'm more than some stupid girl who shot a cow. So, in a way, yeah."

"Fair enough," I said.

We sat in the quiet Jeep for a minute longer. Then I thought about the fact that Julie Haywood had shot a cow. It was funny, and I couldn't help but start giggling.

"Don't you start, Hank!" she yelled.

"I'm sorry, Julie." The laughter grew. "I'm sorry." I tried to catch my breath. "It's funny, c'mon?" I kept laughing.

Julie looked pissed at first. But I smiled, letting her know that it was a mistake, not a death sentence, nor the definition of her being. A few more laughs built up, and I let them loose. Finally, Julie smiled. It only fueled my laughter more. She smiled wider and wider until she joined.

After another cathartic minute of fun, I added, "See, it's okay to be self-deprecating once in a while."

"Okay, but you call me Elsie and I'm kicking you in the balls."

I let out a deep raucous laugh with a head nod. "Deal."

When the laughter faded into silence, the matter of what step in the case to take next needed to be decided.

"Now what do we do?" Julie asked.

"What about your friend, Hope?" I answered. "We should really talk to her."

Chapter 17

Julie pulled down the narrow gravel road that led into the trailer park. We had traveled away from the small urban area of downtown Madison, taking a two-lane highway a few miles out. Like many of the disenfranchised places of Tallahassee, here too, a lack of prosperity blended into an overall canopy of sadness. Most of the mobile homes were in disrepair, with junk stored in the yards and random trash littering the common areas.

Parking her Jeep out in front of a dull beige trailer, I noticed Julie had become tense. She sat stiffly in the Jeep, her palms gripping the steering wheel as if bracing for impact. There was a hesitation about her I didn't understand. In every step of this investigation, even the retraced steps, she had exuded a sense of urgency. The image of Julie in locked arms with the teenage Crystal Daws and their third friend, Hope Bennett, flashed in my mind.

"You okay?" I asked. "You're not still pissed about the cow thing, are you?"

Julie stared blankly past the windshield, ignoring me.

"Hey, you alright?" I asked again.

"Yeah." She pulled the keys from the ignition and sat back in the seat. "It's just that…." She looked down and fidgeted with her keys. "I haven't really seen Hope in like… fifteen years. And before that, it was awkward because of what happened to Crystal."

"Earlier when I asked about her, you said she was a 'mess'." I took an exaggerated look around the trailer park. "I take it she went downhill after Crystal's death?"

"You can say that. Drugs at first. Pot, then more of the hard stuff, had a few kids by different guys, been to jail a few times."

"Yeah, that sounds like a mess."

"I'm not sure how she'll react with me being here, asking about Crystal and all—"

"You want me to take lead?" I asked.

"Well," she smiled. "You've been lead this whole time, but yeah. Could you do all the talking?"

"Sure."

Standing on the concrete slab at the base of the rickety wooden stairs next to the trailer, I paused to look at Julie. I gave her a nod, which she returned, telling me she was ready. I reached up and knocked on the aluminum door. A muted female voice said something from inside. I looked at Julie, and she didn't understand the sound either. A moment of nothing, and I knocked again.

"Who is it?" The voice from inside was louder.

Out of habit, I was about to yell "police," but I held back, giving Julie an indecisive shrug, I wasn't sure what to say. *Private Consultant* didn't have the same ring to it.

Julie was standing next to me and noticed my hesitation. "It's Julie Haywood, Hope. Can we talk for a minute?"

We could hear a few bumps and thumps inside the trailer, but soon after, footsteps neared the other side of the door. It cracked open and a tired-looking face peered out. She looked at Julie, scanned me up and down, and then looked back at Julie. For having once been the closest of friends, Hope Bennett couldn't care less that Julie was standing at her doorstep.

"What do you want, Jewels?" Her tone of contempt matched the scowl on her face.

Julie's professionalism kicked in. "Just want to ask you a few questions; that's all."

"Who's this?" Hope's lazy stare moved back to me.

"I'm Hank Trescott, Ms. Bennett. I'm working with Julie on a case."

Hope pushed open the door and stood with her arms crossed, looking down at us. "Well, I don't know anything about no case, so if you don't mind, I'd like to—"

"It's about the Crystal Daws case." I cut her off. The indifference of people dismissing their ability to help before they even knew what something was about always irked me. My bluntness paid off. Hope's face, although haggard and tired, flashed a genuine, worrisome look before she caught herself and resumed her indignant pose in the doorway.

"I see you still can't let things go, huh, Jewels?" she barked.

"She was your friend, too," Julie said.

"Don't you think I know that? I loved her like a sister, but she's dead, and ain't nothing can change that. I don't care who you got helpin' you or whatever. Can I go back inside now?"

"Hope, I just wanted to ask a few questions. We're not here to bother you. It'll only take a few minutes."

"I don't think so."

Hope reached across the threshold for the doorknob.

"Why didn't you ever talk with Detective Byrd about Crystal's murder?" I blurted out before she could close the door.

Her face crinkled. She looked confused.

"Uh, I did talk to him," she said matter of fact.

"Wait, you did?" I asked. I saw Julie stand straighter. This was news to her as well.

Hope didn't answer. The confused look morphed into panic. Her eyes widened, and she pawed at the doorknob.

"Hope, you said you *did* talk to him about Crystal's death?" I asked again.

She began pulling the door shut before answering.

“Stop! Leave me alone!”

I caught the bottom of the door with my foot and held it open against her effort.

“Hope, please!” Julie pleaded.

“Did you talk to him, yes or no?” I demanded.

“I already answered that and look what good it did. Nothing. She’s still dead, and I’m stuck in this shithole.”

“But what did you tell Detective Byrd?” I asked in haste. She was pulling the door with all her body weight.

“Am I under arrest, *Officer Haywood*?” The venom in her voice was thick.

“No, of course not, Hope. But if you know something—”

“Leave me alone, or I’ll call the real law out here!” Hope screamed.

Julie put her hand on my shoulder. “Let it go. It’s okay.”

I let go of my grip, and the thin aluminum door slammed shut, shaking the entire trailer. Foot stomps from Hope Bennett resonated away from the door.

Looking back at Julie, I asked, “What the hell was that?”

“I told you she was a mess.”

⌘

After directing Julie where to go next, we spent the car ride digesting our contact with Hope Bennett.

“So, why would Byrd keep an interview with Hope Bennett out of his report?” Julie asked.

“I have no idea,” I replied. “From what I can tell, he was very meticulous.”

“Yeah, I think so, too.”

“It definitely seems odd.”

We rode in silence for a few miles. I attempted to make sense out of that train wreck of an interview. I gazed out my window at a vast, open field stretching for acres. It was beautiful farmland. Lush, green vegetation sprouting life from the ground stirred something primal inside of me. I had no idea what crop was growing, but nonetheless, it was impressive.

"What I don't get is why would she react like that?" Julie asked.

"Yeah, I don't know that either," I said. "I just met her. You've known her a lot longer."

"Well, yeah, but I knew the sixteen-year-old Hope Bennett, not the forty-year-old bitch we just met."

Part of me wanted to be angry at Julie for letting the relationship with Hope Bennett sour, but I knew from working homicides that death changes people. Whether it be for better or worse, it changes everyone.

"So, what do you think she told Detective Byrd?" Julie asked. "I mean, it couldn't have been that important if he didn't mention anything in his report, right?"

"Again, I don't know," I answered.

Julie hit the steering wheel out of frustration.

"And you think we'll find the answer going here?" she asked.

Looking out my window again, we drove down the dirt driveway, past the mailbox with *Byrd* painted on the side.

"I hope so," I said. "You think she's home?"

Shadows from the tree line stretched across the front yard, giving the illusion night had already come. The sun was tucked behind a line of thin clouds and sat just above the horizon. Soon it would be dark, for real.

"Yeah, I see a light on," Julie answered. She put the Jeep in park and waited for me to get out first.

The main door was open, leaving the screen door as the only barrier. I knocked, rattling the old door in the frame.

"Mrs. Byrd, are you home?" I called out. "It's Hank Trescott, again. I came here the other day."

There was a quiet shuffle inside. "Yes. Hold on." Mrs. Byrd replied.

Mary Anne Byrd looked annoyed but remained hospitable. I understood this was an intrusion on her time, her house, and her past, but I needed answers.

“I’m sorry to come at such a late hour, Mrs. Byrd, but I was hoping we could come in for just a moment. It’s about the same case I mentioned the other day.”

“We?” she asked.

I looked behind me, and Julie was standing at the base of the steps, off to the side. I waved her up.

“Yes, me and Officer Haywood, from the Madison Police Department,” I answered.

“Oh, yes. Hello, Officer Haywood,” she said, “come in.”

I held the door for Julie, and we stepped inside the living room. Mary Anne Byrd wrapped a long housecoat over her nightgown and tied it tight. She turned off her television at the set by clicking the button in the top corner and sat down on the edge of the couch.

“What can I help you two with?” she asked.

“Well, after I left the other day, I wondered if maybe I missed something related to this case.”

“I gave you everything I could find, Mr. Trescott,” she answered.

It had bothered me that Detective Byrd’s widow had retrieved the case files without my assistance. I accepted it at the time and understood the situation. She didn’t want a strange man going through her late husband’s things, but she wasn’t a cop. A cop left notes and information in all sorts of ways not visible to the civilian eye. In this case, it would take a cop to ensure nothing was missed.

“Would you mind if I took a look around your husband’s office area, Mrs. Byrd?”

She looked put off. But, if Hope Bennett spoke to Detective Byrd about Crystal Daws’s murder, there should be something documented somewhere. I was sure of it.

Awaiting a decision was excruciating. I held my plea for as long as I could. “Please?” I looked at Julie for reinforcement, but she just sat there.

“Fine,” she said. “Let me show you.”

Mary Anne stood up and led me to a small room halfway down the hallway. She opened the door, reached inside, and flicked on the light. As the room lit up, I saw boxes crammed in the corner at both the far sides with a messy desk barely visible in the middle. She stepped slowly into the cluttered room and made her way to the desk.

“This is where’d it be, Mr. Trescott,” she said flatly.

“Okay, that’s great,” I said. “Thank you.”

Mrs. Byrd left the room and went back toward the living room. Julie stood at the doorway, unsure about joining me inside the packed office.

“Now I’m kind of sorry I asked,” I said quietly.

“Holy shit,” Julie whispered. “That’s a lot of stuff.”

I pulled out the drawers to the desk and began sifting through the contents. Knickknacks, police memorabilia, actual junk, and office supplies all filled the drawers. In the bottom drawer were files, and I noticed, markedly, that they had numbers stamped on the tabs in the same sequence as case numbers. A few went back to 1978, back when I was in high school. Curiosity urged me to pick it up and read the case, but I didn’t want to further impose on Mrs. Byrd. What I did notice a gap in the files.

“Got anything?” Julie asked.

“Not really,” I said. “He kept some of his old files in the drawer. There’s a gap, like one’s missing.”

“Crystal’s case?” she asked.

“I don’t think so. His widow brought me everything in a box.”

“Oh, you think it means anything?”

“I don’t think we’ll be able to tell. But if he kept everything in that box, what we’re looking for won’t be in that drawer.”

“Oh, okay,” Julie sounded confused.

"What if whatever Hope told him was important enough that he decided to keep it to himself?" I asked.

"Okay? Like what?"

"I don't know, but there's a reason it's not in the case file."

"That or she's a damn liar, and we're wasting our time," Julie huffed.

There was a loud knock at Mrs. Byrd's screen door. I perked up, and I met Julie's eyes wide with surprise. She shrugged her shoulders and looked down the hallway. Looking back at me, she shook her head. Mary Anne called out to the other late caller.

"Go see who it is," I whispered to Julie. She nodded and walked out of sight.

I kept looking around the desk and flipped through a few notepads that were lying around. Nothing obvious. I pulled open a few smaller drawers, but that proved fruitless. I stepped back and went into full-on detective mode. I slid my hands under the lip of the desk, feeling for any hidden key or secret switch that would lead to a cache of information hidden away since his death.

Nothing. I kneeled and looked for anything suspect, but it was just the plain underside of a desk.

Arguing erupted and began to get louder in the living room. I walked into the living room and was surprised to see Ryder Langston standing in full uniform between Julie and Mary Anne Byrd.

"You and your friend need to leave," Ryder demanded of Julie.

"C'mon, Langston," she pleaded.

"Hey, what's going on?" I interceded.

"You and Officer Haywood are being told to leave immediately!" Langston ordered.

"Why?" I looked at Mary Anne Byrd for an answer.

"You can't just barge in on an old lady and drudge up the past, that's why." Mary Anne began breathing heavily and held her hand to her chest as she spat the words. Earlier she had appeared to be put off, but I didn't think she was this angry at the intrusion.

"I didn't…." I was dumbfounded by her reaction. I looked at Langston. "I didn't barge in. I asked if I could look around, and she said yes."

"Well, she's changed her mind. It's almost nine o'clock, Hank. Round here, that's pretty late, especially for old folks," Langston said.

"Okay, sure." I didn't want to make things worse. "We're leaving."

I gave Julie a quick wave and held the door open for her. I paused at the screen door. Ducking back in for just a moment, I caught the attention of the widow.

"I'm sincerely sorry, Mrs. Byrd, for any inconvenience. But you said this case 'bothered him to the end,' right? Well, all I'm trying to do is continue his work. That's all."

I disappeared through the door before she or Langston could answer. I got into the Jeep with Julie, and she began to drive off.

"Old bat must've called him instead of just telling us no," Julie vented.

"Yeah, I didn't see that coming."

"Did you find anything while you were back there?" she asked.

"No. Nothing."

"Dammit," she yelled. She checked the digital clock on the dashboard and asked, "It's getting late. You want the pull-out again?"

I was reminded of what Katie had brought up in our conversation earlier that morning. Was this a friendly invite out of concern or was there another motive?

"Hello, Hank?" she asked again. "The pull-out? You want it, or are you going to spring for a hotel?"

"Oh, no," I said. "The pull-out's fine, if it's not too much trouble."

"It's okay. I don't mind the company."

I was unsure how to respond, so I let the silence of the ride take over.

A moment later, Julie huffed in frustration.

"What?" I asked.

"I'm a little pissed," she said.

Fearing, but uncertain that I was unable to read Julie's intentions, I gave her an inquisitive look. "Why?"

"Well, we actually got somewhat of a lead in this case, right?" she huffed again. "I mean, after all these years and something actually breaks…."

I was relieved it was about the case and not whatever Katie had suggested might be going on. "Right," I agreed.

"And today, we run into not one but two roadblocks in Hope and Widow Byrd. Both of them basically told us to fuck off. It's aggravating as hell."

Julie let out a high-pitched groan and slapped the steering wheel again.

"Calm down, Julie," I said. "It'll be okay."

"But how, Hank. How?" she demanded. "How can I be calm when these two won't help?"

I thought about Hope Bennett's words and Mary Anne Byrd's reluctance. Julie's inexperience was blurring her vision, but what we saw in both women was just surface tension. There was something worth knowing underneath, and they were hiding something. It was less obvious to Julie, but the possibilities put a smile on my face.

"Are you smiling?" she yelled.

"Yes. I am."

"Alright, now I'm getting pissed at you."

I chuckled. "Do you know why they reacted like that?"

"No!" Julie barked in frustration.

"It's because we're on the right path."

⌘

After picking up food from the only Chinese takeout place in the county, I found myself back in Julie Haywood's living room. The pork fried rice satisfied my appetite, and Julie placed her leftover sweet and sour chicken in the refrigerator. She disappeared into her bedroom while

I waited. We needed to discuss the case and which direction it needed to go.

As Julie stepped out of the bedroom, I was taken aback. She wore a loose T-shirt and matching pajama shorts barely covering her toned backside. There was a small hint of cheek showing below the cuff. I found myself in a trance, fixated on her as she passed by on her way to the kitchen. As she ducked out of sight, I noticed I was holding my breath. She tinkered for a moment and asked a question from the other room.

"I'm pouring a glass of wine, you want one?"

Aside from Victoria and family, I hadn't shared a drink with a woman in decades. I didn't know how to respond.

"Um, sure." I decided not to be rude.

"Is Cabernet okay?"

"Yeah, that's fine." The casualness of the moment between Julie Haywood and me seemed foreign. I was beginning to think, maybe Katie was right.

Julie carried two glasses tucked between the fingers of her left hand and the wine bottle by the neck in her right. She poured two glasses and handed me one before taking a seat on the couch. She tucked her bare legs under her and sipped slowly from the glass. She sat up straight and let her hair cascade down the right side of her face. She looked beautiful in a natural and simple way.

She looked up and caught me in a stare, peering over the edge of the glass. Attempting to hide my embarrassment, I took an extra-long pull of the red wine, staring blankly at the ceiling for guidance. I welcomed the warm flush of the cabernet, hoping to dull the sharp edge of the uncomfortable moment.

"So, um…," Julie broke the silence. "What did you mean, 'we're on the right path'? All I got out of today was a broken-down woman who won't talk and a pissed-off widow who doesn't want to help."

"Let me ask you something," I started. "When you work the street, have you ever made contact with someone who was verbally abusive, uncooperative, and threatened you for just talking to them? Usually, after a complaint of them selling drugs or casing cars, or whatever the illegal activity might be?"

"Sure, of course. At least once a week, feels like," she answered.

"Okay, good." I continued my explanation. "Now, you ever deal with that same person who dog-cussed you one day, but on some other occasion, was nice and maybe even cooperative? Would offer up a consent search of their person out of the blue?"

Julie took a sip of wine while she thought. She pulled the glass away and answered, "Yeah, actually. A few times."

"Why do you think that is?"

"Because…um…." Julie's face crinkled in thought. "Well, I don't know. Why?"

"It's because they *were* doing wrong. The drug dealer was hiding drugs, or the burglar had the loot stashed on him, and they tried their best to distract you by lashing out with empty threats so you didn't find out the truth. It's classic posturing."

Julie sat wide-eyed.

"And those times they were nice and cooperative? Well, they were actually clean that time."

"Holy shit," she said, "so, what you're saying is that Hope Bennett knows something about Crystal's death. She was just being nasty, so we'd cross her off the list, and she could go back to hiding in whatever hole she dug."

"Exactly." I took another sip and let Julie process the lesson. "People naturally push away when there is something to hide."

"But what do you think she knows?" she asked.

"That, I don't know," I said, "but that's what we need to figure out."

"How do we do that?" Julie asked.

"The only thing I can think of is to go back over the case. Try to see where she would've fit in."

"Alright." Julie set an empty wine glass down and got up from the couch. She walked back to the kitchen and returned with the murder book. She plopped it down on the coffee table and flipped it open. "We start at the beginning?" she asked.

"Yeah, probably the best place."

Julie stood with her back to me, refilling her wine glass. With her directly in front of me, I couldn't help but follow the curves of her smooth legs up and down. I turned up my glass, finishing all the wine. She looked back, offering me another with the bottle in hand. I thought, *what the hell.*

"Sure," I told her. I grabbed the book and sat back down. Julie took a seat back on the couch, tucking her legs back under her.

"I think we need to look at the timeline again but with different factors."

"Different factors, like what?"

"Well, at the time or in the moment, some events surrounding a case appear as coincidental. However, if you look at a chunk of time from afar, those same coincidental events don't look like happenstance. A pattern develops."

"I don't really follow."

I pulled out my notepad and flipped to a fresh sheet. "Okay, first, we have Crystal's death." I wrote March of 1993. "In August of 1993, we have Darrell Banks stealing her stolen credit cards from an unknown car, most likely near the Winn-Dixie."

I left a space between those two entries to symbolize Holcomb Byrd's investigation. "Now, you said Hope Bennett stopped being friends with you soon after that, right?"

"Yeah, pretty much the next school year, so would've been a little after August of '93."

I added it to the timeline and looked at it. It was bare and didn't reveal as much as I had hoped.

"Anything else you can think of?" I asked. "Anything of importance happen around that time?"

Julie shook her head.

Over the next few minutes, I flipped through the pages of the murder book, willing the answer to jump out.

"Wait!" Julie suddenly shouted. "Oh, shit."

"What is it?"

"Well…," Julie paused, "Holcomb Byrd died in the fall of '93."

I recalled the local residents at the McDonald's breakfast club mentioning an untimely heart attack had killed Detective Byrd, but I had assumed it was well after the murder.

"Really?" I said.

"Is that one of the coincidences that you're talking about?"

"Could be, sure." But how to make it fit into the puzzle, I wasn't sure. I let the information process. It was an interesting footnote, for sure.

"Anything suspicious about his death? Or was it pretty obvious?" I asked.

Julie shrugged her shoulders. "I don't know." She took a quick sip of wine and added, "That was well before my time, obviously."

Julie Haywood was just a young girl in 1993. Understandably distraught over the death of her closest friend in the world, she would've hardly paid attention to the death of Holcomb Byrd.

"Oh, right. Of course," I said.

Maybe it was the wine causing the swirling of information, but I let this timeline float around in my head, trying to decipher if there was something we'd missed.

Crystal is killed in March and five months later her credit card is stolen. In a matter of two months, the lead detective dies of a heart attack, and someone close to Crystal, who, according to the detailed report, is not questioned, suddenly alienates herself from her life.

I needed more, but my instincts told me that something was there.

"So, did Hope Bennett go into this depressive state after Crystal's death, or are you saying it wasn't until the following fall?" I asked.

Julie cocked her head to the side, thinking back in the far reaches of her memory.

"No, it was the fall." She nodded confidently. "I remember around the time of the funeral, she and I were still close. She would call me at night, and we'd cry over the phone about how we missed her. We started to drift a little over that summer, but that was because her parents sent her off to summer camps while I stayed home. My parents couldn't afford it. But, yeah, it wasn't until the next school year that she stopped talking to me and just fell apart."

"Did you know why she just fell apart?" I asked. "Or did you assume it was because of Crystal's death?"

"Yeah, it was Crystal's...," Julie's face scrunched up in thought. "Well, shit. You know what, I think everyone just assumed, but I'm not absolutely sure."

I nodded.

"You think it was because of something else?" Julie asked.

"I don't know, maybe."

"Damn her," Julie spat. "We need her to talk." She tossed the glass back, emptying it a second time. She reached over to the coffee table and set it down. I could see her eyes beginning to gloss over from the wine.

"We'll figure it out, Julie," I said.

Julie smiled back at me, but it wasn't for the progress we were making. It was for something else. Something more personal.

We sat in silence for a few minutes while I flipped through the murder book. Glancing through the pages, I was trying to make sense of the timeline, not actually reading the reports. I whipped through the supplemental reports and property receipts and rescanned the crime scene photos. I heard Julie stir on the couch. I looked up as she emptied the bottle into her glass. She looked up at me, then down at the photos, and instinctually looked away.

"Ugh, I can't see those," she said. She stood up slowly, the wine making her stance a little wobbly.

"Right, I'm sorry." I placed my hands over them, blocking her view.

Holding the pictures angled so that she wasn't able to see, I flipped through the photos one more time. Studying each picture again, I tried to see what had previously been unseen.

"What was your wife like, Hank?" Julie asked.

"Huh?" The question was out of the blue.

"Your wife. What was she like?" she asked again.

"Oh," I said, setting the pictures down on the table. I searched for the words to sum up Victoria Trescott but found myself at a loss. "Well, she was kind. She was smart. Way smarter than me."

"Really?" Julie asked.

"Yeah, she would always beat me at crossword puzzles and Jeopardy questions, but she would also help me figure out life problems, too. She had this way of explaining how the world worked beyond my eyes, and I swear she was part angel."

Julie smiled, and I caught myself beaming at the mention of Victoria.

"How long were you married?" she asked.

"Thirty years," I said, proudly.

"Wow, that's awesome," she said flatly.

Unsure of why Julie Haywood would ask me about Victoria, I read regret on her face. She stared off into the distance, allowing something to consume her thoughts. She'd nearly finished her wine, and she looked up at me and smiled.

"Well, I guess—" she took the last sip. "I guess I'm going to bed, Hank. In there." She pointed to her bedroom.

There was an awkward pause while she stared at her bedroom door.

"Alright, Julie," I said. "Good night."

"Right, good night." She turned abruptly and stepped into her room. I went back to the crime scene photos, relieved that she had walked away because the top picture was of Crystal lying in the middle of the street. My eyes worked the picture, taking in the corners, the background, the foreground. The details. It was my third or fourth take of the image. Still, there could be things I missed. And there it was. Something I missed.

"What the hell?" I said. I ripped the photo out of its protective sleeve and angled it in a better light. I blinked, set down my wine glass, and made sure I was seeing it right. I pawed at the other pictures in the murder book and examined them as well. There it was, again. Now it was real.

"Holy shit," I said, loud enough for Julie to hear me.

She reappeared in the door frame; her inebriation lessened as she read the excitement on my face.

"What?"

"Julie!" I held up the collection of crime scene photos and added, "I don't think this was a robbery at all!"

Chapter 18

After the wine, Julie brewed some coffee, and we were up into the early morning hours combing through the murder book with a newly added filter. I kicked myself along the way for not spotting this earlier. It had been right in front of me. Julie joked that it was the wine that helped uncover the revelation.

Looking over the crime scene pictures, I had focused on Crystal's body. This was how the killer left her. It was the last connection she'd had to her killer. Her position was expected, consistent with taking a backward fall after being shot. That wasn't new. The bullet holes were the bullet holes, but something else caught my eye. It was slight, and clearly, Holcomb Byrd had missed it. But after comparing it to other pictures, I was certain of it.

Crystal Daws's pants were left unzipped.

At first glance, this registered as peculiar, but the more I thought about it, it completely changed the motive. If the motive changed, then the theory changed, and there was a whole new aspect to the case that went previously unexplored. The other pictures also showed Crystal's pants undone and open at the fly. This could have been overlooked because of her shirt hanging low or the obvious bullet wounds to her stomach catching all the attention. A closer look from a side angle was the convincing shot, which I sold to Julie. This other angle showed Crystal's underwear bunched above the waistline of her jeans.

"I'm sorry, Hank. I'm not following?" Julie asked, cupping her hands around a coffee mug.

"The zipper is down, and her underwear is bunched above her waistline. Meaning that her pants were down, and then they were suddenly yanked up, causing her underwear to bunch at her waistline. It looks sloppy."

"Oh," Julie said. "Oh!"

"Unless Crystal was the sort of gal who would have left the movie theatre with her pants undone and pulled down past her waist."

"Oh, no." Julie shook her head for emphasis. "She'd never— No, not Crystal."

"Right, I didn't think so," I said. "What I'm thinking is that after he shot her, he tried to get her pants down to…, you know." I didn't want to paint a picture that vivid for Julie, but my new theory was that the suspect had intended to rape Crystal Daws after shooting her. "He was interrupted by the responding Officer Langston and yanked her pants back up before taking off."

"Right, right," Julie was excited. "Yeah, because Langston heard the shots, and the guy probably heard him coming, so he was in a rush."

"Possibly," I agreed.

"Wait…," Julie finished her thought and then said, "What if the guy shot her second, like maybe she resisted the rape attempt, and that's why he shot her?"

"Well, I thought about that, but I don't think so."

"Why not?"

I hesitated, because my explanation was in the picture. I pulled it out but kept it facing away from Julie.

"You see," I pointed to a spot on the picture as if she could see it through my eyes. "The buttons or the zipper weren't ripped. From what you've told me of Crystal, she seemed to be the fighting type and would've fought her attacker."

"For sure," Julie agreed. "She would've fought like hell."

"Right, so there aren't any defensive wounds on her hands or arms. Plus, if she was fighting the guy on the ground, the back of her shirt wasn't very dirty."

"Ah, right." Julie sipped her coffee. I noticed she was sitting with her legs together, at the edge of the couch, since she switched from wine to coffee. Instead of down, her hair was now back in a ponytail.

We sat for several minutes, letting the new theory that the murder was sexually motivated, and not robbery, sink in. The quiet hum of her ceiling fan provided the only sound. I thought about this discovery and where it would take us next in the investigation. Moving the motive from random robbery to seeking out Crystal for a sexual assault changed everything. This explained the improbability of Darrell Banks finding her stolen credit card five months after the murder. The murder wasn't about the money; it was about the power and gratification of a sexual assault. When it came to sexual assaults, my instinct told me that Crystal was targeted, not randomly selected. That's most likely why she was shot. The killer wanted her subdued for the sexual assault, and taking the bank bag and her purse was just a smoke screen.

"Hank?" Julie broke the silence.

"Yeah?"

"Why would the guy bother to pull up her pants before fleeing? I mean, why wouldn't he just take off and leave things as they were if he heard the cops coming?"

"Huh," I replied, giving thought to the question. "That's a good question."

"You'd think he would cut and run. Seems risky to stay and try to cover his tracks, right?"

"Yes, it does," I said. "But then, he took the bank bag and purse as a smoke screen, so why not fully commit?"

"Yeah, okay. I can see that too. So, what do we do now?"

I checked my watch, and it was nearly three o'clock in the morning. "Holy shit, it's late."

"Oh, my goodness," Julie said as she spied the clock on her cable box. "I can't believe it's that late."

"It's okay. We can pick this up first thing in the morning. We have plenty to do now."

"Good." Julie got up from the couch, collected all the glasses and mugs, and took them to the kitchen. As she walked back toward her bedroom, I was putting the pictures and other files back in the murder book. She put her hand on my shoulder, and as I looked over, she leaned down and kissed me on the cheek. It was tender and sweet.

"Good night, Hank," she said. She went into her bedroom and shut the door.

⌘

Despite the lack of sleep, I felt the investigative buzz beginning to grow. The half cup of coffee helped, but the excitement of the chase brewed in my soul. The twenty-five-year-old cold case was starting to thaw. I followed Julie to the station from her house so she could check out the clothes that Crystal Daws was wearing on the night of her murder. After getting them from the evidence room, she handed me a large, brown paper bag, the top folded over and taped down along the front. Examining the paper bag, I checked the taped seal on the top and bottom. I trusted its contents weren't tampered with too much by the medical examiner when they removed the clothes from her body. Plus, it was a safe assumption that he was wearing sterile gloves.

"Okay, now what?" Julie asked.

"Well, now we take a quick road trip to Tallahassee and drop this off at FDLE's lab. It's a long shot, but just maybe the killer left his DNA on her pants when he pulled them down."

"Hey, Elsie?" Officer Boone yelled from across the room.

Julie turned with a scowl on her face. "What?"

"The captain needs to see you." Officer Boone had a derisive smile he let linger as Julie walked past him.

"I'll be right back, Hank," she said.

"What's up, Hank?" The short cop leaned against the wall with his arms tucked inside each other and waited until Julie was around the corner. "You guys crack the case yet?"

"We're still going over some evidence, but I'm feeling positive."

"Okay, good." Boone stood up straight. "Heard you guys were digging around some old cases in the courthouse basement."

"Yeah, we looked at a few." I decided to remain non-committal because of Julie's contempt for her co-worker.

"Anything interesting from the time of yesteryear?" he asked. I could tell he was mocking us. I didn't like it, but I didn't want to make trouble when I was still a guest. Especially when we had a big break in the case.

"Not really. Just trying to get a feel for anything that was going on around the time of the murder."

"Okay," Boone seemed unimpressed.

"Were you around when Crystal Daws was murdered?"

"I don't need to answer that, ol' Hank, now do I?"

His response caught me off guard. I was hoping he could shed some light on Hope Bennett's downward spiral in the fall of '93, but I didn't know how to react to his answer.

"Um, no. I guess not."

"You're a goddamn prick, Boone!" Julie snapped as she flew out of the captain's office.

Officer Boone began to laugh. He smiled at me, turned, and walked away, ignoring Julie's comment.

"I know it was you," Julie spat as Boone rounded the corner. "You're such a little shit!"

"Whoa, calm down," I said. "What's going on?"

"Stupid, small department bullshit. That's what."

Julie Haywood was steaming. She paced as she tried to make sense of whatever she had just been told.

"Okay. I don't know what that means, but it'll be okay."

"The captain said there have been complaints of me not pulling my weight on patrol by running around helping you on this case."

"Well, that's not entirely false, right?" I offered.

"But still. I know it was that dickhead who complained. Because no one else has ever cared about me working this case. Ever."

"So, I take it that you won't be joining me for the trip over to Tallahassee?"

"No, I'm sorry. Is that a problem?" she asked.

"Oh, no." I shook off any hint of inconvenience. "I've taken my fair share of evidence over to FDLE. It's been a while, but I think I can handle it."

"Alright." Julie was upset.

"Just fill out a request form and a chain of evidence form, and I'll take care of the rest."

Julie grabbed a few sheets of paper from the evidence prep room and filled them out. She paused while in the middle of the request form.

"What are we wanting done, again?" she asked.

"We want DNA swabs taken from Crystal's pants, but specifically the zipper and buttons."

Julie's face remained blank.

"The killer pulled them down," I pantomimed unzipping a pair of pants for her. "So, he probably left his DNA on the zipper."

"Oh, right. Gotcha." She resumed filling out the request.

"Make sure you spell that out in detail."

Julie finished and handed me the paperwork. Coincidentally, she was called over the radio for a traffic crash out on the main highway.

"Gotta go, Hank," she said. "Thank you for doing this."

"I'll call you if anything comes up."

With the evidence clutched tight, I turned toward the parking lot but was surprised by who was standing behind us. As Julie noticed, she gasped and her body stiffened.

"Aunt Carol, what's going on?" Julie asked.

Carol Daws stood expectantly with a scowl on her face. The quiet I'd seen in her the other day had vanished into something more tumultuous.

"Hey, I'm glad you're here," Julie said, walking closer. She hadn't noticed the change in her aunt. "We're getting some serious headway on the case. Hank and I—"

"I want you to stop this, Julie," Carol said. The use of her formal name as opposed to her nickname of Jewels told me I was right. This wasn't going to be pleasant.

"Stop what, Aunt Carol?" Julie asked. "We're actually making some real progress. After all these years."

"She's right, Mrs. Daws," I added.

"I don't care, Mr. Trescott. I don't." Carol Daws let loose a tear. She wiped it away before it ran down her cheek.

"But I don't understand?" Julie cried. "This is for Crystal. Don't you see that?"

"No, Julie," she snapped. "All I see is someone unwilling to let go of the past. All I see is someone who's dredging up the past. A painful past that I, for one, don't want to relive."

"I…, but—" Julie was speechless.

"As Crystal's mother, I want you to stop this pointless crusade," Carol demanded.

Julie wiped away tears of her own. "I don't know if I can do that, Aunt Carol."

"Julie, don't you see you're the only one who can't move on? You and your friend here are bothering everyone in this town. For what? Some misguided chance to prove something to everyone?"

Julie bowed her head. Carol's words hurt her; I could tell.

"It's always been about Crystal," Julie spoke softly and pitifully, still holding her head down.

"I've watched from afar, Julie. This has nothing to do with my Crystal and everything to do with rectifying the guilt you have over her death. I thought it was *cute* that you pursued this line of work, but figuring out your reasoning is quite sad. Did you really think *you'd* avenge her death?"

"Listen, Mrs. Daws—"

"I have no interest in listening to what you have to say, Mr. Trescott," she said. "I blame you for filling my niece's head with the idea she could somehow rewrite the past. You should go home and leave us alone."

I didn't answer. Julie didn't answer.

"I love you, Jewels," Carol rebutted. "But, please, for everyone's sake, including your own. Stop this, now."

Carol Daws turned and walked away, leaving Julie crying in front of the police department.

"Where the hell did that come from?" Julie said after a moment.

"I don't know, Julie," I said.

"Why can't she see the reason we're doing this? And that we're finally getting somewhere?" Julie wiped another tear away.

I reached up and placed a consoling hand on her shoulder. "It's okay, Julie."

"Should we stop, like she said?" Julie asked.

"No, absolutely not," I answered. "Is that what you want? Is that what you think Crystal would've wanted?"

"No," she answered. Giving thought to the second question, she replied, "I'm pretty sure she'd want me to find her killer."

"Then that's what we do, Julie," I said.

"Why would Aunt Carol act like this?" Julie asked. "I don't get it. I don't get it at all."

"Hope," I said.

"Hope?" Julie was confused. "What do you mean?"

"In cases like these, hope is a double-edged sword. It breeds life into a dormant case, but then it gives life to a grieved soul that believed it had already been healed."

"But we're making progress; why didn't she want to hear that?"

"She's scared," I answered. "In reopening the case, it essentially reopens those scars that she believed had healed. I assume losing her daughter the first time was hard enough but going through another investigation and seeing it end in the same way would be unbearable to her. You can't really blame her for feeling that way, can you?"

"No, I guess not."

"But that's not an excuse to stop," I said. "In homicide work, we speak for the dead, not the dead's relatives, right? Let's let this be more motivation to continue."

"Yeah," Julie smiled as she wiped away the last of the tears. "Yeah, let's do that."

"Okay. It's settled," I said.

"Ugh." Julie let out. "If it's not one thing, it's another, Hank Trescott."

"Welcome to life as a homicide detective," I said.

"Thank you for being at my side," she said.

Julie put her hand on my shoulder as she said goodbye, but unlike the night before there was no accompanying kiss on the cheek. As she walked away, I realized that I had expected a kiss. I wasn't sure what that meant. I secured the evidence in the passenger seat and focused on my upcoming drive. My thoughts moved toward Victoria and her beautiful smile, but her image was unclear in my mind. This irritated me as I tried to figure out why. It was all I could think about on the drive over to Tallahassee.

It felt as if she was in the car with me. Staring at me in judgment.

Why can't you see my image? We were married for thirty years, Hank Trescott.

I glanced in the rearview to check traffic, but the corner of the mirror caught my eye. I began to stare into my own soul. Why was it so hard to see her image in my head? She was my everything in life, and now, for some unknown reason, the simple task of remembering her face was difficult.

I remembered our wedding day, when Katie was born, Katie's wedding, and other cherished moments we'd shared together, but when I focused on her face, the image was blurred. I grew angry and looked back in the rearview mirror to see what was wrong with me.

"Why can't I see her face?" I asked the empty car.

I settled back in my seat and glanced over at the bag containing the clothes Crystal Daws was wearing the night she was killed. The idea of following a lead in the twenty-five-year-old murder grounded me for the moment. It helped remind me of purpose. Victoria would approve.

Another look in the mirror for self-direction, but I paused. An eerie feeling washed over me. For the last thirty miles, there had been a silver sedan about ten car lengths behind me. I'd first noticed it as we both got on the interstate from the State Road 14 exit at Madison. I thought nothing of it at first, but thirty miles later, it was still there, matching my speed. I tried to tell myself it was nothing, but my instincts told me otherwise. In my twenty-two years as a police officer, I had learned many things. One was to always trust your instincts.

Without moving my head, I looked in the mirror to gauge where the sedan was, then checked my speed. Seventy-two miles per hour. I clicked the coast button on the cruise control, slowing down to sixty-seven. The two cars between us quickly merged into the passing lane and made the move past me. The sedan slowed down to keep pace. I gave the cruise control a few more clicks downward, now to sixty-four. The silver sedan inched closer but slowed again.

A single silhouette of a man sat behind the wheel. I couldn't tell age or race or anything much past it being a human male from the distance. I thought about slamming on the brakes to see what they would do, but if I forced a confrontation, I had nothing with which to protect myself.

I had another idea. I suddenly sped up. I pushed the accelerator forward and climbed up to eighty miles an hour. Distance grew between me and the silver sedan, and I imagined the driver's frustration if, in fact, he was following me. Not to my surprise, the suspicious car sped up.

I grabbed my phone and quickly dialed Julie Haywood's number.

"Hey, Hank, that was quick," she said. "You got good news?"

"Not really," I answered. "What are you doing?"

"Oh, nothing important," she said. "Just headed over to a neighbor dispute about one of their dogs crapping the other's yard. I swear I'm the only one working today."

"Well, no good news, but I got interesting news," I teased.

"Oh, okay. What?"

"I think I'm being followed," I said.

"What?" Her tone was fearful. "Are you serious?"

"Yeah, silver sedan. He's been on me since I hit the interstate. Maybe before that."

"Silver sedan, huh?" Julie said. "Can you see who's driving it?"

"No, he won't get close enough to me. But whoever it is, he sucks at surveillance."

"Be careful, Hank," Julie said. "What are you going to do? Do you need me to call the state troopers?"

"No. I think I can take care of this," I said with confidence. "Listen, how long have you known your buddy, Officer Boone?"

"Lance? Seriously, you think he's following you?"

"Well, I'm not sure; I'm just going down my list of suspects. That little nonsense earlier in the hallway, when you went to the captain's office. I asked him if he knew Hope Bennett, and his answer was very odd."

"What do you mean, odd?" she asked.

"He told me that he didn't have to answer me." I let the answer settle, hoping to convey my concern to Julie. "Is he still at work?" I asked.

"Actually, no." Julie's tone grew anxious. "He went home soon after you left. That's actually why I'm humping all these damn calls."

"Does he drive a silver sedan?"

"I've never seen him in one. He usually drives full-size pick-up trucks."

"It could be a rental," I said. "Didn't you tell me he grew up in Madison?"

"Yeah, I mean, we were never friends. He was a little older than me growing up. Actually, he was like a grade or two ahead of Crystal."

"Really?" I asked. "Were they ever friends, or date, or anything like that?"

"No." Julie sounded skeptical. "I don't think so."

"So why would he blow me off like that about Hope Bennett? Do you know if they ever had history?"

"Shit, Hank. I don't know."

"You are not being much help right now, Julie," I said sarcastically.

"I know. I'm sorry," Julie said. "Listen, I have to get out on this call. Be careful and call me if you need to."

"Okay, I will. Bye."

I hung up the phone and watched the silver sedan out of the corner of my eye. Holding strong at eighty miles an hour, he was still about ten car lengths back.

Not knowing much about Officer Lance Boone, I thought about how he fit into this case. I knew he was local and was living in Madison around the time of the murder. He seemed to mock and tease Julie Haywood, the same person investigating a murder he could be responsible for, and in which there was now a breakthrough. Also, I was being tailed all the way to Tallahassee on the same day I had asked him about Hope Bennett and received a weird answer. Plus, he struck me as the type to need power and control in his life, which spoke to his obvious shortcomings. Probably why he went into law enforcement. It is also the basic motivation for sexual assaults.

Exit 209, the easternmost Tallahassee exit, was fast approaching, and I had an idea. I steadily increased my speed up to eighty-five miles per hour with the off-ramp getting closer. The silver sedan kept pace. I held steady in the passing lane as the exit ramp began to open up on the far-right side. The narrow window of opportunity was almost there. Holding pace as long as I could, when the off-ramp bent to the right, and the grass wedge began, I let off the gas and pulled hard to the right, screeching my tires as they barely held traction making the abrupt turn.

I barely missed the exit marker going onto the off-ramp. As I coasted down, I eagerly watched what the silver sedan did. He tried to follow, but other traffic interfered enough that he was unable to make the turn before being met with the guardrail, forcing him to continue west on the interstate. I watched as he slowed, looking for an alternate way to keep chase. The blue Ford emblem on the grill stood out, and I focused hard on what the model was as he passed. I smiled, pleased with the successful maneuver, as I hurried off the interstate and made the turn into town before he figured out a way to catch up. Certain I was successful in losing the tail, I had a couple of stops to make before proceeding to the lab.

⌘

T-ROC, or the Tallahassee Regional Operations Center, was the local office for the Florida Department of Law Enforcement. Wedged between two residential neighborhoods on Tallahassee's east side, it sat inconspicuously and looked more like a state bureaucracy than law enforcement. I pulled in off the main road and rolled through the parking lot, bringing back memories. Working homicides, evidence processing had been paramount, and time was always in short demand. Dropping off evidence directly to the lab, along with an incentive, depending on the lab technician, would usually mean a quick turnaround. In the dusk of my career, DNA had become prolific among criminal cases, and the demand for lab work skyrocketed. But the new science process was tedious and time-consuming, eating away at the demands of the case. The incentives, from bagels to beer to Florida State football tickets, were what made the difference.

With Crystal Daws's clothes in one hand and a bag of fresh bagels in the other, I parked and walked around to the back of the serology lab. I pressed the call button on the door and waited for a buzz.

"Can I help you?" A voice spoke through the intercom.

"Yes, hello?" This was a new step I was unfamiliar with.

"Yes, hi. Can I help you?"

"Um, yeah...." I held up the evidence bag but foolishly realized there was no camera. "I have evidence to turn over for analysis."

"What agency are you with?"

"Talla—" Oops, I thought. Habit. "Um, the Madison Police Department. I'm actually a consultant on the case."

The door in front of me buzzed, clicked, and popped open. I grabbed it and walked inside. The lobby was the same, except someone had replaced the chairs. A woman I didn't recognize sat behind a thick plate of glass with another intercom mounted in the middle. Above the window on the wall read: Evidence Receiving.

Waiting at the window ahead of me, was a young woman with a blonde ponytail wearing black cargo pants and a tan polo with a Tallahassee Police Department Forensic Unit emblem embroidered on the chest. She signed something and delivered it through a push drawer, similar to those at bank drive-throughs. She turned around and gave me a polite smile. The name tag with the police department logo clipped to her belt said, "Headley." I couldn't make out her first name before she turned around. I didn't know her. She obviously joined after I'd left, as she showed no signs of recognition.

A large door to our left opened, and the woman from behind the glass appeared with an empty bin. She took the evidence from Headley, and they chatted for a moment before the evidence tech disappeared through the large door and Headley exited the small lobby.

At least the process was nearly the same as before, I thought.

"Can I help you?" It was the same voice from the outside intercom, only less distorted.

"Right. I'm from the Madison Police Department, and I have this evidence that needs to be analyzed for DNA."

Her look was a combination of annoyance and pity. I wasn't sure why, but I stood there waiting.

"Do you have the request forms?" the tech asked.

"Yes." I pulled them out of my notebook and held them up. The woman reached below the counter, and the drawer opened on my side. I put the form in, and she retracted the drawer. She examined the paperwork from her side of the glass. Apparently, everything was in order. She passed through a chain of custody form, which I signed and volleyed back. Then, she came from behind the large door to the left and took Crystal Daws's clothes.

As I watched the evidence get placed into an empty bin and disappear behind the door, I had an uneasy feeling, like watching a child go off to school for the first time. I hoped everything would go well and prayed there would be no problems.

There was no one behind me in the lobby, so I stepped back up to the window.

"Any chance I could speak to the lab techs?" I asked.

"I don't know," the woman said flatly. "I just take the evidence."

The lab used to be connected, but clearly, the operation had grown in the last ten years, and there was significant separation from intake to analysis. I nodded a *thanks anyway* and exited out the door. With the bagels still in hand, I wandered for a bit, hoping to stumble across the lab. The expansive campus proved too hard to navigate as a civilian with no access, so I headed back to the parking lot for fear of raising suspicions from security. It was a lost cause anyway. I figured everyone I knew from ten years ago had probably moved to other positions or retired.

I sat down in my car and stared at the full bag of quasi-fresh bagels. I fished one out, spread some soft butter over one half, and bit down. Dropping off the evidence that could potentially solve a twenty-five-year-old murder turned out to be quite anticlimactic. I finished the bagel, started the car, and headed out. I remembered the tail from Madison and peered around the parking lot to make sure whoever it was hadn't found me. There was no sign of the silver sedan, and although I had ditched him, it told me that we were getting close. Dropping this evidence had been the right move, and the likelihood that this tail could return or escalate was higher now. There was one quick stop I had to make before heading back to Madison.

After picking up lunch at Canopy Road Café, I headed back to Madison, taking the more scenic route of Highway 90. The two-lane stretch between Tallahassee and Madison running through rural north Florida would make it easy to spot a tail. Keeping a vigilant eye, there were no signs of a tail.

As I hit the outskirts of town, I called Julie Haywood to let her know I was back.

"Hey, Hank. I take it nothing more developed from your shadow on the interstate?" Julie asked.

"No, I was able to shake him as I got into town. And let's say, I still got some moves up my sleeve."

"Did you ever get a look at the driver? A tag perhaps?" she asked.

"No, neither," I answered. "It was too far away to get a tag, but it was a Ford Fusion. I did a Google search on my phone and pulled up the images. I'm positive that's what it was. Probably a 2018 model."

"Okay, I can work with that," Julie replied. "I'll work on that as soon as I can."

Julie quickly transitioned to what was really on her mind.

"How'd it go at the lab? You get a hit?" she asked with anticipation.

"Hit?" I asked, confused. "What do you mean?"

"Did you get a DNA hit from Crystal's clothes?"

"Oh, no!" I said. "That's going to take a least a month, maybe less if I could've given the tech these bagels."

"Huh?" Now, Julie was confused. "Bagels?"

"Never mind. It's going to take a little bit for the lab to get back with us, so we need to focus on the next part."

"Oh, damn. I thought.... Never mind what I thought. So, what *is* the next part?"

Julie's comments made me realize she had never really worked with DNA evidence firsthand and was unfamiliar with the process. Unlike the movies, the science took some time.

"Well, right now it has to be Hope Bennett. I don't see anything else to go on. I say we go at her again. Maybe we tell her that we found some DNA evidence and hope something shakes loose."

In some of my cases, witnesses remained silent, thinking the case rested solely on their testimony. But, when I found corroborating evidence that backed their account, they felt easier coming forward. They wanted proof beyond their words. It was nerve-racking for the investigator, waiting for the witnesses to come around, but in the end, it was worth it. I hoped that Hope Bennett was this type of witness.

"Alright. Well, I'm on until six tonight," Julie said. She abruptly added, "Wait a minute."

I heard her radio squawking in the background and then Julie said, "Ten-four."

"Got a call?" I asked.

"Yeah, teenagers walking through this old lady's yard again after school. I swear I don't think I can take the high-speed excitement, Hank Trescott."

I laughed at Julie. "Someone's got to do it, right?"

⌘

With a promise not to do anything foolish, Julie Haywood sent me Officer Boone's home address. I wanted to press the issue, if there was one, while I waited for Julie's shift to end. I drove to the far east of town to Route 6 and made a left on a small two-lane road. The neighborhood was a mix of mobile homes, manufactured homes, and large family homes with working farmland. I drove slowly so I wouldn't miss my target but tried my best not to look suspicious. As Officer Boone's address approached, there were no cars behind or ahead of me, so I slowed to a crawl as I passed. The house sat back off the road. A two-rut driveway ran the length of the yard and disappeared behind the house. There was a small boat sitting on a trailer in the front, but no silver sedan. Actually, there were no cars. I kept going along the two-lane road until I passed the house completely. I decided that since no one was around, I would make another pass. I found another driveway with a mailbox decorated with painted-on cherries and made a quick turnaround. As I approached the house on my right, I noticed a small structure in the backyard. I studied it as I crept by and realized it was big enough to hide a vehicle.

I continued back to the beginning of the neighborhood and pulled off to the side. Could the silver Ford Fusion be hidden in the structure behind the house? I reconsidered Boone as a possible suspect. He had been abrasive since the day I'd shown up. Clearly, he did not like Julie Haywood, and after he ducked questions about a witness in the case, I suddenly and coincidentally had a tail when I was dropping off potentially damning evidence. Coincidences were unlikely in homicide work, and this was no exception.

"Screw it," I said out loud. I spun around and headed back toward Boone's house. I parked beyond his property where the tree line partially blocked my car from the incoming road. I slipped out of the car and quietly pushed the door shut. I felt as if I was back on the beat responding to a burglary alarm. I scanned my surroundings three-hundred-sixty degrees and began to walk along the tree line to Boone's property. I kept checking the road to make sure any passersby couldn't see me. I didn't need any unwanted attention. As I made the corner of the house, I slowed and peeked around the corner. No dog houses. No motion lights. No obvious booby traps. Although the latter was extremely rare, somehow Officer Boone seemed the type to booby-trap his own backyard. However, the irony was not lost, as I was now creeping around his yard.

After determining it was safe, I made my way to the structure. It was a tall shed, but still large enough for a vehicle to be stored. It had a garage-style door in front and a normal-sized door on the side. I moved up to the side door and tried the door handle. Unlocked. I scanned around once more and twisted the knob. My heart thumped in my chest. The Crystal Daws case could be coming to an end very soon.

I pulled the door and leaned inside. It was dark, and my eyes needed a moment to adjust. It smelled of gasoline and sawdust. I groped the inside of the wall and found what I was looking for. The light turned on, and in the middle of the room, I saw the gleaming green of a John Deere lawn tractor, along with other landscaping tools spread about. I scanned the entirety of the room and there was no silver sedan. Given the amount of stuff in the structure, it was clear a car was never kept in this makeshift garage. Disappointment set in, but it was quickly replaced by panic. I heard the throaty growl of a large pickup truck turn off the road and drive down the two-rut driveway on the other side of the house.

I shut the side door and jumped behind the side of the house as I heard the truck pull around to the back. I slid along the opposite side near the front yard, knowing I would have to run to avoid being spotted. There was no way I could explain this away and have it go well with Officer Boone.

"Shit, shit, shit."

I was just about to make a run for it when the engine cut off, and it went silent. He'd probably hear me running, so I stayed still. Trying to calculate the odds, I figured I would wait until I heard him go inside before making a break for it. My footfalls would go unnoticed only if he was inside and not looking out a window. I didn't hear anything, and before I could move, I saw movement out of the corner of my eye. Boone was halfway into his front yard, walking toward the street. I pressed against the side of the house as if he were looking my way. I peeked around the corner and watched him check his mailbox. He scanned his mail and started to walk back but stopped. Something caught his attention off to my left, his right. Curious, I looked but didn't see anything. Boone stood still in the yard, staring at something. He began walking toward whatever it was as I began sliding toward the back of the house in case he continued to where he could see me.

Suddenly, I realized what had caught his attention. It was my car.

"Shiiiiiiiiiiit!"

Boone stopped at his property edge, looking at my empty car, and then made a beeline straight to the house. Peering around the back of the house, I waited until he was close enough for me to make my way back up the side. As soon as he made it inside, I took off running for the car without looking back. I jumped in, cranked it, and left as quickly as I could. About two hundred yards down the street, I glanced in the rearview mirror to see Officer Boone standing in the road holding his hand up. I couldn't tell from the distance, but I was certain there was a particular finger extended into the air as well.

Chapter 19

"Well, that was stupid," Julie scolded. I had just explained what happened at Officer Boone's house. We were behind a grocery store and parked car door to car door. We called this "fifty-sixing" in my day, the radio code to meet another officer.

"Yeah, I know," I said. "But I wanted to check it out. I don't believe it's a coincidence."

"Lance Boone is an idiot and general pain in the ass, but I don't think he killed Crystal. I mean, I've known him a long time, and well.... I don't know; I just don't see it, Hank."

"Sometimes it's the ones closest around us who we don't see."

"What?" Julie said. "That doesn't make any sense."

"You never truly know what's in someone's heart, Julie. That's all."

She nodded, considering what I'd said.

"Anyway," she changed the subject, "you didn't actually go in or *do anything* at his place, did you?"

"No. I just peeked in the garage looking for the Ford Fusion."

Julie nodded again. "Okay, so if he complains, the best he's got is trespassing, and you're sure he didn't see you?"

"Pretty sure."

"Okay, well, if he didn't see you, he can't arrest you."

"Arrest me? For what?"

"Trespassing, Hank," she said. "That's what you did. You were a cop for how long? Or did you only work homicide your entire career? Never bothered with the little stuff, huh?"

Julie was giving me a hard time as she let a smirk escape across her face.

"Oh, stop it," I said, trying to defend myself.

Julie checked her watch. "I've got another hour before the end of my shift. Can you manage to not get arrested until then?"

I rolled my eyes and smirked back at her.

"What are you going to do?" she asked.

"Um, I'm going to see if Hope Bennett is home," I answered. "Maybe without you distracting her, I can get somewhere with her."

"Okay, good luck." She pulled out of the lot.

As I headed out of town to Hope Bennett's trailer park, I recalled our last encounter. She was a stone wall as far as witnesses were concerned. I considered the twenty-five years she'd had to marinate in whatever mix of alcoholic and narcotic cocktails she used to forget the pain. How badly had it warped her memory? Was she even worth the interview? One thing kept circling back in my mind; it was her statement about talking to Holcomb Byrd that stuck out. I played that scene over in my mind. There was truth and honesty when she said it, surrounded by spiteful gibberish.

As I rolled down the gravel road, I prepared myself. Catching Hope off guard, I was hoping, would work in my favor. Without Julie as a distraction, maybe I could get her to focus on what she had told Detective Byrd twenty-five years ago.

There was no car on the drive pad next to her trailer, but I stopped anyway. I looked around at the neighboring trailers and scanned up and down the street. There were some kids playing about five lots down, but other than that, it was quiet.

I knocked. Nothing. I looked around and listened intently. Hope had proved she wasn't very hospitable to visitors. I backed up and watched the windows for any movement. Nothing. I knocked again and was met with more silence. I walked around, looking at each window. The trailer sat on concrete footers, so from the ground, I was looking slightly up at the windows and unable to see inside. After making it around the trailer, I knocked one more time. Still nothing.

"Crap." I had planned to catch her off guard, in person. Now I was determined to wait or find her elsewhere.

A buzz in my pocket broke my plan formulation. It was the Madison Police Department. A wave of panic washed over me, thinking Boone had made a formal complaint about me.

I took a deep breath. "Hello?"

"Hey, Mister…um…Trescott? This is Tyler from the Madison Police Department."

"Hey, Tyler," I answered. "What can I do for you?"

"Well, um, you have a message from Mrs. Mary Anne Byrd. She wants you to come out to her place when you can."

Relieved it wasn't related to my earlier transgression, I let out a breath before answering. "Oh, okay, Tyler. Thank you. I'll take care of it."

"Okay, great, Mr. Trescott. Bye."

Tyler hung up as the message sank in. Mary Anne Byrd wanted to speak with me. Presumably, it was about her husband and the Crystal Daws case. Or possibly she wanted to apologize for how things shook out the last time Julie and I stopped by. I hoped it was the former.

Standing outside of Hope Bennett's trailer, I decided the interview with her would have to wait. Before I opened my car door, a soft voice called out from across the street.

"She ain't been home fer a bit."

I turned to see the source. An elderly woman was on her porch sitting on a rocking chair, smoking a cigarette.

"Do you know where she is?" I asked.

"Nah' sir. She comes and goes, ah'she pleases."

"Okay, thanks anyway," I said.

"Been gone since you'ins came 'round last." The woman added.

I stared back at the woman. “You mean,” I thought for a moment, “after yesterday? She left after we came by?”

“Yeah, sir. Been gone ever since.”

“And she hasn’t been back?”

The woman shook her head as she took a drag of her cigarette and blew a steady plume of smoke in the air.

“Okay, thanks again.”

Driving out of the trailer park, I had to focus on how to get over to Mary Anne Byrd’s house, but I was stuck on what the old woman had told me about Hope Bennett. *She left soon after Julie and I came around asking about Crystal Daws and hadn’t been back since.* This struck me as peculiar. I was unsure how this fit in, but it all felt related. There was no way I believed it was simply coincidence. Was it guilt on her part? Or did we trudge up painful memories which led her into a downward spiral deeper into the world of drug addiction? I made a note to have Julie check the area hospitals and psychiatric wards for Hope Bennett.

Trekking across the small city took only a few minutes as I found myself on the country road that led north out of town. Now familiar with the old country house, I pulled down the driveway like an old friend coming for a visit.

As I walked up to the house, Mary Anne Byrd greeted me at the door.

“Good evening, Mr. Trescott,” she welcomed. “Thank you for coming.”

The widow’s attitude toward me was in stark contrast to the day before.

“Good evening, Mrs. Byrd,” I replied. “What is it that I can do for you?”

“Well…,” Mrs. Byrd paused as she looked around. “Well, first thing is you should come inside.” She pulled the screen door open, and I followed her inside and took a seat on the couch.

She took a seat opposite me in the living room. I read worry on her face. Something was wrong.

“What is it, Mrs. Byrd?” I asked. “Did something happen?”

“It was what you said to me last night, Mr. Trescott. It made me start thinking about all this stuff,” she started. “Don’t get me wrong, I don’t wish to be bothered by my past, but what you said about continuing on the case and about my Holcomb.”

I held back a response and let the silence push her to continue.

“That was the case that kept him up at night.” She turned to look at the portrait over the fireplace of her husband. “I feared it was the case that cost him his life, too.”

“What do you mean, ‘cost him his life’?” I asked.

“I think he just let that case get the better of him, and his poor old heart couldn’t take it,” she said. “He poured so much of hisself into findin’ out what happened to that girl. And, if I can help you solve this case, then maybe he can be at peace up there in heaven.”

“Help me solve it?” I asked suspiciously. “Is that why you asked me over, Mrs. Byrd? Is there something you know about this case that could help?”

“Well, I’m not sure, exactly. But you’re the detective, right?”

“Sure,” I smiled.

Mary Anne reached over to a side table, pulled the drawer, and removed an envelope.

My pulse quickened. My mind raced, trying to figure out what was in the envelope and what secret it held. I remained calm and let the widow explain herself.

“What is it?” I asked.

“After you left last night, I sat here thinking. About my husband and what he would’ve wanted me to do. For some reason, when you came by that first time, I didn’t think about the old lock box Holcomb kept under the bed. I mean, he kept all of his work stuff in that dusty old office, but that case was more than just a case, like you said. It bothered him. So, I pulled it out this morning and found this in there.”

Mary Anne held up the envelope. It was thin and, from the weight, didn’t contain much.

"What's in it?" I asked.

Mary Anne leaned over and extended her arm out, handing over the envelope. I took it.

"I'm not sure if it helps or not, but it's yours to use."

I peeled back the top flap and looked inside. A key and a small set of polaroid pictures. I removed the key and studied it. It was gold, with an odd-shaped handle that had a number etched on it. My best guess was that it was to a safe deposit box. I carefully removed the pictures and glanced back at Mrs. Byrd. She was looking at the contents intently. She, too, was curious if they could be vital to the case.

I flipped through the pictures like a stack of baseball cards. They were of the Crystal Daws crime scene with which I was very familiar. I made my way through ten pictures with nothing glaring or remarkable about them. Having studied the pictures in the case file for hours, there was nothing new that I noticed. Just more pictures from different angles.

"What are they of?" Mary Anne asked.

"Oh," I looked up at her. "Pictures from the Crystal Daws crime scene."

"Are they helpful?"

"Yes, ma'am. Absolutely," I lied. She wanted another connection to her dead husband, and I wasn't going to deny her. "Do you know what this key is to?"

Mary Anne considered the key as I held it up for her to see. I twisted it around to give her both sides.

"No, can't say that I do."

"Maybe a safe deposit box?" I suggested.

"No, we never had any deposit box. Never a need for one," she answered.

Unless Holcomb had something to hide, even from his wife, I thought.

I scanned the pictures one more time and figured they were pictures Holcomb Byrd had taken himself once he got on the scene. Being an old-school-style detective, he probably didn't want to wait until Crime Scene took them and had to get them developed. This way, he immediately had a copy ready to work with. I remember doing the same until digital cameras came along.

On one of the overalls, showing Crystal's lifeless body in the foreground and the responding patrol cars staged down the street, there was some writing on the back. It was in Holcomb's neat handwriting. It read: *418, 109*, *314*, and *649*. But *649* had a question mark next to it, and it was underlined twice.

"Any idea what these numbers mean?" I asked Mary Anne. It was more a stab in the dark than any chance she actually knew.

"No, I'm sorry, I don't," she replied.

I put the pictures and key back in the envelope and put it in my pocket.

"Thank you, Mrs. Byrd. This was very helpful."

"Will it help?"

"Yes, ma'am."

"Alright then."

Suddenly, I was reminded of what Julie Haywood explained about the timing of Holcomb Byrd's death. While I had his widow being so generous with the case, I wanted to ask her a few questions about his death.

"Mrs. Byrd, may I ask you a few questions about when your husband died?"

Her face grew troubled, and I feared I had overstepped.

"What is it you'd like to know?" she asked.

"Well, really..., what do you remember of that day, you know, *before*? Like, what was he doing that day?"

"You see, that was what led me to look in the lockbox," she said curiously.

I didn't follow. "What led you, Mrs. Byrd?"

"The day Holcomb died; he was in his office going over that case. Then, he suddenly had to leave."

"Oh? Where did he go?" I asked.

"He didn't say," she answered. "He just said he had to go and that '*he*' lied to him."

"*Who* lied to him, Mrs. Byrd?"

"That I don't know, Mr. Trescott," she said. "He just said, 'He lied to me,' grabbed his stuff, gave me a kiss, and out the door he went." Her eyes fell to the floor. "That was the last time I saw him."

"Did you tell anyone else about this, Julie, or someone at the police department?"

She shook her head, dismissing it. "No, because later he had the heart attack, and I didn't think it much mattered. Hadn't thought about really, until you said something last night."

"You're right, Mrs. Byrd," I said, lying to her. "It probably didn't matter."

Everything inside of me told me Holcomb Byrd's death wasn't a coincidence. Something didn't sit right, and I needed to get a hold of his death investigation report. I thanked Mrs. Byrd for contacting me and for the envelope. Next, I headed for Julie Haywood and the police station.

⌘

"Is it too late to get a hold of that report?" I asked Julie Haywood. I met her at the police station following the end of her shift.

"Um, I don't think so." She was in the process of switching out her patrol car for her Jeep. "We can probably shoot over to the courthouse before they close. They've had a trial going on for most of the day. I saw the bailiff's car parked out front, so they're probably still finishing up."

Julie Haywood led the way over to the courthouse and down into the police archives. She moved around the room stuffed with files and microfilm with intimate familiarity. She went straight to a cabinet that encompassed 1993, the same year Crystal was killed.

She opened the drawer and thumbed through several case files. She spied one and pulled it out, fanning it open to glance inside.

"This is it," she looked up at me. "What are you looking for specifically?"

"I'm not sure, but I think it's worth a look after what Mary Anne Byrd just told me," I said.

"What do you think Detective Byrd meant by 'He lied to me'?" Julie asked. "Who is '*he*'?"

"Don't know. That's why they call it detective work. We have to detect!" I joked.

"Ugh." Julie spun around and shut the cabinet drawer.

"Can we take this out of here?" I asked, holding up the case file.

"Yeah, we just have to sign for it."

Julie walked over to a desk at the door of the archive room. She walked back with a clipboard and pen to fill out the paperwork. She listed the case number, her name, and a brief reason. I glanced over her shoulder to see what she wrote for a reason. It read: Detective work.

After locking up the archive room, we exited the courthouse just as the bailiffs were closing down the courthouse. We walked across the street to Lucile's for some coffee. Julie ordered while I dove into the case file.

Out of habit, I began with the autopsy report instead of the report itself. Although it seemed rather unanimous that Holcomb Byrd had died of a heart attack, I wanted to read what was actually on paper from the medical examiner and look for any discrepancies. In a moment of haste, I flipped to the back of the autopsy to double-check the cause of death. Manner of death was listed as natural; the cause was listed as coronary disease. This meant he died of a heart attack as determined by a medical examiner. No smoke here, I thought.

Flipping back to the front, I scanned the part of the report where the doctor performs a visual scan of the body and notes any injuries, bruising, tattoos, scarring, or any irregularities that may pertain to the death. There was mention of various scars and surgical events that came with the normal wear-and-tear of an adult man of Holcomb Byrd's age, but there was nothing noted that would have risen to the level of suspicion.

"No suspicious needle pricks or stab wounds that were missed, were there?" Julie asked as she placed a steaming cup of coffee on the table.

I chuckled, "No, nothing like that."

"Okay, now what?"

"I guess I finish reading," I said. Julie sat across from me and blew on her coffee before taking a sip. She raised a hand, palm up, as if to say, "Don't let me stop you."

There wasn't much else, content-wise, in the report. After finishing the narrative, I let it digest for a moment, allowing the scene to unfold in my mind with the additional information provided by Mrs. Byrd. Information not known at the time of this report. I blew the top of my coffee cup and took a sip.

"So, he was found at Lake Francis, in his car." I started.

"Okay," Julie said. "Does it say what he was doing there or who he was with?"

"No, just parked there alone."

"Okay, who found him?"

"Some dog walker noticed the car was running, and that he was slumped over in the driver's seat."

"So, the dog walker didn't see anyone else around?"

"No. How big is that lake?"

"It's pretty big, why?"

"I mean, is it big enough to not see the goings on from across the lake? This guy, the dog walker says he noticed him on the second pass around the lake."

"Um," Julie considered the question. "No, it's not really that big. I mean, you can't hear conversations or see faces from across the lake, but movements and action, I'm sure you could."

I wanted to go to this area and see for myself, but for the moment, I had to trust Julie and her knowledge from growing up around this lake.

"But why this lake?" I asked. "Maybe it makes sense to a local, but I'm the outsider. Why does he go there? He just figures something out, presumably about the Crystal Daws case and this unidentified *he*, so Byrd storms out of his house. Where does he go? The station to put things in motion or to confront this 'he'?"

Julie gave it more thought. "You know, I had an uncle one time, died of a heart attack. But he was driving when it happened, you know? So, he somehow managed to pull his truck over before losing control of the truck. It was like he knew it was happening and did not want to put anyone else in harm's way. Maybe that's what happened and is super weird timing?"

I nodded. It was certainly possible, but another thought crept into my mind.

"Okay, it's definitely possible that he simply pulled over. Is the lake between his house and the police station?"

Julie sat up straight in her chair, her eyes shot upward while she calculated the route in her head. She looked at me with concern.

"No," she answered. "Actually, it's out of the way."

"So, if he wasn't going to the station, then maybe he was trying to meet with this 'he'."

⌘

Julie and I decided to eat at the Mexican restaurant next to the Old Bookstore, but first, she had to pick up her son after practice. The three of us were going to eat dinner together, and I questioned myself about why that didn't seem foreign. While I waited, I took a walk, allowing the new information surrounding Holcomb Byrd's death to sink in. How was it connected to the Crystal Daws investigation? From Lucile's, I walked north and crossed over Main Street to Four Freedoms Park. I had passed it numerous times since coming to town, and I wanted to see it up close. The small piece of southern heritage, along with a four-sided marble monument, was the centerpiece of the town. The monument was established as a representation of President Roosevelt's 1941 State of the Union address when he explained the four freedoms to the country. The monument was sculpted to honor a fallen soldier from World War II, who was a Madison native. It was commissioned in Madison Square Garden and later moved to the small town. It was to be used as a memorial for World War II casualties, highlighting the local man who was a decorated war hero.

Reading the historical marker that sat at the edge of the park, the freedoms President Roosevelt spoke of were freedom of speech and expression, worship, freedom from want, and freedom from fear. I looked past the marker and up to the monument. Four angelic figures reached out on four sides atop a large marble base. It was quite remarkable. I couldn't help but think, because of her killer, Crystal Daws wasn't afforded the freedom from fear.

In the park, large moss-covered oak trees stretched their limbs across the green space, providing ample shade, while a quaint gazebo sat in the middle. The perimeter walkway was reminiscent of the famous squares in downtown Savannah, Georgia. As I walked, a memory of Victoria and I strolling through the charming southern city while on vacation materialized. We'd held hands like newlyweds and talked about everything.

I shut my eyes, trying to focus on the memory. I remembered the warmth of her hand in mine, the scent of her perfume, and the radiance of her smile. We were so happy. As I recalled her smile, the image of her face began to soften and blur. I struggled to hold on to the memory and follow it deeper into the recesses of my brain, but it slipped through and into oblivion. My eyes shot open, taking in the street lamps lining the walkway of the park.

"Dammit." Why was it so hard to keep her image?

I kept walking, growing angrier every second. I went back to thinking about the case, something over which I had a modicum of control.

Stepping up into the gazebo, I took a look around. It was nice and clean. I pegged it as a popular venue for local weddings and town gatherings. I pictured a microphone set up on the edge to address the crowd staged further into the park, or a band playing music while people danced on the lawn.

Looking out from the gazebo, I was reminded that Ryder Langston was parked somewhere around this end of the park when he heard the gunshots that killed Crystal Daws. I transitioned from a wandering tourist back into homicide detective. There was a small worn spot in the grass in the northwest corner of the park; a clue that cars frequently park there. I stepped down the stairs of the gazebo and walked over to the spot. I paused and looked around.

A pair of headlights flashed me as a vehicle made a turn in front of the park. I glanced at the car but paid it no attention. I continued walking around the park, waiting for Julie Haywood to text me that she was ready to meet for dinner. I checked my phone, but no message.

The dreaded feeling of someone watching me crawled over my skin, and I looked up to see a car slowly rolling past the north edge of the park. My heart skipped a beat as I saw that it was a silver Ford Fusion. It made the turn along the west end towards Main Street where it was caught by the traffic light. I stared hard into the driver's window, but the tint coupled with the low light of dusk and the street lamp's glare made it impossible to see inside. I started walking toward the car to get a better look at the driver. The brake lights dimmed and flashed back on as the car moved forward. Was it the same silver Fusion from earlier?

There was an unseen sense of urgency as I neared the car. Without thinking, I darted in a sprint toward the silver sedan. The brake lights dimmed and flashed as he nearly hit the stopped car in front of him. Now, I was certain it *was* the car from earlier. Before I could get close enough to read the tag, it backed up and pulled around the stopped traffic, screeching its tires in its haste. The sedan nosed into the cross traffic, and the driver recklessly floored it between passing vehicles, nearly causing a collision. Horns blared loudly from the angry motorists because of the near crash, as I continued the chase on foot. Luck granted me perfect timing as the light turned green just after he passed through, giving me the crosswalk. I crossed the street, keeping an eye on the sedan as it sped down Range Street past the courthouse. Without slowing, it turned left and gunned it down Pinckney Street. I sprinted through the courthouse yard, trying to keep up, but the car raced by, blowing through the stop sign and disappearing east several blocks down.

I stopped, gasping for air. Bent over in pain, my lungs nearly exploded. I collapsed to the ground, pulling myself up to a seat on the curb. My head pounded and my lungs ached. Engulfed by the warm sensation of sweat building in the creases of my body, I experienced heat flashes as my brain functions slowly came back online.

"Oh, my…." Panting. Gasping. "That…," deep inhale and exhale, "…was stupid."

I stared down the block, then whipped around to the north to make sure the Ford Fusion didn't double back going on the attack. When I didn't see it, I began to calm down.

As my body stopped throbbing, I tried to gather my thoughts and attempted to recall any parts of the tag I may have seen. Nothing. Dammit! That would've been such a big piece of the puzzle, I thought. But also, with regard to my safety, whoever it was in the Fusion was clearly following me and possibly Julie Haywood.

Still catching my breath, I fished out my cell phone to call Julie and warn her. A text message was waiting for me. From Julie: *We're at the restaurant waiting for you.* It was sent only a minute before, and if she was at a restaurant, in public, there wasn't much reason to alarm her. Plus, I wasn't ready to move just yet.

"Ugh."

Mexican food did not sound as appetizing at the moment as it had five minutes earlier. I finished resting and realized I was sitting outside of the courthouse annex, and more specifically, the Crystal Daws crime scene. I looked around, and then back toward the courthouse and the large silo stretching into the night sky. I studied the façade of the annex and overlaid the image of the old Woodard Theatre and its neon signage.

Finally, after a few more minutes and a follow-up text from Julie asking where I was, I stood without getting dizzy. I stretched out my legs and back and oriented myself back toward the Mexican restaurant. It was a few blocks away on the same street. Suddenly, a thought occurred to me, but I wasn't sure what to make of it. It questioned several things about this case. I stopped and turned back to the middle of the street where Crystal Daws's body lay twenty-five years prior. I stared off into the distance, back toward the park, and found my answer. This changes things, I thought.

Chapter 20

Unable to sleep on Julie Haywood's pull-out couch, I sat at the kitchen table looking over the files of the Crystal Daws case for yet another look. Dawn hadn't broken. It was still dark outside, and still silent in Julie's home. The drip of the coffee pot echoed loudly, and I was hoping to wake Julie, too afraid to step inside her bedroom. I wasn't sure what I was afraid of, but it seemed safer on the couch and in the kitchen.

I added the old Polaroid pictures to the file. I pulled out the crime scene photos and compared them to see if there was something I'd missed. They were the same pictures, taken from different angles. The Polaroids were hazy and not as focused as the more professional thirty-five-millimeter film. I flipped through them, hoping to find the reason Detective Byrd didn't leave his personal pictures with the case file, but nothing stood out.

Exhausted, I leaned back in the chair and took a sip of coffee. I let the warmth flow down my throat and send reinvigorating vibes throughout my tired body. This was the part of an investigation that irritated me. The lull. The lull was when momentum built to what was expected to be the crescendo but somehow plateaued into a standstill.

Hope Bennett knew something, but she was in the wind. Some mystery person, possibly the killer, was stalking me in a silver sedan. Of which, I had nothing to go on to try to identify it or the driver. The case's original detective had left a key and Polaroids in a private box for an inexplicable reason. That same detective's death was now in question; he may have met with the killer just before his untimely death. There was a potential for DNA, but the results wouldn't be ready anytime soon.

A lull.

I wiped my face in frustration, hoping to gain clarity and also wake up a little more.

A door creaked open, followed by soft footsteps behind me. I turned to see Julie Haywood rubbing her eyes, fighting a yawn, and looking tired herself. Her robe was pulled tight, hugging her curves and exposing her bare legs. Although she had just awakened, I felt a pull of attraction and realized I was smiling at her.

"Good morning," I said.

"Morning," she slurred. "Ooh, you made coffee already?"

"Yeah, I hoped you wouldn't mind."

"Ha, no, Hank," Julie said. "Why would I mind a handsome guest making me coffee in the morning?" She poured a mug and sat down next to me at the kitchen table. I turned my head so she wouldn't notice me blushing.

She took a sip and looked at the case file spread out on her table.

"Get anywhere?" she asked.

"Not really." I moved the pictures out of range for Julie. "I took another look at the crime scene pictures and can't quite figure out why ol' Holcomb kept these apart from the case file." I collected up the Polaroids and tapped them on the table like a deck of cards.

"Are they of anything different?" Julie asked.

"No, pretty much the same pictures, just different angles." "So, maybe he kept them aside to keep from cluttering up the case file." Julie had proven consistent with simple logic to questions surrounding the case, but I had doubts.

"Could be, but why keep them in a lockbox only he and his wife knew about?"

Julie shrugged as she sipped her coffee.

"Oh, that reminds me, we need to find out what this goes to." I held up the key that was stored with the Polaroids.

"Okay," she said, "if you think it's a safe deposit box key, there's only like two banks in town he could've used. Unless he went out of town, then obviously, that number skyrockets."

"Given what little I know about Holcomb Byrd, he was a local boy through and through. If it is a safe deposit box, it's here in town."

"Okay, then shouldn't be too hard to narrow down."

I got up and refilled my cup of coffee. While in search of creamer, Julie began sifting through the crime scene pictures.

Before I could intervene, she said, "You were never good at those spot-the-differences-in-the-picture games, were you?"

"Huh?" I was confused.

Julie pulled an overall picture from the stack of thirty-five-millimeter images and grabbed a similar one from the Polaroids. She put them side by side and looked back at me expectantly.

"What?" I still didn't see what she saw. The images were an overall capturing the west end of Pinckney Street. In the immediate foreground were the edges of Crystal Daws's body, but beyond that was the crime scene perimeter, the tape stretched across the street, and the staged patrol cars. I moved from one image to the other and still didn't see it.

Julie held her expectant look, but now added a teasing smile, which elevated my annoyance.

"What is it?" I asked.

"The patrol cars," she said with confidence.

I leaned over her shoulder, close enough that all I could smell was her body lotion. It was distracting as I focused on the pictures.

"See," she said as she pointed to the Polaroid and then back to the thirty-five millimeter. "There are three patrol cars in this one," the Polaroid, "as opposed to four in this one," the thirty-five millimeter.

"Well, I'll be," I said, stunned. "But what the hell does that mean?"

"That I couldn't tell you," Julie said, "but Detective Byrd may have known. See?"

Julie flipped that image over, and it was the only picture with the dead detective's handwriting on the back.

"And those numbers don't mean anything to you?" I asked.

"Nope," she said flatly. "I guess we have to do that thing you mentioned yesterday, you know, detective work?"

I scoffed, and Julie laughed. Clearly, the coffee was working.

"Smartass," I teased.

⌘

Dawn broke and sunlight began filtering in through the living room blinds, lighting up the room. I hoped the new day would bring us one step closer to solving the case. The lull needed to end. If it lingered around too long, the case could turn cold again.

Julie showered and got dressed in time to get her son off to school. I gathered up the case file and sorted the contents back into the binder.

"After I drop off the kiddo, I'll run by First Bank of Madison," Julie said as she was situating the holster on her hip. "If that's a no-go, I'll run over to Madison Commerce and check there."

"Okay, great," I said. "Call me and let me know what you find out."

Julie grabbed her purse and Jeep keys and called out for her son to meet her in the truck. She had filled a thermos with the remaining coffee I made earlier, and she headed for the door. As she passed, I turned, and we nearly bumped into each other.

"Oops, sorry," she apologized.

"No, I…," Julie was only inches away.

She smiled but didn't back up. Her scent drifted up and surrounded me, enveloping my senses. I didn't back away either. Whatever was between us didn't seem so daunting at the moment. However, I was paralyzed about what to do next. Her smile widened, as did mine. Our eyes were locked, and neither wanted to move. Letting myself go with the moment, I moved my head down, holding her gaze, and closing in on her lips.

"Mom, you ready?" Julie's son asked, breaking the growing tension. We each stepped back as if we were oil and water.

"Yeah, bud," she said, dampening her smile. "I'll be right there."

I turned to pick up the case file, and I heard Julie clear her throat.

"I'll call you and let you know what happens at the banks."

"Right," I replied.

Julie disappeared out the door, and I was left standing there, feeling foolish. My thoughts immediately turned to Victoria as guilt suddenly washed over me. Was she watching me from heaven? Was she embarrassed for me? Or was she upset? Although I couldn't see her face, I could hear her voice clearly.

She's lovely, Hank. Give it time, my love.

Really? I asked myself. I was expecting some level of judgment from the woman I married, not encouragement. I wasn't sure what to make of that, especially because I knew, on some level, it was my subconscious talking. Moving on with the case was the obvious distraction I needed.

I picked up the Polaroid where Detective Byrd had written mysterious numbers on the back.

"What the heck do 418, 109, 314, and 649 mean?" I asked out loud. "And why is 649 underlined?"

I flipped the picture around and studied the captured image closely. I focused on the cars, as Julie had figured out the difference was the patrol cars. The numbers were not official times associated with the case, and they weren't officer badge numbers. I let the possibilities bounce around in my mind for a minute, but nothing stuck. I peeled out the closest matching crime scene photo from the stack of thirty-five-millimeters to compare again. There were four cars, not three. This made little sense. I held up the images side-by-side and moved my focus back and forth. Same picture, different angle, but the only difference was the number of patrol cars. The additional car was parked next to the third, slightly up on the sidewalk. It looked like whoever parked it had moved it in a hurry and jumped the curb to get closer to the crime scene.

"What did you see Holcomb?" I asked. I had heard Victoria's voice; maybe the detective would speak to me too.

Silence.

"Figures," I said. I stared at the Polaroid, and the realization of what the numbers meant nearly knocked me over. "It's the car numbers."

Many departments give marked patrol cars a specific number as part of the fleet. It's a way to keep track of them, but it also allows for accountability among patrol officers while in public. It's like giving the cars their own identity.

How to figure out whose cars were whose was going to be tricky. I felt confident there would be an active roster of patrol officers and their assigned patrol cars for today, but from twenty-five years ago, I highly doubted it. If I was going to find my answer, it was going to be at the police station.

I grabbed the case file and headed to the station. I fought the urge to call Julie and have her help navigate how to find this information. There needed to be more time between that awkward exchange from earlier. Ten minutes later, I parked out front of the station, snagged my visitor badge from the visor, and walked in.

"Hey, Mr. Hank," Tyler greeted. "How are you doing today?"

"I'm good, Tyler. Thanks."

"Hey, I got that BOLO out from yesterday about the silver Ford Fusion, but so far nothing back on it," Tyler explained.

"What?" I snapped. "What BOLO?" I asked, confused. I didn't want any attention on the silver Fusion in hopes that it would spook them away. As I built the case, I wanted the killer to have that false sense of security, so when I figured it out, I could drop the hammer without suspicion.

Tyler looked shocked. "Um…, Officer Haywood called last night and said to put out a BOLO for a reckless driver; said the guy nearly ran you over."

"Oh," I replied. That was vague enough not to raise too many questions.

"I mean, I left you out of it, of course," Tyler added. "I just put that it was some random citizen."

"Good, thank you," I said. My tone obviously had changed, and Tyler relaxed a bit.

"Hey, Tyler?" I asked.

"Yes, sir?"

"Could you find out who was driving a certain patrol car back in 1993?"

Tyler's eyes bulged at the request. "Oh, my goodness…. Um, I wasn't even born then."

I rolled my eyes. "Can you do it or not?"

"Um, well…." Tyler picked up a clipboard on his desk and showed it to me. "This is today's roster."

"Tyler…," I said with feigned patience, "1993, March fourteenth, to be exact."

"Ooh." He sat up straight in his chair. "Ooh, this is for the…," he looked around and whispered, "murder."

"Yeah, Tyler," I said, "it's for the Crystal Daws case."

"Right, right." He sat in deep thought for a minute. "Okay. If we have it, it'll be in records somewhere. I can go look in a bit; is that okay?"

I didn't see any other option other than asking Detective Byrd himself.

"Sure," I said, "just call me when you find it."

Moving through reception into the main area, I made my way to the conference room and sat down. I wanted to take a broad look at the case and insert the newly acquired facts into what Detective Byrd had left behind. Abandoning the theory that this was a robbery gone wrong and considering it a planned attack and attempted rape was a huge paradigm shift. This meant that Crystal Daws was targeted, and most likely by someone she knew. The fact that her purse was taken from the scene and her credit card was later stolen from somewhere in town five months later supported the idea that the killer was from Madison and probably knew Crystal.

I pulled out my notes and opened the case file to the beginning of the narrative. I had to start with the crime itself. A pre-planned attack and a random robbery are set up in very different manners. One would take days, if not weeks, to plan. The other could be hashed out in a matter of minutes, depending on the experience level of the criminal.

Crystal Daws and Maynard Preston walked out of the theatre after Preston punched his timecard at 10:02 p.m. Maynard had said that Crystal went back inside to answer the phone. He assumed it was the manager calling to check up on them, but he was just guessing. I had read over the phone records already, and it was apparent that Detective Byrd had exhausted that lead.

But what if it wasn't the manager? I thought. What better way to separate prey from any protective hurdle than to make an innocuous phone call as she walked out of the theatre? Hell, it could've been from a pay phone, adding a layer of anonymity, especially twenty-five years ago.

Nonetheless, I flipped to the phone records in the case file and pulled them from the binder. The perforated paper and handwritten notes in the margin made it difficult to discern. I focused on the time and date column and found the calls made on the 13th until late at night and then back on the 14th starting in the early afternoon. I ran my finger down the column until late night of the 14th. The last entry for the page was at 7:39 p.m. Flipping the page, the next entry was early afternoon on March 15.

"What the—?" I asked. It was understandable that a two-screen theatre in a small town wouldn't field a lot of calls, but there should've been more. I flipped the page back to see the 7:39 p.m. entry at the bottom of the column and then to the next page that had skipped to the day after the murder.

Was Maynard Preston lying about the phone call that caused Crystal Daws to return to the theatre? I sat and thought for a minute. Maynard Preston seemed genuine and appeared to be a good person. But twenty-five years can change a bad person into good, and vice versa.

"Hello, Hank." A salty voice came from the doorway of the conference room.

I looked up across the table to see Officer Lance Boone standing with a scowl on his face.

"Oh shit," I murmured. I had forgotten about my little transgression on his property.

"What's that, now?" he asked.

"Nothing," I said. "Can I help you with something Officer Boone?" I held up my visitor badge. "See, I'm all set here."

"I know it was you came pokin' round my place yesterday. And yer damn lucky the chief says I can't arrest you for trespassing, so I came to warn you. I don't know what you were lookin' fer, but just stay clear, ya hear?"

I gave him the best ignorant smile I could muster. "Okay."

"Okay, so just watch yourself," he said.

"You got it, Officer Boone."

The diminutive officer stood there awkwardly, so I went back to what I was doing. I decided what I really needed was a storyboard, so I could look at everything at once. On big cases, I would pin up key pictures and write out the substantial facts on a bulletin board to help build the case. The overall perspective helped me look at the case from a different angle. As I began packing up, Boone stepped in and started looking over the files as I had them spread out.

"Got any leads?" he asked. The condescending sarcasm in his voice made it obvious that he didn't actually care.

"Not really," I lied.

"What are these?" Boone asked as he picked up the phone records from the night of the murder.

"Please don't touch," I said as I reached for them.

Boone stepped out of the way to keep them from my reach. Unprepared to make something of the situation, I answered truthfully. "Phone records."

"Only reason you must've come trespassing is you and Elsie think I'm some kind of suspect. Not sure how that tracks or why, exactly. So, you want to in-ter-O-gate me, big city detective? Or can you just let me look?"

Boone was hardly a suspect in my eyes, but he could make trouble with the whole trespassing ordeal, so I thought, *what's the harm?*

"May I have them back, please?" I was hastily stuffing papers and pictures back into the binder, hoping he would get the hint. As I collected everything but the phone records, he stood there looking at them. He was analyzing something, what I couldn't figure out. Especially with him not having any context as to how they fit into this case.

"You're missing a page," he said. His sarcasm was gone.

"Huh?"

"You're missing a page," he repeated. "Right here, page ten." Boone leaned over and pointed out that the entries on the afternoon of the 14th ended on page nine, and the entries on the 15th picked up on page eleven.

"What?" I said, confused. "Let me see that."

Taking the records back and scanning just the page numbers, I confirmed what Boone found.

"Holy shit, you're right," I said, astonished.

"Plus, this is perforated paper. Why the hell was it ripped apart and then stapled? I mean—" Boone chuckled at the thought. "I mean, it's perforated for a reason, am I right?"

"I have no idea, Officer Boone." His affinity toward the style of paper used to print the twenty-five-year-old phone records was odd, but it was graciously appreciated. It made sense.

Incredulously, I placed the records back in the middle of the binder. Unaware of the magnitude of the discovery he'd just made, Officer Boone shrugged off the encounter and walked out of the room.

I chased after him and yelled out, "Hey, where's the nearest phone company headquarters?"

Boone turned around. "Nearest?" he chuckled. "Okay, big city. What you mean is the only. AT&T has an office down Range Street. If you hit Bunker Street, turn around. You went too far."

⌘

Like the Old Bookstore, the door hit a chime when I pulled it open, stepping into the AT&T office. There was a hushed murmur of several conversations going on past a partition behind the receptionist's desk. They continued despite hearing the notification of a possible customer. The décor was full of muted tones in beige and gray, accented with fake plants. The company had moved into the twenty-first century, but it had left this tiny branch back in the past. Behind the desk was a round-faced woman wearing a headset. She was busy typing something as I walked in, but she gave me a courtesy smile before continuing.

Having rushed out of the police station after Boone pointed out the missing page, I hurried several blocks here, thinking that this was where the killer's identity had been hidden for a quarter century. I hadn't even thought about how I was going to ask for the information, or even if they would be able to give it to me.

Shit. I cursed myself for rushing. I paused and gathered my thoughts. At best, they'd give me the information that was on the missing page, but then I thought further; it was pure speculation that the killer had called that night. I might get the information only to learn that Mr. Elden was the caller, and he was checking up on his employees.

But why was the page missing? If the missing page contained only legitimate calls, then why take it? And the more I thought about the exchange with Officer Boone in the conference room, the more I thought about his comment about the perforated paper. It was silly, but the point sticks. Why rip it up when it was designed to stay together?

It was evident that someone had messed with it, I realized.

"Can I help you, sir?" The round-faced woman had finished her task.

I turned and smiled at her. She was pretty, with deep auburn hair styled up atop her head and cascading down the side of her face. She seemed to be in her late thirties. She smiled back.

"I have a bit of an unorthodox request," I said. I glanced down at her nameplate. "Penny."

"Oh my, that sounds mysterious," she replied. "I love a good challenge."

"So, I have some phone records, and I seem to be missing a page from it. It was obtained through a subpoena, but like I said, I'm missing a page. Is there any way you could help get the missing data?"

"Are you a police detective or something?" Penny asked.

"More like 'or something', but I am helping out Officer Julie Haywood on the case. My name is Hank Trescott."

"Oh, did you reach out to the custodian of records through the corporate office? They usually handle those things," she said.

This was a roadblock I was afraid of. She was right. Had this been an unfulfilled subpoena request, I would simply contact the custodian of records and resubmit the paperwork. But there is a shelf life, and it does not extend past two and a half decades.

"Well, here's the unorthodox part. It's from nineteen-ninety-three."

What I assumed was a perpetual smile on Penny's face vanished at the mention of the year. Obviously, her level of expertise was surpassed.

"Cell phones weren't really used that much back then, and we can only go back so far because of the amount of data that—"

"Oh no, Penny," I interrupted. "This isn't cell phone activity records. This is from a landline. It's actually a business line that has since closed down."

The perpetual smile returned to Penny's face.

"Oh, well, that changes it up a bit, doesn't it?" she said.

Excitement grew inside at the sound of her optimism.

"What business was it?" she asked.

"The Woodard Theatre," I answered.

Penny's eyes grew wide at the mention of the theatre. Her mouth gaped open as if what I said was inflammatory. Unsure of what line I'd crossed, I stayed silent, waiting for her to say something.

Penny sat straight up and then scanned me up and down with scrutiny. At last, the smile creased her lips.

"Are you…," she paused, "are you looking into the Crystal Daws case?"

Curious as to why she specifically asked that, I responded, "Actually, yes."

Penny nodded in validation.

"Why do you ask?" I said.

"Hold on," she said as she pushed a button on her headset. "Thank you for calling, AT&T Madison Branch. How may I help you?"

I disengaged from the counter to let her talk, but I was met with her hand extended and an index finger telling me to wait. She nodded, waited, nodded, and then spoke, "Yes, ma'am. Please hold."

Penny punched a few buttons on her console and looked back up at me.

"It was because we were friends, me and Crystal," Penny said. "I mean, we weren't close, but we were friendly. I was a grade ahead of her, but then…," Penny's face turned sad.

"What is it?" I said, thinking whatever she was about to say would be beneficial to the case.

"Well," she said, trying to keep from choking up. "I was on a date at the theatre that night."

"Oh," I said, hiding my disappointment. Guilt was weighing her down.

"Yeah, me and my boyfriend went to the late show. We saw that movie with Tom Cruise as the Navy lawyer yelling at Jack Nicholson about 'handling the truth' or whatnot. Heck, I remember waving at Crystal as we left after the movie."

A tear rolled down her round cheek. She pulled a tissue from a nearby box and blotted her cheek and then her eyes carefully.

"So, the rumor is true then. You guys reopened the case?" she asked with enthusiasm.

"Yes, Penny," I answered. "But I really need help with this missing page."

She furrowed her brow and looked around, checking behind the partition as best as she could.

"So, Mr. Trescott, right?" she asked.

"Yes, ma'am."

"So, Mr. Trescott, are you telling me that you have a signed subpoena request for records?"

It took me a moment to realize where Penny was going with the question. I fished out the twenty-five-year-old subpoena from the case file and showed it to her, "Yes, it's right here."

Penny glanced beyond the partition one more time and turned to her computer screen. Her eyes were intense and fixated on the monitor. I heard her fingers pecking feverishly at her keyboard. I left the subpoena out in case, but leaned on the small counter, watching the receptionist work. She was right about liking challenges.

"What was the address?" she asked. I read it off the case file out loud.

A moment later, "Date of the…, you know?"

I rattled off the date from memory.

Penny was still searching, and I couldn't find any discouraging looks on her face as I watched.

"What page are you missing?" she asked with pleasure.

Now it was I who stood there, eyes wide and mouth gaping open. I snapped to and answered, "Page ten."

A moment later, I heard the whir of a printer start up and the sound of a laser jet moving back and forth. Penny scooted her chair to her left, reached down, and presented me with the missing page of phone records from a 1993 murder investigation.

"Wow," I said, "How did you—"

"Let's not bring too much attention to this, Mr. Trescott, if that's okay?" Penny asked in a half-whisper.

I mimed my mouth zipping shut, but with a big smile, I affirmed her request with a nod.

"Crystal was my friend, and I'm glad she hasn't been forgotten," Penny said somberly.

Immediately, she was met with an incoming phone call. I thanked Penny and took a seat in the small lobby area anxiously reading the newly obtained printout.

I verified that the dates and theatre number matched the records I did have. Scanning the call log from the top down, I found what I was looking for. Starting at 9:21 p.m., the same number called ten times inside of fifteen minutes. Then at 9:58 p.m. and 10:03 p.m., a different number called.

"Ten calls from the same number?" I said out loud. That is obsessive behavior and the actions of a stalker. I stared at the number to see if it held any similarity with anything in the case file, but I had nothing. I would have to cross-reference the new numbers to the entirety of the murder book to be sure. I let the information sink in for a moment. The ten phone calls from the same line the night of Crystal Daws's death, followed by two additional calls just prior to her murder.

The revelation of Crystal Daws's pants being hastily pulled back up by her attacker had changed the focus from random robbery to targeted sexual battery. The discovery of the missing phone calls painted a clearer picture of how the killer set up the crime. Watching from a secluded spot nearby, he realized he needed Crystal to be separated from Maynard Preston. He called the phone inside the theatre, drawing Crystal away from the witness. My head shot up, and although I was never a gambler, I was willing to wager handsomely that the second number belonged to a pay phone somewhere on that block.

An airy awareness arose from within the depths of my stomach. It was a long-since forgotten sensation, but a sensation I knew, nonetheless. It was the nervous energy that surged through my body when I was closing in on a killer. I had no doubt the first number that called ten times belonged to the killer of Crystal Daws.

Chapter 21

Penny was unable to help put names to the two different numbers that called the theatre on the night of Crystal's death, citing the need for a current subpoena. However, she did confirm the existence of a pay phone on the courthouse grounds back in 1993, but not the assigned number. Obviously, it wasn't still there, but if my theory played true, it would have been in line of sight to the theatre doors.

Waving goodbye to Penny as I exited the door, I set out toward the courthouse and the original scene. I thought about how fast Julie or I could write up a subpoena and get it served. If Penny's motivation held, I felt confident I could have the account name in a matter of hours. I checked my watch and realized most of the morning had vanished away. Also, I hadn't heard from Julie Haywood about whether there was a safe deposit box that belonged to Detective Byrd.

Without slowing my pace, I pulled out my cell phone and pressed Julie's contact.

"Hello?" she answered on the second ring.

"Hey, you have any luck at the banks?" I wasn't as interested in the answer as I had been before. At this point, the mysterious key seemed unnecessary with the discovery of the missing phone calls.

"Yeah, I'm at Madison Commerce," she answered. "The manager says the key belongs to them. He went to go pull the file or something like that."

"Oh! Okay, I thought that was a bit of a long shot, but okay." I paused a moment. "I want to go check on something real quick, and I can meet you there."

"You got something, Hank?" Julie must've heard the excitement in my voice.

"Yeah, I do." I was smiling. "Apparently, there was a missing page from the theatre phone records, and I just got it reprinted." I paused for effect.

"Wait, you said a missing page?" she asked. "As in, someone took something from the police file? Who the hell would do that?"

I hadn't let my mind run down that rabbit hole just yet. I would rather focus on the case and circle back later. With any luck, finding the killer would reveal all the answers.

"I don't know, but we shouldn't dwell on that for now," I said.

"I bet it was that asshole Boone," Julie spat. "That son of a bi—"

"Julie, he actually pointed out the phone records were missing a page." The other end went silent.

"Huh?" I could tell she was in disbelief. I explained how he noticed the missing page and my subsequent trip to the AT&T branch.

"Boone did that?" she asked. "Lance Boone?"

"Yeah, we can talk about this later," I said, not wanting to get distracted. "But I'm at the courthouse right now. I'm going to check on something and then I'll meet you at the bank, okay?"

"Yeah, okay."

"Oh, hey? Julie?" I caught her before she hung up.

"Yeah?"

"Do you remember where the pay phone was at the courthouse?" I asked.

The line went silent as she thought about the question.

"Um, I remember one inside in the main lobby area," she said. "I mean, for the public that is."

"What about one outside?"

"Oh shoot...," she said. "Yeah, I think there was one, just don't remember where."

"It's okay," I said, "I'll figure it out."

I got the address for Madison Commerce and hung up with Julie Haywood. As I did, I realized that the awkwardness from this morning had gone undiscussed. But there was progress in the case, and that was the main priority. The lull was breaking. Following the lead was a more pressing matter in my mind, and I was positive it was in Julie's mind as well.

Crossing over Pinckney Street, I scanned the lawn of the courthouse. There was no old shell of a phone booth. Not even one of those half-open booths that were more common just before the cell phone boom. Walking up the western stairs, I checked the corners of the courthouse, looking for any remnants of that phone. On the southwest corner, there was an unexplained concrete pad that was not symmetrical with the other corner. I walked around the entirety of the courthouse and there was only the one little pad. This had to be it, I thought. I walked over and stood at it, facing the courthouse, figuring the pay phone would've faced outward. I spied down Pinckney Street toward the annex where the old Theatre was. I could see the front doors. Easily.

Knowing more about the case than when I started, I was now convinced this was how the murder played out. The killer obsessively called the theatre, trying to talk to or harass Crystal for whatever selfish motivation. When his calls were ignored, he went to the theatre to take action. But he needed her alone to convey his message, which could only happen after closing. He waited here, at the payphone, watching. He made a well-timed call to separate Crystal from Maynard Preston and seized his opportunity once Preston left the area.

Feeling validated, I needed to catch up with Julie for that subpoena. It was paramount to the case. I headed toward the police station where I'd left my vehicle. Out of curiosity, I glanced north across the courthouse grounds and could see the gazebo underneath the mossy live oaks in Four Freedoms Park. I stopped and looked, considering the scene, and then wondered what else I was missing.

⌘

At the bank, Julie Haywood and the branch manager were waiting for me in his office. A mid-forties man with salt and pepper hair, a thin build, and a firm handshake greeted me as I arrived. The magnetic name tag on his lapel read, "Jim." The framed diploma on the wall from Florida State University School of Business read *James R. Conrad.*

"Officer Haywood filled me in a little on the case you guys are working; that's crazy," said Jim.

I shot a wary glance over at Julie, curious as to how much she actually had divulged.

"Is that right?" I said, cryptically.

"Yeah, and Madison Commerce will be glad to cooperate," he added. "Plus, my daddy and the late Mr. Byrd were good fishing buddies, so—"

"Outstanding," I answered. His connection didn't factor into our decision to look inside the deposit box. However, I never turned down help from a citizen, no matter the personal motivation. "So, shall we?"

"Yes." Jim got up and buttoned his jacket. "Let me make sure the room is ready for you. Our policy is that we only allow one client at a time in the room."

"Okay, thank you," Julie said.

After Jim exited his office, I told Julie the rest of the details concerning the missing page, Penny the round-faced woman, and the ten obsessive phone calls made to theatre followed by the two from what I believed was from a payphone at the courthouse. I played out the scenario of how I believed the murder happened, given all the new evidence.

"Whoa," Julie said, "that makes a lot of sense."

"Who does the number belong to?" she asked.

"I don't know. That's why we need to get a subpoena cranked out as soon as possible," I said.

"Want me to—"

"If you two would follow me, please?" Jim Conrad stuck his head back in the office. He gave us a flat-handed wave.

"Sure," Julie said.

I checked my watch and figured, unless there was a confession note to the Crystal Daws murder or a small treasure of pirate gold in the safe deposit box, we had about fifteen minutes to spare.

We followed the branch manager to the edge of the lobby, down a small hallway, and into a vaulted room lined with safe deposit boxes. Each had a small, numbered plate attached on the outside just above a keyhole. Some boxes were wide and flat, others square and narrow. The corresponding number from Detective Byrd's mysterious key belonged to a box the size of a mailbox.

"Jim, will you tell Hank when this box account was opened?" Julie asked. The question was forced and out of place, which made it that much more intriguing. I looked up at Jim.

"It was the day before he died, actually."

"Really?"

Julie's eyes widened and her brow raised in a look of confirmation.

"Yes, sir," Jim added. "Does that mean something to the two of you?"

"No," Julie chimed in. "It's just a coincidence." I kept silent as I inserted the key and opened the safe deposit box. I knew Julie was lying to him. We both knew it was no coincidence. We both knew that whatever was in this box, Holcomb Byrd had put it there for fear of it falling into the wrong hands.

As I slid open the box, I could feel Julie and Jim, the branch manager, step closer and look over my shoulders with curiosity. Light poured into the box, revealing a single brown folder. It was well-aged and thick with equally aged documents. It looked familiar, but I thought, how could it? I never knew Holcomb Byrd. I had never worked for the Madison Police Department, so why did this folder look familiar?

"What is it?" Jim asked.

"Looks like a case file?" Julie answered.

Then it hit me. "Back at his house, there were a bunch of case files in Holcomb Byrd's desk drawer. I remember looking in the drawer and noticing a case missing. Or at least a space where a case file could have been."

"You think this is it?" Julie said.

"Yeah, I do."

I reached down and carefully lifted it out of the box. I scanned the rest of the box for anything else, but it was empty. The tab on the folder had a case number sequence, suggesting it was from 1982. I flipped open the folder to see it was another murder case Detective Byrd had worked.

"Will there be anything else?" Jim asked.

Julie had an expectant look on her face, and I shook my head.

"No, Jim," Julie answered. "Thank you so much for your help."

"Alright, then. I wish you two the best of luck, and let me know if I can be of any further assistance."

Branch Manager Jim Conrad exited the small room and headed toward the lobby, leaving Julie and me in the room. The case was gaining significant momentum, but the awkward moment from the morning still hung in the air. I feared that Julie might bring it up, so I focused on trying to figure out the meaning of Holcomb Byrd storing a forty-year-old murder case file in a safe deposit box.

"How does this case play in, Hank?" Julie broke the silence. I was relieved it was about the case.

"I'm not sure."

"Well, what case is it?" she asked.

I held it open and scanned the top sheet. I recognized Holcomb Byrd's neat penmanship on the cover page, but I was taken aback when I realized it was completely handwritten. The case was a relic. Paying attention to the details of the case, I read a few of the highlighted spots to answer Julie.

"Looks like the murder of a guy named John 'Jack' Branson, November 19, 1982. He was shot to death in his home that night, around 8:20 p.m."

Lacking the motivation to continue, it wasn't clear to me how this case was connected to the murder of Crystal Daws, so I stopped reading.

"Does that sound familiar to you?" I asked Julie.

"No, not really," she said. "I was two years old when that happened."

A sharp pang hit me in the gut at the mention of how old Julie was in 1982. Recalling the year, I was in college, dating Victoria at the time.

"Well, we can take a trip down memory lane later," I said, getting annoyed. "I think we need to get on that subpoena as soon as possible so we can get a name on that old landline."

"Okay, sure thing," Julie said.

I slid the safe deposit box shut and locked it. I kept the case file tucked under my arm and followed Julie Haywood out.

Once outside, we were met with the glare of the mid-afternoon sun. Julie slid on a pair of sunglasses as I squinted at the brightness.

"But if that case wasn't important, why did he secretly stash it in a safe deposit box?" Julie asked. "I mean, why wouldn't he just lock it away at the police department?"

Without too much judgment, I gave Julie a raised eyebrow in response to her last question. I didn't want to mention that her department didn't have the best evidence integrity given the state the Crystal Daws case was in. And that case was thirteen years newer than the one he'd hidden.

"Okay, okay," Julie conceded. "But still, why hide it, and why hide it the day before he died?"

"Those are great questions to ask, Julie," I said. "But they're going to have to wait."

"Wait, why?"

"We need to find out who belongs to that number that called the theatre that night," I said. "So, we need to get that subpoena going."

Julie processed the situation and looked down the street to the south. She seemed hesitant, and internally, I questioned her experience writing subpoenas. Maybe the hesitation was because she wasn't sure how to construct one.

"I still find it odd, though," Julie said.

"Listen, we've read through the Crystal Daws case over and over, you more so, right?"

"Yeah."

"So, you see or read anything, I mean *anything,* where a murder from 1982 or Jack Branson was mentioned?"

Julie paused and thought for a moment. "No."

"There you go."

Julie still hesitated.

"Listen, I'm not saying it's not connected. Hell, it's mysterious as hell that Detective Byrd squirreled away this particular case a day before he died, especially after he left his wife saying, 'he lied to me'. But the fact is, we have a real tangible lead that needs to be followed."

"Yeah, you're right, Hank."

"I know I am." I smiled. "We can dive into it later if you like."

"Yeah, alright."

"So, back to the station? Crank out that subpoena so we can solve a murder?"

"Actually," Julie looked back to the south. "I have a better idea."

⌘

The drive from the bank only took a couple of minutes, but I was confused after pulling up to the curb in front of the Old Bookstore. *How was this a better idea than getting a subpoena*? I quelled my annoyance building inside. Julie Haywood's lack of experience in murder cases warranted a little patience. I checked my watch and decided that it was worth ten minutes. After that, I was going to drag her to the courthouse to file a subpoena.

"Here?" I asked, following Julie inside the bookstore.

The door chimed, and Cade McCoy perked up from behind the counter.

Julie turned quickly toward me. "Yes!"

"Hey, guys, what's going on?" Cade asked.

"Where are those old phone books?" Julie asked, while walking past the counter and deeper into the store, not waiting for an answer.

"Uh, phone books?" Cade was trying to catch up.

"Yeah, didn't your Grandpa keep a bunch of old phone books from Madison?" Julie asked. "I remember seeing them in here somewhere."

As Julie disappeared in the back, I stayed up front with Cade. He grabbed his cane and struggled to stand up, but he managed and headed toward Julie.

"Um, try in that first room under contemporary titles," Cade offered.

There was no way this was going to work, I thought. I checked my watch, and Julie had seven minutes left.

"Why…?" Cade spoke. "I mean, what do you need old phone books for?"

Julie mumbled something about detective work, but I couldn't quite hear what. I moved closer.

"You guys have a lead on the Crystal Daws case?" Cade asked.

"We have a phone number that called the theatre a bunch of times the night Crystal was killed," Julie explained.

"Okay…," Cade sounded skeptical. "I mean, it was a theatre, what's odd about someone calling a bunch of times? It's not like the internet was prevalent back then. You couldn't quite Google movie times like you can today."

I stepped into the small bookshelf-lined room behind Julie as she searched each shelf carefully. She spun and looked my way, then glanced at Cade.

"Well, the page that contained those phone calls was actually missing. Probably been missing for twenty-five years," Julie said. "And the calls were from the same number within like an hour of each other."

"Wait, so—" Cade interrupted. "You don't think it was a robbery gone wrong anymore?"

Julie stopped her search to look directly at Cade. He stood on the threshold, leaning against the opening for stability. "No," she said. "We think she was actually targeted. But for what reason, we don't know yet."

I knew Julie trusted Cade, but I was glad she didn't divulge the fact that Crystal Daws's pants were pulled down and replaced during her attack. That was an intimate fact about the case only the killer would know.

"Wow, that's a twist," Cade said. "Did you guys find evidence other than the phone calls?"

Julie stayed silent.

"Let's just say we feel confident in the theory," I answered from behind Cade.

"Okay, I was just curious," Cade said. "I jus—"

"Found it." Julie announced, interrupting Cade.

"What?" I was startled, and my body immediately stiffened with anticipation. "Found what?"

"The 1993 phone book for Madison County."

"Oh," I deflated somewhat. Making a direct match for the number is what we needed, not a needle-in-a-haystack search. Julie had three more minutes.

Flipping through the thinnest phonebook I had ever seen; Julie scanned the pages up and down.

"Are you looking for the number and hoping it'll be in there?" I asked with heavy skepticism.

Julie sneered at me and pulled out a business card from her pocket. She pressed it on the page and scanned the columns of numbers. She moved down each column, going line by line, then flipped the page. On the fourth page, her shoulders sagged, and a grin appeared wide on her face. She turned to face me with a gratifying smirk.

"They were in numerical order," she said with pride. "It's called detective work."

I chuckled at her comment and passed it off, allowing her the moment.

"And?" I snapped. "Who does it come back to?"

"Linda Bramwell," Julie said.

"Who the hell is that?" I vented.

Anticipation for the revelation was short-lived. My annoyance and aggravation had reached a tipping point. This was a completely new name, and that created more questions than answers.

Julie looked as perplexed as I, which, for a Madison resident and not recognizing the name, was not a good sign.

"I don't know, Hank," she said. "Name doesn't ring a bell."

We both turned and looked at the bookstore owner.

"Sorry, doesn't ring a bell for me either," Cade admitted.

"Wait," Julie said. She set the phonebook down with the page open to Linda Bramwell's entry and grabbed another phonebook.

"Let's check another phone book," she said.

"Good idea," I said, grabbing a third phonebook. Julie scanned 1992 while I looked through 1994. We found Linda Bramwell with the matching number from the theatre in both of the adjacent years.

"Well, at least you know you have the correct name attached to that number," Cade added. He turned and walked back to the front.

"Well, we obviously need to figure out who the hell Linda Bramwell is and who was living with her in 1993," I said. "Are you sure that name doesn't sound familiar?" I asked.

Julie shook her head no.

"You grew up here and knew Crystal, right? You're telling me that last name doesn't stick out?"

Julie was slow to answer. Her head was elsewhere, and it added to my annoyance.

"Hey? I need you right now," I told her.

"No, Hank," she said. "I can't think of anyone by that name."

Julie was getting annoyed as well. Any time you get an answer that leads to yet another question in any case, it is frustrating. The frustration doubles when it's a murder. I would imagine it's exponentially higher when that murder is of a loved one.

"It's just that our theory goes to shit if it's not someone she knew, you know?" I explained.

"Yeah, I know," she said.

"What are y'all going to do now?" Cade called out from the front. Julie grabbed up the phonebooks, and we stepped around to the front of the store.

"I'm going to take these, okay?" Julie said, holding up the phonebooks.

"Yeah, sure thing," Cade said. "Whatever you need."

"What's the next move?" Cade asked again.

"Figure out how this Linda Bramwell fits in the puzzle," I said.

I looked over at Julie. She was sorting through something in her head. I wondered if it was case-related, or maybe it had to do with our near kiss this morning. Lost in deep thought, it was hard to tell which of the issues she was dealing with. Either way, I thought, both needed to be resolved.

"Hey, maybe we should take a coffee break or something?" I offered.

"Huh?" Julie snapped out of her reverie. "Coffee?" she replied.

"Yeah, I figured we could gather our thoughts," I said. "A lot has happened in the past few days."

"Um, no," she said. "I need to go check on something." In a flash, Julie Haywood shoved out of the door, got in her Jeep, and pulled down the street.

"Well, damn," Cade said.

"Yeah." Confused, I stood there thinking I'd missed something with Julie. Did I say something to offend her? Did I piss her off asking about the Bramwell woman?

"You could try Facebook." Cade said, breaking the silence.

"How would that help?"

"Social media will be the downfall of our civilization, but it is one helluva a resource if you want to find someone, just so long as *they* have Facebook," Cade explained.

"Okay, it's worth a try."

Cade scooted his chair over to the rolltop desk and clicked away at the computer. His own profile popped up with a picture of him and a pretty blonde woman on a boat. He was bare-chested, and she was in a revealing bikini, both holding up beer cans in a posed cheer. There was another side to the ex-cop bookstore owner that I wasn't aware of.

"That's Eve." He could sense my curiosity. "She's a professor at the Community College."

"She's pretty," I said.

"Yeah, she's pretty cool."

Thinking back to my courtship with Victoria, I remembered taking several trips to *The Rez* back in Tallahassee. Short for *The Reservation*, it was on Lake Bradford situated on the south side of the city, near the airport. Owned by Florida State University, it was a popular place for college students to have outdoor, recreational fun. We would go swimming with friends, and Victoria would wear what would've been considered a revealing bathing suit back then. She was fit, beautiful, and in Cade's words, "pretty cool." I focused on her face within the memory, but I could not get past her vibrant smile. Her face eluded me again.

Dammit.

"You okay, Hank?" Cade asked.

He must have read the disappointment on my face. "Yeah, I'm fine."

Cade hit a search function and typed in Linda Bramwell's name. A long list of the same name appeared on the screen. Cade scrolled down, showing at least two dozen Linda Bramwells.

"Popular name, I guess," Cade said.

"Any chance you could narrow it down geographically or age or anything like that?"

"Yeah, I can try."

Scanning the list on the screen, I noticed there were some variations of the name. Some had additional names or middle names, or what I assumed were maiden names. Katie had shown me her Facebook profile one time, and her screen name was Katie Trescott Anderson, her maiden name along with her married name.

Then, a name caught my eye.

"That one," I said pointing to the screen. "Click on that one."

"Linda Branson Bramwell," Cade read aloud.

After clicking on the name, her profile came to life. The woman held a modest pose in front of the Methodist Church around the block from the bookstore. She looked to be in her sixties, with gray hair cut at the shoulders. She held a tired look hidden behind a forced smile, which would deceive most into thinking she was content with her life choices. I could see through her façade. A darkness followed her around like a tormented memory.

"Yeah, she lives here in Madison," Cade confirmed. "Says she was married to Lucas Bramwell in 1992. Attends the United Methodist Church and was born in Madison, all according to her bio." Cade turned around in his chair. "You think this is the lady your theatre number comes back to?"

"I think so," I answered. "Her middle name is Branson."

"That mean something to you?" Cade asked.

I turned and disappeared out of the store. Following the door chime, I could hear Cade's voice trailing off, "Oh, come on—" is all I made out. But I wasn't leaving. I needed to see it with my own eyes. There was no coincidence. Holcomb Byrd had secured a case file detailing the murder investigation of John Branson, and now this woman, Linda Branson Bramwell, surfaced in the Crystal Daws investigation. It was time to find out why.

Walking back into the bookstore with the Branson murder case file, I held up a twenty-dollar bill.

"I'm buying if you're flying," I said.

Cade grabbed his cane, popped up on his good leg, and held out his hand.

"There won't be much flying, but I can manage a coffee run." Taking the money, he asked, "I'm confused about what's going on. What am I missing?"

"Detective Byrd hid this case file in a safe deposit box the day before he died. No one knew about it, not even his widow. It's of a murder investigation he worked in 1982, where a guy named John Branson was shot in his own home. Now—" I stopped my explanation and opened the file, carefully looking for validation. "Yep, there it is." I pointed down to the file and looked back at Cade. "His wife and witness in the case was *Linda* Branson."

"And that's who the number comes back to in the Crystal Daws investigation?" Cade asked.

"Exactly."

"Oh, shit," Cade said.

"Oh, shit, is right," I replied. "Better make it a large, with two sugars, one creamer. Something flavorful. Surprise me," I said, "and get whatever you want."

"Oh, right." Cade moved toward the door. "I'll be right back."

Taking advantage of the quiet bookstore, I sat down at Cade's desk and began reading the files. I commandeered a notepad and pen from a drawer to jot down notes as I read. My heart rate elevated, and I needed several deep breaths to slow it down. I didn't want to overlook anything in my excitement. Something told me the answer to Crystal Daws murder was in this file, and all I had to do was find it.

⌘

For most of this case, I'd been the driving force with the help of Julie Haywood. We were resuscitating it back to life from its once dormant existence. Now, with the latest information, this case was dictating its own speed. It had come alive. The connection between the missing phone number and the 1982 murder of John Branson had delivered a shockwave, waking it from a once-frozen state. Time to hold on for the ride, because this was the fun part.

By the time the door chimed, announcing Cade's return with the coffees, I was fully submerged in the murder of John Branson. From the extensive report, the man was an abusive bastard on top of being an alcoholic. Detective Byrd included synopses of several incidents of abuse where John was listed as the suspect, even one where he was arrested for hitting his wife, Linda. All had the common theme: John Branson, while intoxicated and belligerent.

On a late November night, officers responded to the Branson home for a report of a disturbance, but when they arrived, John Branson had been shot in the back and lay dead on the floor. Branson's wife, Linda, was there with her two children, James and Charles. The officers recovered a rifle on the scene with a spent casing still in the chamber. A second casing was found on the floor near where the rifle was recovered.

That night, the responding officers took Linda in for questioning about the shooting. They figured she was fed up with being beaten and had reached her boiling point. She then took an opportunity when John's back was turned and shot him. After getting her calmed down, Linda admitted to shooting her husband. She detailed years of abuse to her and her son, Charles, whom she called "Charlie." She explained that John was Charles's stepfather, but the younger son, James, they'd had together. For some reason, John focused his insecurities and anger on the stepson and wife, leaving his own son, Jimmy, alone.

Detective Byrd wrote in his report that Linda Branson was unable to provide adequate details about how the shooting occurred. She offered vague admissions that lacked the specificity Holcomb Byrd needed for his investigation. He had suspicions about her statement, especially when she couldn't quite explain how to shoot the rifle. Knowledge of how the bolt had to be pulled back on the rifle to extract the spent casing and load the next bullet seemed foreign to the woman who had supposedly just shot her husband with a rifle.

At this point, Detective Byrd turned his focus to the boys. He wrote that he noticed the younger of the two, James, had blood on his hands, and Charles had a fresh welt forming on his cheek.

Earlier at the crime scene, Holcomb noted that there was a bullet lodged in the top of the doorway, just above where John's body lay. Measuring his height, John stood around six foot four and the bullet wound was in his upper back. From where the round struck the doorframe and where John was shot, Detective Byrd determined the angle of the shot originated from a lower point of aim than what Linda's five foot eight inches would've been. Both boys hovered around five feet tall, Charles, being older, had a few inches on James.

Detective Byrd was further able to add the trajectory, proving the origin of the shot was about three feet off the ground. Too low to be consistent with Linda Branson's statement of standing with the rifle shouldered as she shot her husband.

Moving on to the two boys, Byrd was able to elicit a confession from the younger brother who cited he was sticking up for his mother and older brother. He boasted about being the protector of the family. The boy had proudly explained how to shoot the rifle, rack the bolt, and feed the chamber with another bullet. The only inconsistency Detective Byrd noticed was that James said his father was walking toward him when he shot, not away as the entry wound suggested.

Flipping over to the probable cause affidavit Byrd had filled out a few days after the homicide, he had charged the boy with murder and based it on the shot placement in John Branson's back.

"Jesus," I said. Looking up at Cade, "The damn nine-year-old shot his father."

"What?" he said incredulously.

"Yeah, looks like they were looking at a self-defense angle, but Detective Byrd determined the boy shot him in the back."

"Okay, so how does this help the Crystal Daws case?" Cade asked.

"Well, Linda has two sons, close to the same age as Crystal. One's an obvious killer, and I'm not sure about the other son, but my money says that one of them placed all those calls to the theatre, then showed up later and killed Crystal Daws."

"If they arrested the younger one, James?" Cade clarified. I nodded. He continued, "would he have still been in some sort of juvy or something in 1993?"

"Good question," I said. "We need to figure out if he was locked up for shooting his father when Crystal was killed. If he was locked up, that would narrow it down to Charles."

I almost told Cade to pull up the Department of Corrections website on his computer to search for James Branson, but he was arrested as a juvenile, and all of those records would've been sealed. There was no database I had access to that would provide this level of information.

Sifting through the file, I looked to see if Detective Byrd had included any case disposition paperwork or anything regarding his sentence but didn't find anything. An eleven-year difference between the murder of John Branson and Crystal Daws was pretty long, considering the latter was at the hands of a child. Most juveniles I arrested who were near the mark of adulthood were treated as such. Nine was on the extremely young end. My guess was that he entered some type of group home under the care of court-ordered social counselors and remained for ten or so years.

With some prodding of court documents, Julie Haywood, as an active law enforcement officer, would be able to see what James Branson was sentenced to for the murder of his father.

"Do you know James Branson?" I asked Cade.

"Doesn't sound familiar, no," he said.

"Really? Aren't you from around here?" I asked.

"No, I grew up in Jacksonville. My grandfather lived here and left me the bookstore. I've only been here about eight years," he explained.

"Oh, okay," I said. "And that name doesn't ring any bells? Maybe 'Jimmy' instead of James?"

"No, still nothing," he said, "but I bet Jewels would know."

"You're right again," I said. "Where is she?"

I checked my phone, and there were no missed calls or texts from Julie.

"She said she had to check on something earlier, but she's missing all this progress," I said.

"I'm not sure where she is either."

I continued sifting through the documents. "Hey, here it is!" I was surprised to locate the court disposition for the case.

"What does it say?" Cade asked.

"James Branson was ordered to eight years in a court-ordered program followed by five years of probation and court-ordered counseling."

"Eight years, huh?" Cade said, "For shooting his own father."

"He must've been quite the asshole, this John Branson," I said.

"Must have."

"But that means he wasn't locked up when the Crystal Daws murder happened."

"Yup, you're right about that," Cade said.

Glancing over the murder case again, I reread the highlights, making sure I didn't miss anything. It seemed pretty straightforward. Asshole drunk abuser gets shot by his family member. Detective Byrd had been thorough with the case. Looking over the names of the involved parties, something stuck out, and I wasn't sure what to make of it. The last name of the older brother, Charles, was Langston.

"Do you know Charles or 'Charlie' Langston?" I asked Cade.

He thought for a moment. "Um, no," he said, "I don't think so. But isn't Jewels' police friend named Langston?"

"You mean Ryder Langston?" I asked.

"Yeah, that's it," he replied.

"You think they're related?" I asked.

"Maybe," he said, "but you know who would know?"

"Julie," I said flatly, knowing that Cade was messing with me.

"Yep."

I emptied the cup of coffee Cade brought from his run to Lucile's. I looked for the old address of Linda Branson in the phone records and asked if Cade knew where it was.

"That I do know," he answered. "It's on the east end of town."

Cade provided some guidance on how to find the address. I gathered up all of the files and my notes from the Branson murder and headed out the door.

"Hey, Hank?" Cade called out, "You miss it?"

Feeling the excitement of the case coming to fruition was apparent, even to the bookseller. I smiled at the question, knowing he was referring to my return to homicide work. Investigating deaths holds such high importance that the weight of each decision in the investigation is balanced on justice or failure. In that balance, I found my purpose, the seeker of truth.

"Yeah, I do," I said.

Chapter 22

Before trying the old Branson address, I ran by the police station in search of Julie Haywood. After leaving the Old Bookstore, my attempts to call her cell phone went unanswered. Every instinct told me to find James Branson and see what he knew about that night back in 1993, but going without Julie seemed ill-advised. Everything pointed toward Branson being the person who'd killed Crystal Daws. However, I lacked the motive. Why would this guy want to kill Crystal Daws? His name was nowhere in Holcomb Byrd's investigation. He was not a love interest, past or present, and wasn't connected to Crystal that anyone had known about. There was nothing tying Crystal into owing him money, legitimate or otherwise. And nothing noting that Crystal was engaged in anything high-risk in her life or on that night. Nothing that I had learned answered the question of why he would want to kill her. Why would he call her obsessively, wait for her after work, attack her, pull her pants down, and shoot her in cold blood? It seemed personal, yet there was no trail that I found where her path crossed with James Branson.

No physical evidence existed, either. There was nothing tying him to the scene or Crystal. The strongest link I had was the phone number that belonged to his mother at the time, calling the theatre. Back then, had Holcomb Byrd possessed the same evidence, he most certainly would've followed that lead, making the probability of closing the case by arrest pretty high. With a twenty-five-year lapse, there was no guarantee of anything panning out without accompanying hard evidence.

Walking into the front of the police station, Tyler was closing down his computer and cleaning up his station.

"Hey, Tyler, have you seen Julie?" I asked.

"Oh, Officer Haywood?" he thought for a moment. "No, I haven't seen her."

"She's not on a call or anything?" I was beginning to worry.

Tyler spun around to his computer and shook the mouse, waking up the screen. He studied it for a second and stood up.

"No," he said. "Nothing on the CAD. Plus, isn't she off today?"

She was off, but something had pulled her away, and I assumed it was work-related. Had it been personal, I hoped she would've said something.

"Okay," I said. "Thanks for checking."

"No problem, Mr. Hank."

Tyler went back to cleaning up his station. I pressed my temporary badge clip to the sensor and pulled the door behind reception open. Before stepping through, I asked Tyler if he'd seen Ryder Langston.

"No, I believe he's already off for the day, too," he answered. "Officer Boone is here if you need someone."

"Okay, thanks again, Tyler," I said.

"Sure thing."

Before the door shut behind me, Tyler called out.

"Oh, Mr. Hank, about the patrol roster from 1993?"

I stopped, letting the door hit me on the backside. "Yes, Tyler?" I answered immediately. "What did you find?"

"Nothing."

I let out an audible sigh, much like air sputtering out of a balloon.

"I'm sorry, Mr. Hank," the kid said. "The department doesn't keep patrol rosters that far back. That's something that's just thrown away."

"It's okay, Tyler," I said, calming down. "Thank you for looking."

"Anytime, Mr. Hank."

I let the door close all the way behind me and stepped into the nearly empty room. Business hours were done, and the place had cleared out.

Julie had earlier explained that, with the exception of patrol officers, everyone else worked day shift hours and was on call at night. I wasn't sure what I could get done without Julie Haywood.

"Help looking for what?" a voice called out.

Searching above the cubicle walls, I saw the top of a brown-haired man walking down the side. It was Officer Boone. Tyler had mentioned he was at the station.

"Nothing," I answered. "Don't worry about it."

He stepped around the corner to face me near the prisoner benches.

"C'mon," he said. "You trespassed on my property. The least you can do is level with me. What did you need Boy Wonder's help with?"

Worried Officer Boone might start trouble with the trespassing issue, I decided to cave. I fished out the Polaroid of the crime scene with the missing patrol car. I paired it with the eight by ten glossy of the crime scene taken later by forensics.

Asking Boone for help felt like a Hail Mary pass in the fourth quarter with only one receiver against multiple defenders. "Do you know who drove this car?" I pointed to the patrol car off to the left, pulled up on the curb. "It's missing from this picture." I handed both pictures to him.

Officer Boone considered each one and then went back and forth from image to image. Finally, he flipped the Polaroid over and read Holcomb Byrd's cryptic numbers. However, I saw recognition in Officer Boone's face, and his shoulders sagged slightly.

Officer Boone let out a, "Huh," as he continued to stare at the pictures.

"Do you know whose car it is?" I asked with rising concern.

"If I do, will you tell me why it's important?" he asked.

"Uh," I was unsure what to tell him. I knew that Julie despised this guy, but there was a genuineness in the way he asked. Almost as if he was excluded and wanted in. I felt uncomfortable making this decision.

"Well, uh," I stammered.

"Fine." He handed the pictures back to me. "Don't tell me. But the car belongs to your buddy, Super Cop."

Officer Boone started to walk away, but he'd spawned more questions.

"Wait, Super Cop?" I asked.

"Yeah, Langston."

"That car belonged to Ryder Langston?" I asked, "Are you sure?"

"Wow, I thought you were this great detective," he said facetiously. "Yes." He pointed at the picture. "That car belongs to Langston."

"You're sure about that?" I probed.

"Yes, man. I'm sure," Boone said. "I know because I got that piece of crap after him when I was a rookie. Car 649. I ran that damn thing into the ground before they gave me another."

"The underlined number was his patrol vehicle number?" I asked.

"Yep," Boone validated.

I started processing this information. Byrd left his house the day he died saying, "He lied to me." Given that the Polaroid pictures were kept in a lockbox at the detective's house, was he referring to Ryder Langston as the "he"?

"Still not going to tell me, huh?" Boone broke my train of thought.

"Oh, well…," he said, walking away. "Dick move, though."

I considered informing Officer Boone of all the updated information in the Crystal Daws case, but I held back on the wishes of Julie Haywood.

"Let me ask you this first. Why do you want to know?" I asked.

"If you don't want me to know, then don't tell me. It's fine." He lowered his eyes, and a frown formed on his face.

"You feel left out, is that it?" I asked. I could see it in his eyes. "You want in on the action."

His eyes widened. "Nah, you got it all wrong."

"Do I?" I asked. "Then why help at all? Boone, you could've just let me struggle with this after hearing me talk with Tyler, but you didn't. You were curious. Hell, you probably got a little jealous after seeing—"

"I ain't jealous of nothin." He cut me off. "I mean, yeah, I see you and Haywood running around town, but…, I ain't jealous."

"C'mon, Boone," I said. "Cut the shit. You don't have to impress me; hell, we barely know each other. But this is a by-God murder investigation. Just say you're interested."

Boone considered my counterpoint. He bit the corner of his lip, fighting against his own self-preservation and ego. I looked at him, raising my eyebrow, waiting for his admission.

"Yeah, okay," he admitted. "Of course, I'm interested. It's a damn *murder* investigation. I just never thought you and especially Haywood would get this far."

"Well, here we are," I replied. "And she's a good cop. Is that why you've been giving her a rash of shit lately? You were jealous?"

"I wouldn't say that," he said.

"I would," I said bluntly. "There's no room for jealousy or anything of the kind when it comes to murder investigations. Hell, there's no room for it in police work in general. It's uncalled for."

"Yeah, alright. I got it. I'm sorry. So, what do these pictures have to do with the case?" he asked.

"I'm not exactly sure, but they were important to Holcomb Byrd. I think he was on to something and was trying to straighten it out, but he wound up dying of a heart attack," I explained.

I checked my notes and read Linda Branson's address circa 1993 to Officer Boone.

"Do you know where that is?" I asked.

"Sure, it's north of town, almost to Pinetta," he said.

"Give me a second. I may need your help," I said, pulling out my cell phone. I tapped Julie's number in the call log, and it started dialing. The phone rang, but again, went unanswered. I hoped she was okay.

"Care to check an address with me?" I asked Officer Boone.

⌘

As dusk settled in the western sky, it left a deep orange that glowed behind the tree-lined highway running north of town. Following Officer

Boone in his patrol car, I had recommended we drive by the location to first see if anyone was home and if any cars were in the driveway. If there were, Officer Boone would run confirmation checks to see if the cars belonged to Linda Bramwell or James Branson. If we got a hit, then we would attempt contact.

Boone had been insistent about driving separately, so he didn't have to drive me back to the station afterward. I didn't fight him on that decision.

Eyeing the passing numbers on the mailboxes, I knew we were getting close to the Branson's property. Boone's taillights brightened, and I noticed he was slowing down. Nearing a stop, he pulled off to the side. I caught a mailbox as we passed, and we were still a ways from our target.

Boone's arm flung out his window, and he waved me up.

"What's going on?" I asked.

"Hey, I got a call. It's not super far away. Should only take me about thirty minutes to handle it," he answered.

"Okay." I looked at him expectantly.

"Just wait for me to get back," he said.

I looked around as night settled over the countryside. I didn't like the idea of Officer Boone being there to begin with, but Julie's absence created that problem. I really didn't like the idea of waiting, either.

"C'mon." He must've read my face. "Please?"

"Sure," I answered. "But I'm going to drive up closer and watch for a bit until you get back."

"Okay, cool," he said. "Just don't do anything until I get back."

"Yup, alright."

Boone spun off and headed back toward town to answer his call for service. I pulled back on the road and headed north, hoping I didn't have to wait for Boone and that Julie Haywood would call me back.

I dialed her number once more but didn't hit send. I realized I had called her several times and left several messages. I wondered if it had something to do with this morning and our near kiss. Was she mad at me? Or was there something else wrong? Either way, I was getting worried.

Passing the target, I glanced over, catching a glimpse of the property. Moving by at forty miles an hour at night, I wasn't able to catch many details. I killed my lights and pulled onto the shoulder. No traffic was in sight in either direction, so I flipped around and drove over to the neighboring property. I pulled off the road into the shadow of a copse at the end of the wood line. I turned off the ignition so I could watch in silence. Rolling the windows down for air allowed a cacophony of chirping crickets and croaking frogs to fill the quiet.

From this vantage, I could see the front half of the property. A darkened home, aged and unkempt, sat near the road, but the clearing ran much deeper and out of my view. My pass, below the speed limit, offered no reconnaissance, so I decided to sit and wait. I noticed my instinctual desire to snoop around had been resurrected. I wanted to find a better observation point to watch the Branson property, but I remained in the car, letting the warm air roll through along with the sounds of the countryside.

A quick breeze blew through my open car, followed by the staccato plops of rain falling on the roof and windshield. I rolled up the window but left it cracked at the top. The intermittent drops quickly intensified and soon blurred my view of the Branson property, further diminishing surveillance. I closed the windows and sat helplessly in the quiet car. I looked at my phone. There was no word from Julie, not even a text or a missed call.

"Where the hell are you?" I said out loud.

It made no sense, as we stood on the brink of discovering the possible murder suspect, that she was missing in action. This was *her* case. What else could she possibly have going on in this little town that could be more important? I grew aggravated but decided that I would have to let it go for now. If she couldn't be here, and I had to hand the arrest over to Lance Boone, so be it. Whether it was him or Julie

Haywood making the arrest, it didn't matter. Either way, a murderer was going down.

That reminded me of something. I reached under the seat and pulled out a small triangular zippered pouch. Being followed from Madison to Tallahassee, with evidence in tow, had prompted me to stop by the house and grab my gun. It was one thing to silently stalk my suspects, but if they knew I was coming, that would change the dynamics of how I needed to conduct business.

I unzipped the pouch and removed the Glock 19. The textured grip felt attached to my hand as I held it tight. It had been forever since I'd had held a weapon, let alone fired one. Working murders, I rarely needed it, but it had always been on my hip when the time came. Waiting for the rain to let up, I thumbed rounds into the magazine, inserted it into the well, aimed down at the floorboard, and charged the gun, loading one into the chamber. I held it out toward the darkness, focusing on the sights along the top of the slide. I prayed I didn't have to use it. I slid it into the paddle holster and affixed it to my belt loop, letting it rest on my hip.

After half an hour, the rain began to lessen, but I received no word from Officer Boone. I tried calling him, but, like Julie's, his phone just rang. I assumed he was unable to resolve the issue as quickly as he'd thought. I turned on the windshield wipers, and they cleared away the blurry sheet of water, allowing me to see. Noticing the rain had nearly ceased, I rolled down my windows again. A cooler breeze, thick with moisture, seeped in. I took in a deep breath, letting the cool, damp air fill my lungs, as it had gotten stuffy inside the car.

Surrounded by the dark of night, the lights from the Branson property stood out. I peered out of the windshield with a pair of binoculars, but from this vantage, I could only see the front of the unkept house. Everything was the same.

A break in the clouds brought out a near-full moon, illuminating the land enough to see further onto the property. The heavy rain had silenced the symphony of insect activity, and there was a hushed quiet this far out in the countryside. The lingering breeze of the night storm rustled nearby treetops, creating the only sound.

Suddenly, in the distance, I heard a woman's voice yell out, "Stop, Goddammit. Let me go."

I peered through the woods to see any movement to go along with the words, but I couldn't tell where it was coming from. Positive about what I'd heard, I figured it came from deeper on the Branson property, on the other side of the woods from where I parked.

"You're hurting me, you asshole," the voice yelled out. "Let me go"

The voice was panicked. I heard a mumbled voice too low for me to make out. I assumed it was whom the woman was yelling at.

"Julie?" I thought.

I disabled the dome light, slowly squeezed the door handle, and slid quietly out of my car. I pushed the door shut and began walking around the wood line in search of the voices. Moving stealthily through the night, I tapped the outline of the gun resting on my hip.

Making my way around the copse, I stood fully on the Branson property. Remaining under the shadows of the timberline, I crept toward the back of the property.

The woman's voice had calmed, but I could hear what sounded like, "Let me go, now." I honed in on the voice and stalked my way further into the property. Double-checking the house at the front, it remained dark and seemingly vacant. Moving slowly, I stopped at the edge of the tree line that ran from the highway. I knew my parked car was just on the other side of the thicket. The property opened up to a much bigger plot, cleared and vast. In the darkness, I could tell it was several acres and spanned to my right and left. To my left, the land dipped into a valley, as I could see the top of the far wood line lower on the horizon than on the right. Several structures were scattered about the property. I could see amber lights glowing, casting a shadow on the buildings. It was too dark to tell if they were houses, barns, or something else. To the right, the earth rose up a hill, and all I could see was the dirt driveway that ran past the first house, winding up the hill and leading somewhere out of my view. A glow came from the top, leading me to believe there was yet another structure on this property.

A sharp buzz on my thigh startled me. Unsure if an insect was stinging me or if I had found a thorny bush, I glanced down, trying to remain quiet. It was my phone.

Seriously, now? I thought.

Quickly pulling it from my pocket, I hoped it was Julie, or even Boone, so I could relay what I'd heard. It was neither. It was a state government number which confused me. I fought the urge to ignore the call, but something told me it was somehow germane to this case.

In a hushed voice, I answered, "Hello?"

"Hank Trescott?" A man asked.

"Yes, this is he."

"Soloman Blanks from FDLE crime lab. Is this a good time? I know it's getting late."

Blanks' name registered somewhere in my memory, but I was too focused on the crime lab part. There were very few reasons a lab technician would call me this late.

"Uh, sure," I said, not wanting to take any time to actually explain what I was doing.

"I tried calling Officer Haywood, but I got no answer. I saw your name on the submission sheet, so…," Blanks paused, and given my situation, I didn't say anything. He continued, "I'll be brief, and we still need to confirm our findings, but I wanted to let you know we got a hit on the evidence you submitted for testing."

"Really?" I asked, abandoning the hush.

"Yes, it was really quite bizarre, but it matched a Department of Corrections submission to an inmate's release in 1991 and tied to a murder case back in 1982 from the Madison Police Department. The suspect in that case is the major donor in your case. Now, for reasons I can't explain, I can't provide a name in the '82 murder, but I can give you the case number if you'd like to write it down."

"Is it James Branson?" I said flatly.

"Uh, well...," Blanks's hesitation was enough to confirm the hit.

"It's James Branson, and the reason you can't tell me is that he was a juvenile back in '82, right?" I asked.

"Um, actually, yeah. It is," Blanks admitted.

"Where'd you get the hit from? You know, the sample that matched?" I asked. I knew it would make a difference. But if my theory was right, I already knew that answer, too.

"The zipper, as well as the top button on the victim's pants."

The validation made me smile. There was a tremendous relief that accompanied the validation. Both were satisfying. Even in the dark of night, hiding in the woods in the middle of nowhere Madison County. I nodded, knowing that soon, Crystal would finally have her justice.

"Thank you for calling and letting me know, but I need to go," I said.

"Oh, yeah. Of course," Blanks said. "But, hey, one more thing."

"What?"

"There was a minor donor as well. It was small, but enough to build a profile."

DNA evidence was a still growing aspect of homicide work when I was still with TPD. But I knew that oftentimes the technicians would discover multiple donors from a single piece of evidence with one being more prevalent than another. Outside of the major donor, those peripheral donors, or minor donors, would sometimes cause issues within the case.

"A second suspect?"

"That's out of my area of expertise, but there was definitely a second profile."

"Did you get a hit on that one, too?"

"No, no hit on the minor donor."

"Okay, well, that makes things interesting."

"But I can tell you that the minor donor is related, closely, to the major donor. They're definitely family."

Movement caught my eye straight ahead.

"Shit." I ducked further into the wood line and returned to my hushed tone. I had so many further questions, but now wasn't the time to take a deep dive into the forensics.

"Listen, I got to go. Thanks for calling."

"Alrigh—" I hung up and stuffed the phone back in my pocket.

The movement was of a figure I saw moving under the amber glow of a porch light sitting atop a larger building. The angle of the building cut my view, so I moved out of the shadow and into the clearing. I kept my footsteps silent, thanks to the downpour softening the ground. As the far side of the building came into view, I realized it was a large, multi-car garage that probably doubled as storage for farm equipment. The figure was a man moving to an open bay of the garage. I crept closer and saw the backside of a silver Ford Fusion with tinted windows parked within. I froze in place, making sure this was not an illusion. I side-stepped further into the clearing to get a better angle, looking deeper into the garage.

"No, you assho—" The woman's voice was muffled. A few more side-steps and I could see the man placing duct tape over her mouth. Her hands were bound in front of her and at her ankles. Her eyes bulged wide with fear as he shoved her helplessly into the trunk of the Fusion.

Instinctually, my hand reached back to my weapon and pulled it from the holster. I married up both hands, squeezing the grip in my palms, holding the gun out in front of me. Preparing for a confrontation, I continued on toward the garage.

As I neared, I focused on the woman being held against her will. It wasn't Julie Haywood. Her disheveled, curly, blonde hair frayed out over the top of a gag wrapped around her head and into her mouth. A stretch of Duct tape covered her mouth in addition to the gag. Her eyes streamed tears of horror. Standing just outside the bay door, I heard the man tinkering with something behind the wall out of my sight.

I had no choice but to take action. I glanced back at the woman. I realized she looked familiar. We locked eyes as she saw her way through the darkness. It was Hope Bennett. She was terrified.

What the hell was she doing here? I thought, but at the same time, I was relieved it wasn't Julie.

Something clanked behind the wall, and Hope's eyes moved to my right. She looked back at me intently and then slowly back to my right. She was telling me he was coming.

"I'm sorry, Hope." The man said. His tone was low and eerily calm. "I just can't let you go."

I crept up outside the bay door and steadied myself. I wanted to keep the element of surprise.

"I know what I've promised in the past, Hope, but this time it's different," the man said. I could tell from hearing his voice that he was standing in front of where Hope had been. "Now, it's time to go."

Hope's muffled refusal went ignored, followed by what sounded like a struggle over a trunk lid. The man's intentions were clear, and it was time to act.

Stepping around the wall, into the open bay door, the man spun in surprise and staggered back as I advanced. He had been trying to close the trunk lid on Hope Bennett. Thrusting my gun into his face, I yelled, "Don't move. Back away from her, now!"

"How the fuck?" The man gasped. He continued to back up, deeper into the garage. His hands flew up in surrender.

Hope was trying to scream through her gag as I moved past her, driving toward the man.

"Are you James Branson?" I demanded.

"Go to hell, you can't be in here," he replied.

I asked him again.

"Fuck you, what if I am?" he said. "What are you going to do about it? You're not a real cop. Not anymore."

"That's true, but step back before I shoot you."

Branson moved back, but his hands lowered. This allowed me to get between him and Hope Bennett. I held the Glock steady with my right hand, and blindly reached into the trunk with my left, trying to help Hope

Bennett get out. Being bound at the wrists and ankles, she tugged at my efforts, pulling me off balance.

"Since you ain't no cop, you're just a goddamn trespasser. I have every right to defend myself," Branson announced.

"I'm stopping you from kidnapping someone, you asshole," I said.

"Nope, looks like *I* stopped a trespasser from kidnapping someone," he countered.

I struggled to keep my gun aimed at Branson and help Hope free herself from the trunk without taking my eyes or focus off of my murder suspect. I needed to get to my phone, and the sudden realization I didn't have any handcuffs caused a panic I couldn't show Branson.

Reaching up toward Hope's face, I grabbed the gag from around her head and pulled it free. I could tell she was making headway, but I felt a hard pull toward the trunk. I turned to see what it was. She was straining to sit upright and needed me to offer counterweight, so I pulled harder. As she managed to get the momentum, I whipped my head back to Branson just in time to see a tire iron crash on top of my arm.

"Fuck!" I yelled out at the pain. My gun fell to the floor as a sharp sting sent a shockwave from my arm to the rest of my body. I retracted my arm as it went numb. I moved toward Branson, but he shoved me against the car and ran into the night. I picked up my gun with my left hand and aimed it at the fleeing man, but I had no shot as he disappeared into the darkness.

"You okay?" I asked Hope. She was climbing out of the trunk, peeling off the duct tape from her face. She nodded confidently as she gasped for air.

"He killed Crystal. It was him. I told the old detective back then, but nothing ever happened," Hope cried. "I'm sorry."

"It's okay," I said. "Stay here. Can you get to a phone and call for help?"

"Yeah. I think so," Hope said steadily, working to get out of her bonds.

Letting instinct guide me, I hooked a hard right out of the barn, allowing my eyes to adjust to the night while scanning for movement. Hoping to see Branson fleeing, I swung out wide from the corner of the barn to prevent an ambush, training my weapon at the hiding spot. He wasn't there. I heard footsteps, heavy and fast, moving away to my left. I remembered the dirt road that led up the hill and started running toward it.

As I kept listening, my eyes widened, taking in the night scene. I caught movement up the dirt road, and as I followed it, I saw the silhouetted outline of Branson running at the top of the hill.

"Stop!" I yelled out. He glanced back but never slowed.

Running faster up the hill, I was fueled by the thought of bringing justice to a victim who'd waited over two decades, further motivated by Julie and her earnest pursuit of this case, and spurred on by a town that should know a killer wasn't allowed to go free.

As I reached the top of the hill, my breathing labored. I slowed to control my breathing and scanned the area. The amber glow from before was from another house. A different, modern house, unlike the one at the bottom of the property. I stood in the backyard, and I could see the glimmering light over the back porch. The dim light made the house seem big. I kept moving, focusing on the shadows, looking in the crevices for Branson. The sting in my arm began to lessen, returning the use of my right arm. Leading with my weapon, I searched the backyard for Branson.

Hurried footsteps in the wet grass caught my attention. Branson was on the run again. I broke into a sprint after him. He headed for what looked like a carriage house offset from the main house.

"Stop, you asshole!" I yelled out again.

Branson kept his stride committed toward the carriage house. Instinct took over again. I broke left toward the back of the structure, hoping to cut him off. As I made the corner, I lost sight of him and prepared for the confrontation. Again, I swung wide around the first corner, and there was nothing. I moved quickly and began to swing wide for the next. I heard Branson fiddling with something around the corner. My weapon up at the high ready, I cut the corner ready for anything.

He had armed himself with an axe, but his focus was trained on the front of the carriage house, not the rear where I stood.

"Drop it, asshole!" I screamed.

His head whipped around with a frightened look stamped on his face. Both of us were panting heavily, but clearly, I had the advantage. Branson didn't move, but he didn't submit, either.

"Drop the axe," I said, calmly between breaths.

Branson looked panicked. His eyes widened, switching his focus from me to the Glock in my hand, tightening his grip on the axe. He was thinking about attacking. I could read it on his face. It was a what-do-I-have-to-lose look. With my distance and weapon advantage, I held steady.

"It's your move, Branson. Drop it. Don't do anything stupid."

Branson studied the axe. My finger was ready on the trigger. Then, he tossed down the axe and squared up to me.

"Something stupid, huh?" he said with confidence. "Like coming onto my property alone, trying to take me in."

This wasn't a surrender. It was a challenge and only served to confuse me.

"What are you talking about?" I asked.

"You're worried about me, when you should be worried about yourself."

Branson looked past me. There was recognition of something, not searching for thought.

This time, my instincts failed me. A blinding light popped into my peripheral vision, and I was suddenly paralyzed. A sharp pain to the back of my head followed and grew exponentially stronger. Powerless, I watched numbly as my view went from Branson to the approaching earth. I fell helplessly, ending with a thud on the wet ground. I blinked and gasped, trying to understand what had hit me. I heard muffled voices from above but nothing intelligible. I feared the attack would continue. I had to recover somehow. I grabbed for anything, trying to get back to my feet, but I was immobilized and lying helplessly on the ground.

Chapter 23

It felt as though I was floating uncontrollably in a tunnel of motionless water. Drifting in stagnant water unable to move, speak, or even think. At the end of the tunnel, somewhere off in the distance, I heard voices arguing. Muted and low at first, but the more they spoke, the clearer the voices became. Pain radiated in the base of my skull, but I began to grab hold of my faculties.

"Jimmy, go!" one voice said. It was a man's voice. Deep, southern, and familiar.

"You gotta do it, Charlie," Branson said back. "You hav'ta get rid of him."

"I'll take care of it, but you have your own mess down the hill to deal with, don't'cha?"

"Right," he said.

Charlie? I fought through the pain, trying to place the name and where he fit into the Crystal Daws investigation. James Branson had a brother named Charles who went by Charlie. How'd did I miss him? Where in the hell did he come from?

Branson turned and headed down the hill. "Thanks," he said. "I owe ya, Charlie Ryder."

"Charlie Ryder?" I muttered, as I pushed myself off the wet ground to my knees. Sloughing off the heavy cloak of the crushing blow to my head, I focused on the figure who stood before me. I fought through a thick cloud of confusion in a two-front battle. In one battle, I must stop

James Branson. The other, dealt with this Charlie. However, there was a reason his voice sounded familiar. It was Ryder Langston.

"Langston?" I asked. "What the hell are you doing?"

"I tried to warn you, man." He stood with a shotgun by his side. I eyed the buttstock, figuring that was what nearly caved in my skull.

Steadying myself, I began to rise and realized something monumental. "Shit. You're his goddam brother, aren't you?"

"Don't move!" he screamed.

I froze. The black void of the shotgun barrel inches from my face was enough motivation to keep me kneeling on the wet ground, motionless. I could feel the moisture seeping through the knees of my pants. "Don't move!" This time, I could sense the sheer panic and anxiety in his voice. "Dammit, I said don't move," he barked.

Frozen, but still gasping for air, I struggled to catch my breath. I was doing my best not to get shot. Still on my knees, I slowly lifted my arms in surrender. Glancing down at the empty holster on my hip, I realized my gun was lying elsewhere.

In twenty years as a cop, this was my first encounter with a gun pointed directly at my face. While investigating countless shootings, murders, and deaths, and hunting down the worst killers society had to offer, I had never been in a situation like this. I didn't care for it, and I sure as hell knew I hadn't missed out. My thoughts swirled as I attempted to analyze where I'd gone wrong. What did I miss? How did I end up like this?

A smirk bent the corner of my mouth as one thought broke through all of the confusion, even at a time like this. It wasn't of life's regrets, uncontrollable panic, or thoughts of the afterlife. Nothing flashed before me and only this thought brought me calm in such a dire situation. It was of her.

Had she not died of cancer, none of this would've ever happened.

With death looming in the form of a shotgun blast to the head, the eerily clear, vivid image of her face brought me peace. I could see every perfect imperfection as if she were in front of me. Was this the end? Was

I on my way to see her? I lowered my arms in submission and suddenly everything became clear. Everything aligned. I heard the echo.

"You covered it up for him, didn't you?" I asked.

Langston's head perked up from behind the shotgun. "What?" he said. "Covered what up?"

"It was James Branson who waited outside of the Woodard Theatre for Crystal Daws to leave. He killed her. Langston lowered the barrel of the shotgun, surprised at hearing I had connected his brother to the case. "And you caught him, didn't you?"

"How?" he stammered. "How— how did you figure that out?"

"You were too close not too." He looked at me incredulously as I summarized my reasoning. "Parked by the Four Freedoms Park, you heard the gunshots and took off running as any good cop would. It only took you a few seconds to get there, even on foot. Trust me, I made the same run, thanks to Branson."

"So, what does that prove? It proves nothing," Langston said.

"Nothing, you're right," I said, "but when you got there, you found him on top of her, didn't you?" I paused to see his reaction. "He had her pants and underwear down to what, about her knees? But that's when you noticed she was already dead from the gunshots."

A worried look appeared on Langston's face. He raised the shotgun, unsure of what to say.

"That's when you interceded, right? You pushed him off, told him to run?"

"Can't prove that either."

I laughed followed by a smile.

"No, but I can prove you were the one who pulled her pants back up. You were the one who staged the scene and probably told Branson to grab her purse and the bank bag to make it look like a robbery."

"How can you prove that?" he asked.

Knowing I had nothing to lose, and that just maybe, I could appeal to Langston in some way by explaining the evidence. Plus, the evidence was already out there. Regardless of if he shot me, he was going to be exposed. Maybe he would see me as an advocate instead of shooting me with his shotgun.

"Your DNA is on her clothing. Specifically, the buttons and zipper of her pants," I explained. "Branson's is on there too, from when he pulled them down."

Langston's eyes widened. His eyes darted around wildly in thought.

"C'mon Ryder; the dominoes are falling. I hope you see that." I paused, and he became lost in thought. He was reeling from what I'd said. I had him on edge. I took another chance. "Tell me about Holcomb Byrd."

Langston looked put off. "What about him?"

"He figured it out, didn't he? He figured you had something to do with it, and what? He confronted you about it right before he died?"

Langston didn't answer.

"You didn't kill him, did you?" I asked.

My accusatory tone set Langston off. "No, of course I didn't kill him," he said. "He came to me with some damn Polaroid he took. Said my car wasn't in the picture but was there later in the other crime scene photos."

"That's it?" I asked. "Hell of a leap to make off that photo."

"No, he said there was a witness who said Jimmy had something to do with it," Langston explained. "Byrd came at me saying I was lying about something. Poor bastard coded out from that heart attack before we finished talking. After all that, when the witness didn't come forward, I let it all die with the old man. Until now, that is."

"A witness?" I asked, "Who?"

Langston nodded down the hill to where Branson ran off and where I had caught him trying to kidnap Hope Bennett.

"Of course," I said. "That's why she was so difficult with us; she *had* talked to Detective Byrd, and then he suddenly died. No wonder she was scared."

A thought occurred to me. "You know he's going to kill her, right?"

Langston shuddered, then raised the barrel of the shotgun back at my face.

"I can't help her anymore. She learned to keep her mouth shut for all those years, and now, you come along and—," Langston trailed off. "Goddammit, why'd you have to come here?"

"Please, don't let him get away with it, again," I pleaded. "You can still stop him."

"Shut up, Trescott," Langston's voice cleared. He stepped closer.

Off in the distance, two pistol shots fired, sending the report up the hill. Both of us looked toward the bottom of the hill, both unable to see what had happened. But we knew that Hope Bennett was just murdered.

"Goddammit, Langston!" I snapped. "What kind of cop are you? You could've stopped that."

"Shut up," he said. Sorrow and pity were thick in his voice. "I am a good cop."

"Then what are we doing here?" I asked. "Go stop him and turn him in."

"I can't," Ryder said. "It's complicated."

"That's a load of crap. I don't get it," I said, shaking my head. "You have everyone fooled."

"What do you mean?"

"Wait…." I had a thought. Now it made sense. "It's atonement. Isn't it?"

"What are you talking about?"

"This whole Super Cop persona you put on," I said. "This bullshit you're fooling everyone with. You're atoning for letting a killer go free. It's your punishment for failing Crystal Daws. You figure if you solve enough crimes, do the right thing for so long, you think that absolves you from the sin you committed all those years ago?"

Langston's face scowled. "Something like that."

"Probably why you never took a promotion or anything. Some misguided self-punishment."

"Whatever, man."

"Don't let him get away with it again, man. Come on."

"Shut up, Trescott."

"What did he ever do for you?" I said.

"YOU'LL NEVER UNDERSTAND, DAMMIT!" He screamed, "YOU'LL NEVER KNOW!"

Suddenly, I was reminded of the old murder case Holcomb Byrd had in the safe deposit box. It was about James Branson killing his father. Byrd had detailed the years of long-standing abuse Charles had endured at the hands of his stepfather, John Branson. It made sense. Ryder felt indebted to him.

"I do understand," I said.

Between heavy breaths, Ryder looked over the shotgun into my eyes. "Huh?"

"He slayed your dragon," I said. "That's why."

"What?" Langston's face crinkled in disgust. "Dragon? What the fuck are you talking about?"

"You were being abused by your stepfather. I imagine you tried to do something about it, probably fought back, told Mom, ran away, stuff like that, right?"

"Yeah," Langston said.

"But none of it worked. The harder you fought, the more the abuse, right?"

Langston nodded. Through the amber glow of the house light, I saw his eyes water.

"You're the villager and your stepdad was your dragon, get it?" I said. "Then one day, a knight in armor shows up and slays that dragon, freeing you from the abuse. Now, you feel like you owe him."

"Yeah, okay," Langston said. "Something like that."

"But in this story, he's not a knight. Yeah, he saved you when you were boys, but he killed a girl, for what? Because she didn't pay him any attention? Because she wasn't interested in him? And now," I nodded down the hill. "He's done it again."

"I can't, man," Langston said. "I just can't."

"COME ON!" I yelled. "Let me go, she could still be alive. Don't add another murder on your conscience."

"Shut up!"

"No, you shut up," I snapped. I felt rage building inside. I slowly got up from the ground and stood before Langston. He maintained a height advantage, and the loaded shotgun was now pointed at my chest.

"Stop fucking around, and let's go down there and arrest him," I said. "We can sort your shit out later."

"Can't let you do that, Hank."

"Why not? How long will you have to atone for Hope's murder?"

Langston didn't answer.

I backed up from behind the carriage house and into the open backyard. A plan to make a run for it popped into my head. I scanned the side of the house for any weapons and to see if that axe Branson discarded was within reach. There was nothing available.

"Stop moving, Hank," Langston said. "I mean it."

"I'm getting tired of you pointing that thing at me, Ryder."

"Goddammit, man," he said.

"I know you don't want to shoot me," I declared.

"I have no other choice."

Langston's voice grew flat. Life faded from his eyes and suddenly, he was a dispassionate killer. He pulled the shotgun tight to his shoulder and lifted the barrel. I suddenly realized moving out into the open was a mistake, as there was nowhere to go. I closed my eyes, knowing that it would be quick, and I would be in the arms of Victoria when it was over.

Two rapid shots exploded. Deafening shots blocked out all sound. I inhaled one last time, hearing only the sound of air filling and leaving my lungs. My heartbeat thumped rapidly. Expecting horrific trauma, I waited to feel the searing, hot, double-aught buckshot tearing through my body, but it never registered. I took another breath. Then, I was shoved from the side.

"Hey!" Julie Haywood yelled. "Hank? You alright?"

"What?" My eyes shot open. Haywood stood at my side, her gun out at the ready, and Ryder Langston lay writhing on the ground in pain. His shotgun appeared to have been kicked several feet away.

"You alright?" she asked again.

I blinked in utter confusion, unable to comprehend what had happened. I was about to be shot, but now my would-be shooter was on the ground.

"Uh…," I looked around, but first, I took a couple of quick breaths, restoring needed oxygen to my body. I scanned myself and did an internal check for unexplained pain. Nothing. Answering Julie, I said, "Yeah, I think so."

"Here." Julie kept her weapon trained on Langston and handed me her handcuffs. "Cuff him."

"Uh, yeah. Sure." I took the handcuffs and moved to Langston's side. I flipped him over to his stomach and secured him.

"Ow, shit," he said. He was bleeding from his thigh. I rolled him back over and sat him up. Scanning his injury, I realized he was losing a lot of blood. The denim covering his upper thigh was already saturated with dark red blood.

"You have a tourniquet?" I asked.

"In the garage," Langston answered. "There's some rope in there you can use."

"Stay with him," I told Haywood, and I went to fetch the rope. Stopping suddenly, I asked, "Hey, the other guy? Branson?"

"Handcuffed to a post in the barn." Haywood answered with a smile.

"Really?" I said, incredulously.

"Yeah," she nodded, still holding the smile.

"Damn, Julie!"

I ran and got the rope Langston mentioned. As I fixed the rope high above the wound, a siren's wail grew louder, and flickering red and blue lights rose up the hill. The engine of a Crown Victoria roared as it cleared the hill and pulled into the backyard.

Tightening the rope around Langston's leg, I knew I wasn't going to be able to tie it off tight enough for it to be effective.

"Julie?" I called. She looked my way as I explained what I needed. "Go in the garage; find some sort of a sturdy stick about a foot or so long and anything we can tape it down with, like duct tape or something."

Langston's eyes started drooping, and his breathing slowed. He was losing a lot of blood.

"Hurry!" I added.

Despite his wrong-doings, Ryder Langston had his reasons for covering up Crystal Daws's murder, but I'd rather he was judged here on earth instead of dying in my arms.

Running back, Julie handed me a long screwdriver and a roll of duct tape.

"Perfect," I said, sliding the screwdriver between the rope and Langston's thigh. With as much torque as I could manage, I twisted the screwdriver clockwise, cinching the rope down on his leg. After two turns, Langston hollered out in pain, proving he still had life in him.

"Here, hold this," I told Julie. She reached in and held the makeshift windlass while I furiously wrapped Langston's leg, tourniquet and all, with the duct tape.

Jumping out of the car with his gun drawn, Lance Boone ran up to Julie and me.

"Goddammit, Hank!" he scolded. "You couldn't wait just a goddamn minute for me to get back, could ya? Shit!"

"Sorry, man," I said, finishing off the makeshift tourniquet. "I heard a woman yell for help."

"Whatever." Boone looked down at Langston, handcuffed and shot. "Whoa," Boone said. "What in the hell did I miss?"

I looked at Julie, and she looked back at me, unsure of how to respond.

"A lot, apparently," Boone said in our silence. "Am I correct in that I saw a guy handcuffed to a post down there with Hope Bennett?" he asked.

Julie nodded. “Yeah, will you go deal with him, Lance? He’ll need EMS, too. Graze wound to the head and arm.”

Both Officer Boone and I paused and looked at Julie Haywood in disbelief over her assessment of Branson.

“Damn, girl,” Boone said. “I missed everything. Dammit.”

Officer Boone walked back to his patrol car and began ordering additional units from the Sheriff’s Department and EMS to help with the scene. After relaying the gist of what the scene consisted of, I heard him tell the dispatcher to get ahold of the chief and that he wasn’t going to be happy.

Chapter 24

"Where the hell were you?" I asked Julie.

James Branson and Ryder Langston were both in custody and on the way to the hospital for treatment. Branson was headed to the local hospital for the minor graze wounds, and Langston was enroute to Tallahassee as a trauma alert. A few deputies from the Madison County Sheriff's Office arrived to assist with the crime scene. .

"That's a helluva way to say thank you for saving your life," Julie said.

"I…, I," I stammered, lost for words. I settled on, "You're right."

I chuckled and lowered my head. She did save my life. It occurred to me that as Ryder Langston was about to end my life, Julie Haywood had scaled the hilltop and fired from somewhere behind me, in the dark, from a considerable distance, managing to effectively hit her target, thus saving my life. It was a remarkable feat.

"Thank you," I said. I moved in close to her without thinking. I threw my arms around her and hugged Julie Haywood tightly. Her body was pressed into mine. She embraced the hug, and I felt her submit to the moment. She reached her arms behind me and held me tight. Loosening my hold, I leaned back, cupped her face with my hands, and pulled her in for a kiss. My lips met hers. They were warm and inviting. It was soft and sensual, yet with subtle power from knowing I'd escaped death because of her actions. I held the kiss and let it linger before slowly backing away.

"Wow," she muttered as I stepped back. "Um…, you're welcome."

I laughed, and she giggled. She looked up at me with a gleam in her eyes, and I locked into her stare. Finally, with all the commotion surrounding us, I stepped back.

"I must've called you a thousand times," I said. "How'd you know I was here?"

"Ha," Julie said, pulling her phone out of her pocket. "I didn't."

"You didn't." I was confused. "Then how'd did you know to come here?"

"First of all, it was eight times you called, a little shy of a thousand." She held up her phone. "And secondly, is it possible I was able to come to a logical conclusion that led me here that *didn't* involve the great Hank Trescott?"

"You heard the echo?" I said, smiling.

She nodded, returning the smile. "I heard the echo."

"But how?" I asked.

"The auto burglaries," she said.

"The what?"

"The auto burglaries I found while trying to find out when Banks had stolen Crystal's credit card," she explained.

"I thought that was a dead end," I replied. "What changed?"

"It was the name Bramwell. From the theatre number. I didn't recognize it at first, but I knew I had heard the name before."

"So, where'd you go?" I asked.

"Back to the station, to look at those reports. I went back over them."

"I thought we ruled out the burglaries and figured that it went unreported."

"Well, it sort of did," Julie said.

"How?"

"Do you remember the criminal mischief report that was bunched in with the burglaries?" she asked.

I shook my head.

"Didn't think so," she said. "Well, turns out the Bramwell vehicle was parked in the overflow lot at Doris' Diner, where one of the other burglaries was reported. It was written up as a smashed-in back window with nothing taken, but the vehicle was registered to Linda Bramwell."

"No way," I said.

"Yes, so I looked into her and the vehicle. Found out she had a son by the name of James Branson who had been pulled over in that car a few times before the criminal mischief and after. I investigated him and found out that he went to high school with Crystal. Did some more digging and found that he had been locked up as a juvenile for murder back in 1982. I also remembered Detective Byrd's case from the safe deposit box and figured there was no coincidence, and it all meant something."

Julie's face turned serious for a moment. "That asshole was still holding onto Crystal's purse months later. I figured Banks saw it, smashed the window to grab it, and the shithead had to report the damage because it was his mother's car. He just left out the part of the murder victim's purse in the backseat."

"Good for you, Julie Haywood," I said. "You sound like a real detective."

She blushed.

"So, I found an address for him and headed this way to check it out. When I got here, I saw Branson running down the hill and going into the barn. I followed and saw that he was trying to force a woman into the trunk of a car. Hope Bennett, can you believe that?"

I shook my head with a smile.

"No wonder we couldn't find her," she added. "So, I confronted him, and the asshole came at me with a tire iron, so I shot him."

Julie paused a moment.

"Apparently, I just grazed him, but it was enough to knock him down so I could cuff him to a pole. I was shocked to see Hope, and she was equally shocked to see me."

"So those two shots I heard were you?" I asked. "Jesus, I thought it was Branson murdering Hope."

"Yeah, that was me, and no, she's safe. Then I heard some yelling, here, up the hill and came running. Lucky I did, because when I got here, Langston had a shotgun to your head."

"Well, I'm glad you got here when you did, Julie. Thank you."

"And another thing, did you know this Branson asshole is stepbrothers with Ryder?" she asked.

"Yeah, I recently found that out as well," I smiled.

I moved closer to Julie Haywood. Soon, the chaotic circus of crime scene processing, the brass brooding, and the media buzzing would all kick off, and I expected to be separated from her for the rest of the night. Inexplicably, I wanted to kiss her again. She wanted me to, as well. I could see it in her eyes. They were inviting. I leaned in, and she moved closer. Both of us smiled, knowing it was going to happen.

"If you think I'm cleaning up your mess, Haywood, you can go fuck all the way off." The pompous voice of Lance Boone killed the moment. We pulled back from each other to reveal Officer Boone standing a mere three feet away.

"Stop trying to make with the help, Julie, and let's get to work," he added. I assumed I was the "help," to which he was referring.

"Sure thing, Lance," Julie said, swiping a loose strand of hair and tucking it behind her ear. "You got it."

"Alright, then," Boone said. "Ah, shit. Is that Channel 6? How the hell'd they get here so fast?" Boone stormed off toward the stretch of road in front of the property. "Let's go, Haywood."

"He's right," I said.

"At least he called me Julie and not Elsie," she mused.

"That's true," I said. Considering the gravity of everything, I felt obligated to ask, "You okay?"

"Yeah, I'm still trying to process everything," she said.

"You did nothing wrong, Julie," I said. "This was an active investigation, and both suspects were trying to either harm you or me when you shot. This is a no-brainer."

Julie smiled with a sheepish look and glanced away. "The shooting I got."

"Then what are you processing?" I asked, confused.

"You." Julie walked off toward one of the assisting deputies.

"Me?" I said to myself, not quite sure I understood Julie's answer.

⌘

What had been a long night stretched long into the early morning hours of the next day. The Florida Department of Law Enforcement sent a "shoot team" to assist with the investigation and whisked Julie Haywood and me off to the Madison County Sheriff's Office for interviews. Being a subject officer, Julie was allowed two days before making a statement. It was so she would be clear-headed when providing the details of her deadly force application. When Julie waived her two days and chose to make a statement that morning, the agent in charge urged me to convince her to wait. My rebuttal was that she had lived with the murder of Crystal Daws for twenty-five years; finally finding her killer and bringing him to justice was more important than waiting for a clear head.

When my turn came, I described every step Julie Haywood and I took, including the discovery of Darrell Banks, the assistance of Mary Anne Byrd, the missing phone records, the death of John Branson, and the phone call from the lab explaining James Branson's DNA was on Crystal Daws's zipper. The interviewing agent soaked up my words while the other furiously worked his phone, presumably sending texts to a team of agents asking for verification of everything I said. I knew this because his phone would chime; he'd show it to his partner on the sly. They'd pause, and one would ask about something I had spoken about. Not having the luxury of texting during my days of interviewing homicide suspects, I used to have to step in and out to get clarification in person. Sometimes we slid notes under the door, so I saw the convenience in the practice. However, I found it quite interruptive and informal.

After what felt like several hours, the agents left me in the interview room alone. How many times had I walked out of the interview room and left the subject alone, stewing in a cauldron of thoughts? Hundreds? Maybe more. Being on this side was different. I took the moment to reflect on the Crystal Daws case. After spelling out the case to the agents, I was able to look at it, as a whole, from start to finish. Oftentimes, in the middle of a case, it's hard to see everything. Sometimes crucial evidence isn't as crucial when looking from afar. But that's what counts, the case as a whole. It's what the prosecutors want, which leads to convictions.

Upon the discovery of how Crystal Daws's pants were pulled down and back up, the motive changed from robbery to sexual assault. It narrowed the focus of the investigation, but still, no other suspects emerged. Even when James Branson's name popped up, the motive and the why remained unknown. Julie was unable to shed any light on the relationship Crystal Daws may have had with Branson. This aspect of the investigation left me uneasy until I heard the full story from Hope Bennett.

Back at the Branson property, Julie Haywood and I had cornered Hope while we waited for FDLE to show up and take over the scene. We needed to know what secrets she had harbored for a quarter of a century.

After being rescued, Hope spoke of James Branson's unrequited love for Crystal Daws as borderline obsessive. But the obsession was a quick onset, which is why no one in Crystal's circle knew about it, except for Hope. She hid this information from Detective Byrd with the promise that James would transfer his love from Crystal toward Hope. This lasted only a few months until Branson became abusive toward Hope. He even threatened to kill her over what she knew. Hope vowed silence to escape his wrath but built enough courage to tell Holcomb Byrd what she knew. Instead of watching James Branson get arrested for what he'd done, she'd caught word that the old detective had suddenly died. Figuring James had something to do with it, she'd become terrified and vowed to keep her mouth shut. The guilt and anguish of it all led her to drop out of school, diving into a harsh life surrounded by alcohol, drugs, and misery.

Reflecting on how Hope had spelled everything out to us, I was satisfied she'd provided the why and that it was going to get him convicted.

Adding to that was the confession of Ryder Langston. After surgery to remove the bullet that shattered his femur and femoral artery, he was met with FDLE agents at the hospital. He reiterated what he had told me while holding a shotgun to my head. He explained that, on that fateful night, he'd found Branson on top of Crystal Daws. Discovering Branson had shot Crystal, Ryder told him to run off with the purse and bank bag. He was the one who pulled up Crystal's pants, misdirecting the case. Langston agreed to testify against his half-brother in exchange for consideration of his crimes. On behalf of the State Attorney, the FDLE agents asked what my wishes were, as I was the one he was about to shoot, had Julie not come along. Knowing the guilt that had plagued Ryder Langston for the past quarter century was almost punishment enough, I had only one request. Take the one thing he used to assuage his guilt—the job. I relayed that I would not press charges if Ryder Langston never wore a badge again. He would have to live in shame without the protection of a badge.

James Branson made it easy for the FDLE agents. He clammed up and requested a lawyer. The agents seemed put off at first, but given the amount of physical evidence and eyewitness accounts, the agents saw the case as I did, solid. The fact that it was a twenty-five-year-old murder case meant nothing.

⌘

My body stiffened up as I waited outside the sheriff's office for Julie to finish her part. The early morning sun had lifted above the horizon, and its rays broke through the tree line. I was on the edge of celebration or complete shutdown. I needed coffee or a bed.

Slowly, with trepidation, Julie stepped out of the sheriff's office doors. She smiled at me. I smiled back.

"Hey," she said.

"Hey," I said back. "How'd it go in there?"

"Fine, I guess." She shrugged her shoulders and looked around. "I'm not in handcuffs, so I guess they think I'm good."

"Of course, you're good, Julie." I stepped in close to her. "You saved my life. And Hope's life, too."

She leaned in and we hugged. Her arms wrapped tightly around me; her head nestled on my chest. She felt familiar and inviting.

"It's weird, ya know?" she said.

"What is?"

"Looking back, it feels surreal. But, damn," Julie smiled in reflection, "we just solved the case."

I nodded.

"I mean, we solved *THE* case, Hank."

"What's weird about that?" I asked.

"I don't know. It's just strange. It's like—" Julie trailed off from her thought.

"You don't know what to do now?" I offered. "You've had this case hovering over you for most of your life, and now that it's solved, it's not there anymore. It's not normal, when you think about it."

"Yeah, you're right," she said.

She leaned back in for another hug.

"So, what do we do now?" Julie asked. "I mean, what do big city detectives do after solving the big case?"

I smiled, looked around, and found the answer. Down a few blocks, I saw a sign that made the decision easy.

"We get breakfast."

Chapter 25

Walking into Lucile's, Julie Haywood's hesitation was unmistakable. She scanned the dining area before cautiously walking through to her usual table in the back. She looked uneasy and nervously locked eyes with me from across the table.

"You think they know?" she asked.

I shook my head as the waitress greeted us with freshly poured coffee.

"Know wut, honey?" the waitress asked Julie, overhearing her question.

"Oh…uh…, I was talking about something at work."

"Alright, let me know ween y'aller ready to order, 'kay?"

"Yes, ma'am," I said.

Alone, Julie asked again. "You don't think anyone knows yet? I mean, this is a small town. Hard to pass gas without anyone hearing about it."

I giggled. "No." I took several sips of the hot coffee, needing some rejuvenation. "Breathe, Julie, and take a second. Calmly look around."

We both quietly turned our heads, looking at the other patrons and employees of Lucile's.

"Look," I said. "No one is gawking or whispering. It'll be okay. Everyone will know soon enough. Enjoy the moment."

Julie accepted it and sat back, letting her shoulders relax. She, too, enjoyed the coffee.

"It's odd, knowing something as big as Crystal's case getting solved before everyone else does, right?" I asked Julie.

"Sure is," Julie said, hiding a smile. "So odd."

We ordered breakfast and tried to talk privately about the events from the night before. We talked about filing official murder charges on James Branson after getting a few hours of sleep. After FLDE's investigation, he was going to be charged with attempted murder on Hope Bennett, aggravated assault on Law Enforcement officer Julie Haywood, as well as aggravated assault on me. Three heavy felony charges would hold him long enough for the murder charges to be written up. Therefore, no need to rush.

"You should handle writing the probable cause," Julie said to me.

I smiled and shook my head. "Nope. I'm not the cop in this little outfit, remember? You are."

"Yeah, but c'mon, Hank." The worried look on her face was easy to read. "You would be better suited, don't you think?"

"Julie," I said calmly, "I think you doubt yourself too much. You can absolutely handle this; lest you forget, you're the one who actually solved it. Julie Haywood, not me."

"What do you mean, 'I solved it'?" she repeated. "We both found Branson, but you found him first."

"Sure, that," I answered. "But that's not what I mean."

Her face scrunched in confusion. "What *do* you mean, then?"

"Think about it, Julie," I said, drinking the last of my coffee.

"Hank," she whined, "I'm tired. Actually, I'm pretty goddamn exhausted, and I'm too tired to think right now. Can you just—"

Julie's eyes widened, and she stiffened in her seat. I realized she was looking past me; something behind me pulled her attention. I flipped around to see. It was Carol Daws.

Subtly, I turned back around to look at Julie. She was a mixture of excitement, tears, sadness, and relief all pent up, ready to explode. Mrs. Daws made her way through the restaurant, visibly raising the anxiety level in Julie Haywood. She gave me a what-do-I-do look. Putting my coffee mug to my lips, I forgot I had just emptied it. I slid out of my chair, excusing myself from the situation. This was a conversation Julie needed to have alone.

"I guess someone passed gas, huh?" I said with a smirk.

Julie rolled her eyes with a, you're-no-help look.

"Aunt Carol, hey."

The quietness surrounding Carol Daws had returned. However, I could see a spark beginning that just needed a push. It sat waiting, ready to ignite with the confirmation Carol needed to hear about her daughter's case. This was the side of hope she'd held onto.

"You did it, Jewels." Carol's eyes welled with tears. Julie began crying along with her. "Some agent from the FDLE called me and told me what you did."

Julie let out some inaudible noise as she rose from the table and reached her arms out for a hug. Carol Daws let loose a tidal wave of emotion as she raced to embrace her niece, causing a stir within the small-town diner. Patrons gawked curiously at the spectacle, wondering about the reason. I smiled at the scene as it brought me joy.

"Thank you, Jewels," Carol managed to say between sobs. "Thank you."

Catching a killer provides a certain satisfaction in homicide work. All the sacrifice that goes into an investigation: the blood, the sweat, the tears, countless hours spent away, is difficult for all. Providing some level of closure and seeing the real effect it has on a victim's loved ones holds a different level of gratification. It is the true motivation of homicide work. Watching Julie and Carol Daws embrace, I felt a warmth surround my soul, as if Victoria were at my side, telling me, "Job well done."

The waitress began to refill my mug.

"What's this about?" the waitress asked.

"Closure," I said.

My answer didn't provide any help, and after pouring the coffee, she stood there watching Julie Haywood and Carol Daws chatter back and forth about never giving up hope.

I took another sip, simply enjoying the moment.

The waitress leaned over the counter. "Does this have anything to do with all the cops out on State Road 145 last night?"

I kept the mug pressed to my lips, trying to ignore the question.

The waitress gasped, "Wait, does this have to do with that old murder of that girl?"

Impressed at her deduction ability, I turned and gave her a wink, still holding the mug to my lips.

"It does, doesn't it?" she said. "Did they make an arrest, finally? Is that why Mrs. Carol is—"

The waitress stood up. I smiled at her, and she scurried off somewhere behind the counter. Another patron caught wind of what Julie and Carol Daws were talking about and joined the conversation.

Five minutes later, a familiar face stormed through the front door of Lucile's. The abrupt entrance caught my attention, but seeing the look on Maynard Preston's face put me at ease.

"News travels fast," I said aloud.

"Jewels!" he yelled across the restaurant, catching everyone's attention. "Jewels, is it true?"

Julie Haywood played coy for probably the first time in her life.

"Is what true, Maynard?" she said with a smile.

Preston rushed over to the table where several people had surrounded her and Carol Daws.

"Don't mess with me, girl," he retorted. "Is it true?"

"That we caught Crystal's killer?" she said. And as the group collectively held their breath in anticipation, Julie added, "Yes. It's true."

Maynard Preston, with teary eyes, scooped up Julie Haywood in a bearhug and picked her off her feet.

"That's great news, Jewels," Maynard said as he let her down. "Seriously, I don't know how you did it, but damn girl, you did."

A buzz from my pocket pulled my attention away.

"Hello?"

"Hey, it's Cade McCoy, are you with Jewels?" he asked.

"Uh, yeah," I said.

"I've been calling her all morning. I heard that something big went down last night, out at the Branson property. I figured you two had something to do with that."

I smiled even though he couldn't see me. "Yeah, you could say that."

"Did you guys make an ar—" Cade went silent. "Hold on, here's something on the news about it."

Assuming Cade was calling from the bookstore, a blurb about the shooting and pending cold case arrest had probably interrupted his thought. Over the din of the restaurant, I could hear something in the background at the bookstore.

"I'll be damned." Cade finally spoke. "You guys did it, didn't you?"

Not wanting to spoil any accolades for Julie Haywood, I told Cade where we were and told him to come get the answer firsthand.

"I'll be right there," he said.

Lucile's was at the end of the block from the bookstore, but given Cade's physical limitations, the walk took him an extra few minutes to get there.

Cade entered the side door facing Pinckney Street and slid in next to me at the counter.

"Look at her!" Cade said.

Julie's beauty shined through from the center of the small crowd. There was a genuine smile on her face. The looming sadness that seemed to follow Julie Haywood had dissipated into a joyful relief. Relief in knowing that Crystal Daws's death was no longer a mystery. Relief in knowing that her killer would have to answer for his actions and that she could truly move on with her own life, free of the guilt and burden she'd carried for so long. I was happy for her.

"Yeah, she deserves this," I said.

"Oh, no doubt," Cade agreed.

Cade leaned over the counter toward the waitress and ordered a cup of coffee, then stood next to me, watching the pother slowly grow with citizens and various people within Julie and Carol Daws's circle.

"Is it safe to say, Hank, that you've found your next chapter?" Cade asked.

"Excuse me?" I wasn't sure to what he was referring.

"That first day you came into the store, you said you were looking for the next chapter in your life," Cade explained. "Did you find it?"

Along the way, running into Julie Haywood and helping her on the case, the purpose just manifested itself. It wasn't until Cade McCoy pointed it out that I realized I had found it.

"Huh," I said. Looking over at Cade, I answered, "Yeah, I guess so."

"Good for you, Hank," he said. "Good for you."

Cade's coffee was delivered, and he managed to walk over to Julie without spilling it. Julie welcomed him to the fold, and she remained at the center of attention. She fielded questions about the shooting and following certain leads. She was careful not to allow too much out into the universe, explaining to everyone that they had to uphold the integrity of the case.

The impromptu celebration continued for nearly a half-hour with no real end in sight. After eating my breakfast, I quietly stepped away and outside of the restaurant. Julie didn't need me any longer, and I was just happy to be of service. Someone had driven my car back to the police station, so I made the short walk a few blocks away.

Cade's words echoed in my mind. Victoria would be proud, I thought. Going from nothing to focus on and no purpose, to helping right a twenty-five-year-old wrong. The sense of pride was instantly overwhelming. Tears welled in the corners of my eyes as I held back from crying. Knowing Victoria was smiling down on me was such an incredible feeling.

Halfway back to Tallahassee, the coffee wore off and extreme exhaustion was bringing me down. I checked my phone and there were no notices. I flicked open the dialing pad and called Katie. Good conversation would keep me awake.

"Hello?" she answered.

"Hey, Katie, it's Dad," I said.

"Hey, Daddy, how are you? Still working that big case?"

"Well, funny you should ask."

⌘

The cemetery was quiet for midday. The sun warmed the day to a nearly unbearable heat. Her memorial stone rested in the shadow of a small dogwood tree whose leaves were bright green and spread wide, soaking up the sun's energy. The newly carved marble was neat and clean, the etching crisp and sharp, something Victoria would have appreciated.

"Well, I did it, Torey," I said. "I found purpose like you asked."

A gust of wind blew, rustling the dogwood leaves. Reflecting back on the case, Victoria had been right about my passion for detective work. She had been right about a lot of things. The case, the chase, and all the complexities that came with an investigation were captivating. It enveloped me to the point that I got excited about the next case just as one ended. But therein was my problem.

"What do I do now?" I asked. "I don't think they have any more twenty-five-year-old murder cases lying around. I'm willing to bet they're fresh out, no thanks to me. Plus, they only average like one murder every two years, so I'll have to wait another twenty-seven years."

Silence from the cemetery was all that answered.

"Yeah, I don't know either."

For the first time in weeks, the uncertainty of my life crept back into my consciousness. However, this time was different. Before, I didn't have any validation that I could still do the job. I proved that by helping Julie Haywood. Moving forward, I needed to find somewhere the job needed to be done. With that notion, the uncertainty faded.

I stood at Victoria's grave a little while longer. There was a comfort in that spot that I hadn't expected. It was peaceful. However, at the same time, my exhausted body and mind reminded me it was time to sleep.

"Good-Bye, my darlin'," I said. "I love you."

⌘

I awoke sometime the next morning with the sound of the doorbell ringing. Slow to get out of bed, I felt various aches and pains shoot alarms throughout my body. It hurt to move. Flashes of my encounter with a shotgun to the head reminded me of the pain's source. My heart rate quickened at the memory. But I'd survived, and the killer was caught. That was enough justification.

By the time I made it down the stairs, the visitor had left. On the front porch was a bottle of Dewar's and two red plastic cups. Scanning the driveway, then the street, I didn't see anyone, but I knew who had left the gift. I had forgotten, but it was tradition. And Mike Durgenhoff was a man who honored tradition. With a grin stretching across my face, I knelt down and picked up the bottle and cups.

"You're right, brother," I said, holding the bottle up as if he were there. "Every closed case deserves a drink."

I shut the door and looked at the clock.

"Even at 8:49 in the morning," I added.

Setting the cups down and opening the bottle, I gave it a good sniff. The pungent sting of the scotch reminded me of all the shared cups Mike and I had had over the years. A lot of scotch meant a lot of justice. I poured a small amount into each cup and tipped mine up for a shot. I let the sting linger.

I hit the remote and turned on the local news. I let the drone of the television go on while I poured myself another drink. I savored the second, knowing that before-breakfast alcohol was a dangerous way to start the day. I patted my pants looking for my phone. I wanted to call

Mike and tell him to come join me, but my pockets were empty. In my haste, I must've left my phone upstairs.

There were several missed messages when I found it, but I figured I could answer them later. I dialed Mike but got his voicemail.

"Hey, Mike, thanks for the scotch," I opened. "I take it you heard about the case over in Madison. It got tough, but apparently, so am I. Call me later and we can toast in person. Thanks, again."

Back downstairs, I finished the second drink and closed the bottle. The news was hitting the top of the hour, and the lead was the Crystal Daws story. The news outlet had found archived footage from 1993 to run with the current story. The footage was surreal, capturing Detective Byrd orchestrating the scene from behind the crime scene tape. The story cut to footage taken from the Branson property the day before, and then, to James Branson's mugshot as the reporter explained the connection. The story was watered down and only provided a few highlights from the case. Excerpts were cited explaining there was an eyewitness to the murder who'd finally come forward along with newly discovered DNA evidence from the crime scene. At the end of the story, there was a close-up interview with Julie Haywood standing in front of the county courthouse.

"And we're here with Officer Julie Haywood with the Madison Police Department and a cousin of the murder victim, Crystal Daws. Officer Haywood was ultimately responsible for closing the case, which was twenty-five years in the making. Officer Haywood, how does it feel to finally find justice?"

"Well, um, it's not really about how I feel, but knowing that Crystal's killer was finally brought to justice. That gives me joy as well as closure," Julie answered.

"Can you provide any insight on what led to the reopening of this case?" asked the reporter.

"Well, to be honest, I've always considered it open. It's the reason I became a police officer," Julie said.

"Wow," the reporter said. "Well then, what got you over the hump, so-to-speak, and led you to make an arrest?"

"Well, I needed help. And I learned that every case has a voice, and I had to listen and find the echo," Julie answered.

Choking on the scotch, I went into a coughing fit brought on by the sound of my philosophical words. Catching my breath, I wiped away the spillage and laughed at myself.

"I can't believe she said that," I said.

"The echo, huh," the reporter said. "Very interesting. Did you have any help on this case?"

"Yes, I would like to give a special thanks to our case consultant, Hank Trescott."

Shutting the television off, I was stunned that Julie gave me credit on the case. I was flattered, but recognition was never a motivator in homicide work. However, it was nice to see Julie Haywood get all the attention for the case. I hoped it would open more doors for her, not only in her career, but in life. She'd harbored the guilt of Crystal's death for so long; being free from that must have its own reward, but actively solving the case was impressive.

Staring at the bottle of scotch, I weighed the options of drinking my breakfast or actually eating some food. The slight buzz from the earlier cups urged the liquid choice. *Why not both?* I thought, in a stroke of genius. Pouring another cup, the doorbell chimed.

"Mike must've gotten the message," I said. I grabbed the bottle of scotch and both cups and made for the door.

Pulling open the door, I was caught off guard when Julie Haywood stood at my doorstep and not Mike Durgenhoff.

"Julie?" I asked. "What are you doing here?"

"Hank," she seemed disappointed. "Did I catch you at a bad time?"

"Oh, no," I stammered, doing an awful job at hiding my inebriation.

"You've been drinking?" she asked.

"Uh, well..., kind of."

"I'm sorry. I should've called," she said.

"No, no..., I thought you were—" I said, embarrassed. "I thought you were someone else."

"Oh," Julie's disappointment grew.

"My old partner, Mike," I said. "We would always toast with scotch after closing a murder." I offered up the bottle and cups.

"Oh, okay," she said, with some relief.

However, there was still something weighing on Julie's mind. In the short time that I had gotten to know her, I'd found she had trouble addressing things that bothered her.

"Something wrong?" I asked.

"The other day, what did you mean, I solved the case?" she asked.

"Oh. You drove all the way here to ask me that?" I asked.

"Well, uh...," Julie looked away, embarrassed.

"First of all, come inside," I said.

Julie Haywood stepped in, and I showed her to the living room.

"Scotch?" I offered her the second cup.

"It's a little early, isn't it?" she said.

I set the bottle and cups on the counter and turned to Julie.

"So, what did you mean?" she asked again.

"I meant just that, Julie. You solved it."

"But I would've never figured out Banks, or the DNA, or Ryder. None of that. That was all you. You figured out all that stuff. I was just riding your coattails."

Julie had missed the biggest piece that goes into every successful case. "That's all true," I said.

"Okay, so why did you say that 'I solved it'?"

"Julie, had it not been for you caring about the case, keeping it alive for all those years, you would've never thought to ask for help."

"I don't understand."

"Sure, you do," I said. "I would have never been involved if you had let it go. You could've easily let me walk out of that bookstore and not thought twice."

Julie bowed her head in thought. I wasn't sure why my statement weighed so heavily on her, but it was enough for her to show up on my doorstep.

"I guess you're right," she said.

I poured myself that next drink along with one for Julie. "Traditions are meant to be honored and shared, Julie Haywood."

She smiled and took the cup. We tapped rims and drank.

"Is that the reason you came here?" I asked. "To ask me that?"

She smiled again, but this time, there was a sparkle in her eyes.

"Not the only reason," she said.

"Oh?"

She set her cup down on the counter and leaned into me, pressing her body against mine.

"There was something else I wanted to ask you," she said.

I reached around the small of her back and pulled her closer, our lips mere inches away. There was no crime scene beckoning, co-worker hovering, or killer on the loose. It was our time, and time was something I had plenty of. I closed my eyes, reached forward, and pressed my lips against hers.

The End

About the Author

William Mark grew up and still lives in Tallahassee, Florida, with his family. He attended the Tallahassee Community College where he graduated with an AA degree, and then went on to the Florida State University where he graduated with a BS degree in Criminology minoring in Psychology.

After college, he attended the Pat Thomas Law Enforcement Academy in Midway, Florida. William has over twenty-five years of police experience that includes assignments in Homicide, and he was a member of the department's Tactical Apprehension and Control (TAC) team.

William and his family, a wife and three beautiful children, are active members in their church, avid Florida State Seminole fans, and they enjoy traveling. William has published four novels with Southern Yellow Pine Publishing, *From Behind the Blue Line* (Award winning novel), *Crossing the Blue Line*, *Lost in the Darkness*, and *Where Light Cannot Reach.*

William is a member of the Tallahassee Writers Association.

www.ingramcontent.com/pod-product-compliance
Lightning Source LLC
LaVergne TN
LVHW091027080826
845145LV00002B/378

* 9 7 8 1 5 9 6 1 6 1 3 7 5 *